Also by Doug Richardson

Lucky Dey Thrillers
> *Blood Money*
> *99 Percent Kill*
> *Reaper*
> *American Bang*
> *Hip Slick and Dead*

Other Fiction
> *The Safety Expert*
> *Dark Horse*
> *True Believers*

Nonfiction
> *The Smoking Gun: True Stories from Hollywood's Screenwriting Trenches*

A LUCKY DEY THRILLER

DOUG RICHARDSON

THE NIGHT IS NEVER BLACK

los angeles

Velvet Elvis Entertainment
6038 Tampa Avenue, Suite 366
Tarzana, California 91356

Copyright © 2018 by Doug Richardson
Cover photo © www.journeysinlight.net
Cover design by Karen Richardson

More information at www.dougrichardson.com
ISBN: 978-0-9990366-0-0
Library of Congress Control Number: 2018904548

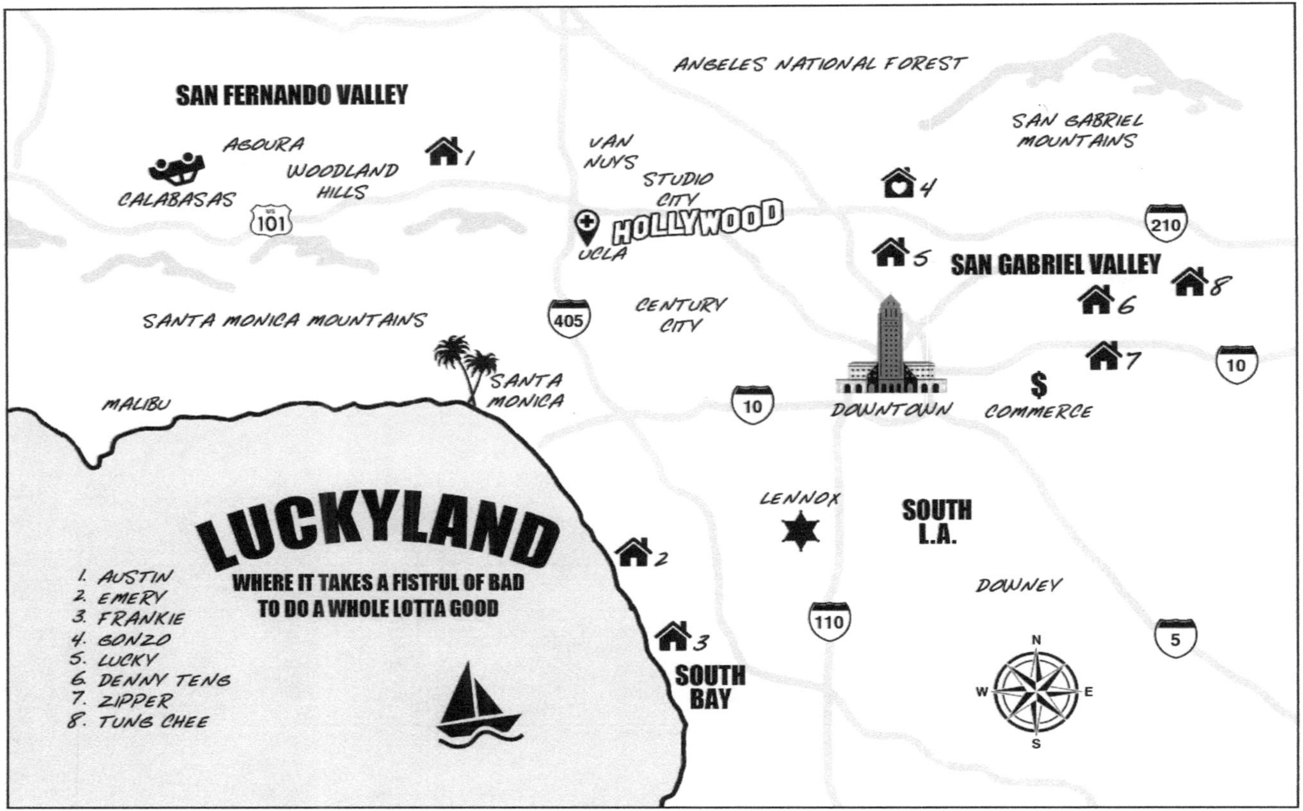
ANGELES NATIONAL FOREST
SAN FERNANDO VALLEY
AGOURA
WOODLAND HILLS
CALABASAS
101
1
VAN NUYS
STUDIO CITY
HOLLYWOOD
UCLA
SAN GABRIEL MOUNTAINS
4
5
SAN GABRIEL VALLEY
210
8
6
7
10
SANTA MONICA MOUNTAINS
405
CENTURY CITY
SANTA MONICA
MALIBU
10
DOWNTOWN
$
COMMERCE
LENNOX
SOUTH L.A.
DOWNEY
2
3
SOUTH BAY
110
5
N
W
E
S
LUCKYLAND
WHERE IT TAKES A FISTFUL OF BAD
TO DO A WHOLE LOTTA GOOD
1. AUSTIN
2. EMERY
3. FRANKIE
4. GONZO
5. LUCKY
6. DENNY TENG
7. ZIPPER
8. TUNG CHEE

November

1

Copper City, California.

The shovel blade was barely penetrating. Underneath the earthy crust were eons of pressure-formed rock and continually decomposing granite that demanded force better suited from a diesel backhoe. With each downward strike, the steel edge practically bounced before it dug. But the violence generated by Lucky, unfazed in his mission-like effort to turn over yet another shovelful of dirt, would eventually evolve into a single, man-sized grave.

"Said you had a place," Mr. Teardrops had said. "Where we could, you know. Get it on. Said you'd even bring a shovel. Whatever. Bring it. Don't bring it. 'Cause I'm gonna cut you into so many pieces the coyotes are gonna feed on what's left."

"Sounds like a plan," Lucky had agreed, knowing even in the fluidity of a phone conversation that he'd reached a critical decision. A turning point from which there might be no return. Lights out. Dead and buried in a hole of his own design.

With the peaceful resignation of a condemned killer with a noose around his neck, Lucky met the hostile O.G. under a rock formation that roughly resembled a hand reaching up to God. The agreement had been for each man to come alone, but Lucky fully expected Mr. Teardrops to arrive with an arsenal of human backup. But perhaps Mr. Teardrops carried the same emotional weight as Lucky—a man so far over the edge he was either ready to take another life or meet the ultimate fate—because he had landed at the site on time and alone, armed with identical dueling knives—fixed blade, bayonet style—one for Lucky, one for himself.

"Funny," remarked Lucky. "I brought two of something as well. Shovels. Figured we'd dig the grave first. Save the survivor half the work."

Despite Mr. Teardrops's venomous protestations, Lucky began the difficult dig. He kept hacking at the earth and turning over shovelfuls of sand until his antagonist quit frothing at the mouth and joined in. A testy conversation ensued with Lucky suggesting Mr. Teardrops tell the tale—and remind him of just why the thick-necked gangster was demanding blood for blood. Until that moment, Lucky hadn't the faintest idea as to the nature of the bad guy's beef or need for recompense. He only knew there was something the man was more than willing to murder or die over. As the men tore into the earth, Mr. Teardrops admonished and complained and shed actual tears, sometimes swinging the shovel over his shoulder like an axe, pounding the dust like he imagined it was Lucky's head. Other times, Mr. Teardrops howled at the sky with the rage of a caged wolverine.

And Lucky just kept digging.

As the O.G. gangbanger's history unfolded, he told of how his younger brother had survived a gunfight with Lucky in an incident initiated with a simple traffic stop. The shooting had led to prison and been followed by a meth addiction and suicide. The assignation Mr. Teardrops placed on Lucky had culminated in the mano-a-mano showdown in the desert. It was unusual for Lucky to let himself get strung into such a willfully reckless brush, but the invite had come at a time when he'd been as close to hopeless as he'd ever felt. It had been a Halloween to forget, climaxing with more blood than even Lucky could stomach and the tragic loss of someone dear to him, for which he'd been blamed. Somehow, a noontime collision on a desolate landscape stretch of landscape near Copper City seemed deserved. And it was there where Lucky would either die or pivot into the second half of his near forty-year life.

Once the bereaved brother had been exhausted of both spit and words, Lucky leaned on his shovel and shared a story about a lost younger brother. *His own.* Murdered on a Kern County roadside and left to incinerate in a car fire. For a minute, Lucky felt like he was back in Alcoholics Anonymous, circled up in folding chairs with fellow addicts sharing the pain.

"So, what'd you do about it?" asked Mr. Teardrops. "You get who done it?"

"I got off a shot," admitted Lucky. "Hit the perp. Tried to convince myself I'd finished him off. But after all this time, I'm thinking otherwise. He's still out there."

"So you understand why it had to come to this." Mr. Teardrops had resumed an aggressive stance, hulking shoulders rounded and full of flex, his whitened knuckles around the shovel handle.

"But it don't at all," disagreed Lucky.

Lucky had already clocked the body language of his opponent—athletic pose, weight on the balls of his feet, hips locked. Only Mr. Teardrops hadn't yet readied his shovel blade to strike. So, when Lucky saw the man twist his torso and the beginning of an arm cock, he closed the distance and struck downward with his shovel's cutting edge. Before Mr. Teardrops could lower his blade, Lucky closed the distance and cracked down on the gangster's ankle. There was a cartilage-crushing *crunch*. The joint gave way. Dust plumed when Mr. Teardrops's body slapped the dirt. Next, Lucky hooked the prostrate man with the shovel's flat shoulder and pulled until Mr. Teardrops was flat-backed in the half-dug grave.

"No, no, no, no!" squealed the gangbanger, arms unconsciously up and fending off a deathblow that would never come.

"Think your little brother wanted you to die like this? I sure as shit know mine wouldn't."

"Dude!" sobbed Mr. Teardrops. "What I got left but my pain?"

Pain. Lucky was filled with it. Whatever path he was on, Lucky knew something had to change. *He* had to change.

So, in the hours that passed, Lucky sat at the edge of the shallow hole, shovel across his knees, sun drying his sweat until his skin was chapped. There both men eventually talked of everything from heartbreak to the paper-thin divide between vengeance and justice. In that lapse of time, Lucky was reflective, claiming he'd rather live in a world where Mr. Teardrops was out there, alive, breathing the same air, wrestling with the demons of right and wrong.

Finally, the men became thirsty and starved, so Lucky drove Mr. Teardrops to a high-desert Dairy Queen. The duo powered up on burgers and DQ Freezes and said their goodbyes a short hobbling distance from a Glenn County hospital trauma center. But not before one last exchange.

"Still don't get why you didn't kill me," replayed Mr. Teardrops.

"Believe in God?" asked Lucky.

"Supposed to. I'm born Catholic."

"My daughter believes," finished Lucky. "And though I'm not sure about God, I believe in her. And she believes there's a purpose to everything."

April

Monday

2

"It's an awesome neighborhood," offered Austin Andrews, his salesman smile on full and rehearsed beam, capped teeth as bright as those of the Osmonds. "Close to the schools. The markets. But, hey, it's Calabasas. What's not to like?"

"What's this neighborhood called?" asked the homely woman in the back seat of the luxury car, a late model Mercedes S class. Leased. At $799 a month, Austin couldn't technically afford the deep blue German beast. But because he continued to advertise himself as one of the West Valley's top real estate agents, he couldn't afford *not* to look the part.

"Well," paused Austin. "It's a Calabasas zip code. But I know what you're asking."

Austin knew precisely what she was asking. Calabasas, like so many Southern California burgs, was divvied up into neighborhoods with their own priceless monikers. The Oaks. Hidden Hills. The Highlands. Malibu Creek. Palatino. Las Virgenes Park. Each neighborhood implied a certain social status. But somehow the tree-lined middle-class streets of eastern Calabasas had escaped the neighborhood name game. Or worse, Austin was suffering from memory slippage. For the life of him, he couldn't recall.

"Revolution Acres," he spun, coining the neighborhood name out of thin air—inspired by a pair of nearby streets, Paul Revere Drive and Declaration Avenue.

In the front passenger seat was a matron of Eastern European extraction. She tipped out at something Austin guessed was near seventy years old, casually attired in a gold-spangled T-shirt and jeans with a yoga and cardio-maintained body that rivaled women half her age. Her forty-year-old daughter, Austin's backseat passenger, might've been best described as fleshy, a child with a late-night addiction to designer vodka and frozen bonbons rebelling against her über fit mother.

Austin guessed it was the girl's mother who was going to be shelling out the down payment on the home, thus he'd insisted the mom sit beside him, up front, with the better view of the neatly sidewalked streets. Old-growth deciduous maple and elms in spring fervor fronted the largely middle-income-sized homes, considerably marked up due to the fact that their foundations were a mere eighth to a quarter of a mile outside the subpar Los Angeles Unified School District.

"What age are your kids?" inquired Austin, eyes in his rearview mirror in search of the daughter's pie-faced expression.

"She has a sixth grader and a freshman in high school," answered the alpha mother before complaining. "LAUSD is the worst. Destroys me that my grandbabies share classrooms with so many…"

The mother's words trailed into silent unmentionables. Austin privately disagreed, but the salesman in him nodded his understanding. It wasn't difficult to fill in the blanks based on a cornucopia of most likely prejudices held by the mother—not that he wasn't beyond his own enmity towards others. If it had been a later hour and he had been more than a few martinis deep into his habitual day's end comedown, he might have dropped jokes about all the names used to describe Calabasas by both locals and outsiders. There was Cala-Baghdad, Cala-Bumfuck, and Cala-Badass, the latter coined for all the bad-behaving hip-hop and rap artists who'd settled into the many hilltop mansions behind guarded gates. Women from the area were often referred to as Cala-bitches or Cala-bimbos. The men were Cala-bastards, himself included, despite having left the tony township long ago.

"How many houses do we have to see in this hood?" griped the daughter.

"Two to show you today," answered Austin, buoying back with extra cheer. "First one's my own listing up around the next corner. The other is at the other end of Revere. Won't take long at all."

There was a genuine sheen to the morning. Intermittent rain showers had wet all the streets and left every leaf and blade of grass iridescent. The air smelled of chlorophyll and must, spilling into the car's interior through the back right window, which the daughter kept cracked and whistling.

Austin needed the sale like plants demanded carbon dioxide for survival. Creditors were closing in at such a nightmarish clip—blowing up his every communication link, from emails to texts—that he'd begun utilizing disposable prepaid cell phones to conduct his day-to-day business. Gossiping colleagues suspected he was dealing drugs. *If only*, he laughed to himself. Selling cocaine or meth or even prescription meds would have at least resulted in a positive cash flow. In Austin's wallet was a single ATM card, but if he'd so much as attempted to withdraw twenty dollars from his account, the transaction would have produced an insufficient funds message.

I'm broke as an aging fag joke.

Accordingly, instead of delivering buyers to multimillion-dollar listings, Austin was reduced to praying he'd split a commission on a three-bedroom mid-century property in the one section of Calabasas that didn't even rate a neighborhood name.

Revolution Acres? Ha. As if.

Austin began to worry he'd been kissing up to the mother a notch too obviously. He needed to keep the daughter engaged and feeling that, in him, she'd found a trusted advocate. He flicked the right-hand turn signal and gave another looksee into the rearview mirror, hoping to make some positive eye contact with his dreary back-seat passenger. Instead, his eyes fixed through his rear windshield and onto the sudden yawning of an oncoming truck grille. A Dodge pickup. Austin was easily able to distinguish the chromed Ram logo before he heard the thrum of the V-8's engine. His shoulder blades clinched in autonomic fear of a sudden impact. Only the jacked-up Dodge swerved a hard left, nearly kissing the leased Mercedes's rear taillight before barreling past. Metallic teal green, a pimped-out show truck. A Nissan sedan, mere feet behind and drafting the pickup's bumper, surged by. White. Arcing around the upcoming street corner, the tandem vehicles blew by the Mercedes like it was a brick with no wheels. While the Nissan hugged the asphalt, the top-heavy pickup's inside wheels appeared to practically come unglued from the pavement.

"*Oh, Gospodi!* Oh, Jesus!" chirped the mother.

"Christ, what was that?!" chimed her sullen daughter, suddenly animated.

"Teenagers," excused a breathless Austin, thinking with his tongue instead of his brain. "No matter where you go, there they are, am I right?"

"Nearly gave me a heart attack!" angered the mother. "They're gonna get somebody killed."

Austin slowed his car, easing into the same turn. He hoped to unholy hell the speedsters had vanished into the ether, leaving the street clean and idyllic. To help erase their nerves, Austin tried to refocus both women on the mission.

"Boys or girls?" asked Austin. "Your middle-schooler and ninth grader?"

"One of each—" began the daughter before her mouth stalled, her voice trailing as Austin braked quickly. Her mother sucked in a lungful of air.

The street was framed by rows of neatly kempt homes, stripes of perfect sidewalks with nary a crack, and a sky partially obstructed by green, fully foliaged trees still dripping from the rain shower. Fouling the enchanted scene were those two formerly speeding vehicles. Stopped. The pickup truck appeared to have rolled, coming to rest on its side against the trunk of a tall, thick-bodied eucalyptus. The white Nissan was angled in the middle of the street with both doors swung wide open. The sedan's driver, an ebony teen in a baggy neon sweatsuit, stood sentry at his door while his passenger, a tattooed, teacup-sized black youth in a bright orange knit cap, positioned himself in front of the pickup's peeled front windshield and aimed a pistol into the cab. With fourteen successive shots, he emptied his magazine into the upside-down, still seat-belted bodies.

The sounds of gunshots penetrated Austin's German car's heavy insulation like the popping of distant fireworks, creating an eerie disconnect from the violence only forty yards beyond the iconic Mercedes medallion. The Nissan's driver, his hair braided into knots with rubber bands that matched his togs, gripped a pistol nickeled with a heavy bore. When he took a threatening step toward Austin's Mercedes, the mother reflexively howled in staccato heaves.

"BACK UP, BACK UP!" screeched the daughter.

But Austin remained frozen, appearing like the proverbial deer caught in a poacher's spotlight. His eyes stayed fixed on the Nissan's driver, as if telepathically sending a set of simple pleas.

I am not a threat.

I will never identify you in a lineup.

I will not cooperate with the police.

Just please, please, please let us live.

Then *thunk!* And the sound of the Nissan's passenger door slamming shut cut the cord of the stare-off. The driver cocked his head as if he'd heard "C'mon, c'mon" from his gunman passenger. With his leash clearly yanked, the driver broke off, swiveled back into the sedan and let the inertia of the car surging forward swing his own door closed. Austin heard himself breathing in with a mild, allergy-season wheeze, then felt words rising.

"Call 911!" he found himself coughing while unhitching his seat belt and leaning all his 240 pounds into the door.

"You get back in the car!" screamed the mother.

"CALL 911!" he barked back. "CALL IT NOW!"

Austin's legs felt unsteady, nearly ready to collapse under the weight of his newly acquired belly fat—a full forty-four pounds in the past two years. The gym had beckoned but he'd fallen so far behind on the payments he hadn't dared to show his pudgy face. His quadriceps ached as he pushed his fallow muscles into an awkward run, rushing toward the tipped pickup. Austin expected blood. After all, he'd consumed days of movies and cable television. But the violence that filled his eyeballs was sickening. Slashes of red were everywhere. Punctured with oozing bullet holes, both victims were black-haired, Asian, limp, and draining fluids. The passenger's jaw had partially sheered into a gaping death maw.

There was also the money.

Hundred-dollar bills were splashed between the dead driver and passenger. Some were still banded in ten-thousand-dollar-currency paper straps. Other Benjamins were simply loose and spattered in red. A small, partially unzipped gym bag held onto the rest of the cash. Bundles on top of bundles.

A hundred thousand dollars? Two hundred thousand? wondered Austin. *And what, if anything, would happen to me if I just reached in, grabbed the moneybag, and sauntered back to my car?*

Austin caught himself. Despite the horror, the instinct of his money woes was calling his subconscious. He remained staring at the duffle until he noticed the voice. Tinny. Urgent. His eyes followed the sound to the ground between himself and the pickup's displaced front windshield. In the gutter was a mobile phone with a badly cracked screen, activated and identifying the user at the other end of the line as Zipper.

"Hello?" the voice kept asking, though to Austin it sounded like a squawk. "Hello! Stop fuckin' with me, ese. What's goin' on?"

Magnetically, as if being lured to the phone, Austin crouched to pick it up. He didn't know why he did it, but would later excuse it to being in shock; that or an involuntary need to seek help for the victims.

"Jesus fucking Christ!" complained Zipper, his voice getting richer as the speaker got closer to Austin's ear. "Do we have Tung Chee's money or what? You half-assed noodle nigga better answer me!"

"Hey…uh…who's this?" stuttered Austin, his own words wavering as his body shook.

"The fuck you say?" pissed Zipper. "Who this?"

"I…I'm the guy at the accident," finished Austin, his eyes slashing across the landscape. Neighbors had begun to leak from front doors, but weren't venturing much further than their welcome mats.

"What accident?"

"There was…" confused Austin. "Men with guns. Did you call 911?"

"Did I…What? Who is this? Put on my cuz!"

"I'm…I'm Austin Anderson and I'm here," he continued to stupidly stammer. "And it's okay. I asked my clients to call 911—"

"Where's my boy, Tu'an?"

"Who?"

"The phone you're talkin' on, fool! Tell that seaweed sucker I wanna talk to him before I reach through and cut your goddamn throat."

"Don't think he can talk right now," swiveled Austin, once

again filling his eyes with the wrecked truck cab and the horror of those two dangling bodies, both dead and bled out to an obvious mortal conclusion.

"And why the fuck not?"

"'Cause I think he's dead," relayed Austin, almost robotic. "Think they're both dead."

3

Overkill, Lucky thought. That was most lawyers' answer to everything when it came to litigation. It was militaristic; overwhelm the enemy with swarms of legality from motions to delays to every bit of attorney trickery until the other side can only yell uncle and settle.

"Not sure I need all this," voiced Lucky, the on-the-ropes Los Angeles County sheriff's detective. He sat uncomfortably at one end of an expansive granite-topped conference table. One glass-walled suite peered into the next, giving the illusion of transparency. *What a crock*, thought Lucky. These were corporate lawyers whose prima facie occupation was concealing the sins of their masters. To Lucky's immediate right was the always crisp-suited Conrad Ellis, Lucky's sometime *consigliere* and a man wealthy beyond human reason. Next to Conrad was one member from his phalanx of attorneys—a chilly blonde best described as human vanilla—though with a vast curriculum vitae of experience negotiating against city bureaucracies.

"Best defense is a strong offense," defended the attorney, whose name Lucky could never seem to remember. Perhaps it was because upon her dry, prosecutor-like presentation he'd privately nicknamed her Ms. Vanilla. "County would like nothing more than for you to just resign. Quit. Walk the hell away."

"Purpose of outside counsel is that they're on your side," added Conrad. "And your side alone."

"Deputies' union is on my side," defended Lucky for amusement alone. He knew it was a weak argument.

"You don't believe that," said the attorney. "Otherwise, why would you be here?"

"One word why I'm here," replied Lucky. "Connie."

"As a favor to him?" she asked. "Or a favor to yourself?"

"Connie's been solid to me and my family," stated Lucky, flat and affect free. Truth was, Lucky didn't trust any lawyers, be it those working for his union reps or Conrad's battalion of business button-ups. "A real friend. So, I trust Conrad."

"And I *trust* this law firm," thumbed Conrad. "And advocates like her will fight for you and only you. On my command. That simple. So, my advice to you is to let her help."

Lucky allowed a cleansing breath, rested his gaze on the floor-to-ceiling window and the twenty-two-story view. The rainstorm had left the air unfiltered. From the Century City office tower, he could see from the Sepulveda Pass all the way to the Hollywood Sign overlooking cozy Beachwood Canyon. Cotton-ball clouds hung over the hills that divided the Basin from the San Fernando Valley. Somewhere further east, out of sight, was Altadena and the family he'd been separated from. Though it had been nearly five months, the wound from the forced detachment was still fresh enough to bleed.

"Lucky?" the lawyer asked, standing erect. Her suit was smart, light gray with tartan lines, and tailored to best flatter her plus-sized frame. "The question is, what do you want? What's the outcome that you most desire?"

Outcome?

Lucky's number-one desire was to be reunited with his family. Though he'd never married Gonzo nor legally given his name to her son Travis, he had a genuine bond with them, not to mention his adopted daughter Karrie. And their absence from his life had proven more crushing than he could have imagined. But that wasn't the subject at hand. After a career publicly decried as "dubiously dangerous" by newly named County Sheriff Paul McGill—as well as a much-publicized recent domino effect of tragedy and death from which Lucky was eventually exonerated, but darkly tainted—the sixteen-year veteran was considered too hot to handle; a veritable catalyst for violence. The Sheriff's Department wanted to quietly retire Lucky. But he wanted to continue serving in some form of frontline duty.

"Don't wanna take a desk," answered Lucky. "Not just to keep my pension. Me on forced admin duty? Certified shit show."

"Understood," said Ms. Vanilla. "But what kind of leverage do we have if they refuse to return you to a position you approve?"

Zero. Zip. Nada. Lucky knew it like he knew the meaning of *Miranda*.

"Would you ever think of returning to Kern County?" asked Conrad.

"Too far away…" Lucky was shaking his head. Conrad understood. Plus, there were no actual gutters to patrol in shit-kicker Kern. Just illegal weed farms and miles of backyard meth labs.

"In the last letter from the County it's pretty clear what they'd like is for you to step away from the job," said the attorney. "And in my one off-the-record conversation with a county lawyer, you were twice referred to as a 'shit magnet.'"

Lucky didn't nod his agreement, though he had heard the phrase more than once before. The last utterance was from Gonzo right before she'd kicked him out of the house.

"County seems to believe," she continued, "that the only

unknown is what you're willing to accept in the way of a settlement. Pension at X. Benefits vested up to Y."

"Union already argued the same," said Lucky.

"Fine. So, you want to know what does Vignam, Brent, and Herschowitz bring to the party?" she asked rhetorically, dropping the firm's name like a thousand-pound block of marble.

"No. I want to know what *you* bring to the party," finished Lucky.

"What we bring…what *I* bring…" chuckled the attorney, "is some serious push. Conrad's a valued client. The senior partners here have relationships in all levels of the local power structures. A whisper here and there? And when the County recognizes that we are your sole counsel in the dispute? Maybe they discover some extra wiggle room in their offer and the final outcome is your returning to the kind of duty you desire."

Lucky leaned forward, sifting through the open file between them until he came up with a Xeroxed letter. He spun it toward the attorney.

"Says I'm unfit for duty," said Lucky. "Their statement of fact."

"Statement of fact or just the first salvo of a negotiation?"

"Yeah," said Lucky, "but how do you know I'm not?"

"You're not what? Fit to be a cop?"

Lucky raised his eyebrows. A challenge.

"I'm not supposed to know," she replied. "I'm supposed to be your lawyer. Your advocate and your advocate only."

That much Lucky knew. She didn't know him beyond the man who sat cross-legged in the high-backed executive chair. For that matter, neither did Conrad, really. At least not well. It was the oft-repeated complaint about Lucky. He wasn't good at letting people in—even Gonzo and Travis. But Karrie? She might be the exception. Lucky wasn't her birth father. That man was deceased. But Karrie, who was legally emancipated and only weeks away from turning eighteen, had taken Lucky's last name nearly a year earlier. During his months of paid suspension, she had introduced him to her Muay Thai workouts, the Brazilian martial art she'd become addicted to. In turn, Lucky was teaching Karrie how to surf.

"It's a process," reminded the attorney. "And nothing happens overnight."

"Like sucking cement through a straw," added Conrad.

"In the meantime," continued the lawyer, "for the sake of your case you must keep a seriously low profile. No trouble of any kind. Nothing that would give the County a stronger case that you *are* a shit magnet."

"Some things easier said than done," smirked Lucky.

Ms. Vanilla put her hands on top of the table and leaned in.

"Harsh question," she parried. "Did you ever once think it was just that kind of *fuck you* attitude that got you into this pickle?"

Lucky knew all too well why he was in the lawyer's office. He was who he was. No apologies. It had always been a matter of time as to when the bureaucracy would drop a ton of bricks on him. His life, though, would remain all about what he could get done before someone eventually found a way to put a stop to his beating heart. Between old enemies and those yet to be identified, Lucky knew he wasn't over his catalytic behavior.

4

San Gabriel. 12:45 p.m.

Karrie was in full chase, but her choice in footwear made her rush that much more difficult. Four-inch, flesh-toned pumps, shiny, but not nearly as slick as the freshly waxed corridors of Coolidge Elementary. The part-time volunteer had an interview after school for an internship, thus the heels, the uncomfortable black pencil skirt, and the frilly white blouse in lieu of her usual tie-dye T-shirt, boyish denims, and Sharpie-decorated Chuck Taylors.

"Kaarriiee," pled five-year-old Min. Tiny fingers splayed, one of the child's hands was reaching back for Karrie, the other swallowed in the mitt of the school's matronly vice principal.

"It's just a drawing!" Karrie appealed, stuck between attempting to keep up while remaining respectful of the older woman in authority.

"Not your fault," said the vice principal, slowing. "It's just policy. Now, go back to your job."

"But she *is* my job!" cried Karrie.

A crayoned drawing on simple white paper stock waved in the vice principal's hand as the pair disappeared through the doors to the school's administration offices. Slightly winded from the terrible worry that infected her, Karrie slowed to a stop and steadied herself in those toe-crushing heels. She was Min's occasional shadow, an assignment best described as a helper assisting a student who hadn't yet adjusted socially. Over the past few months, Karrie's kindergartner had shown signs of social awkwardness, sometimes impenetrable by her teacher. Karrie, who was hoping to major in child psychology, had volunteered at the school district as a way of beefing up her pre-college resume. Min Lee Teng—or Mini, as the other kids called her—was Karrie's first charge. If Karrie had wondered if the pair had formed a connection, the answer had come in Min's reaction when pulled from the classroom. The five-year-old, who would usually utter no more than soft whispers to anyone besides her parents, squealed and called out numerous times for Karrie from the doorway of room 8K all the way to the main office.

When Karrie's wits returned, along with a personal reminder that she wasn't even a school employee, she went back to the classroom to quietly gather her things. Her return was more interruptive than the teacher would've liked, as every one of those twenty-seven babylike faces swiveled as if it were Karrie who had caused the screeching disturbance. She waved a silent *I'm sorry* to no one in particular and crossed to the rear corner, where she discreetly bent down to pick up her backpack. On the shelf next to it lay a pastel blue folder with Min's full name neatly handwritten across the top. Underneath, Min had copied her three-letter moniker in red, yellow, and purple crayon. Without asking permission, let alone even passing a glance toward the teacher, Karrie stuffed the folder into her backpack, zipped it shut, and pivoted for her exit.

"Bye, Miss Dey," said the boy nearest the door.

Karrie turned, smiled back, and finger-waved, noting the rest of the class signaling a sweet so-long. All those young faces, the light in their eyes as rich as the rainbow-decorated room…It filled Karrie's heart just enough to mend the temporary rupture from watching poor little Min being dragged away.

5

Agoura.

"You are swearing under the penalty of law that this statement is true," explained the sheriff's detective for the umpteenth time.

"Yeah, yeah," agreed Austin Anderson, already exhausted, yet unable to jettison the mental images of those two murdered Asian men in the pickup truck—nor that gym bag stuffed full of cash.

By noon, the murder scene in east Calabasas had been roped off with sheriff's vehicles and miles of crime scene tape covering the residential street from end to end. The lookie-loo neighbors had pretty much lost the shock or excitement at being eye- or earwitnesses to a deadly shootout once they realized that while the investigation was unfolding there would be little coming or going from their homesteads. Pending completion of forensics, the picturesque neighborhood promised to be an island of no exit or return until dark.

Soon after sheriff's officers had arrived, they quickly assisted Austin into the back seat of an SUV radio unit. Over the span of three hours, investigators came and went, sharing the back seat with him and offering Starbucks coffee while seeking answers to a litany of obvious, witness-related questions. Between friendly interrogations, Austin could see the edges of the crime scene and the technicians in their disposable jumpsuits and shoe coverings gathering physical and photographic evidence. Across the street, in two separate black-and-whites parked grille to grille, the real estate broker's pair of prospective homebuyers sat in their respective backseats facing their own round-robins of questioning. At some point during the afternoon, Austin wisely reckoned that he wouldn't be selling the duo a house in Calabasas or, for that matter, anywhere on planet Earth.

Eventually, Austin and the team of sheriff's detectives retreated to the closest headquarters, the Malibu/Lost Hills Sheriff's Station in nearby Agoura, where written witness statements were composed, pored over, and signed. From the first question to the last, Austin was honest, yet circumspect, and careful to a specific point—re: his own personal safety. Not that he was afraid of death. Of late, he'd often pondered if suicide were going to be the only way out of his financial predicament. But a self-inflicted death would have to occur on his own glamorous terms. The idea of dying at another's hand—in a crime, no less—was rather unappealing.

Thus Austin's recollections of the morning were crisp up until the gunshots, at least when he talked to the authorities. In an act of self preservation, he claimed only to have seen two black men of average height, one indistinguishable from the other. He wondered if the detective thought him racist, but would rather that than risk getting even more caught up in the crime. The make and model of the getaway car was no more specific than a newish, whitish sedan. And the part about picking up the mobile phone and talking to a man the screen had ID'd as Zipper was left out of his statement altogether. It was that precise sort of self-preservation that Austin credited for never having gotten into a fistfight, as well as further proof of his wont to stay alive.

Snitches get stitches, Austin heard his sub-brain repeating. For the life of him, he couldn't recall where he'd picked up the rhyming mantra.

"There's no more you want to add?" the gin-blossomed old detective pressed, hoping the confines of the windowless, prison-cell-sized interview room might provide adequate pressure to squeeze more details from the real estate man.

"For the life of me..." Austin shook his head. "Hey. Is my car still part of the crime scene?"

"Behind the station in the motor yard," said the detective. "Sorry to hear you might not be sellin' nothin' on that street for a while."

"Who knows?" Austin tried to joke. "That one property I was gonna show might get a price reduction now that somebody can't pass up."

"Glass half full kinda guy, huh?"

"I sell real estate," smirked Austin. "Means I gotta be full up and ready with a smile."

"Selling rainbows and sunshine. I get it."

"I call it hope and happiness," said Austin. "But same thing."

The detective was just swinging the door open when Austin remembered a missing puzzle piece.

"The victims," Austin suddenly said. "Who were they?"

"Can't say. Not 'til the families are fully notified."

"Right, right. But were they...I mean, they from Calabasas?"

"Were they local? Hell no. Way east. Alhambra or Monterey Park or some such land of Asian enchantment. But we'll sure as heck figure it. Why they were so far from home, you know?"

"Drug deal gone bad, ya think?" asked Austin, chummy.

"Why you ask that?" returned the detective.

"I remember the money. Saw it all over," shrugged Austin. "I dunno. Read about that kinda thing. Or a crime show. I don't sleep so good. Watch a lot of late-night stuff."

"We'll be in touch."

Austin nodded his acknowledgment without even trying to put any more pieces together. He just wanted to get out of that airless room. It was after 9:00 p.m. when he was finally handed the keys to his leased sedan. A smell lingered, a stale blend of that mother and daughter and Mercedes leather. *Ugh*, he thought of the mash-up of scents. *Kim Kardashian Fleur Fatale* meets *Kirkland Signature Body Wash.*

He damned his own overly particular nose, cracked the windows, and accelerated the short six miles east to a tony enclave called Amestoy Estates in Encino. Snuggled between the freeway and Ventura Boulevard, the flat Valley zip code sported groves of old-growth oak trees, gated private driveways, and the kind of street addresses that became a successful real estate broker. If only it hadn't been another one of Austin's illusions. The home where he'd been allowed to plant his flag belonged to his ex-wife—the same ex whose heart he'd crushed some twenty years earlier when she accidentally discovered his secret homosexual love life. The subsequent divorce had led to his self-exhumation from the queer closet. He'd since referred to the big day as his proclamation of independence, annually celebrating the date like a birthday. In turn, his brokerage career blossomed and, with religious alimony payments, a new friendship grew between the two exes. She had recently remarried a retired dermatologist and had offered their detached garage/converted guest house to Austin in exchange for looking after their menagerie of cats while they were away on vacations. Austin didn't care for cats. But his ex and her doctor hubby adored travel and were gone what seemed like half the weeks of the year.

Despite the day's trauma, Austin plodded through his usual routine. He parked on the street, retrieved the mail, and turned off the house alarm, but never paid note of the other vehicles on the street—especially the pair of headlights that had stalked him all the way from the Agoura sheriff's station to his Encino address.

He fed the cats, making certain to refill their water bowl before emptying the litter box. The rest was as simple as resetting the alarm, exiting through the rear kitchen slider, and following the curved brick path around the swimming pool to a dollish guest-house covered in ivy and blooming white jasmine. There was no alarm in the granny unit—barely five hundred square feet of living space with room only for a couch, kitchenette, cramped bedroom, and shower-only bathroom. Watercolor paintings from his ex-wife's semester of Valley College art classes both decorated and covered up the defects in the peeling wallpaper.

In the eleven months Austin had camped there, he'd mem-orized the distance between the pavers, usually navigating the twenty-six steps from the rear of the residence to his guest unit in near darkness. Sometimes it was twenty-six paces of peace; others, it was a twenty-six brick paver countdown to the depressing truth that lay on the other side of the guesthouse door. Bills. Credit notices. Red-striped bank statements. Both the kitchenette and coffee tables were blanketed in piles of financial problems, some-where amongst them a handwritten list of bankruptcy attorneys to dial. The night before, Austin had promised himself that today was the day. After showing the mother and daughter the two Calabasas properties, he was going to retire to the privacy of his humble hut and at last begin the process of declaring insolvency. But the day had already proven traumatic enough. Before he'd left the sher-iff's station he'd promised himself an appointment with a freshly plucked lime from one of the property's trees and a fizzy tumbler of tonic mixed with his favorite discount vodka.

God bless Costco.

Not only was there no security code to enter the guesthouse, but Austin had never so much as been issued a key. The assump-tion was that there was nothing of value to steal either before *or* after the broke-as-a-joke ex-hubby had moved in. With his only guide being the ambient light, Austin gauged where the front doorknob was, found the brass orb in his hand, twisted it, and pushed. That's when he felt a hand grip the back of his neck, as if the jaws of the dark itself had lunged from behind and bit down with a supernatural force.

Austin recalled being propelled through the door before crumpling against the arm of the corduroy sofa just feet inside the threshold. He was too shocked to release a shout or call for help, at first assuming he'd simply lost his balance and tripped—the shove, simply gravity overwhelming his own graceless and overweight body. That fantasy was quickly snuffed by an unexpected voice.

"Right there. The couch is good."

There was a blast from a cell phone flashlight. Austin saw shapes and felt extra-large hands grasping through his jacket to the hairs on his chest, wrenching him into the cushioned seat. He heard the seams in his imitation Armani jacket rip, sounding the alarm that his lousy day was about to go from very bad to down-right rock bottom. He shielded his eyes against the glare.

"Let's start with what you told the cops," demanded the voice.

"What…who are you?" squeaked Austin.

"Who do you think I am?" The phone swung and lit up a face. Asian. Topped by a swoop of anime hair tinted green. "Z, man. You 'n' me already talked!"

"Z?" freaked Austin, utterly lost.

"Zipper, motherfucker! You picked up my cousin's phone!"

"Sorry!" Austin found himself apologizing. "I didn't know… I…I was just there. In shock."

Zipper swept the tiny living space with his phone light, found the one window, and pulled the blinds shut. He flipped the light switch next to the door, igniting a single torch lamp to the left of the sofa. He was taken aback by the tightness of the space.

"You're drivin' that luxe whip and livin' in this shithole?" regarded Zipper. "You're one of them tapped-ass motherfuckers, lyin' to the world. And you drive like a slow-assed ol' woman."

Austin was more than confused, mouth open in a half-formed word when Zipper chose to clarify things.

"You were at the sheriff's," stated Zipper. "We followed you and your Mercedes to this backyard shithole. You with me?"

Austin nodded, not entirely certain what he was agreeing to.

"My two cousins are the ones killed dead in front of you. Yeah?" annoyed Zipper.

"Yeah," shook Austin, focusing below Zipper's cartoon hair on a pair of silver-gray eyes like a wolf's.

"Did you tell the PD about the phone? You and me talkin'?" angered Zipper.

This was when Austin caught his first real glimpse of Zipper's muscle act, a half-Samoan steroid junkie called Fungo. Shaved scalp. Body builder. He wore a pastel wifebeater and what looked like a bone necklace.

"Now, what you say?" pressed Zipper.

"Say to who?" said Austin, still befuddled.

"The phone?"

"No. Okay? Yeah. I left that part out."

"What else you leave out?"

"Nothing."

"So, tell me what you say to the PD about the faggots who killed my cousins."

"Your cousins?"

"Fungo?"

The muscle head's open palm slapped the top of Austin's head.

"They were black. White sedan. Kinda new," stammered Austin.

"But you saw 'em?"

"Yeah."

"And black's all you got?"

The lie in Austin rose—as did the guilt. When he talked to the cops he'd purposefully left out specifics that might identify the killers. He'd heard too many stories and watched even more fear-selling news accounts of gang members applying retribution to witnesses. Yet the faces of both Calabasas gunmen might as well have been forever etched on the inside of his eyelids.

"Yeah," guessed Zipper. "You lied about that. That's 'cause you, my man, are a lyin' liar."

Zipper bent at the waist, stepping so close to Austin they could trade whiffs of each other's breath. The Asian man was of average height but stick thin, his elegant arms gesturing down to the green fingernails that matched his hair.

"Can't have you lyin' no more," threatened Zipper. "You gonna tell me every little bit about who did that shit to my family. What they look like. What they wore. Then after we get outta here you gonna call the cops back and tell 'em those same two niggas showed up here and beat your fat ass as a warning for testifying. That way you'll have a reason why you remembered."

It was too much too fast for Austin to follow. But he didn't want to ask questions for fear Fungo might slap him again. He would later quantify that first strike as a mere attention-getter. At Zipper's prompting, Austin regurgitated all he could resurrect about the shooting: the height, weight, shade of skin, scars, even the facial expressions of the killers. He relayed the specs of the car down to the Nissan Sentra's paint. Metallic ivory. At the end of the forty-minute recitation, Austin remembered the second part of Zipper's demand.

"Okay. You want me to inform the sheriffs I was just assaulted by the same two men I saw kill your cousins?"

"Unlock your phone," demanded Zipper. "I'm putting my number in it. You're gonna sticky-stay on the cops like you was liquid nails. When you hear anything from the cops you gonna call me with it and leave nothin' out. You get?"

As Austin fumbled with his cell phone, a question mark landed across his face in regards to Zipper's instruction. "When I call the cops, what kind of fictitious assault should I describe that they'll believe?"

As if on cue, Fungo rested his fencepost of a shin across the realtor's quadriceps and pinned Austin's legs just before palming the top of Austin's head like it was a basketball. As the half-Samoan chest-flexed with the cocking of his right fist, Austin got himself a close-up look at the tribal-styled necklace. What he'd imagined were bones turned out to be teeth—human teeth—each drilled through and hung on a thin loop of cable.

The impact of Fungo's fist striking his jawbone rattled the real estate broker's brain. Austin recalled a low, subwoofer-like vibration as his vision turned to gray TV static. Then he lost all consciousness.

6

Eagle Rock. 11:21 p.m.

The apartment was temporary. A sublet. That way Lucky wouldn't have to remove what little of his own property remained inside the Altadena bungalow he co-owned with Gonzo. She hadn't pressed the issue. Perhaps it was because neither wanted to take the last step to finalize their split.

The old walk-up was comfortable enough. It was on the top floor of a postwar, six-unit complex perched at the end of a nearly empty hilltop cul-de-sac. The large living room window had a partial sunset view across the east end of the San Fernando Valley.

Lucky was coming home from a late evening physical therapy session. For years, he'd been treated three times a week by a self-professed physical terrorist, building up his core to better protect the steel rods and screws used to harness his long-beleaguered back. Still sore, Lucky climbed the tight flights of wooden steps, most of them nearly walled in with painted plywood shearing. Once inside the apartment, he deadbolted the front door behind himself, unsheathed his backup Sig .45, and rested it on the kitchen table along with his two spare magazines.

Lucky couldn't count how many rented flop boxes he'd crashed in without ever really moving in, normally reserving any second bedroom for all the unpacked boxes he'd cart behind him.

But not this time.

Light was leaking from under the spare bedroom's door. Lucky eased toward the slice of light. Hoping not to disturb Karrie, he quietly cracked the door open, peeking in to see her under the full flare of the overhead lamp, dressed, and splayed belly-down on the bed like a child half her age, her strawberry-blonde hair a wild frizz covering her entire face. Fast asleep.

Only weeks away from eighteen, Lucky thought. It was wonderment that she was living with him, even if only half the time. The other nights she remained with Gonzo and Travis at the bungalow, insisting on *sistering* her unofficial younger brother. How far the father-daughter pair had come in less than three years. Since he'd rescued her, Karrie had insisted on rescuing him—at least, the best she could in her young capacity. Dedicated to a fault, she offered unconditional support and affection.

He was pivoting toward his own bedroom when the floor creaked.

"Don't turn off the light," moaned Karrie, not quite awake.

"Okay," replied Lucky.

How many times had there been that simple ask and reply? Since she'd tucked herself under his protective wing, Karrie had always slept with the light on. When she'd first moved in, he would flick her light off to save on the electric bill—much like he'd done with his younger brother when they were kids, practically living alone while their mother was working or sleeping around with strange men. Karrie had eventually confessed that she hadn't slept in the dark since she was six and the living nightmare of a childhood she had attempted to escape by running away to L.A.

But her new city had been less than kind. Forty-eight hours alone, imprisoned in a cargo container in pitch black, awaiting further sexual abuse had scared the piss out of her, reinforcing her insistence on sleeping with the light on as well as her affection for Los Angeles.

"What I think I love most about it here?" she'd recently confessed during an evening, post-movie walk. "The night is never black. Like, ever. You know? Not black like it was inside that thing I was in. In L.A. there's always some kind of light. What's it called?"

"Ambient light," Lucky had said, picturing L.A.'s endless horizontal suburbia. From streetlamps to porch lights to cars traversing the landscape, the ambient illumination reflected against the atmosphere, leaving the city in a permanent nightly gray-black glow.

"I find it really comforting," Karrie admitted before joking, "God help me if the power grid goes down."

"Then I'll be there to hold the flashlight," Lucky had warmed.

Tuesday

7

While Lucky snored his way through the night, Karrie awoke early, gathered a pre-packed sports duffle, and hurried out into the dawn. Her first stop was the Muay Thai gym in Monrovia due east. There, she sweated out her demons, showered, and happily dressed in her jeans, T-shirt, and green and black Converse before the short drive to San Gabriel and her morning gig as Min Lee's shadow.

Because she was a part-time volunteer at the grade school, parking was not afforded her. The closest non-metered parking she could find was a four-block hike—time enough for her to devour a 7-Eleven breakfast sandwich and a sweet chai tea. The walk was sunny, crisp, and full of purpose. The only unanswered questions in Karrie's mind were if she'd get to the school on time and whether or not little Min would even be attending kindergarten that day. The images of the crying student being dragged off by the vice principal had been Karrie's last thoughts before sleep and the first when her eyes had blinked open to an alarm clock reading 5:45 a.m.

Before it was chained shut with a padlock, the side gate to the playground was left open for fifteen minutes after the morning bell. With perhaps five minutes to spare, Karrie swerved from the sidewalk through the gate and bee-lined across the painted asphalt for the classrooms.

"Kaarriiee," squealed a tiny voice from behind her.

Spinning seventy-five degrees to the left, Karrie caught sight of Min's happy face on the other side of the cyclone fence that separated the empty playground from the sidewalk. Min slapped the chain-link in a rush. Karrie ran to her, bent low, zeroed in on the little girl, and touched her fingers through the stiff wire.

"Hey there, little bug!" grinned Karrie. "I missed you."

"I missed you toooo," squeaked Min, unusually vocal.

The child pulled at her keeper toward the gate as Karrie tracked her from the other side of the fence. Once they both arrived at the opening, Karrie knelt and prepared for Min to jump into her arms. Karrie was folding her arms around Min when the five-year-old was painfully yanked backward and out of her grasp.

"Ooowww!" cried Min.

"Who are you?" accused a suited Asian man in polished black shoes, his cigarette smoker's teeth revealed behind a set of fifty-year-old lips. "You are not her teacher!"

"She's my shadow," tugged Min, face full of tears and upset.

"I'm her shad—" Karrie was reaching again for Min when the man's free hand struck out, straight-arming her with a violent snap to her right shoulder.

The rest was quick—a cocktail of rehearsal and instinct. Karrie wheeled with her left side, wrapping up the man's stiff arm before delivering a hard sideways stomp. The man's knee caved sideways with distinct pops from both MCL and ACL ligaments. He was howling before the rest of him collapsed to the blacktop.

Then instead of recoiling in shocked regard at what she'd just done, Karrie swept down and scooped Min into her arms and charted a sharp course to the classroom. She didn't look back. She simply held the child tight, defensive to a fault, until the pair was ensconced in room 8K.

The classroom was in chaos with the first fifteen minutes of the school day dedicated to noisy indoor play. As only a five-year-old could, Min was off to the corner where the Duplo building blocks were stored the moment her little feet touched the floor. She slid the plastic crate from the bottom shelf and was constructing an imaginary house in seconds flat.

"Karrie, help," begged Min.

Karrie sat on the floor, distractedly reaching into the box to supply Min with more building pieces. She was shaking, replaying what she'd done, her heart in a torrid giddy-up. Had it been self-defense or assault? She couldn't say. The only fact was that she'd left the suited man who'd delivered Min to school that morning splayed on the empty asphalt, crying in pain. How long before the police would arrive? Sooner still, the vice principal? This time, to drag *her* from the classroom.

I am so fired.

Karrie's thoughts hurried ahead. She might even be arrested, hauled off to jail. God, she'd have to call Lucky. As much as he'd understand, would his opinion of her be somehow damaged? She couldn't bear that. Then again, if anyone would understand, it would *have* to be Lucky. He loved her, cared for her, got who she was. And wouldn't he have done the same thing? Around the time her mind was swimming in fears and images of what a night in jail might feel like, the teacher clapped her hands and called the classroom to order.

"Go on, Mini," whispered Karrie. "Get to your seat." The child scrambled, leaving her shadow to return the Duplo blocks to the crate.

Any minute now, Karrie whispered in her head.

Her eyes kept flicking to the classroom door, fully expecting some kind of authority to walk through in search of the strawberry-blonde assailant. The room clock ticked. The Tuesday morning routine of daily shares and walking through some rote learning of numbers and the ABCs continued without interruption. Then came recess, circle talk, and story time. The kindergarten teacher asked Karrie if she'd read to the class as a whole. With Min seated on her lap assisting with page turns, Karrie tried with all her muster to keep her voice from audibly quavering with abject fear. Nobody appeared to notice. When noon finally arrived and Karrie was set to excuse herself for her afternoon sociology class at Pasadena City College, she was left with a new worry:

Why the hell has no one come to question me?

With sunglasses masking her uncertainty, Karrie crossed the busy playground and the locked side gate where hours earlier she'd felled the man with the polished shoes and smoker's teeth. As she hurried the long way around to the school's main entrance, there were no calls out to her from school staff. Nor was she accosted by any authority. On the long trek back to her car, she cancelled out the rest of her day, choosing to skip her afternoon class and reconnoiter with Lucky instead. She speed-dialed him on her phone.

"Hey, it's me," she said, nearly breathless. "Blowing off my afternoon class. What about that surf lesson you promised me?"

8

West Hollywood. 1:32 p.m.

Frankie Coleman was not only late for her lunch, but she smelled of cigarettes and hated herself for both foibles. Over her professional career, she'd successfully curbed her habit of making people wait, an attribute she blamed on B.W.S.—or Beautiful Woman Syndrome, as she'd once heard it coined. As a teenager living in America's rural South, she had quickly discovered the power of her looks and eventually parlayed them into a Miss Tennessee crown and first runner-up to the Miss America title.

But that was a long time ago.

Frankie realized she was fresh out of breath mints and gum as the valet held open the door to her Porsche Cayenne. She dug around in the center console hoping to come up with even a Life-Saver to mask her stink.

"Jeeeeezus," she bitched, giving up and finally exhuming herself from the sedan.

The valet gave her the ubiquitous up and down, considering how she towered over him. Combined with her height, fairer than fair skin, and sweep of short, dark, chocolate brown hair, she made a head-turning snapshot, every inch of her designed to disrupt male attention. Dressed in a simple white blouse, tan capris, and matching heels, she caught her reflection in the restaurant doorway and thought to herself, *At least that much is working for me.*

"Sorry I'm late," Frankie beamed as she swung toward a side booth. The restaurant was one of those undersized Third Street bistros designed to appeal to the local showbiz and progressively political elite.

City of West Hollywood. Land of the free, home of the gay, she singsonged in her head.

"I'd wait ten minutes in Hades for you," grinned Ram, otherwise known as Mayor Ramon Avila. The fifty-year-old elected leader of the City of Angels slid from the booth and stood soldier erect, his six-foot-four frame drawing attention from the other diners. The bronze-skinned pol and the towering, forty-year-old banker made a statuesque pair, exuding a star power not lost on the mayor's other lunch guests.

"You're smoking again," whispered Ram after Frankie left a faint lipstick mark on his cheek.

"Never stopped," she sweetly twanged, as if owning the bad habit would mitigate any judgment from the mayor or his guests. "My last and only vice."

"Frankie Coleman. This is Ernst Kruger from Kapperman-Kruger Investment Group of Austria. And I'm not sure if you've met my old DWP pal Catalina Rincon."

Frankie reached across the table and shook Kruger's thin hand. His bony fingers were soft with little grip, his face elongated and strangely grim-looking. As she passed her hand off to the pixie-sized Catalina Rincon, she received an unmistakable power squeeze coupled with a smooth, toothy smile.

"Nice to meet you," Frankie drawled, fully aware that after eighteen years in Los Angeles any thickness in her accent was more performance than authentic. Truth was, her default lilt was more Tennessee twang than honey-tongued. *Born and bred trailer trash.* She was proud of how high she'd flown—from selling Girl Scout Cookies and kisses at truck stops to piloting a private bank that was mere weeks away from an IPO.

"We've met," clipped Catalina, known as Cat to those close to her. "At the Friends of the Foundry fundraiser. That was at Bergamot Station?"

"That's it," nodded Frankie, not having at all forgotten her first introduction to the petite Latina. Cat's reputation had come with a warning label. Colorful, calculating, *and* criminal, if the rumors were anything close to true. Whatever had happened, the tiny power player had somehow sidestepped liability and was still a trusted friend of the mayor and an inner circle of money bundlers and power brokers.

"And how's the banking world?" Catalina inquired, stinging Frankie with a knowing familiarity, as if Ram had told her everything. "On schedule for the IPO?"

"Only if I get my way and the attorneys don't," replied Frankie, almost smug, deftly using her quip to pivot away from Catalina to the Austrian investment scion. "Tell me who you think are slower…American finance lawyers? Or the Swiss?"

"Oh, the Americans, I'd say," smiled the aging investor. "Institutionally speaking, the Euros tend to know where their bread is best buttered."

Frankie had done her research. The Austrian investment banker was fourth-generation rich, his family's wealth and holdings dating back to the First and Second World Wars, after which they'd strategically moved their assets to Switzerland. Frankie was out to sell the man on doing his US banking with her boutique establishment, Aegis & Angels Partners, Ltd. Ram had promised the introduction. This was Frankie's audition. Clearly, the mayor's pal, Catalina Rincon, was along for more than Ram's amusement.

"Ram tells me you were a Miss America," shifted the Austrian.

"Oh, Ram," Frankie teased. "You didn't tell me I was going to have to bring my crown to lunch." After a nudge to the mayor, she returned her attention to the investor. "I was, in fact, only a contestant. First runner-up. Not bad, but not a winner. Guess I peaked at Miss Tennessee."

"I like country music," swung the investor.

"And I love depositing buckets of Euros in my bank," she said, her baby blue lamps leveled on her target. She let her lips glide back across her competition-perfect teeth. "I know. I'm direct. But I'm also confident in my abilities. Just four years ago, all I had was an idea and the phone numbers of two billionaires. I sold them, and Aegis & Angels was born. And now, here I am."

"And she's still goddamn pretty," added Catalina, a bit forward, adding a scent of sexual tension to the moment.

Frankie swiveled to Catalina, her short coif gently bouncing like perfect daggers stylishly hanging from her scalp. The hair, as well as the rest of her look, was part of her sell. A natural blonde, Frankie had started coloring her locks dark brown soon after quitting on her Hollywood dream. Once she'd set her sights on an international finance MBA at UCLA, she had quickly learned that a brunette in glasses was taken far more seriously than a blonde ex-Miss with a nasally Tennessee tongue.

"Thank you." Frankie looked at Catalina. "I try."

"Seriously," added Ram. "If I wasn't mayor, my wife would send me packing for just looking at either of these two. Let alone sharing a lunch."

Okay, thought Frankie. *The table is set.*

Sex on the mind was generally a good start to a sale. Frankie had long ago learned that men liked to be teased. It was fuel for their natural fantasies and often served as a warm foundation for shoptalk. She was a woman who was alluring, confident, and didn't mind a little innuendo. Moreover, she could deliver hard, cold numbers on terms like arbitrage, bid-to-cover ratios, credit default swaps, interest-sensitive viabilities, and risk-weighted assets.

"Sir," restarted Frankie.

"Please. My name is Ernst," insisted the investor.

"Very well," she continued. "Apart from the very public charity work we've done with Ram's office over the past few years, I know you wouldn't be here if—pardon the expression—you hadn't already looked up the skirt of my business."

Frankie could've glanced to her right and captured Catalina and Ram's reaction to her sexed-up line of attack. Instead, she kept her gaze fixed on the old Austrian to measure to what degree he might involuntarily blush or swallow. A little color to the man's ears or cheeks would be just right. Too much red in the face or a lower lip quiver might reveal she'd crossed a line. No reaction whatsoever might say the investor was either homo- or asexual and disinterested in provocative wordplay.

Despite the investor's practiced Euro-cool of feigned indifference, the lobes of his ears practically glowed crimson from the blood rush of titillation.

"By my estimation, you must have cash laid off in various US institutions to the tune of two to three hundred million," Frankie pressed with greater confidence. "A flyer with my bank, say, of twenty-five million? I'd show you how we're doing better for our depositors than banks with ten times our assets—"

Almost in unison, Mayor Ram's and Cat's faces suddenly turned upwards to Frankie's left, the aging investor's eyes being the last to swerve.

"Three of four of my favorite people at one table," interrupted Denny Teng. "What are the odds?"

"Or only in L.A.," added Ram, his long arm stretched past Frankie, hand open for a grip.

The basketball-player-tall Dennis Teng, dapperly dressed in an ivory linen suit, stood over the booth, megawatt smile beaming back at them all like the Cheshire Cat of *Alice in Wonderland*. His thirty-five-year-old crop of black hair casually planted over a pair of sharply expressive eyebrows.

"Denny Teng in white. Don't you look dashing," offered Catalina. "What's the occasion?"

"Trying to sell a chunk of my investment cap to Hollywood," replied Denny.

Frankie faked a smile while trying like hell not to appear nervous or caught off guard. But her insides had gone from fully self-assured to those of a crumbling cookie. She slid from the booth and, despite her height, had to stand on her tiptoes to kiss Denny's cheek.

Then, out of her lunch companions' view, her left hand pinched Denny's thigh just enough to send a nervy message.

"How's my sugar man?" she feigned, stuffing her jones to rush outside through the kitchen to suck back a cigarette.

"Too bad my wife's real Chinese, otherwise *she* might wanna call me that," joked Denny.

"Not a Chinese thing?" asked Ram.

"'Sugar man' has different connotations," replied Denny. "Take my word for it, not worth going into detail."

"You are not real Chinese?" asked the Austrian investor in what sounded like a putdown. He was clearly put off that he'd yet to be introduced to Denny Teng.

"American," returned Denny, offering his hand. "Chinese-American on paper. But I'm So Cal born and raised. Denny Teng."

"Who, I might add," interjected Frankie, "is also doing lots of bang-bang business with A&A."

"Bang-bang?" asked the investor. "Is that a new American financial term?"

"I represent a lot of Pacific rim companies who need to get their money from there to here," explained Denny. "Frankie's my stopgap. And let me tell you, her international group makes the complicated so much easier. Genius bank."

"Join us?" offered Ram.

"See that hungry-looking trio in Armani?" nodded Denny across the restaurant. "They're waiting to pluck my feathers."

"Like that's gonna happen," smiled Frankie, trying not to look semi-thrilled at the prospect of Denny making an exit sooner than later.

"Nice meeting you, sir," smoothed Denny. "Cat? We need to catch up. Ram? You owe me a dinner."

"My office will call," assured Ram.

"Frankie, my platonic love," finished Denny, "always a joy."

"Love to your wife," patted Frankie, returning to her seat in the booth. "Now, where were we?"

"Small town, your big city," remarked the investor.

"It's a who-you-know town," added Catalina.

"And by that definition," winked Ram, "my city is very, very small."

"Eight million people," smirked Frankie before her punchline. "One hundred stories."

The table erupted in laughs. It calmed Frankie, whose insides were still a tumult. Just knowing Denny Teng was sharing the same restaurant air gave her an under-the-skin case of the heebie-jeebies. If that Austrian investor—or anybody else in the banking universe—suspected her business with Denny Teng was less than legitimate, her precious IPO would be dead in the water—as would her career in finance. It was as if all of a sudden, from the height of a high wire, she felt how far her fall would be. And that was to a place worse than the trailer park from which she'd vaulted herself.

That worse place being prison.

Thirty feet away, Denny Teng was seated at a four-top table with his broad swimmer's back to Frankie and her lunch companions. If anything, he felt buttressed by the chance encounter. Encouraged. To his rear were partners in both crime and future fortunes, particularly in regard to his banker and his friend, the mayor. Across from him were a trio of Hollywood movers and shakers he was hoping to impress with the gap funding he was willing to invest in their various movie projects. Yet despite his bounty of business prospects, Denny couldn't shake the thousand-pound invisible anchor that he felt hanging from his ankles, threatening to drown him and everything he'd worked for. The anchor had a name. Chinese. And it rhymed with *fuck me*.

That name was Tung Chee.

As the power brokers in Armani suits joked and cajoled their moneyed link to mainland Chinese financing, Denny smiled, laughed at their jokes, played the game. Still, there was the anchor front and center in his cerebral cortex.

Tung goddamned Chee.

Dumb-assed fobby fuck, complained Denny to himself. This despite never having met the man. Denny didn't even know what Tung Chee looked like. Tung Chee was but a name on a list. A long list. It was a profitable list that Denny had been mining for almost a year.

Denny didn't know the details, but something had gone horribly wrong in Calabasas. *And why the hell Calabasas?* What was the mainland moron doing banking in the West Valley—miles and miles from the SGV?

Disaster, thought Denny.

"You following all this?" asked one of the power brokers, sensing perhaps that Denny had checked out of the lunch conversation.

"Not just following. I'm miles ahead of you," disarmed Denny with a charmer's grin. Not quite a lie. In his perception, the three men across from him were in the business of screwing over investors. They looked to Denny as their next bird in hand, soon to be defeathered. Not that he minded. His game was to play the lamb until he found the route to screw the screwers back. To him, that was business. Men or women screwing over other men and women for profit—or at its most basic, dog eat dog. Capitalism was Darwinism at its most pure.

At least he was back in the moment. The game. He'd once again shoved Tung Chee to the back seat of his brain and concentrated on the showbiz pitch. It's the least he could do, considering the knowledge that Tung Chee would soon return like a rectal-reminding hemorrhoid.

9

Malibu. 6:45 p.m.

The sun hung low, pinched between a filmy vanilla layer of clouds and the high-priced cliff estates atop Point Dume. There was a slight chop to the water, making the ocean glitter. Fifty yards beyond the break, Lucky sat astride his surfboard, Karrie alongside him, the cold onshore breeze buffeted by their wet suits. It had been over a decade since he'd taken up the waves, the last sojourn feeling like a failed attempt to recapture the best part of his youth. This time, it was Karrie's interest in the sport that had brought him back. The evenings they'd shared on the water returned him to the clarifying sensation of getting lost in the pocket of a wave, the smells, the brine, the familiar taste of sea salt on his lips.

And he was grateful.

It was no surprise that Karrie had proven an excellent student.

In an eyeblink she'd picked up the basics: the pop-up, board positioning, life-saving duck dives, and Eskimo rolls. Within a week she was already catching wave shoulders and chasing down clean faces. If only he'd had a GoPro camera to catch her first cutback—textbook, arms wide and low, butt pointed at the beach as she turned a crisp one-eighty into the break and escaped the churn. She'd screamed in existential delight as she flipped off the top, caught some air, and splashed down.

"Did you see that? Did you see that?" she'd squealed.

He surely had. Every foamy millisecond.

At the end of each session, and before they chased one last wave, the pair would sit side by side on their boards, the swells rolling underneath them as they talked, shared, and tried to make up for the father-daughter time they had missed out on during Karrie's first fifteen years. As the sun was collapsing behind the cliffs, Karrie replayed the sequence of events from the last thirty-six hours: five-year-old Min's removal from Monday's class; their happy reunion that morning; the sudden assault by the Asian man with smoker's teeth; and her swift, knee-collapsing retaliation, followed by an oppressive fear of imminent arrest.

"Then nothing," she finished. "Nobody came. The yellow teeth dude just kinda vanished. The morning was like normal Tuesday classroom stuff."

"You probably embarrassed him," surmised Lucky. "Guy admitting he got his ass kicked is hard enough. By a blonde chick in tie-dye, well…" Lucky let it hang. He'd made his point.

"Can't be the end of it," she argued. "I mean, the school's got cameras everywhere. It's on tape."

"Unless there's a complaint, doubt anybody's gonna look," said Lucky before shifting back to a more curious point. "The pictures the girl was drawing. What are they about?"

"Disturbing," she admitted. "But that's why I'm her shadow. Besides already being diagnosed as dyslexic, she's super shut down. There's stuff in that little noggin of hers that's pretty weird."

"Like?"

"Hard to describe her pictures. There's all these lemon-yellow suns. Flowers. Happy house on the outside. But some dark, weird stuff happening inside. There's this recurring character. Purple and green like Barney the dinosaur. Only she named it the Monster Chihuahua."

"Monster Chihuahua?" chuckled Lucky, wondering if heard her correctly.

"I can show you the pictures. After they dragged her out of the class I put her art folder in my backpack."

"Pretty bold of you. Why?"

"Dunno. I just did it. There was a gun in the last drawing. That's why the office got their panties all in a bunch. I mean, Jesus. She's only five. She's not gonna shoot up a school. She probably saw the gun on TV."

"Sucks," finished Lucky.

Though it was a public beach, access to Dume Cove was severely limited by the megamillion-dollar real estate that occupied the overlooking cliff. Unless surfers were willing to hike from southerly Paradise Cove or the westward side and Point Dume Beach, which was far around the point, a key or a gate code was required for access to the steep trails leading to the sand. When he was a South Bay surf punk, Lucky was more concerned about running into packs of the MLO—Malibu Locals Only gang— than getting busted for trespassing or illegally bypassing gate locks. Some of his reckless youth had proved advantageous as a police officer, especially his knack for beating a variety of locks.

Lucky wasn't going to let his position as a sheriff's deputy— suspended or otherwise—prevent Karrie and him from a surfing shortcut. They'd parked near the end of Cliffside Drive, suited up, and cut toward the cliffs on a path between a eucalyptus tree–lined estate and a newer property under a massive renovation. The rein-forced steel gate, illegally installed to prevent public beach access, had a mechanical push-button combination lock not unlike those used in government buildings. In the bad ol' days, teenaged Lucky would easily defeat any kind of strike plate with a sturdy credit card or thin cable inserted into the gap. But in the 1990s, most mega-rich homeowners had installed the supposedly pick-proof five-button locks. Non-electric. Weather resistant.

On their first trip to Dume Cove, Lucky had approached the blockade with amusing calm. After asking Karrie to hold his surfboard, he had knelt and dug his fingers into the sandy topsoil, sifting until he had a handful of powdery dust. After a brief examination of the buttons, he blew the dust onto the lock, certain that unless the buttons had been recently scrubbed with an alcohol-based cleanser, the tiny dirt particles would cling to wherever oil had been deposited—either from bodies or, more likely, some kind of chemical sunblock. Once he'd identified the most-used buttons—and knowing the lock required three unique numbers—it was just a matter of identifying which of the only six combinations would release the latch. The code turned out to be 5-2-1, easily memorized and repeated with each of Lucky's and Karrie's subsequent visits.

"More shades of a misspent youth," Karrie had remarked. Lucky's reply had been a less-than-proud wink. And from then on, to any curious neighbors, Lucky and Karrie appeared as welcome guests who'd been granted the gate's access code.

It was practically night by the time Lucky and Karrie climbed the switchback trail from the beach to the gate. The sky had slipped past twilight to near dark. Lucky held both surfboards while Karrie felt the buttons and keyed the code. There was a question stuck on her tongue, one that she'd been waiting to ask when the time was ripe. As the gate swung free, so did her query.

"Did you love her?" asked Karrie in a total non sequitur.

"What?" wondered Lucky. "That's a pretty stupid question."

"Not talking 'bout Gonzo," clarified Karrie, tucking her fish-tail surfboard back under her arm. She let Lucky lead the way on the weedy path to the street, a lone streetlamp as their beacon. "I meant your police officer trainee. The one that was murdered. Deputy St. George."

"Oh," breathed Lucky. "Shia."

"That's her."

"Did I have thing for her?" Lucky shielded his discomfort while seeking the right words.

"I mean, she was *sooo* beautiful. You two were in a patrol car for, like, five months. And…"

…*And I was briefly accused of her murder.*

"Suppose you could say I did," relived Lucky. "Different, though. Not like I love you. Or Gonzo."

"You know what I mean."

"C'mon."

"You don't have to tell me. It's not like you and Gonzo were married."

"We bought a house together. We were committed. Do the math."

"So, you didn't."

"Love her?"

"Hook up."

"'Scuse me?"

"Okay. Have a fling."

"Really, Karrie?"

"I know," she admitted. "Why do I wanna know? Why is that any of my business…which it's not, by the way."

"Then why ask?"

"'Cause I wanna know."

"Wanna know what? If I cheated?" Lucky's voice had turned from cautious to sharp and uneasy.

The trailhead emptied to the asphalt stripe of Cliffside Drive. Lucky's '99 Crown Victoria, recently and incongruously outfitted with a Thule surfboard rack, was parked on the opposite side, seventy-five yards to the east. Lucky turned toward it, expecting Karrie to remain in his increasingly annoyed wake. He angled across the blacktop.

"Ow, shit," Karrie bitched. She stopped suddenly at the trail's edge, utilizing her surfboard as a crutch so she could remove a sharp pebble that had sneaked into her mesh and neoprene water shoes. Lucky, who carried the car keys in an aqua-pouch around his waist, enjoyed the brief distance, thinking perhaps by the time she'd caught up with him her inquiry would've been altered or, even better, permanently corked.

"Just gonna start the car," he called back, wanting to get the heater working, fully expecting the usual chill once he'd peeled off his wet suit. With the breeze, the air felt like a muscle-hardening forty-five degrees Fahrenheit.

Karrie spanked the heel of her shoe to make certain the pebble had come free, slipped it back on her foot, and resumed her tack, already a hundred feet to Lucky's rear.

She never heard the car—at least not until it was upon her.

From out of a shadow it came, low to the ground and accelerating—a compact electric vehicle in a hurry. Headlights extinguished. She would never see the make or model, nor remember anything after her head struck the windshield. Karrie felt her legs leave the ground, kicked out from underneath her. Something snapped. *My surfboard*, she thought in that warped instant of consciousness with no regard whatsoever for her body. Then it was lights out. Brain motors cut. All that before Karrie even returned to earth.

Lucky's ears were first to catch the sound. There was the slightest chirp of rubber against road upon the initial surge from the shadows, followed by the quiet scream of an electric motor winding up. His eyes followed, catching up to the Chevy Volt's slate gray skin as it sped past. A warning stuck in his throat, unable to find the breath to release before he heard the collision. There was the slap of a body going limp combined with the dull double-clunk of Karrie's surfboard severing as the impact spun it into the air. The crack of Karrie's head slapping the windshield pierced the dark like a gunshot. Under the lone streetlamp, Lucky saw her body rotate midair, legs one way while her partially stripped wet suit flung the other.

In his mind, Lucky saw himself rushing forward, catching Karrie in his arms, or at least breaking her fall. Only reality returned as she collided with the street with nothing whatsoever to cushion her body. To the ears, it was sickening. To the eyes, Karrie was barely a visible yellow and black speed bump in the road. Motionless. Lucky would remember the silence that followed, as if his ears were still filled with seawater. He raced forward, grabbing at his aqua-pack for his cell phone. He would never recall if he talked to the 911 operator. All he had were images, flashes of memory, and the sensation of too much of Karrie's sticky, warm blood coagulating in her strawberry-blonde hair and onto his fingers.

Lucky cradled her like a baby, commanded her not to die, and waited a lifetime for the sirens.

10

He'd wanted to tailgate the ambulance. If he could, Lucky would have drafted the emergency vehicle, riding every inch of roadway bumper to bumper until his arrival at the nearest trauma center. Yet he also knew he was the sole eyewitness. A Cliffside Drive homeowner who was in her front garden tending her rose bushes by flashlight had called 911. She'd heard the shock of the impact and had frozen briefly before hurrying out her gate to see Lucky's shadow sprinting for his daughter.

The first responders were two pairs of L.A. sheriffs in radio units. While one duo of uniforms attended Karrie, the other pulled Lucky away in an attempt to get an early statement. Lucky struggled with the youngest deputy, an obvious trainee, and insisted on staying with Karrie until the EMTs arrived. Either the rookie didn't hear Lucky identify himself as a cop or Lucky hadn't expressed as much when he thought he had. When he had tried to push his way back to Karrie, the trainee hooked him, spinning the distressed father back around. Lucky met the youngster with a palm heel to the nose. It was reflexive. Unthinking. Cartilage was mashed, a spit of blood issued, followed by the slight buckling of the young man's knees.

In a blink, Lucky was gang-tackled to the asphalt, cuffed, and fitted into the back seat of a black-and-white. Eventually, while a team of paramedics mobilized Karrie, the deputies were able to sort out exactly who Lucky was: a fellow sheriff; the hit and run victim, his daughter. Out of earshot from the growing throng of curious neighbors, off-the-record cell phone calls were quietly dialed to assess Lucky's reputation as a cop. The trainee, who was burning mad and threatening to file his very first 243B charge—the California penal code for battery on a police officer—was harshly sidelined by his training officer with a strong suggestion that he invent a less incendiary scenario to explain his broken nose.

"Like your dumb ass tripped over your untied boot laces," suggested the training officer, a sergeant with some ties to Lennox Station, Lucky's old stomping grounds.

Lucky's brain felt fractured, one half wanting to chase after the ambulance while the other needed to cooperate with the authorities on scene in order to get as many sheriffs and LAPD assets searching for the driver of the Chevy Volt. Moments before he was cut loose to follow the path of the EMS transport, a report was radioed in. Deputies had discovered an abandoned Chevy Volt in the Zuma Beach public parking lot, front hood with a human-sized dent, the windshield caved to the bull's-eye where Karrie's head had made impact. Left behind were residual blood and strands of strawberry-blonde hair. A quick computer search of the VIN number revealed the car had only just been reported stolen.

Still wearing that wet suit stripped to his waist, Lucky drove the '99 hard. Per L.A. County emergency protocol, the ambulance crew had radioed their destination—the Los Robles Medical Center in Thousand Oaks—to the sheriffs. The twisting route to the hospital was via Kanan Dume Road through the Santa Monica Mountains, the low-lying desert range that separated the west San Fernando Valley from the Pacific. As he raced through tunnels and along steep ledges, Lucky worked the numbers. Los Angeles and thereabouts had long worn the crown as the bank robbery capital of the United States, but had recently earned a second title: America's leader in hit-and-run accidents. Almost nightly, victims were left bleeding and often dead inside the stripes of city crosswalks. Many blamed the ugly statistic on the overwhelming number of illegals living in the Southland and the state's insistence on providing them with driver's licenses. The undocumented. Migrants. Mostly from Mexico and Central America. Lucky was reminded of another one of So Cal's dubious achievements. It was the nation's uninsured driver capital.

Facts aside, the Chevy Volt that had struck Karrie bore none of the usual trademarks of the garden-variety hit and run. Though the car was reportedly stolen from a restaurant valet stand in Culver City, the run-down hadn't happened in the act of escape. If anything, the scenario reeked of someone lying in wait. No headlights. The license plate lamps purposefully extinguished. The choice of a nearly silent, all-electric vehicle could be construed as a conscious act of stealth. Was it a targeted hit? Or was it some kind of bizarre flavor of thrill kill?

Kill?

Lucky hadn't yet entertained the thought that Karrie might be dead. Murdered or accidental. Until that moment she was, at least in his mind, no more than injured with a few broken bones and a lousy bump on her head. With the car windows down and the cold air rushing through the Crown Vic's cabin had come another chill. Lucky had begun replaying the scene in his mind—over and over—Karrie's shadow tossed ragdoll-like into the ocean air before crumpling to the pavement. How could she not have been seriously injured? Or dead? She'd left blood where her head had met with the windshield as well on the road where she had lain, not to mention on Lucky's hands, which had since dried red.

Karrie, dead? No. No. And no!

Lucky couldn't imagine that the rundown had been meant for him. Dark as it was on Cliffside Drive, it would be hard to mistake Karrie's slightness for his six feet of height, buzzed scalp, and muscular build. She was just five-four and, wet suit aside, impossibly feminine. So, why her?

With every mile, Lucky felt a creeping guilt. Had somebody aimed the car at her as a message for him?

The list of those who might want to hurt Lucky was long. As he escaped the mountain range and the lights of Westlake Village loomed, Lucky thought of the Kasabians. Namely Chris. Were he and the Armenian mob behind the attack? Or might it have been an older foe like Greg Beem? *Assuming that Greg Beem was even alive...* Names rushed into Lucky's brain along with all the faces of those who had motive to do him harm. Too many to count and hardly enough time.

Once at the hospital, Lucky didn't bother searching out a legal parking space. He left the Crown Vic in the fire lane and, still barefoot, burst through the emergency room's automatic doors. He swept through the waiting room to the admitting window, the soles of his feet slapping against the polished linoleum.

"I'm looking for Karrie Kaarlsen!" he barked, hoping his state of undress and body language would inform any and all as to the urgency.

"I'm sorry, sir," said the calm, apple-faced nurse protected by an inch-thick pane of Plexiglas drilled with holes for visitors' voices to pass through. At the bottom was a document slot. "Who are you asking for?"

"Karrie Kaarlsen...or Karrie Dey," corrected Lucky. "Seventeen. Head trauma."

"The hit and run?" she asked.

"That's her. I'm her father."

"I think they…" she began before giving her words a serious rethink. She swiveled in her chair, opened the door directly behind her, and called back. "The hit and run?"

Lucky saw the woman nod, her fat body in Lane Bryant nurse-wear perfectly balanced on her seat's caster wheels.

"What I thought," she continued. "Trauma docs worried they couldn't stabilize her, so they called the helicopter. Just airlifted her to UCLA Med."

"Jesus, really? Westwood?"

"What did you say your name was?"

"Deputy Lucas Dey," said Lucky. "Spelled D-E-Y."

"I don't think your name came up on next of kin," said the nurse, her fingers tapping her keyboard with a rhythm. "Driver's license database had an address in Altadena. We called and spoke to a Ms. Lydia Gonzalez."

"You spoke to her?"

"Just reading the notes on the screen, sir."

"Do the notes say if she's critical? Alive? Stable?"

"Says airlifted UCLA Med," she answered dryly. "Do you need directions?"

Directions? No. What Lucky needed was a helicopter. Instead, he was relegated to navigating thirty-plus more miles of evening traffic, all while his heart was coming undone. He'd never experienced such pain, not even when he'd lost his younger brother. He was gripped by fear, pure unmitigated terror. The thought of losing Karrie brought tears to his eyes. His brain was cycling, moving from anger to recrimination to fear, over and over. Back in the driver's seat of the '99, he was trying to collect himself when his phone trilled. Gonzo's name appeared on the screen.

"Yeah, hi," Lucky quickly answered, his voice betraying him—his throat so constricted he practically squeaked. "You got the call?"

"What happened?" asked Gonzo.

"Hit and run," he replied.

"How bad?"

"I dunno. Had to stay behind to make a statement. Then they sent me to the wrong fucking hospital."

"Where are you?"

"All the way out in Thousand Oaks."

"Jesus!"

"Heading to UCLA now. Where are you?"

"Almost to the 405," said Gonzo. "Travis is with me."

"You're gonna beat me there. I'll get there as quick as I can."

"Drive safe," she said by habit, as if she were sending him off on a simple sortie to the supermarket for a gallon of milk. "You know what I mean."

"You too."

It had been two-plus hours since Lucky had climbed from the ocean and the cold air had at last penetrated his core. He took a moment and moved to the back seat where he stripped off his wet suit, replacing the damp neoprene with denim, a hoodie, and a pair of flip-flops. Upon returning to the front seat he noticed a slick piece of paper trapped underneath his windshield wiper.

A goddamn parking ticket?

Lucky reached around and snatched the paper, preparing to crumple it and toss it clear when, for some reason, he recalled the advice from his lawyer.

Low profile. Nose clean. Not even a parking ticket.

While turning the ignition key with his right hand, Lucky unfolded with his left what he thought was a summons to pay a fine. Only it wasn't the printed slip he expected. It was post-card-sized stock. Slick. A real estate broker's advertisement with a silhouetted home against a palm tree sunset. Inserted was a retouched photo of a smiling, dark-haired, strong-jawed man. The copy read:

Austin Anderson
The West Valley's Number 1 Broker
"I guarantee top dollar for your house!"

Lucky re-crushed the card, flipped the wad into his back seat, and punched the gas pedal.

11

Encino.

Along with never having suffered the unkindness of a fist to his face, Austin often prided himself on his survival instinct. Furthermore, since he'd paraded himself as a straight male most of his life, he'd never suffered a lick of gay discrimination—at least none that he could arguably measure. And now the ugly hole he was in, not to mention the bruises on his face, was partially of his own making. When he woke from unconsciousness, Zipper and Fungo were barely a memory. For the briefest moment, Austin thought all of it had been just a liquor-induced nightmare—the accident on Revere, the killers, the dead Asian men in the truck…

…even that tempting gym bag stuffed with hundred-dollar bills.

But as he noticed the half-empty towering bottle of Kirkland brand vodka, the pain had come—a rush of knives emanating from his jaw surging northward into the underlining of his skull—and with it, awareness.

He had barely been able speak when he dialed 911 the night before. By the time the LAPD arrived, he'd found a bag of frozen peas to hold against his face and had already begun sipping tall vodka and diet tonics through a straw. He made two sets of statements—one to the LAPD since they policed Encino where he'd been assaulted; the other to sheriffs who had jurisdiction over Calabasas. Both included the lying canard that he'd been attacked by the same pair of black men he'd witnessed murder the two men in the turtled pickup. The lie wasn't as hard to tell as he had thought it would be. He was, after all, a real estate agent. If Austin hadn't yet learned how to sell a story, he wouldn't have deserved that once-true moniker as the West Valley's number-one broker.

After swallowing a double dose of Advil PM chased by a fourth cocktail, Austin had passed out on his bed, waking just shy of noon the following day, his face glued to the long-defrosted packet of peas.

"Jesus," he mumbled aloud, stunned his lips even worked. A look in the bathroom mirror revealed that half his face was black and blue and swollen, his jaw oddly cockeyed. "What the fuck?"

Although the LAPD officers had suggested he visit the nearest ER or doctor to have his jaw looked over, Austin had somehow managed to convince himself that he just hadn't imbibed enough ibuprofen to stem the mass of inflammation. Advil or Motrin he could afford. A doctor visit, he couldn't. His private insurance coverage had long since lapsed. And of late, when he'd suffered anything worthy of a physician's attention, he'd dressed down, parked his Mercedes far from the hospital, and utilized Southland emergency rooms—none anywhere near his real estate stomping grounds—and claimed he was indigent.

Austin pillaged his ex-wife's medicine cabinet in search of more serious painkillers. He found a bottle loaded with Vicodin and, after considering his ex's feathery weight, popped triple the recommended dose.

Finally, nearly twenty-four hours after he'd received the heavy blow to his face, Austin drove west to Thousand Oaks and the Los Robles Medical Center. Perhaps it was the hydrocodone haze that caused him to grab a handful of those slick postcard flyers. From the Quiznos sub shop—where he'd sandwiched his luxury sedan into a compact car spot—to the emergency room entrance, he semi-buoyantly stuffed the four-by-five-inch advertisements under windshield wipers and into car door jambs. Austin was so high on opiates that by the time the double doors of the ER automatically slid open, he honestly could have said he was feeling no pain whatsoever. There were some eleven or so people in the waiting area with a stripped-to-the-waist surfer dude occupying the attention of the single admitting nurse. Austin found a seat near the registration window, fanned the leftover postcards like a deck of cards, and momentarily fixated on the surfer's physique.

Not that I have a snowball's chance in Hades of bedding such a stud, dismissed Austin.

Attractive as Surfer Man was, the broker suspected his kind didn't bend the gay way. But Austin was still fond of looking. He especially liked the way the surfer's wet suit dangled, partially peeled from the man's torso as if meant to tease. The man's muscles were tensed. Urgent. Surfer Man's right calf was mostly exposed, revealing a tattoo inked across smooth skin. Austin tilted his head, at last making out the artwork as something resembling the Grim Reaper. Austin startled as Surfer Man raised his voice and looked poised to slip his fingers into the window's holes and rip the Plexiglas clean from the reinforced frame.

As it turned out, Surfer Man was Austin's last distraction before the pain returned. In that middle ground between an opiate high and pure torture, Austin found a moment of clarity. While still waiting for his name to be called, his eyes were drawn from the TV screen and fixated on the multitude of security cameras installed on the ceiling. The room appeared covered from all angles, every tick of every human being collected, recorded, and stored under the lenses' high-definition gaze.

Security, indeed.

And with that, an idea formed.

When Austin's turn came he mumbled his symptoms, signed the variety of government assistance forms, and was fitted with an ER bracelet and ushered through the basic triage procedures before being wheelchaired down to radiology for an X-ray. All the while, he played a game with himself by trying to pick out every security camera, counting them off in his pounding skull.

Nineteen, twenty, twenty-one…

He was X-rayed and CT-scanned. Both revealed a mandibular fracture. After that he was IV'd, pumped with a Darvocet drip, and parked in pre-op until dawn, when an oral surgeon was scheduled to wire his jaw shut. With that constant flow of painkillers, dosed appropriately to keep him in a womb-like miasma, he was happy to wait until whenever. After that, he'd revisit his genius idea, turn it into a full-fledged personal safety scheme, and perhaps even salve his financial worries.

12

The private waiting room was compact to the point of suffo-
cation—windowless and reserved for families in shock while
loved ones unconsciously tried to make it through hours of emergency surgery. Gonzo had been first to arrive, her sixteen-year-old
son Travis accompanying her on the long, fevered drive from
Altadena. The two were informed that Karrie was in surgery and
were shown to the seemingly airless little room whose occupants
remained in an emotional holding pattern. Lucky arrived shortly
after. The trio shared awkward hugs before retreating to separate
corners of a rectangle no larger than the average middle-class dining room. Lucky answered Gonzo's questions in an unconscious
monotone, reciting back most of what he could recall from the hit
and run, playing more to the glass-protected lithograph framed on
the wall than mother or son. After that there was little said. With

all the unexpressed tension there was barely room for small talk. It had been more than three months since Lucky and Gonzo had even spoken to each other.

"So weird," said Travis, shattering an almost twenty-minute silence. "This is what Karrie was trying to make happen. You know? The four of us all together again."

"Albeit under slightly different circumstances," muttered Gonzo, sarcasm thick.

"Yeah, but…" shrugged Travis.

Gonzo crossed her Latina stems, as long and poetic as the day Lucky had met her, then attempted to relax her shoulders against some rather stiff couch cushion. Lucky spied as she slipped her fingers underneath that spray of soft, black kink to massage her own stiff neck. He could read the strain on her like a roadmap where all highways led directly back to him. His faults. His malignant errors. His lousy damned judgment. It was as plain as her face that she'd already blamed him for whatever calamity had befallen Karrie. Without any evidence to the contrary, Lucky wasn't in a position to argue.

"I need to find out what's happening," lurched Lucky.

Opening the heavy door, he felt a whoosh of air as if he'd unsealed something. The noise of the busy hospital hit him, a reminder of the waiting room's vacuum-like quality. Hermetically sealed. Soundproofed. A design meant to mute the wails from bereft families unable to contain their grief. As he sighted down a nurse practitioner, Lucky heard a voice behind him.

"Coming through!" sounded a male attendant in scrubs and disposable booties, guiding a rolling cot. Two more nurses flanked the bed with a fourth technician pushing from the rear. Attached were two IV stands holding three bags of various fluids that snaked through clear tubes into a comatose, fully intubated patient covered by an inflatable blanket.

Lucky could see a shaved head encircled by a crown with six screws penetrating the skull at ninety-degree angles. The patient's face was black-and-blue, swollen, and almost devoid of any features.

Lucky didn't recognize her at all. But somehow he knew. Karrie!

"Jesus," he uttered as she passed.

Trailing were a pair of surgeons; the elder of the two, a cue-balled, slight man in scrubs, chattering away in a thick Israeli accent.

"S'cuse me," stopped Lucky. "But that's my daughter!"

"Yes. I was just coming by," stalled the neurosurgeon, who motioned to the waiting room door. "Are you all here?"

"There's only three of us," replied Lucky, subconsciously fearing that the odd number would become a permanent scar; a hellish reminder that Karrie might never be part of them again.

"I'll be right with you," said the neurosurgeon in practically a whisper, his voice as warm as it was comforting.

The passing minutes felt like they were sealed in an airless coffin. Before the surgeon returned, Lucky had only been able to report to Gonzo and Travis that Karrie was alive and unconscious, with her head connected to an erector set–like apparatus that appeared to be holding pieces of her skull in place. His dire description caused Travis, whose general affect leaned toward the stoic, to collapse into sobs.

The neurosurgeon, who introduced himself by his birth name, Uziel, suggested the broken family sit before he calmly rattled off the emergency procedures Karrie had received, followed by a breakdown of those yet to come. It was a wash of medical information loaded down with acronyms that Uziel patiently unpacked, the first being TBI, traumatic brain injury. The massive blow to the back of Karrie's skull had caused so much swelling that the doctors had to induce a coma before installing drains to relieve the ever-increasing pressure against the walls of her skull. She was alive but remained critical. The following hours and days would inform them more as to her likelihood of survival.

There was more. Karrie had suffered a fractured pelvis. Her right femur was shattered and would require significant reconstruction, as would her ankle. There were hairline fractures in her left ulna and severe bruising to her right kidney, which had temporarily stopped functioning.

Gonzo, ever the cool warrior, was full of queries that Uziel calmly answered. If Karrie came through, it was a safe bet to expect some brain damage and extensive rehab. *How bad?* The surgeon could only shrug his answer, describing the brain as a complex organ capable of untold miracles. It was all going to be about what happened if—and whenever—consciousness returned and Karrie's will to recover.

"But will she still be Karrie?" begged Travis at one point.

"I've had patients who could never walk or talk again," answered Uziel, a gentle hand squeezing Travis's shoulder. "And I've had others who were able to dance and compose symphonies. It will be up to your sister. But right now I'd like to work on having her survive the night."

And that was it. When the kind doctor exited the room and the door clicked shut behind him, the vacuum returned. It was as if all the air had been sucked out with him. The uncomfortable trio was left stunned in suspended animation.

"Someone's going to need to be here," began Gonzo. "At least until she's out of the woods."

Though Lucky was nodding his agreement, his mind was already elsewhere, making moves on his own mental chessboard. He couldn't get the pictures of injured Karrie out of his temporal lobe. There was a reason why she was at death's door. Somebody was responsible. And that person was somewhere out there, beyond the walls of the hospital.

"Lucky?" asked Gonzo. "You good with that?"

"Yeah," he answered almost remotely. "You're good to stay here for a while?"

"How long's a while?" she asked, already suspicious he had some hidden motive.

"I dunno. First shift," he hedged. "Whatever that is."

"Travis has school tomorrow," argued Gonzo. "I have a shift that, okay, I can maybe move around. You, on the other hand, are on suspension with pay. Forgive me when I ask where the hell you gotta be other than right here?"

"Somebody did this to her. I gotta—"

"Gotta what?" she interrupted, voice elevating with every syllable. "Sherlock Holmes this shit in some hope against hope you figure out that this is *not* all your fault?"

"I know that's what you think," fought Lucky, feeling guilty as charged. "There's just a few things I need to look over."

"You're on suspension!"

"Just a few hours!" Lucky angered.

"You guys are being really loud," worried Travis.

"Room's practically soundproof!" spat Gonzo. Then she drew a deep, calming breath. "Sorry," she refocused, thumb and index finger pinching the bridge of her nose. "I can't think right now. Not clearly."

"I'll drive Travis home," Lucky offered. "If you can move your shift it's greatly appreciated…And yeah. This is probably all my doing. Karrie either got in the way or—"

"And it's probably the Armos!" finished Gonzo, meaning the Armenian mob. Five months before, things had gone horribly awry when the assistant sheriff asked Lucky for a favor that had culminated in an escalation of bloody violence that had burned all the way to the doorway of their Altadena bungalow. In the aftermath, Gonzo had sent Lucky packing, setting their official split in motion. "This is Armenian tit for tat. So please let the sheriffs handle it this time."

"And if it's not?" asked Lucky.

"Then it's some other shit come back to haunt your ass." She pinched the bridge of her nose again, a sure sign of an oncoming migraine. "Karrie took your last name. Your place is not out there, whipping up dust, hoping to make things right. It's here. With her. Your daughter."

"Just a few hours," promised Lucky. "I'm not abandoning her, you, anybody. That could never happen."

"You gotta ask Travis if he's okay with you driving him home."

"Trav?" asked Lucky.

The teen simply nodded his answer.

The normality of family hugs or be-well kisses were dispensed with as a need for distance prevailed. Lucky opened the door for Travis and chinned his silent appreciation back at Gonzo. He left her alone, elbows tucked at her sides, and clearly feeling taken for granted. And when Lucky had promised himself that he'd make it up to her for the umpteenth thousandth time, he swallowed the thought with the keen knowledge that he'd never be able to make it all up to her. His hole was too deep and Gonzo's heart too wounded.

It was almost 2:00 a.m. when Lucky dropped Travis at the Altadena bungalow. The drive had been relatively silent. The teen played a game on his phone while Lucky's brain spun in search of a scenario that made sense of the hit and run. Travis had more than once suggested that maybe—*just maybe*—it had simply been an accident. The young man was a geeky repository of odd facts and figures. Because of Lucky's and Gonzo's cop careers, Travis had gained an interest in crime. On the drive, he'd brought up the chances that Karrie's circumstance was merely an accident— another random hit and run in the L.A. parade of cars that ran down innocent pedestrians. The best Lucky could muster in return was a glimmer of hope that Travis was correct. An accident was just that—an accident. No conspiracy. No malice aforethought. No blame need be assigned to anybody but the Fates.

If only my shit were that simple, lamented Lucky.

Upon returning to his Eagle Rock sublet, Lucky searched Karrie's room for her backpack. Since those serene, lolling moments before the surfing duo had caught their last wave, a nagging thought had stuck in Lucky's craw—Karrie's ugly conflict with the man with the smoker's teeth, along with the revelation that the troubled kindergartner she was paid to shadow had crayoned some kind of objectionable art that had concerned the school's administrators. Lucky couldn't imagine what a five-year-old could have drawn that might have proved so abhorrent. The school was probably following some ridiculous politically correct dictum and nothing more. But he needed to see them for himself.

When Karrie's backpack turned up nowhere in the apartment, Lucky looked for the keys to her Prius. When he couldn't find them anywhere he grabbed a tactical pen, went outside, and shattered the car's left rear window—a move he'd later admit was rash instead of simply efficient. He reached inside like some smash and grab artist, withdrew Karrie's backpack, and, while reclimbing the rickety stairs, encountered a petrified neighbor, a worried old bat who'd suffered too many failed face-lifts and often complained to Lucky about dogs barking in the distance. She had a cell phone at her ear, ostensibly calling 911 about the vehicle break-in.

"Daughter couldn't find her keys," informed Lucky, holding up the backpack for the nosy knob to witness. "But please tell the nice 911 operator I found what I was lookin' for."

Back inside the apartment, Lucky unzipped the book-heavy bag. The first item he found was Karrie's keys, easily identified by the pink pepper spray canister hanging from the ring. He couldn't imagine how upset she must have been to lock her keys in the car. Next he pulled out school textbooks and notepads until he landed on the very obvious kindergarten folder fashioned from pastel blue construction paper. Lucky stretched for a light switch, flipping on the pan lamp suspended over the kitchenette table. The folder was stuffed thick with twenty-plus drawings. At first glance the contents appeared to be standard five-year-old's renderings—the expected depictions of animals, stick-figure friends, small-fisted doodles, swirls, and crayon scratches. But six drawings in, Lucky slowed, stopping to settle on something equally simple in skill, yet far more composed.

An idea was at work in the picture. The first image that caught Lucky's attention was a yellow sun in the upper left-hand corner—precisely as Karrie had described. The sun looked as if scribbled excitedly in a series of childlike orbits until it resembled an oblong gumdrop with single-stroked streaks jutting away. Taking up the outer ridges of the page were black lines forming a box, atop that a triangle, the basic and universal outline of a house. Arranged within the house was a mixture of bumblebee-like figures—five in all—drawn like smaller yellow gumdrops but striped with horizontal black slashes. Atop the bumblebees' bodies were frowning human faces with even more black markings across their eyes.

Masks? wondered Lucky.

To each side of the bumblebees were cartoon dinosaurs—at least Lucky thought them to be dinosaurs from either his own interpretation or Karrie's characterization. It was very much like she had described, the dinos looking like the kids' show's big, silly dinosaur—purple and green and almost amorphous-shaped but for their black eyes and big, spiked tails. *Yeah, like Barney*, confirmed Lucky.

"Monster Chihuahua," repeated Lucky, only he wasn't as amused as he had been the last time he'd sounded out the name.

Min's versions of Barney were hardly benign. She showed elongated claws. Menacing. Not quite the stuff of children's half-hour television.

Lucky flipped to the next drawing. It was eerily similar to the former. Another yellow sun. A warm house. Multiple Barneys left and right, only these bore jaws with sharp teeth. *More Monster Chihuahuas.* But in the middle there were only three bumblebees, all masked again, the largest bee with a blob of red crayon scratched on top of its head. Lucky studied it, compared it to the drawing before, and moved on to the next. And the next. And the next. All were familiar in context, with the house and family of bumblebees fearing those purple blob-formed Barneys. One drawing had four bumblebees. Another showed two. All had at least one bee with red crayon scribbled somewhere on its frowning face.

Static filled the room, the soft hairs on Lucky's forearms stood at attention. It was as if an unconscious connection had been made. How could the drawings of a five-year-old possibly be linked to Karrie's hit and run? It was mystifying. *A helluva reach*, argued Lucky at himself. With that, reason fought its way into his mind. The drawings were likely just those of a socially troubled kindergartner. After all, why else did the five-year-old girl require some kind of minder? A shadow? By attaching invisible strings to the hit and run in Malibu, was he just trying to assign blame away from himself?

Self-psychoanalytical bullshit!

If history had taught Lucky anything it was that he was a lousy armchair shrink, especially when practicing on himself. He was better off trusting his instincts, the microscopic beads of sweat on the back of his neck, or, for that matter, the static hairs on his arms.

It was already past 3:00 a.m. Lucky's to-do list was getting longer at an hour when there was little, if anything, that could be done. Per his promise to Gonzo, he was due back at the hospital at 6:00 a.m. He grabbed his phone and began tapping out a text. It was the usual: apology first, excuse after—a rationale for his being delayed. After three failed attempts at composition, backspacing all the way to the start, Lucky quit on the bad idea, switched over to his contact list, and clicked on a familiar number. After five rings a groggy voice croaked, "Who dis?"

"Frosty-man. It's Lucky."

"Lucky…shit. What time is it? Was sleepin', ya know?"

"You're too young to need sleep," replied Lucky. "Need help with something."

"Can we do this somethin' when it's light outside?"

"You know my little girl?"

"Yeah. Kung Fu Karrie. She got a need to kick my ass again?"

"Something's happened to her," pressed Lucky. "C'mon man. Do me a solid and wake the fuck up."

Lucky exited the apartment, not forgetting the security procedure he'd taught Karrie—a defense against the landlord, who had a creepy reputation for letting himself inside to "inspect his property." Lucky grabbed the tube of lip balm he kept above the doorjamb and rubbed a fingernail-sized smear over the lock. That way, if somebody entered without permission, the keyhole would appear clean. If plugged, the apartment was safe to enter.

So far Lucky had kept Karrie safe from the creepy landlord. Not so much everything else.

Wednesday

13

For Tung Chee, Wednesday had begun almost exactly like Monday. Only now, Tung Chee Liu from Guangzhou, China, paused before opening his front door and forced himself to take a deep breath before gripping the knob. His right hand remained in the front pocket of his bathrobe, fingers wrapped firmly around the loaded snub-nosed revolver he'd borrowed from a relative.

On Monday, Tung Chee had been unarmed.

For Tung Chee, the Temple City house had been love at first sight—albeit via an internet real estate application. The home boasted three bedrooms, two and a half baths, a recently remodeled kitchen courtesy of IKEA, original oak floors, and even an arched front window facing a large queen palm. The Spanish-style bungalow was vintage Southern California and American middle-class. Nestled on a quiet sidewalked residential street, the home's driveway led to a detached garage with a basketball hoop affixed over the door. At only 1,900 square feet it was hardly a palace. It was, though, a certified step up from the family's high-rise apartment in China's smog-choked Guangzhou.

The married father of middle-school twins had made a success of himself in China. He and his brothers had banked millions after taking over their family's leather goods factory and retooling it to manufacture counterfeit designer handbags for export. Ten years later, with the correct connections and a six-figure investment in a hot sauce business in nearby El Monte, Tung Chee, his wife, two young children, and mother-in-law only three years older than himself, had been issued visas and made it to the USA.

As was his habit, Tung Chee had been the first to rise that fateful Monday morning. He had performed a series of ritual stretches before pulling on a robe and padding from his back bedroom to start the teapot. He'd shuffled to the front door to the driveway, where he'd seen two newspapers wrapped in plastic: the *Los Angeles Times* and *Chinese Daily News*. As he'd looked blearily out the door of his east-facing bungalow, he'd welcomed in the light he imagined existed only in the Golden State. He'd closed his eyes in gratitude. Monday had begun as a good day—the day he would start his second business in the USA; the day he would become a true diversified American entrepreneur. He was going to invest in a chain of nail salons. A franchise deal. And he would be paying cash.

Like so many Chinese nationals before him, Tung Chee had bought a house in the corridor that stretched from the edge of East Los Angeles all the way to the City of Arcadia. For fifty years the long trickling migration of moneyed Asians to the flatlands of the San Gabriel Valley—or the S.G.V., as locals had branded it—had in many unhappy eyes turned the swath from Anglo-white with an accent of south-of-the-border brown, to a widening ribbon of yellow.

After that grateful breath of morning air, Tung Chee had

reopened his eyes only to see a black man with a backpack walking towards him up the short path to his door at a resolute pace. The man was thick, wearing black jeans, a Hawaiian shirt, a designer L.A. Dodgers cap, and the kind of wraparound sunglasses worn by athletes. In one gloved hand he had held both Tung Chee's newspapers.

"My man, Tung Chee!" Mr. Aloha had greeted with a wave and a pearly Chiclets grin. "And a good morning to you, sir."

The homeowner's uncomfortable but conditioned response had been to wave back, force a wary smile, and generally assume he'd simply forgotten his neighbor's name. This despite the fact that he couldn't recall ever meeting a neighbor of African-American extraction.

"Goo' morning—" nodded Tung Chee with a half bow, unconsciously pulling his robe closed to cover his small but protruding belly—a recent acquisition he proudly blamed on his affection for craft beers and Taco Bell.

"Got your Monday papers for ya," said Mr. Aloha, holding them forth.

Tung Chee was ready to accept the double bundle and form a thin-lipped thank-you when he discovered the stranger had closed the gap between them to uncomfortably close. That's when the black man straight-armed a glove into the homeowner's sunken chest and delivered a balance-shifting shove. Tung Chee stumbled back over his own threshold. By the time he'd caught his balance, the front door had been shut and bolted, and both he and the stranger in the baseball cap were inside.

"Shh," warned Mr. Aloha, a single gloved finger to his lips. "You'll wake the family."

Considering the volume of footfalls he heard coming from the kitchen, Tung Chee was pretty certain his family was already awake. As he swiveled his neck to warn them, he discovered two more black men clad in classic blue Dodgers caps and those same cheap wraparound sunglasses worn by Mr. Aloha. Only both men were tattooed up to their necks and slinging pistols like natural appendages. The bigger of the pair was yoked from prison-yard workouts. His hair was arranged in knots held by neon-colored rubber bands. Tung Chee thought he'd heard one of them call the smaller gangster Lil Rod, but felt he couldn't yet trust his ear for the way some American black men tongued their English.

As Mr. Aloha backed away, Tung Chee felt a strong hand pinch his neck like a vise. The immigrant's legs were kicked out from underneath him and his face thumped the hardwood with a slap. It was like those bad dreams when he missed a step while descending stairs, only this time he didn't jerk awake before crashing to earth.

"Easy now!" reprimanded Mr. Aloha with an element of surprise in his voice. "We're professionals. We've done this game a hundred times before. So, Mr. Tung Chee? Do exactly what we say and we'll be done in time for brunch. Chicken 'n' waffles. Everybody cool. What you say?"

Tung Chee recalled the biggest thug forcefully assisting him to his feet and steering him to the fully enclosed dining space. From a wooden chair, he watched Mr. Aloha lower the blinds. One by one, Tung Chee's family was assembled, their mouths stuffed with socks and secured with loops of clear strapping tape. All but Tung Chee were zip-tied and placed on the floor. Tears streaked every terrified face.

"We're gonna start with your wifi password," calmed Mr. Aloha, setting up a laptop computer on the dining room table.

Frozen, stuck in the moment, Tung Chee seemed to forget how to speak, let alone in English. Before Mr. Aloha could repeat the wifi question, the larger of the thugs swung and gouged his gun across the hairline of Tung Chee's wife. While the children screamed through their gags, blood spilled across the poor woman's face.

"Stop! Please!" cried Tung Chee, his subconscious finding the correct words.

"Then answer my friggin' questions," calmed Mr. Aloha after

a moment staring down the big thug. "Take a breath. I'm sure it'll come to you."

"FOBBY 1-2-3-4," released Tung Chee without thinking.

"You say 'FOBBY'?" Mr. Aloha forced a chuckle, hoping to lighten the mood. "Now that shit's funny. You didn't think of that. Musta been the kids?"

Mr. Aloha correctly entered the password, which was clearly the work of one of the two girls, their black hair—unkempt from a night of hard sleeping—falling over their terrified faces, their hands laced into submission. FOB stood for Fresh Off the Boat. Fobby was a slur for Asian immigrants more utilized by the ABCs—or American-born Chinese—as a form of derogatory demarcation between themselves and more recent immigrants.

"After we're done today," lightened Mr. Aloha. "You're gonna get one of the little ones to enter a new password. Somethin' not so easy to steal, like 'Chairman Mao Can Suck My Smelly Old Socks' or some other random phrase that computers can't pick. You don't have to. Just helping. You can do way better than FOBBY 1-2-3-4."

"What you wan'?" trembled Tung Chee.

"Lil' man," ordered Mr. Aloha. "Kitchen towel for the missus?"

"Man? I ain't goin' pussy this early in the mornin'," spat the smaller thug. "She need a towel? You go on."

After a momentary standoff, perhaps giving away who—if anyone—was in authority, Mr. Aloha disappeared into the kitchen, returning seconds later with a fresh rag. He squatted, began to wipe the wife's bloody face, then queued up his rehearsed speech.

"Here's what it is," began Mr. Aloha. After cleaning off what blood he could, he pulled out his smartphone, punched up a screen, and worked from his notes: "You're Tung Chee Liu. Your wife is named Mei. Your daughters are Alix and Bai and they were born in Guangzhou—I pronounce that right—Guangzhou?"

"Yes," nodded Tung Chee.

"Moving on," continued Mr. Aloha. "You left China with cash.

Dollars. American. Sunk close to seven-fifty into your little house here. Our research says you're sittin' on another million or so. All I want is half that. So, when I'm ready, you're ready, and the bank opens, we're gonna make a substantial withdrawal. That assumes your shit is in a bank instead stuffed in General Tso's mattress."

"I have bank," agreed Tung Chee.

"Good then," straightened Mr. Aloha. "Now, since *my associates* don't get along so good with your family…" Mr. Aloha let his glare land on the gun-toting thugs, clearly addressing them as much as the immigrant clan. "I think we all can agree it's best that they drive you to your bank and go get what I asked for. Me along with the camera on the computer here will keep an eye out while they're gone. Once we have finished our transaction, we say our so-longs and nobody gets wise."

The bigger of the two thugs, the man with the neon-bound braids, appeared to like the suggestion.

"Yeah, man," said the thug. "I could go for a drive."

"But I don't—"

"Nuh uh," Mr. Aloha's head shook slowly. Chest puffed, he was feeling back in control. "Don't go sayin' you don't have it or can't get it. See? This is my business. It's a referral business. Know what that is? That means you were recommended by one of your friends. You know? Some other fobby who we pulled the exact same game on. And before we're done today, you're gonna name me three of your fobby friends, family members, or some dudes you don't like. And one day we will do the same to them. It's good business. And we trust nobody will go to the cops because you know what we know—that you and yours never declared that cash when you entered these United States. So, according to the cops, it's like nothin' ever got stolen. Follow all this?"

Tung Chee only nodded.

"And if you go to the cops?" warned Mr. Aloha. "How long you think before somebody comes along and burns down your house, kills all your loved ones?"

"Not? Long?" gulped Tung Chee.

"We have an understanding," said Mr. Aloha. "So. On to the next part. Where are we going to collect our half million dollars?"

"That money," said Tung Chee. "I need for something else today. How you know I need money for Monday?"

"Dude? I dunno what you sayin'—"

"It Monday!" angered Tung Chee. "I make investment today. In nail salon!"

"Nail salon? No shit?"

"How you know?"

"I don't. But maybe you can put that shit off 'til tomorrow?" suggested Mr. Aloha. "Now time's tickin'. Where's your money?"

Tung Chee's jaw tightened. Finally, he relented.

"Calabasas," he spat.

"Calabaghdad?" Mr. Aloha laughed, as shocked as he was amused. "That's West Valley. Why so far away?"

"'Cause it far away," replied Tung Chee, angry. "And bank was having special on safety deposit rental."

"Smart and cheap," nodded Mr. Aloha. "What's that axiom? 'Makin' a million ain't hard. But keepin' a million?' Whatever. Calabasas is a haul and back. Better you get movin'."

14

San Gabriel.

Standing outside the private school, Frosty had to rejigger the notion that he was over his discomfort. It wasn't quite xeno-phobia. He wasn't afraid of *the other*. He was afraid of *being* the other. Or perceived as such. As the moms and dads and nannies filed in, delivering their young charges through the gate to the playground, he found himself stuck on a double dilemma. As a favor to Lucky he was surreptitiously there to identify a kindergart-ner by the name of Min, a task he had assumed would be as easy as pointing out the Klan member at a Crips convention. After all, how many five-year-old Asian girls could be enrolled?

A lot, he gulped.

Better than half the students were Asian. At least to Frosty's eyes. On the other side of the playground fence must have been fifty jet-black-haired five- to seven-year-old girls in white blouses and miniature tartan skirts. The other parents and attendees were Caucasian. Some of the nannies were Hispanic.

And I'm the one black dude staring in at 'em from the outside.

Frosty felt uncomfortably conspicuous, something he thought he was cured of. He'd been born and raised in one of the most racially diverse cities on the planet. However, he'd grown up south of the 10, and as a child had rarely ventured from the mostly black and brown City of Compton. Gangbanging had been his destiny and he had done that and more until his radical religious conversion, which had been, oddly enough, spurred on by Lucky and Karrie Dey. Both his mama and gran'nana had long said the whippet-thin twenty-one-year-old had been birthed with the Lord in him. To them it had only been a matter of the day and date when the Jesus seed would sprout and bloom. When it did, Frosty and both women moved out of the hood into a north San Fernando Valley rental.

Ever since he began walking with Jesus, those old *feels* of the reverse xenophobe had all but vanished. As long as Frosty lived in Christ, he felt practically colorless.

But *invisible*? That was a bigger ask.

Frosty squatted, grabbing a handful of cyclone fence for balance.

"Hey Min," he said not too loudly. If he was lucky, a kindergarten-aged head would turn. Perhaps even a little voice would reply. But all he received in return was a wall of sound—the normal morning squeals, screams, and giggles expected from a playground chock-full of young children getting in their last licks of fun before the bell rang. Frosty upped his volume. "Hey, lil' Min!"

A nearby boy, his arms wrapped fully around a blue rubber ball, ran up to the fence.

"You want Mini?" asked the six-year-old.

"I do, yeah," replied Frosty.

"Don't think she's here," said the boy. Then his eyes swiveled and his eyebrows arched. "Never mind. There's Mini right there."

Frosty twisted to the boy's sight line. Hopping from the back seat of a polar bear–white Range Rover was a small girl, short black hair and pigtails that might've served as antennae, her left hand stuck in the mitt of a twenty-something Asian man in an oversized suit and red tie. When Frosty turned back to say thanks, the boy with the rubber ball had already padded off.

"Thanks, kid," said Frosty to nobody in particular. He pushed up to his feet, circled around behind the Range Rover, clicked off a quick camera phone photo of the vehicle's license plate, and hustled back to his borrowed car, an aging station wagon with chipped, white stenciled lettering on the doors and rear window reading *Valley Missionary Baptist Ministries*.

When the twenty-something in the ill-fitting suit returned to the Range Rover, Frosty set up his tail. The rest was a cakewalk. The unaware-he-was-being-followed driver piloted the luxury SUV due south to an entrance to the San Bernadino Freeway and aimed toward the heart of downtown. The overly cautious manner with which the driver operated the Range Rover—keeping to the slowest lanes and some seriously early braking—allowed Frosty to calculate that the car wasn't his own. Like it belonged to a boss of some kind, more than likely the child's mother or father. That would make sense out of the silly-looking suit. The twenty-something behind the wheel was a low-wage earner—or even some non-paid intern—at least that's what Frosty suspected. It was a seasoned guess. Frosty was good that way. His instincts. That natural study of human behavior was what had earned him the rep as the dangerous man he had once been—before becoming a top garden associate at one of the Van Nuys Home Depots.

The Range Rover exited at Alameda Street, carefully working its way toward the old railroad yards and adjoining warehouse district. Block after block of brick and mortar slaughterhouses and indoor livestock processing plants had long since been gentrified into a tony arts district. From fashion designers to Hollywood producers, the two- and three-story structures were fortified and repurposed to offer a modern mashup of chic office space, live-in lofts, restaurants, and coffee bars. After a moment's pause, and still buoyed by the belief that the driver was clueless of his tail, Frosty snapped a ticket from an automated dispenser and trailed the white Range Rover into an underground parking structure. The brakes of the borrowed church station wagon squeaked conspicuously on the downward trajectory. Frosty slid into a spot marked *guest* and quickly followed the young driver's footsteps up a stairwell to a heavy third-floor fire door. Frosty stood on the landing, inhaled a lungful of musty air, and pulled the door open. He expected to discover a corridor leading to a distribution of smaller office suites. Instead, he saw glass—floor to ceiling—along a sixty-foot corridor. On the other side of the thick pane was a bustling office. Well-appointed in a modern-meets-industrial motif. Cubicles. Most of the visible employees looked young, Asian, and dressed to impress, their heads dutifully in their work. Halfway down was a pair of double entry doors built from distressed oak and framed into the glasswork. One of those doors was halfway open, the Range Rover's driver frozen—stuck, almost—staring down Frosty.

"That's him!" pointed the driver. "That's the asshole who followed me."

The door swung wider and the immaculate Denny Teng appeared, eyebrows angled with concern.

"Hell yeah, I followed you," lipped Frosty, coolly giving meaning to his chosen nickname. He instinctively dismissed the driver and aimed his question at the impressively tall Denny Teng. "That white Range Rover. That yours?"

The angry driver released the door and marched directly at Frosty, his over-sized suit flapping like clipped wings.

"Whoever you are, get the hell out," demanded the driver in his best manly display.

"He work for you?" directed Frosty. "Been on his ass since the grade school. Dipshit clipped me pullin' away from the curb."

"What?" The driver slowed, incredulous. "I didn't touch you."

"Touched my ride," replied Frosty. "Not my car but I was the man drivin' it. Rear left fender. Come look!"

"He's lyin'," defended the driver.

"Hit me and took off. That's hit and run, man. You lucky I didn't call 911."

"Bullshit!" popped the driver.

"Why don't you both lower the volume?" injected Denny. "Let's just go take a look."

"Hope you got insurance."

Frosty pushed the fire door open and held it, waiting to follow the worried driver and his boss down the steps into the garage. There, he showed Denny the station wagon's left rear taillight, which, despite all the dents and rust on the heap, looked freshly smashed. Before the driver could summon a protest, Frosty walked Denny around to the Range Rover's front right bumper—the section he claimed to have been struck with. Sure enough, the Ranger Rover's fender showed a fresh dent and scuffing.

"Boss, I swear I didn't—"

"Why don't you get back to your cube?" suggested Denny in a calm capitulation.

The defeated driver gave Frosty one last dismissive once-over before retreating up the stairs.

"First, my sincere apology," said Denny.

To Frosty's ear, Denny's words didn't sound the least bit apologetic. They were tinged with the sort of condescension he'd heard his entire life from those who assumed he was little more than a poor-assed black man.

"How about we leave insurance out of it?" suggested Denny. "And we come to some kind of cash settlement right here and now?"

Frosty pondered a dollar figure, quietly amused that had the Range Rover's owner flattened himself and his thousand-dollar threads against the oily garage floor and peeked underneath the adjacent Toyota, he might have spotted the three-foot galvanized steel pipe Frosty sometimes carried for protection. After shoving the station wagon into park, Frosty had quietly gashed the old car and kicked away the taillight debris before easing across the lot and giving the Range Rover's bumper a heavy smack.

If both his vandalism and deception were sin, Frosty would be able to live with it.

"All right," said Frosty, pretending to have been aggrieved. "Station wagon is a certified shitmobile. So, no real foul. How about you cough up a coupla Benjamins to my church and we'll leave the rest for you to figure out with your driver dude or whatever he be."

"He's one of my interns," clarified Denny before offering his agreement with a handshake. "He works for me. At least, he does until I fire his dumb butt. I'm Denny Teng."

"Name's Roscoe," fibbed Frosty, gripping Denny's hand. "You some kinda business baller?"

"Baller?"

"I mean, come on. Interns? That means they work for free, feel me? You gotta be somebody for a buncha nobodies to wanna slave for nothin'."

"Not slaves," grinned Denny, uncertain if he'd been baited into uttering the word in front of a black man. "Interns get paid in opportunity and education."

"S'okay," played Frosty. "We all slaves to Jesus. Whether we know it or not. Now, how about them Benjamins?"

"Come on back upstairs and we'll take care of ya," winked Denny.

"Two hundred and a validation sticker for the parking," followed Frosty.

"Not a problem," said Denny, "since I own the building."

"Like I said. Baller."

Yeah, he's a baller, Frosty repeated in his brain. *But gangster too.* Not like the O.G.s or the bangers he knew or had crossed warpaths with in his former Compton days. The man who'd introduced himself as Denny Teng gave off an altogether different bad boy vibe. *Like razor blades hidden in an ice cream cone*, thought Frosty.

Sweet. But don't lick too long.

15

Westwood.

"You're still here," mused Lucky. It sounded almost like a question instead of a not-so-surprised statement of fact.

"So it appears," replied Gonzo, legs crossed, eyes stuck to the trade paperback in her lap, something new and literary she'd found in the hospital's gift shop. She was seated in a new waiting room, nearly identical to the hermetically sealed one for the emergency room; only the fourth-floor space had a small vertical window overlooking Westwood Village.

Lucky had returned just past 6:00 a.m. In lieu of an apology, he had given Gonzo a grateful shoulder squeeze before slipping back into the ICU. The eighteen-bed unit took up a full corner of the wing, the isolation "cubes" encircling a central mission control of doctors and critical care practitioners. Karrie's glass-encased unit was in the center directly opposite a nurses' depot with so many screens it resembled a NASA monitoring pod.

Instinct slowed Lucky at the threshold. He processed the visual impact as if he had been rocked by a rogue wave. Stretched across an angled bed was his dearly adopted daughter, all matter of tubes and wires snaking from underneath her hospital gown and gathered into a bundle before connecting to a myriad of IV bags and digital equipment. The only sounds were low beeps from the telemetry monitor interrupted by the pump of the ventilator every three seconds. With every forced rush of air delivered through an endotracheal tube inserted into her larynx, Karrie's chest rose and fell, her body appearing more mechanical than of flesh. Attached to her head was that same orbital crown of screws relieving the pressure building inside her skull. Karrie's face was almost entirely black and blue. Almost lifeless. And without a single strand of her trademark strawberry-blonde hair, she could have passed for an unconscious cancer patient.

Lucky slid a chair over and sat beside her. He first stroked her fingers then slid his calloused digits into hers. Karrie offered no grip whatsoever in return, so he chose to gently hold her fingers in his.

"Jesus God," he found himself whispering, not so much in prayer but suddenly pondering the prospect. His thoughts on God were complicated and he sure as hell didn't want his own unredemptive sins and selfish plea to spoil Karrie's chances at recovery.

"Talk to her," urged Uziel.

His steps professionally muffled by rubber-soled clogs, the Israeli doctor had crept in behind Lucky. "Head trauma patients often remark that even while comatose, they could still hear their loved ones speaking to them."

"How is she?"

"Hoping we get her stable enough so we can get the orthos to fix what can be fixed. Less traumatic than having to rebreak her bones."

"And what about her head?"

"Bleeding has stopped but there's still too much swelling," whispered the doc. "I can relieve only so much with the screws before having to remove pieces of her skull. Once we get the brain under control, I wean her off the pentobarbital and see whose coma it really is. Hers or mine."

"So, this might be it? She might not ever wake up?"

"Keep talking to her. Sing her some songs. Perhaps even the ones you sang when she was a baby."

Lucky shook his head.

"I wasn't there," admitted Lucky, the sadness of the statement settling to his marrow. "Truth is, she pretty much adopted me before I did her."

"Then my guess is that she chose you for a reason," salved the doctor. "Listen to me. The mind has a mind of its own. And I've seen some special, special things."

"If I sing she might gag on her ventilator just to make me stop."

"Ah. We are vocally ungifted, both you and me," smiled the doctor.

"They should issue club cards. Lifetime members of the singing impaired."

"Don't sing, then. Tell her some jokes. Even the unfunny ones. It all counts." With that, the doctor patted Lucky's back before exhuming himself from the cube to resume his rounds.

Lucky sandwiched Karrie's fingers between both his hands. He bowed his head and searched for a joke.

"Right," he said. "Okay. So, this Hollywood a-hole in a Lambo blows through a stop sign. Deputy in a black-and-white pulls him over. Says, 'Sir, did you realize that you just ran that stop sign?' A-hole goes 'Hey, man. I slowed down some. You gonna write me up? Whatever.' Deputy grabs the dipshit by the collar, drags him out the car, starts beating him senseless with his baton, then says, 'Sir, would you like me to stop beating you? Or just slow down some?'"

It was one of Lucky's favorite jokes. And he half expected to catch just a quiver from Karrie's lips as if unconsciously attempting to form a smile. Yet nothing was returned. Not a flinch. Not a tick. Her facial features remained lifeless, her hands and arms as limp as death itself. The only movement she gave back was the involuntary lift and deflation of her lung cavity from the automated ventilator. The sound was metronomic. *Kummm-pahhh. Kummm-pahhh.*

"S'okay," squeezed Lucky. "I know you're laughing inside that little bald head." Then Lucky mock gasped. "Whoops. You probably didn't know. Sorry. Guess that secret's out of the bag."

After two hours telling bad jokes at Karrie's bedside, Lucky returned to the private waiting room. He was only partially surprised to discover Gonzo in the very same seat, glued to the very same tome—a half inch deeper into the literary tale, a testament to the appetite with which she read.

"Thought you had a shift to catch," broke Lucky.

"She's our daughter," said Gonzo. "Official or otherwise. We're all she has."

"She deserves better."

"No *and* shit."

"You sleep?"

"Nodded off here and there," admitted Gonzo. "Don't have to ask you the same."

"Show you somethin'?" asked Lucky. His tail had found the chair opposite hers. He had his phone out and was punching up a photo. "What you make of these?"

Gonzo accepted his phone, stared a good long while at the first pic of Min Lee Teng's drawings, and swiped through the rest one at a time.

"What are these supposed to be?"

"Kid's drawings. Kindergartner."

"What's that have to do with anything?"

Lucky filled Gonzo in on Karrie's two days before the hit and run—at least as best as he could based on Karrie's recitations—from the child's suspension to Karrie's reflexive kneecapping of Min Lee Teng's driver, the thin man with the smoker's teeth.

"And Karrie felt concerned enough to bring the rest of the girl's drawings home?"

"There's some serious worry in those scribbles."

"Could be a TV show the little girl watched," shrugged Gonzo. "When Trav was five he drew all kinds of weird shit."

"Bad Barneys versus captive bumblebees?"

"I recall one pretty strange drawing," said Gonzo, rubbing her face. "Trav had Donald Duck leaving a trail of bird poop for Mickey Mouse to eat as snack food. Just as weird."

"Maybe. But I also wanna trust the hairs on the back of Karrie's neck," argued Lucky. "She's earned 'em."

Gonzo flipped the phone back to Lucky. Before he'd even snatched it from the air, she'd returned her eyes back to the book in her lap.

"S'pose you want to run it down anyway?"

"Just kick over a couple of rocks. See if anything crawls out," Lucky answered.

"Really?"

"Cursory at best," he relented. "Frosty got me a line on the child's father. He didn't like what he found."

"And what'd Frosty find?" Gonzo couldn't help but follow with an eye roll, not exactly quick to forget or forgive the danger the former Crip had once visited upon their family, let alone trust a scintilla of what Frosty had to say.

"Dunno," said Lucky. "But Frostman knows his bad guys when he comes across one. I'll be back in a few hours."

"You're leaving me? Thought this was supposed to be your shift?"

"You're right. My bad. Okay if I pass off the deets to you? Check this guy out for me?" Inside, Lucky kicked himself. On the list of asshole moves, this one was top ten.

"You're impossible."

"I am what I am." Lucky meant it to sound self-deprecating. Instead, it landed cold and narcissistic.

"You really think this is all about Karrie?" queried Gonzo

more rhetorical than otherwise. "And not about some violent, stu-pid Lucky shit you started?"

"So what? If I prove it's not about me…that mean we still have a chance?"

"We? As in us?"

Lucky watched the muscles flex in Gonzo's proud jaw. Her head tilted ever so slightly. Her deep brown eyes were unblinking gun barrels, leveled and straight.

"Keep your phone on," she finally replied. Then she snapped her book shut and left it as a placeholder on the chair before van-ishing out the door without so much as a so long or good luck.

16

Alhambra.

On most days, Zipper Ling felt like an identity wreck. A single unflattering incandescent bulb screwed in above the bathroom mirror illuminated his self-examination. Feet squared on the bathmat, Zipper washed and shaved his face before combing his hair and applying the all-important color and/or gel. He stared back at what his mother had made—a mutt with dirtied DNA—Cambodian, French, and who knew what else? Zipper's mom, Linh, and his birth father had emigrated to the United States in the late nineties. Shortly thereafter, a baby boy had arrived. On the child's birth certificate the hospital had inked Kevin Trin Pham, born at Garfield Medical Center in Monterey Park.

As early as Zipper could remember, he'd loathed the name Kevin. So Anglo, so *ugly American*. He'd eventually understand his parents chose it to help him assimilate. But Zipper had been born before the cultural coin had flipped—when instead of melting into the *pot Americana*, it had become more fashionable to be identified as a pure *something* instead of an indecipherable member of USA's human stew.

Zipper's dad had invested in a number of bargain basement nail salons, but with success, had begun to fritter away the profits playing the stock market. The addiction ended with his mysterious swimming-pool death. Linh had long claimed it was an accident. The idiot was drunk. A sad calamity was all it was. But Zipper felt the murderous truth all the way to his skinny bones. Mother was the culprit.

Zipper's mom remarried. For convenience. This time it was a Chinaman with beaucoup money to invest in her nail business. *A fucking FOB*. And just like that, Linh Pham from Vietnam became Linh Ling. And young Kevin Pham became Kevin Ling.

As usual, Zipper had woken just minutes short of noon to a familiar smear of color on his pillow. It was the neon green dye of which he'd recently become so very fond. Hungover from a night of chasing cocaine hot rails and rum cocktails with Red Bull, he'd quick-showered then appeared in front of that tell-all bathroom mirror. In the reflection was Kevin Pham or Ling as well as every dirty name he'd ever been called: *Rice Ball. Dog Eater. Ironing Board. Socket Face.* At age fifteen, when mixed-up Kevin Ling attempted to pigment himself as solely Vietnamese, he coined his very own nickname: Zipper—from the derogatory Vietnam War epithet, *Zipper Head.* He felt embracing a demeaning name was far better, far cooler, then being labeled with that cracker name *Kevin.*

With a flatiron, Zipper groomed his custom cut into the Japanese anime look he desired. After achieving the proper arc and swoop—half-covering one eye in a sharpened, silky black waterfall—he applied the temporary spray coloring in a slash across the tips. It was his middle finger to the world.

I'm not anything. I'm Zipper.

The day ahead unfolded on his mental calendar. He'd first be required to visit his mother to see what chores she had for him.

His official title at the chain of thirteen strip-mall salons was Vice President of Operations. Only Zipper preferred his own job description: *Fingernail Rancher/Flunky Number One.*

His primary chore was to manage the ebb and flow of South Asian nail girls. When the girls weren't applying enamel microshimmer or opalescence for minimum wage plus tips, Zipper pimped them out to the local sex trade. The money was small scale compared to his mother's primary scam—selling fake fingernail franchises to the FOBs. She was careful about choosing her marks. The newly landed Chinese were paranoid about communist spies looking for proof they had looted the motherland and were ripe for Linh's gambits. And before a swindled fobby could cry foul, he'd get a visit from Zipper and Fungo. One look at the big Samoan wearing a necklace threaded with human teeth and the complaints would end.

My mom, the murdering, extorting bitch, complained Zipper. *Was it my fault she tried to rip off the one stupid fobby some other crew had also marked for their own rip-off?*

Since Monday, Linh Ling had been on a warpath. Last time she had spoken with Zipper's cousin Tu'an, he and his brother had been waiting, as planned, for Tung Chee outside his bank in Calabasas. All the useless Chinaman had to do was give them the cash for the new nail salon franchise he thought he was buying. But something had gone terribly wrong. Now, her money was gone and her sister's sons were dead—presumably gunned down by a pair of ghetto gangbangers trying to move in on her business. Linh Ling was demanding her son find out who was responsible. Zipper, the mutt in the mirror with the anime haircut, had been pushed to the cusp of turning from no worse than a pimp and part-time leg breaker to a full-on, revenging gangster.

Zipper had decided on a simple wool peacoat over a white T-shirt and a pair of stovepipe jeans when his phone sounded— an unknown number requesting a video call. *Probably somebody's burner phone*, he figured. One of his nail whores wanting to prove she was under the weather via some sort of visual shtick. Before accepting the call, Zipper positioned the phone's lens close to his face so the first thing she'd see was his unforgiving gray eyes.

"What stupid excuse you wanna make today?" he growled upon answering.

But as Zipper pushed the screen further away, he came to realize it was a man's face glowering back—puffy white with horrific bruising.

"This's what you did," informed Austin Andrews, maneuvering his own phone's lens closer to the swelling from Fungo's hammering fists.

"What you sayin' to me?" asked Zipper, unable to decipher.

"My jaw," grit Austin. "They had to wire it shut!"

"Hard to understand you," annoyed Zipper. "Why you bothering me?"

"I. Got. My. Jaw. Wired. Shut!"

"Man, whatever you're sayin', I'm not gettin'. You either got information for me or you don't."

Austin nodded in the affirmative.

"Westfield Topanga," Austin tried to say.

"West Bumfuckistan? Nuh uh. I'm boss man. You come to me."

"And I don't go east of the 405," replied Austin, referring to the north/south freeway as some form of red line in the sand. "You come to Westfield Topanga. Text me when you're coming."

Austin hung up. The call ended.

Zipper stood, stupefied. That broke-ass prick was setting terms now? Clearly the jaw-cracking strike from Fungo hadn't set that real estate tool on the correct course.

Faggot, prick.

17

Downtown.

Angelenos trade small talk about the ebb and flow of traffic the way those in other parts of the country chat about the weather. To Lucky, the mysterious way the traffic surged was a salve. Even when it slowed to a crawl, it affirmed that the city was alive. The freeways and boulevards were the arteries and vessels carrying white and red blood cells, elements, nutrients, oxygen, chemicals—legal or otherwise—and even valve-clogging plaque through a massive five-thousand-square-mile body.

As birds fly—or Gonzo in her LAPD helicopter—the distance from UCLA Medical Center to downtown Los Angeles was just over ten miles. But at gutter level, the height most comfortable for Lucky, it was fifteen miles of rubber meeting pot-holed asphalt. Choked with millions of residents and commuters in fuel-swilling cars that were owned, leased, or stolen, unregistered and not.

The Crown Vic ate up Sixth Avenue, its grille aimed toward the skyscrapers of downtown. Lucky calmly shifted from lane to lane, safe enough for his own conscience but leaving the speed limit behind, his mind fixed on Karrie and the film clips in his head. One scene was of Karrie's silhouette, flipped into the air by that stolen Chevy Volt. The second was set in the ICU—Karrie's face, pale and bruised in half shadow, her lively freckles faded to naught, and the oppressive yet life-sustaining sound of the ventilator pushing air into her chest followed by the automated hiss of her exhales.

Lucky hungered for someone to blame, someone whom he could bloody with his fists until he came within a hair's breadth of losing his life. And still all he had was a name and a downtown address.

Who in the bejesus was Dennis Teng?

The child's father? An uncle? It was perhaps the thinnest string he'd ever run down. Behind those God-awful clips reloading and playing back in his head, there was a nagging doubt that all he was doing was sprinting ever further from the truth. That he himself was to blame for the hit and run. It was a message meant for him from some old enemy with a grudge. Most probably, the Armenians—making Gonzo correct yet again on nearly every one of her complaints about him.

The South Vignes Street address Frosty had sent Lucky was familiar enough. The rescued three-storied former meat plant was only blocks east of the Los Angeles Sheriff's Department's central HQ on Temple Street, the same division where only months before he'd manned a detective's desk inside the Major Crimes Bureau.

Before my violent shit hit the fan.

Lucky circled the block, noting obvious ingress and egress from the building before he parked at a distance close enough for further observation. He was looking for foot traffic in and out, and cars entering and exiting the underground garage. Once he'd pegged it as a generally quiet business with few comings and goings, he discarded the idea of blending in with public traffic and stumbling into the office space as if some kind of lost salesman.

So, as Lucky turned the key to lock his Crown Vic, he still hadn't a glimmer of what game he was going to play once he entered the building. There was no legend in the lobby, sending a message that visitors would need to know where they were going. But Lucky didn't know much beyond the address itself.

A bell rang, a dainty, digital signal that the single elevator car had arrived. The faux-galvanized door slid open, revealing a tall Asian man in a smartly tailored suit. His eyes met Lucky's and both men instinctively measured and assessed the other. The once-over Lucky received from the dapper Asian was typical. Or so he assumed. Moneyed men tended to size him up as working-class, if not a cop then in the same league as a plumber or air conditioning repairman.

"Denny Teng and Associates?" asked Lucky the moment the man's eyes left his.

"Third floor," replied the man, aiming a hard right for the exit door as if in a hurry. "Can't miss it."

Lucky saluted his thanks then stepped into the elevator, taking in the Oriental-carpeted interior and polished brass handrails. The design smelled of money and cool, not unlike all those Culver City and Santa Monica offices housing entertainment biz over-lords and their arrogant attention to style over substance. When Lucky stepped off, he was faced with that floor-length wall of glass and double oak doors.

Money and *power*, read Lucky.

Still without a notion as to how he'd play it, Lucky pushed through the door into a small, glassed-in reception area. Behind a raised partition sat a classic front-office girl, the top of her burgundy-colored hair barely visible as she manned both the incoming phones and a computer screen. In keeping with the name on the door, the business-attired beauty on the early side of her twenties was of Asian extraction.

"May I help you?" she smiled warmly as Lucky eased nearer.

"I'm from the city Disability Department," Lucky lied, flipping the switch on a standard authority play. He pasted on a winning grin as if he were one of the legion of well-paid Los Angeles regulatory agency drones with a you-can't-fire-me air. The municipality had so many hundreds of codes to follow that businesses were fairly accustomed to drop-in inspections. Fearful of getting a poor grade, building managers rarely asked for any identification.

"I'm investigating an ADA. complaint," informed Lucky.

The terrifying ADA, a.k.a. the Americans with Disabilities Act. To a small business, the only human scarier than a disability inspector was one of the myriad of ADA trial lawyers—or   disability trolls—seeking the smallest of infractions over which to sue.

"Complaint?" she asked as if on cue. "Are we out of compliance?"

"Ancient building," shrugged Lucky. "Hard for remodels to hit every mark. Do you have an office manager who can walk me around?"

"That would be Annie," said the receptionist. "She's out sick today. Let me call back and see if there's anybody who can give you a tour."

"Consulting business?" asked Lucky, pretending to be curious.

"Yes, sir."

"What kind?"

"Mr. Teng has many enterprises. But the consulting part is helping US companies interface with Chinese business, manufacturing. That sort of stuff."

"Sounds above my pay grade," joked Lucky.

"Mine too." She winked. Her flirting was obvious, nervous. Lucky couldn't tell if it was because of who he was or who he pretended to be.

"No hurry," said Lucky. "City pays me no matter what."

"Can I have one of our interns get you an espresso, latte, infused water?" she asked.

"All good here," said Lucky, trying, but not entirely succeeding to hide a sneer at the pompous selection of libations.

He did an about-face in search of a seat. Above the corner sofa unit was a collage of framed photos and magazine articles expensively mounted. The articles were mostly from Asian magazines, their precise languages a mystery to Lucky. Centered in every photograph was the same tall fellow Lucky had just encountered on the ground floor. The graceful gent always appeared smiling, confident, and immaculately attired. Interspersed were photos of the man posing with political and financial luminaries of Los Angeles.

Lucky quickly recognized a photo of the man with Mayor Ramon Avila.

"Denny Teng?" Lucky guessed.

"That's the man," said the receptionist. "You just missed him."

Hands in his pockets, Lucky continued his perusal of Denny Teng's wall of fame and what it said about the man. The pictures… the luxury setting…everything reeked of more than money. It smelled of *power*. To do business with Denny Teng was to be in a fraternity of designer-suited muscle men—the movers and shakers of the world. Was it a façade? Lucky couldn't divine as much. But when taken in the context he presented, Denny Teng was a man cloaked in power.

Then, while closely inspecting Denny's facial features, Lucky silently asked, *Did you hurt my little girl?*

He couldn't imagine a reason why a man of such a potent and politically connected disposition would have a thing to do with the mysterious hit and run of his daughter.

"Family man?" asked Lucky.

"Proud daddy of a little girl," answered the receptionist. "Five years old two weeks ago. Little Min. Such an adorable little button."

"I'll bet," said Lucky, confirming the nearly invisible filament that bound him to Denny Teng. Karrie was Min's shadow…whatever that meant.

I'm on a fool's errand, he reprimanded himself at the slenderness of his nefarious suggestion—the idea that this Denny Teng had a hand in Karrie's dire situation. *And I'm on this errand while Karrie lays in a goddamn coma.*

Despite his doubts, Lucky found a seat, spreading out on the sofa pretending to be a man without worry. Before him lay a carved antique door, horizontal and repurposed as a coffee table. Lucky reached for one of the magazines, all neatly feathered in a row, their names a panoply chosen to show off the owner's basket of interests: *China Business Review, Hong Kong Monthly, Us Weekly, the Hollywood Reporter, Variety.* Lucky was inches from choosing one when the *whoosh* of the glass door swinging inward convinced his eyes to flick upward. Limping across the threshold was a thin man, leaning hard on an orthopedic cane, his wispy black and gray hair swept in a comb-over.

"Anybody need me, you know where I am," monotoned the man without as much as a glance to the receptionist.

"Better put some sunblock on that dome," she smirked.

The man couldn't help it. He smiled, his lips pulling back over two rows of yellow teeth.

Smoker's teeth.

Lucky plucked one of the magazines without regard and blindly thumbed through it before easing to his feet.

"Bathroom?" he asked, already knowing full well the door marked *Men's Room* was at the end of the corridor outside the entry.

"Oh. Sure," answered the receptionist. "Out the door and to the right."

Opposite the men's room was the fire door leading to the stairwell. As Lucky shouldered the door, his ears keyed on the disappearing footfalls from the flight above followed by the metallic squeak of a closing door. Lucky headed upward, lamenting the days when he could vault two steps at a time. Now if he climbed too aggressively he'd feel the steel pedicle screws and rods that buttressed his lower back. There was a familiar tightness, a sincere lack of flex where the fusion had initially been forged. Four years since the surgery and still didn't feel entirely whole. The closest he'd felt to his old self was when riding the waves, a gift he credited to Karrie.

The staircase emptied onto a rooftop recently tarred and regraveled. The smell of the midday sun penetrating the molecules of coal and petroleum licked at Lucky's nostrils along with a hint of burning tobacco. Leaning on his cane was the man with the yellowed teeth, a cigarette already lit and dangling from his lips.

"There you are," boomed Lucky, the surprise announcement meant to catch Limping Man off guard. It worked. The man with the smoker's teeth appeared taken aback by the gregarious stranger with the buzzed scalp. Lucky continued, "Sorry. Tryin' to quit. But was sittin' there just jonesing for a smoke and you walk by on your way to, you know. I admit it. Got zero willpower. Wouldn't have a stick to spare, would ya?"

"You saw me?" asked the man, still off-kilter.

"Guess you didn't see me. But hey, that's me. Mr. Wallpaper," replied Lucky, offering a hand in introduction with a well-worn fictitious name. "Dave McAlevy. City Disabilities Office."

"Wayne," answered the man, shifting the cane in order to properly shake hands.

"Wayne?" repeated Lucky.

"Well, it actually Wang. Wang Zhang. But since moving to America, Wayne sometime easier."

Wang reached into his jacket, removed a pack of Pall Mall Reds and shook loose a fresh smoke.

"Old school," remarked Lucky at the brand, removing the cigarette with his fingertips and inserting the stick between his lips. The truth was that he hadn't smoked since the awful murder of his little brother. Yet the physics of handling the filtered smoke remained second nature. Before Lucky could ask, Wang offered a light from a disposable Bic lighter. "Thanks."

"You investigating my office?" asked Wang.

"Your office?"

"Officially, it Mr. Teng's office," conceded Wang. "But he's never around. I'm his VP of operations."

"Thought that was the man I bumped into getting on the elevator," said Lucky. "Tall guy, smiling eyebrows?"

Wang regarded Lucky again, eyes charged with a sudden distrust.

"You inspecting what again?" asked Wang.

"Nothin' to worry about," assuaged Lucky. "Random complaint. Promise I'm way easier to deal with instead of some asshole ADA lawyer."

"Americans. You like your regulations."

"Where you from?"

"Mainland. China."

"No shit?"

"You?"

"Local. Born and raised."

"You never leave?"

"Got as far as Kern County. But that shit-kicker life didn't work out." Lucky shifted gears, addressing Wang's obvious orthopedic cane and limp. "New knee?"

"Emergency ACL surgery."

"Oh. Had me one of those. Right knee. How'd you pop yours?"

"Softball team," lied Wang. "Slide into second base at my age? Equals bad idea."

"Not sexy," judged Lucky, pulling a deep drag of smoke. He suddenly missed the habit. As he released a plume of nicotine exhaust from his lungs, he realized he was gazing dead west. From the four-story perch, he could see the concrete outline of the Hall of Justice building where the Sheriff's Temple Street Division was headquartered. He briefly allowed himself to imagine that somewhere inside the Hall a meeting was going down between the top brass and some fat-assed attorney, plotting how best to separate Lucky from his badge. Then some additional words rang inside his skull, but in his lawyer's voice—Ms. Vanilla.

For the sake of your case you must keep a seriously low profile. No trouble of any kind. Nothing that would give the county a stronger case that you are indeed a shit magnet.

Lucky felt the barrel of Wang's cane gently graze his knee.

"How you do yours?" asked Wang. "Better be good story if mine not so sexy."

"More embarrassing than sexy," returned Lucky. "Put my hands where I shouldn't have."

"Put your hands where?" Wang offered a curious, if lascivious, smile, his lips still pinching the last licks of his own cigarette.

"Teenage girl," revealed Lucky. "Little blonde thing. Truth be known it was my own damn fault. Before I knew it, she'd locked up my arm, turned me sideways, and hammered a foot into my knee. Collapsed me at the joint. Pop goes the anterior ligament. I go down. Strangest place too. Dropped my ass right in the middle of a grade school playground."

Wang's eyes stared back at Lucky. Slack, without a measure of guilt or embarrassment. Only a deep, unadulterated suspicion.

"Who you really work for?" angered Wang, who Lucky guessed was some ten years older than him and four inches shorter. He imagined if the man were to strike, it would be with the cane. So, before Wang had so much as cocked it, Lucky swiveled left and gripped the aluminum shaft by its extension bolts. Lucky wrenched the cane away and maneuvered the handle as a hook. Wang was snagged under the calf of his bad leg. The man with the smoker's teeth tumbled to the new tar without a struggle, his lungs releasing a rushing wheeze.

"Okay," started Lucky. "That's twice this week you ate the dirt. The only difference about this time is whether you get up again."

"Who are you?" coughed Wang.

"Sorry," said Lucky. "I'm the man standing. That means my questions go first. Why'd you wanna hurt the girl?"

"Don't know what you're—"

Lucky pinned Wang in the sternum with the cane's rubber foot. Next, with the heel of his cross trainer, he readied himself to apply pressure to Wang's knee brace.

"Think my girl hurt you?" threatened Lucky.

"Don't-don't-don't!"

"Meter's runnin'."

"I'm gonna sue."

"Only one thing I got of value," hissed Lucky. "And you put her in the ICU."

It was a bluff that cops used every day in interrogations—tossing out accusations in hopes of excising confessions. They could even legally lie to a suspect if it might result in information. It was the threats and intimidation parts that crossed the statutory line. Lucky produced his smartphone, aimed the lens at Wang's face, and thumbed the video record function.

"Baseline," established Lucky. "Is your name really Wang Zhang?"

"You really filming me?"

"Answer the question. Is your name really Wang Zhang?"

"Yes."

"From mainland China?"

"Yes."

"And you work for this Denny Teng guy?"

"Yes."

"Are you really gonna sue me?"

"Bet your ass!"

"Did you have anything to do with the hit and run?"

"What hit and run?" asked Wang.

"Did Denny Teng have anything to do with the hit and run?"

Wang's face tightened. His eyes glared into the lens. His lips pulled back over his yellowed teeth.

"No," he emphatically voiced.

"But you brought Denny Teng's daughter to school yesterday?"

"You stop this!" angered Wang. "You can't do this to me!"

"Funny. Because it's happening to you right now," shrugged Lucky. "And I'm the one doing it."

Lucky pocketed his phone. He could've ventured further. Applied pressure. Delivered pain. But up until then he'd only threatened Wang with the athletic shoe to his knee. He'd never once applied any weight. Not that he was unwilling. Considering

Karrie's critical condition, he easily could've ground every pound he could muster into the man's just-repaired joint. He even imagined how much work it would take to bust the stitches until Wang bled through his khakis. It might have even elicited a confession. But what good would a confession matter if Lucky were locked up for assault? And whatever about his hanging-by-his-fingernails career, Lucky had a responsibility to Karrie to stay out of trouble. So far, all Wang had suffered was a backward stumble to the tar roof—nothing worthy of a criminal complaint.

But halfway down the stairwell to the first-floor fire exit, Lucky was second-guessing himself. He wasn't at all sanguine that Wang had something to do with the hit and run, let alone to what degree and why. All Lucky knew for sure was that Wang was the man Karrie had felled. Perhaps with a little extra drilling, more answers would have surfaced. Then again, considering the immediate rot eating away at his stomach lining, a confession or even a reply in the affirmative might have resulted in Lucky tossing Mr. Wang Zhang off the roof. It might have even been a satisfying way to end the conversation. But not necessarily just.

18

Woodland Hills. 2:11 p.m.

"Okay, shit-stick," accused Zipper, index finger accusingly cocked. "You got us here. So this better be gold on gold."

With extreme purpose, Austin Anderson had chosen a pedestal table in the food court centered in a concourse spilling over with lunchtime shoppers. Wherever the eye looked there was either high-resolution video signage or take-out stands from the everpresent Panda Express to the trendier Blaze Pizza.

"He doesn't look comfortable," grit Austin, getting more accustomed to speaking through his wired jaw. "Maybe you should send Mongo Man to get us some frozen yogurt."

"Fungo," corrected Zipper. The big man was feeling as awkward as Austin had guessed. The trio was surrounded by a melange of mostly mommies, nannies, and young children. "Now, what you got?"

Austin regarded Fungo with caution, wondering if the over-sized Samoan cared that they were under surveillance. The public space was like so many in the post-9/11 universe. Security cameras covered nearly every possible angle, every megabit continuously uploaded to the cloud—to data farms from Utah to Uzbekistan. Austin's gamble was that Fungo wouldn't even try to hurt him if Zipper gave the order.

"Know what I got?" mustered Austin. The steel holding his mandible in place covered the egg-sized lump of abject fear in his throat. "I got debts. Not proud of 'em. Doing my best to keep the ship afloat. And now cuzza you I got medical bills for this shit."

Austin gestured to his jaw.

"You better not be tellin' me I came all the way out here for jack shit," warned Zipper.

"All I did was witness something," whispered Austin forcefully, saliva welling in his cheeks. "I didn't ask for any of this. I didn't ask for you or him or my broken fucking jaw. But here I fucking am. I'm willing to make a deal."

"A deal," grinned Zipper. "You're shittin' me?"

"You want information?" asked Austin. "You want the names of those black killers? When the cops ID 'em I'll pass it on to you. But you gotta help me out first."

"Like, pay you?"

"There's money in this," garbled Austin. "I saw what was in that truck."

"You got no idea the kinda game you're messin' in," Zipper growled.

"I don't know your game. But ask me if I give a shit!" Austin pounded his fist before he hissed. "I got the leverage. You got the money. So, let's make a deal."

"Walk with us out to the parking lot," goaded Zipper. "Fungo'll make you give a shit."

"Nuh uh," said Austin, chin wagging left and right. "I'm not a badass like you. I know that. I'm just a middle-aged, self-loathing queen who's tired of being on the short side of a deal. I know leverage. Been a while since I had it. And now that I got it I'm gonna use it. From this point on, only time you see me is face to face. Public places like this. Lotta security cameras. Won't find me at my ol' house. Until we're square, I'm not even at my office."

"Fuck you," spat Zipper, only his words were betrayed by his body language. He sat back and let that cascade of tinted hair guard half his face. "Fungo. Go get us some ice cream."

"What you say?" asked the big man.

It was the first time the big man had spoken, his words soft as tapioca coming across his lips.

"Ice cream," repeated Zipper.

"Froyo," corrected Austin. "Something simple. Chocolate-vanilla swirl."

Fungo slid his chair away.

"Somethin' with strawberry," said Zipper, waiting for Fungo to step away before continuing. He leaned back into Austin. "Last time. What. Do. You. Want?"

"For starters, five thousand in cash," said Austin. "Call it a retainer. That much keeps me workin' for you."

"That it? Five stacks? Like I got it stickin' outta my asshole?"

"Not gonna screw you. Never screwed anybody. I sell real estate. Good at it. For me it's a fee—for getting you what you need—I'm going to sell you a property."

"A property. Like a house?"

"You get to flip it, rent it out, hang onto it until it appreciates," reasoned Austin. "I don't care. I get the commission. You get your information as it comes in. All legal. On the up and up."

It was, of course, a gross rationalization of a shakedown. Convincing Zipper to purchase a property made it seem as if the transaction were on the up and up—at least when compared to trading information for a bag full of cash. That and Austin felt he was owed for the pain and suffering he'd received for merely witnessing a crime. Zipper might've been a criminal. But Austin wasn't going to stoop so low.

"You got some stones. You think you got leverage? I'm thinkin' my man Fungo didn't hit you hard enough."

"Any harder and it might've killed me." Once again Austin used his index finger to indicate his fractured jaw. "What good would I be then?"

"Yeah, well, the decider in this shit isn't me," admitted Zipper. "So, whoops on you."

"If you're not the boss then why'm I even here?"

"I'll get back to you on that." It was hardly a concession on Zipper's part. To both men it rang like a polite segue, a route to exit the conversation. "Where can I find you?"

"Not gonna tell you," supplied Austin, as if he'd rehearsed the line in a mirror. "All you gotta know's that wherever you find me there's gonna be cameras. For my security."

Zipper knew his mother would never, not for a cheap second, buy into Austin's paranoid payola game, let alone consider entering some kind of real estate deal. No. Until Austin offered them some kind of tangible information, the play would be to simply leave the debt-drowning agent to his own imaginative devices. Allow their silence to drive him batty, make him worry that he had overplayed his hand.

"*Your father overplayed his last hand*," was the most Zipper's mother would ever say in regard to that untimely death in the swimming pool. "*Mark my words when I say you will never see me overplay mine.*"

19

Downtown.

On the list of scents Frankie Coleman loved, the suites at downtown's Crown International Hotel would have made her top twenty. The owners of the hotel, nicknamed the Downtown Crown, had gone to Herculean lengths to keep the establishment fresh and comfortable while never yielding to those who sought to renovate the old girl into something more modern. The aged kissing cousin to the more stately and famous Los Angeles Biltmore was known as much for discretion as it was for its turn-of-the-century design. For moneyed patrons requiring clean sheets, warm towels, and suites to rent by the hour for midday liaisons, the Crown was downtown's high-end no-tell motel.

"I think it's the fabric softener," she said, perfectly pleased to lie naked until dry, spread across the unmade bed on her stomach.

"I mean, it smells like someone sayin', 'Curl up, close your eyes, take a nap on me.'"

"Be my guest." Denny Teng had already showered and toweled off, leaving the soft, white bath sheet on the floor for maid service.

"C'mon. Hang out with me," purred Frankie. "We can order in something. Lunch. Hungry?"

"Already late for a *late* lunch," shrugged Denny. "Rain check?"

"Frankie don't give vouchers. Not for a fuck 'n' run."

"That's all I am?" he grinned. "A fuck 'n' run?"

"Asked the man who can't wait to get dressed and get out," she said slyly. "Look at me. I'm still *nekkid*."

"That how they say it in Tennessee? *Nekkid*?"

"Did you know they got a joke about guys like you down home?" she said, rolling over and sitting up, back braced against a pile of down-filled pillows. Her spray tan was an expensive head-to-toe paint job. And though bronzed like a Playboy Playmate, Frankie didn't require Photoshop. Her armor against rejection was to make sure Denny saw what he was forfeiting.

"Fuck 'n' runs?"

"Chinese fellas," she skewered. "Well, certain Chinese fellas."

"Cue ethnic slur," he said, his good-natured façade applied to a fault.

"What do you call a Chinaman with a big dick?" she teased.

"What?"

"A Cock-Asian," she deadpanned before busting out into a girlish, body-shaking giggle.

"I like it." Denny's eyebrows arched. "Gonna tell it to Ram."

"Without attribution," she warned.

"Text you if he laughs."

"Wait," she stiffened. "You're having lunch with the mayor? Right now?"

"Downstairs," teased Denny. "Should I give him your best? How about a selfie?"

"You will not!" She found herself pulling the sheet up in an unconscious act. "Does he know?"

"About this? No. But I can tease him if you want."

"What if he sees me getting off the elevator?"

"So, stay here," solved Denny. "Text you when we wrap up."

"Asshole. I have a bank to run."

"Oh, that," he winked. "I'm just messing. Ram's not down-stairs. We're meeting at the Biltmore."

"Screw and you," pissed Frankie. "For that I oughta charge you an extra vig on your per deposit fee."

"But you won't." Denny finished dressing, his dreamy, for-tified six-foot-four figure draped in a linen suit that looked like threaded wheat. He slipped into a pair of Gucci loafers left neatly pointed toward the door, grabbed a sparkling water from the mini-bar, and was gone without a formal farewell. There was nary a hint of romance; no sweet kiss goodbye. Theirs was a relationship built on convenience and healthy doses of mutual suspicion.

On the elevator Denny found himself unthinkingly tap-ping the glass bottle with his gold wedding band. *Clink. Clink. Clink.* He suffered no measure of guilt for the cheating. For him, everything with Frankie Coleman—from the sex to their spurious banking—was business. Any anxiety he felt was from the sting of her words, no matter how much sweet molasses they had been served with.

Cock-Asian.

It wasn't the first slight slung in his direction. His life had been full of them. All this despite his obvious good looks, an all-American resume—from high school swimming to Ivy League education. Dartmouth. Still, to hear it from a woman like Frankie—a certifiable smoke show—was as if every damn day someone appeared to remind him of what he was. Chinese. *Chopstick-American.* Frankie had uttered something racially insulting once before. During some pillow talk, he'd tried wrapping his tongue around her patented twang. Between her giggles, she threatened to call him her *Chinkabilly.* He'd laughed with some genuine gut, but now recalled how much it had hurt.

As Denny crossed South Grand Avenue to the Biltmore's back

door, he felt he was looked upon as Asian first, businessman second. Mayor Ramon Avila had built his political career mostly on race. Now that he was laying the groundwork for a run at governor, having a Chinese face at his side during the campaign would speak volumes to the six million California voters of Asian extraction.

Looking up Grand Avenue, Denny couldn't quite see Chinatown. But at only a half mile away, he felt its pull like it was some kind of magnet, identifying and reminding him of the cradle in which he was born. Given the chance, he'd set fire to the entire ten square blocks. Starting with the gas ovens in the kitchen of his grandfather's restaurant, he'd watch the flames feed outward, frenzied and out of control, until consuming every carved front door and cheesy neon sign.

"Denny boy!" cried Ram from his petite booth in the Biltmore's famed Cognac Room. The recently restored hotel bar boasted impossibly high ceilings, engraved to their original articulation, Tiffany fixtures, and scrolled, spiraling pillars. But with one bartender and a singular guest the space appeared almost ghostly.

"Mayor's private bar?" asked Denny, his grin and charmed nature on full wattage.

"Doesn't open 'til five," replied the mayor with a broad it's-all-me gesture. "Sometimes they let the mayor use it as an office away from the office. Hungry?"

"Starving," sat Denny, drumming the table with the flats of his fingers.

"Gotcha covered." Ram held up his arm while pointing downward at Denny. "How about a bar menu sampler for my friend over here?"

"Very good, sir," nodded the bartender. "Something for your guest to drink?"

Denny noted the wedge of lime in the tall, clear tumbler of fizzy water the mayor had been drinking. He wondered if Ram had secretly ordered a shot or two of top-shelf vodka to his usual club soda.

"Guinness on tap?" asked Denny. The bartender agreed with an Irishman's wink.

"Fan of the dark stuff?" asked Ram.

"In all shapes and sizes," quipped Denny. "I try not to discriminate."

"You're pretty quick. Might have to find you an office to run for."

"Are you recruiting?"

"Always searching for allies. The more like-minded I can get in the political pool, the merrier."

Denny let the gleam of his teeth fake his concurrence. He understood, but disagreed with modern political ideology's focus on amassing people who thought and maneuvered exactly alike. In one of his college papers, he'd referred to the cesspool of similar ideologies as intellectual incest—an opinion he would not share with Mayor Ramon Avila. After all, Denny knew he was going to be used and was already looking for the chance to use the mayor right back.

"Why I wanted to see you…" segued Denny.

"Really? You interested in elected office?"

"Not yet…I meant *why* I asked to have lunch with you."

"Lemme guess," began the mayor, readying a joke. "Your sojourns into motion-picture financing have left you with too many young and willing actresses to service. And you wanted to know if your friend Ram could assist with the overflow."

"I'm not quite there yet."

"At the point where the dam has crested? Or tasting the fruits of the entertainment tree?"

"Why I wanted to have this talk," eased Denny. "I need some detective work done."

"That so?" The mayor leaned back. "Business-wise? Or personal?"

"In a general kind of a way, I think," fibbed Denny. "I don't know these showbiz guys. And by their reputations, some of them seem to wanna shake my hand as much as pick my pocket, know what I mean? Would feel better if I had a private somethin' or someone who could look under their hoods."

It wasn't entirely a lie. Any information Denny could bundle on a potential business partner or competitor was always a bonus. But there was a more primal reason Denny required some private sleuthing. His number-two man, Wang Zhang, had messaged him in regards to a violent encounter on the office's rooftop. The assailant fit the description of the rough-looking man Denny had encountered when leaving. With Frankie already waiting in the hotel suite, Denny had been in a hurry and had politely directed the stranger to his third-floor office. The stranger had then gone on to falsely identify himself as a city disabilities inspector and followed Wang to the rooftop, where he'd roughed him up. For what reason? Who did he work for?

And why the hell does he have an interest in me?

"Anything to help Denny Teng become an even wiser investor," remarked Mayor Ram.

"I remember you once saying you had this private investigator guy. For—what's it called?"

"Oppo," answered the mayor, meaning the political dark art of opposition research. "What can I say? It's a city full of snakes. Never a bad idea to know what somebody is hiding."

"He like a real private eye? I mean, I've never had to hire someone—"

"My guy is a background investigator for the city," bragged Ram. "Ex-cop. Sheriff's Department. But moonlights for a price."

"So, he might—"

"Mark Baba," wagged the mayor. "Righteous guy. Discreet to a fault. He'll look up the asshole of the devil if it's what you need— even blow out the fires of hell, if you know what I'm sayin'. Glad to hook you up."

20

Lucky's love/hate relationship with smartphones seemed to be in constant beta mode, as if he were always fighting the urge to put each infernal device under a giant boot heel and crush it like a cockroach. From his perspective as a cop, youths' obsession with the virtual panorama on their tiny phone screens had given rise to untold potential victims, disconnected from reality and unaware of their immediate surroundings. Lucky would often catch Karrie and Travis distracted and sneak up from the side or behind and scare them. His excuse was that if reason didn't work, perhaps he could terrify them into vigilance.

Man's newfound instinct to video an event rather than involve himself was another sore point with Lucky. Potential Good Samaritans had become videographers instead of crime stoppers— chronicling of the *who* and *where* of a certain situation without the context of the all-important *what* and *why*. In Lucky's opinion, cops had been caught in the act of police misconduct as often as they'd been maligned for some one-sided, grainy moving image that just showed the biased perspective of the camera phone's operator. Context free and viewed countless times on TV news and streaming sites, the videos provided an electronic execution by millions of capricious eyeballs with no trial or presumption of innocence.

While hamstrung in near-standstill freeway traffic, Lucky pulled out his phone in rare appreciation of the technology's investigative attributes. The northbound leg of the 110, otherwise known as the Pasadena Freeway, was a double stripe of bumper-to-bumper cars winding through the low hills beyond downtown. Highland Park. Mount Washington. Eagle Rock. A fender bender ahead had been enough to turn the Southland artery into a parking lot. It was up to the drivers stuck in traffic to make the most of the delay. Lucky had chosen the fallow moment to reexamine the camera phone footage he'd recorded earlier.

"Did you have anything to do with the hit and run?"
"What hit and run?"
"Did Denny Teng?"
"No."
"Did you bring Denny Teng's daughter to school yesterday?"
"Stop this! You can't do this to me!"

The answers to the latter questions betrayed the earlier baseline queries Lucky had forced. Wang's face tightened like a drum skin and his irises showed slight wobbles. Both were autonomic indicators of deception—or so said science. Lucky wasn't big on using tech or clinically tested techniques to divine truth from fiction. He'd always trusted his own instinctive response. But considering his present predicament—the vortex of Karrie, career, and his innate need to do the right thing, he'd begun to second-guess himself and had sought additional confirmation.

Or confirmation bias.

He considered forwarding the phone vid to Gonzo, as if that

might exonerate him from feeling that Karrie had been viciously run down because of his own debatable behavior. But Gonzo might argue that Lucky's one-man lie detector routine was anything but scientific, let alone trustworthy, especially when the subject was under duress.

But the lining of his gut and those antennae-like hairs on the back of his neck continued to inform as well as ask probing questions. Such as, *Why on God's green earth would a power player like Denny Teng want to hurt Karrie?*

"How is she?" Lucky asked, fully ignoring the hands-free law regarding cell phone use while driving. At a warp speed of under four miles per hour, he figured he was safe.

"Back in surgery again," choked Gonzo, her voice box constricted. "They're drilling more holes to release the pressure."

"She's young and healthy—"

"She nearly died again, Lucky!" hammered Gonzo. "The anticoagulants sent her blood pressure down to almost nothing. Then they crashed her back into surgery and started drilling. I don't even know if she's made it out."

Just her tone left Lucky breathless. His skin tingled with fear and guilt.

"Can't lose her…" he found himself whispering before resuming his composure. "Okay. I'm heading back your way—"

"You get anywhere?"

"Nothing that can't wait—"

"Did you find out who did this to her or not?"

"Might have."

"Who?"

"Don't have the driver. Don't have motive. Just a possible name."

"So, you're getting somewhere?"

"Yeah. Somewhere. But somewhere isn't always a destination."

"Don't stop," she suddenly permitted. "I'm not leaving her… or the hospital."

"Like I said. I'm turning around."

"No. I got this. You get him…or whoever it was."

Traffic ahead was beginning to lose its stickiness. Lucky slumped in his seat. He was split. Dreadfully so. Painfully hung up between the dilemma of returning to the ICU and his hell-bent desire to disembowel whomever the son of a bitch was who hurt Karrie. And now Gonzo, who'd generally served as his voice of reason, was encouraging him to press on with the hunt. The question wiggling up Lucky's spine was in regard to Gonzo's agenda. Was she animated about lynching whoever hurt Karrie? Or had she decided to use his righteous wont as a buffer to keep a physical distance between the two of them?

Lucky arrived at his destination—a four-block section in the suburb of Highland Park—a bygone business tract, gratefully devoid of Southern California's ubiquitous brown stucco *strip mall–itis*. Behind a corner brick building that doubled as a coffeehouse and hot yoga studio was a parking area slotted for only eight cars. The Audi convertible was just as Lucky had recalled—candy apple red with a leather interior the hue of rich vanilla. When he'd installed the GPS device he wasn't quite certain how much longer she'd possess the car. He'd guessed it was a standard lease. Thirty-six months. As far as he knew, the vehicle had been refreshed and resold and the present owner was currently getting his or her ligaments stretched out in a steamy downward dog pose. But the travel patterns had given Lucky confidence that it probably was *her*. The lithium battery in the digital tracking unit had lasted as advertised. In the nearly eighteen months he'd been keeping occasional tabs on the car, its routes had been consistent. The late afternoon visit to the yoga studio was nothing more than a practiced pit stop.

Lucky pulled the '99 up behind the Audi, kissing close to its bumper—effectively pinning the convertible in its space. Under the rear bumper he found the magnetized device precisely where he'd installed it, only covered in grime and road tar. He pocketed it, wiped his fingers off on the hem of his jeans, ambled around to the sidewalk, and entered through the café section of the yoga studio. Behind the barista bar was a floor-to-ceiling window, partially clouded from a roomful of sweaty bodies twisted into human pretzels—all women, from what Lucky could determine, each postured on her own colorful mat. Scanning for faces and making a positive ID through the spotty semi-fogged glass was an undoable adventure. Making it that much more impossible was the spandex-togged barista obstructing his view. She was guiltily admiring the rugged looks of the obvious non-customer while also currying a feminist disdain for his clear and present stares into the yoga studio.

"Looking for something?" asked the barista, instantly regretting that her tone sounded more coquettish than that of a stoic defender of the clientele's privacy.

Lucky lowered his gaze to the young woman, a sultry Sephardi in her mid- to late twenties, her body revealing an obsessive worship of workouts. It sucked him back to a time when it was easy to assume that someone so stunning was one of those actress-model wannabes who had migrated to Los Angeles for a shot at fame. But in the recent decade, he noticed spectacular-looking women seemed to sprout from the desert earth—too many to count.

"How long?" asked Lucky.

"How long have I what?" she replied, still acting more game than guardian.

"In there. The stretchy-bendy class?" Lucky nodded toward the studio on the other side of the glass.

"It's called Moksha," she quickly corrected, dispensing with the tease after sensing Lucky's lack of sexual interest. "It's a ninety-minute session including cool-down."

"Concludes about what time?"

"Think they're around the halfway point."

"Fine," finished Lucky, already swerving for the door. "When she's finished in the sweat lodge, tell her I'm in the ice cream joint across the way."

"'Scuse me? When who is finished?"

"You'll both figure it out."

Lucky swung through the door, squinted into the sunshine, and debated returning to his car for his Wayfarers. Instead, he checked his watch, a newer model TAG Heuer, a gift from Gonzo a couple Christmases back. The back plate of the timepiece was engraved with affectionate words and was the closest thing to a wedding ring he'd ever worn. By the time he crossed the boulevard he was in the shade of the Ice Cream Shoppe's awning, no need for sunglasses. Considering his forty-five-or-so-minute wait, he ventured inside, ordered up a Karrie favorite—a Neapolitan banana split with the works. He'd meant it to be a burning reminder of his mission, but the sweetness of the treat proved more guilt-inducing than motivating. He chose a sidewalk table, rocked uneasily in a flimsy plastic chair, and barely spooned at the sundae as it indifferently melted into a warm soup.

"Who the fuck do you think you are?" blustered a woman in the middle of the crosswalk. Almond-skinned face flush from her workout, her tangle of hair was yanked into a topknot, and she was walking on a razor line at Lucky. "You blocked me on purpose!"

"Catalina Rincon," stated Lucky, not deigning to stand for the bantam-sized lady. She was tinier than he'd imagined, barely one hundred pounds. Hardly the killer he had envisioned. He gestured to the chair opposite him.

Teetering on the curb, Cat stood in her neon trainers and matching workout apparel. Lululemon, Lucky noted. He'd purchased the same brand of attire for Gonzo the same Christmas he'd received the love note on the TAG chronograph.

"Who are you?" she seethed.

"We know each other," Lucky played. "Just never officially met. I'm Lucky Dey."

For a micro moment, she blanched, as if the name had struck her.

"Lemme help," Lucky continued. "You tried to have me killed."

"Don't know *what* you're talking about—"

"Not me exactly," smirked Lucky. "Your former business partner. Julius Colón. Whoever you had shoot up his pizza shop? You know. The one down in Compton? I nearly got punctured in the crossfire."

"Don't know a thing about that. But you are parked behind me, so if you would please move your car?"

"Sit. Cool down. Won't take a minute or two." Lucky could see that the gears in her mind were well-oiled, whirring, and measuring countermoves that might extricate her from the very literal and physical checkmate Lucky's Crown Vic had imposed behind her Audi.

"How'd you know where to find me?" she countered, not yet deigning to take the open seat, but willing to brave an approach.

"Try to keep tabs on potential threats. Was entertaining watching you extricate yourself from that whole Water and Power meltdown. Nobody gets away that clean without being connected. So, there. I answered. You wanna get onto your next whatever? Sit."

"Whatever you're looking for, tellin' you straight up I'm gonna be zero help to you." Cat sat anyway, her workout bag and rolled-up yoga mat on her lap in a posture of pure defense.

"Before you help me—and you *are* gonna help me—I'm gonna tell you *why* you're gonna help," leaned Lucky. "One. This ain't about you. And two, just like this little surprise meetup, I know stuff about you that you'd probably rather forget."

Locked onto her chestnut eyes—a pair of becoming orbits that had surely charmed a cavalcade of politically linked men and women—Lucky recalled a recent summer in a Sheriff's black-and-white, his return to uniform duty in Compton, his sparkplug trainee named Shia St. George, and the near cataclysm that had been her first week on the street. Cat Rincon had played a role in that overheated tumble of deadly dominoes. Ever since, Lucky had pinned the former DWP board member as an enemy.

"Denny Teng," said Lucky. "You know him?"

"Maybe."

"Know him well?"

"What if I do?"

"You do or you don't. Get real with me or I'll make a firepit out of your little red car."

"It's insured."

"Gonna be hard to collect if you're strapped in when I light the match."

"That's a threat," she stated, trying to sound unaffected but squeezing ever tighter to her yoga gear.

"You gotta ask yourself what's the easier play," reasoned Lucky. "Testing my bad side? Or just coming up with the answers I need?"

Cat visibly squirmed, though Lucky was more focused on her jawline for a signal of unease—an involuntary swallow reflex. He registered two gulps before her ever-so-minimal shift into a more cooperative bent.

"Denny Teng. He's a friend of the mayor," she finally replied.

"Tell me something I can't Google."

"Only know him socially," shrugged Cat. "Seen him at some of the same events. Fundraisers, museum galas, what have you."

"Let's speak a language that you understand," forced Lucky. "You're an operator and a criminal. I know it. You know it. I need you to utilize that special acumen of yours and give me something real. I wanna get inside Denny Teng's loop without stepping on his Gucci shoes. And I want it in a matter of hours. How do I make that happen?"

"Introduce yourself," she said dismissively. "Now you're in his loop."

But Lucky had already introduced himself—at least his visage and the threat of violence—to one of Denny Teng's employees. With a man as close to power as Denny Teng appeared, Lucky had thought the better move would be something less direct. Sideways. Or even a backdoor approach. If he could find the back door.

"Oh, I will introduce myself," replied Lucky. "But in my own way, in my own time. Now. Denny's loop. Who else is in it?"

Cat's eyes squinted. Like she was applying some kind of bullshit filter.

"I don't think you have anything on me," she floated with some pretend steel in her reserve. "I think this is a bluff. I think I should phone the city and have your crap-mobile towed. And then after I make a few calls to my *friends* at City Hall—and I do have lots and lots of friends—I'll see how you like eating all the shit that's gonna rain on your pretty head."

"Julius Colón," Lucky repeated.

"Never heard of him."

"He's dead. And it wasn't your people who got it done. That one's on me. By my hand, in case you question my personal resolve to bring the hurt. That leaves my Catalina Rincon problem. And I haven't yet decided on how your story ends."

Lucky let his glower spell the rest. The threat. The fatal weight of his meaning. His eyes never left hers. The stare lasted until she wiggled in her seat, back on her mental heels, unnerved.

"Frankie Coleman," Cat finally revealed. "About all I know. Denny Teng and her."

"Affair? So what?"

"He's married. She's a former Miss Something. Big private banker, tight with the mayor. You know, where there's money, there's Mayor Ram. And this Denny Teng guy's some kinda operator himself. No way a guy like him and a woman like that are only doing each other."

"More."

"Serious. That's all I got. Gossip. But you want inside Denny's thing, well…"

"Phone," said Lucky, gesturing to her bag. "Gimme."

"Why?"

"Think we're past you second-guessing me. Phone. Let's have it."

Reluctantly, Cat fished for her device, entered the unlock code, and slid it across the table. Lucky tapped at the screen succinctly.

"This is my phone number." Lucky flipped the phone back to her. "You're gonna find out for me where this Frankie is, where she's going. Then you're gonna call me."

"Excuse me? Aren't you the cop? Finding out shit is what *you* do."

"And now *you* are my snitch."

"*Snitch*," she sneered. "Disgusting sounding word."

"Hey. If CI or 'confidential informant' boosts your self-esteem, be my guest." With that, Lucky stood, looming. "If you get the urge to call in those hitters who missed murdering your ex-partner, just make sure they don't fuck up again. Otherwise you won't survive the week."

When Lucky's boots landed in the crosswalk he was confident enough that Cat Rincon would behave. In the eighteen months since he'd tagged her as a potential risk, he'd assessed her to be more pragmatic than vengeful. Her escape from prosecution, let alone actual incarceration, was an impressive Houdini act. She was so thoroughly buttressed by attorneys with connective tissue to City Hall's ivory towers she had barely gotten a sniff from the District Attorney. Her only punishment had been to tender her resignation from the Department of Water and Power board.

Even after all those dead bodies down in Compton.

But that was only a history lesson. It's what lay ahead that burned Lucky. It was nearly 5:30 when he pointed himself in the direction of Westwood and the Ronald Reagan UCLA Medical Center. In the weekday rush, the traffic was a block-by-block slog. Karrie liked to call it *crush hour*. It brought to mind perhaps the one thing about Los Angeles Lucky's runaway-turned-adopted daughter loathed about the city. He had tried to get her to see the traffic from his arterial perspective. *The life of it.* But so far, that was an argument he hadn't won.

It was 6:22 when Lucky finally collected the automated ticket to enter the hospital's parking garage, a six-story structure that charged the sick and the visiting premium prices despite their lot in life. On the elevator up to the fourth floor, he found himself crowded in by a five-deep crew of suited administrators, all credentialed with laminated IDs slung around their necks as if they were International Olympic Committee royalty. The only sound on the muted ride came from Lucky unconsciously scraping the barcoded garage ticket across his neck stubble. He caught a glower thrown by a runt of a man hiding behind a pair of tortoiseshell eyeglasses. Lucky catalogued the man's gold Rolex Daytona and tasseled loafers and didn't hesitate.

"You look like a man who can answer a parking garage question," Lucky deadpanned. "What do I pay the machine when I exit? One healthy kidney or do I just pony up the copay?"

The fourth-floor doors slid open before the bespectacled bureaucrat could muster more than a gape-jawed comeback.

Then the spell unfolded.

As soon as Lucky turned the first corner after the elevator bank, he found himself oddly disoriented, like he'd stepped into a carnival of funhouse mirrors. Everywhere he spun, the hospital corridors appeared identical with white-on-white paint triple-striped with gurney bumper rails and hand sanitizer dispensers fixed on the walls every twenty feet. Not until he calmed his feet and took measure of himself and a deep cleansing breath did he at last accept that the fear of losing Karrie had warped his entire being into a metaphoric vise. A superficial sheen of sweat leaked from his pores. He read the posted signage and managed to find the ICU's family waiting room. Lucky expected to find Gonzo where he'd left her, legs crooked, book cradled between her knees.

"Oh, hey," perked Frosty, straightening in the seat where Lucky had expected to discover Gonzo.

"Where's Gonzo?" was Lucky's first salvo, followed by a more acute examination of the welt below Frosty's right eye and the twisted tissue stuffed in his nostrils. "What the hell happened to you?"

"The wifey. Or whatever you call her? Gone home for a change," replied Frosty. "And before she left…" Frosty motioned to his face then opened his palms in acceptance.

"She clocked you? What the hell for?"

"Guessin' she didn't know you put me on the family visitor list," shrugged Frosty. "So, maybe she meant it for you."

"Probably."

"Still. Nothin' I didn't have comin'," admitted Frosty, finding his feet. "If I were her? Yeah, don't think I'd want the guy that tried to put a bullet in her man's skully prayin' on her daughter in a coma."

"How long ago?"

"Hour. Hour and a half. Said you'd be along soon. So, I thought I'd hang out until then."

"Thanks for comin'," deflated Lucky before suggesting, "You should get some ice on that."

"Was hit way worse by your daughter," smiled Frosty. "Hung out for a while with her."

"No problem getting in?"

"Nah. Whispered in her ear. Let her know He was up there watching. Watching over y'all."

"Appreciated," said Lucky, uncomfortable.

In many ways, Lucky had saved Frosty's life and, quite possibly, the young man's soul. Reciprocating with Lucky was nearly impossible. Yet that wasn't going to stop Frosty from seeking out potential cracks in the veneer he might penetrate.

"Whatever I can do," said Frosty, his alien-like arms enfolding Lucky with a warm embrace disguised as a bro-hug. Lucky appreciated the gesture, but unconsciously slapped Frosty on the back to cue the separation.

"Stick around then, will ya?" pled Lucky. "I'm gonna look in on her for a bit, but might have to cut out on that other thing."

"Got somethin' to stick on that downtown guy?"

"Maybe…But what it is I don't exactly know yet. Hoping to have a new door to kick down."

Despite Karrie having withstood yet another procedure in which more drill bits penetrated her priceless skull, to Lucky's eye little, if anything, had been altered in the ICU room. The life support and monitoring systems ticked and hummed. The intubation pipe, curled and taped to Karrie's mouth, kicked with every mechanical breath forced into her lungs. Seeing her so slight and still delivered a second punch of vertigo. Lucky grabbed the arm of the chair next to the bed and steadied himself, only to buckle under a transitory weakness. His knees caved and he sat, his body heaving. They weren't quite sobs. But his body succumbed to emotions he hadn't felt since days after his brother had passed.

"Fuck me," Lucky mouthed, his arms clamped hard around himself. "Jesus, please…" he whispered to the static air. "If you are what you say you are. If you're what she believes in, then give me her pain. Please. Take your shit out on me. I can take it. Hell. You know I deserve it. She's already had more than her share of this world's bad side. So, please…please…please…"

Lucky's plea was interrupted by a buzzing in his pocket. He dug for his phone. A text message from Catalina Rincon landed on his screen. Displayed was Frankie Coleman's name and an address in Manhattan Beach, zip code included.

As if I'm gonna mail a freakin' letter.

He briefly pondered if it was a setup. Cat could've phoned up the same hitters who'd attempted to gun down Julius Colón, demanding a kill on Lucky as a matter of recompense. But any second-guessing would have to wait. He had squeezed Cat Rincon for intel and she had produced.

The medieval-looking apparatus encircling Karrie's cranium made it impossible for Lucky to leave her with simple kiss on the forehead. So, he touched her hand, stroking it with a knuckle while he whispered:

"Hang in there, kiddo. We're not done yet."

21

City of Commerce. 10:02 p.m.

"Think about it," blabbered Mark Baba, pausing his speech only long enough to swig from his tumbler of ginger ale and lime. "Callin' your city 'Commerce.' It's stupid genius. I mean, when I was a kid growing up next door in Downey, I just wondered at what a weird name to call a city. Commerce. But the older I got and the more I thought about it, I finally figured it out. Genius. You gonna build yourself a private little hamlet of a town, a municipality friendly to business and only business. Come bring your factory, your manufacturing and everything. Your damn card casino?"

Mark Baba, known as Babylon to most everybody who knew him, opened his arms wide as if to embrace the massive poker room that was the Commerce Casino. The utilitarian space was more convention hall than Las Vegas gambling emporium. Its only fanciful lighting was the red-flared signs over the fire exits. The room itself was choked with poker tables, nearly every felt-top crowded with players of every imaginable ethnic flavor, size, sex. The garble of voices was muddied by the sound of the exchange of poker chips and the tinkling of ice swirling in Babylon's glass as he gesticulated with practically every animated syllable.

"Zone for general domiciles? Not here," Babylon carried on. "Don't move your damn family here. 'Cause but for the card casinos and after-hours truck deliveries, we're gonna roll the sidewalks up in our town called Commerce. We don't need to build any schools, no parks for kids to play. Which means you don't even need real cops. Hire a security company to patrol. Any real crime happens, hire out the County's for police work. Pay 'em by the job. Brilliant, man. Frickin' brilliant municipal business model."

Denny Teng was nested atop the bar stool opposite Babylon, his solid posture and lengthy trunk dwarfing Babylon's fireplug frame. The sixty-year-old ex-sheriff's deputy had a ruddy face abused by acne and a lifelong taste for high-test alcohol from Everclear to home-brewed corn liquor. And though sober for eleven years, Babylon hadn't lost a lick of his loquacious nature. Denny Teng had been fully warned by Mayor Ram that the former detective could talk the chrome off an exhaust pipe. He'd also been told Babylon was strong enough to tear telephone books in two; ask and he might demonstrate. While Babylon babbled, Denny tried to picture the kind of body beneath the rumpled khakis and cotton shirt. Ripped and pimpled from steroid abuse or scarred like a scrapping dog? The only true giveaway to the man's age was the pair of tortoiseshell readers that hung around his neck on a silver chain.

"Know why they call me Babylon?" asked the ex-cop. "Because I babble on and on. And I know it. Not somethin' I'm proud of but, hey. I am what I am. My momma's boy through and through."

"Which one is she?" asked Denny. "Your mom?"

"Where the hell is she? Good question," scanned Babylon. "Usually not too hard to spot. Just trip your eyes across all the poker heads until you land on a little puffball. Her hair is snow white. And whadda you know, there she is. Eleven o'clock. Table against the wall."

"And she's ninety?"

"Ninety-one. Seriously. Plays three nights a week. Had to start bringin' her here because she kept clipping all the old men at the ol' folks home."

Denny laughed.

"No shit," confirmed Babylon.

"She have a curfew?"

"I'll tug the leash at eleven. Have her tucked in and snug in her Depends by midnight."

"So, this guy…" Denny tried to segue.

"The guy who harassed your guy…"

"Roughed him up."

"Say you got video?"

As if he'd been waiting for the invitation, Denny reached into his slacks' front pocket, produced a thumb drive, and placed it in Babylon's meaty palm.

"If he's got a face," smiled Babylon, "I promise I'll ID the ass-hole. Might take a day or two but I'll tag him."

Babylon produced a large-screened smartphone and plugged the thumb drive into the port. By the time he'd lifted those read-ing glasses the video series was rolling. Four security cameras had recorded Lucky. The first revealed colored images of Lucky enter-ing Denny Teng's downtown lobby. The second was a high angle from inside the elevator. The third camera, dark and in higher contrast, tracked Lucky crossing from the elevator bank to Denny Teng's office's oak doors. The last and cleanest moving images were from a camera mounted above and behind the office receptionist. From that angle, Lucky's features were finely detailed down to the threads of his pullover.

"Son of a bitch!" ticked Babylon, the vein in his neck swelling. "I can do better than putting a name to the asshole's face. I frickin' know the bastard."

"You know him?!" Denny wasn't sure he heard Babylon correctly, considering the decibels of casino noise clogging his ears.

"I do, I do." Babylon turned the phone screen to face his potential client. "That guy is Sheriff's Deputy Lucky Dey. Least I think he's still on the job. And not just Sheriff's, by the by. That asshole's a goddamn Reaper."

"Reaper? Like a killer?"

"Not like that," corrected Babylon. "A gang within certain sheriff's stations. You know, motorcycle clubs. Like that. Gotta patch in. Only you gotta get inked up. Like this one."

Babylon shifted, pulling his shirt to the side to reveal a tattoo on his shoulder.

"That's a Reaper?" asked Denny Teng, confused. The ink job was freckled and dark and looked nothing like Death carrying a bloody scythe.

"No. That's my station. Vikings. My club. Fraternity, you know? At Lynwood we had Vikings. Lennox was the Reapers. Same shit. Different station. That's all," finished Babylon before shifting gears. "But damn. You got Lucky Dey lookin' up your business. Lemme ask you this. You got dirty laundry to hide?"

"I'm a businessman."

"Hey. We're in the City of Commerce. It's all business here. Didn't I tell ya?"

"I don't have a godforsaken clue what he'd want with me."

Denny wasn't exactly lying. He could count on all his fingers and toes the number of illicit transactions he had to worry over. Just which particular crime was Lucky on to? Was it an official investigation or...

"Do you think he's working outside his sheriff's job?" queried Denny. "Like you. But for someone else?"

"Like a competitor?"

"Or a former business associate?" wondered Denny, giving up zero in the way of specifics.

"Dunno 'til I have a go."

"When can you start?"

"After I drop my mom at her crib. Shouldn't be too hard. Except the Lucky part."

"What do you mean?"

"Man comes with a rep," warned Babylon. "Package you don't wanna open."

"What if I made that part of the job?" implied Denny, voice weighted with gravitas. "What if I needed you to open that particular package?"

The ex-cop rocked back on his stool as if to get a wider picture of the lanky businessman. He lowered those readers from his face.

"Suppose that depends on how a man like yourself defines 'open.' Figuratively? Or physically? But, hey. Don't answer just yet. Let's see what I find out, then we can discuss the semantics."

22

Manhattan Beach. 11:27 p.m.

The address supplied by Cat Rincon was to a four-story Highland Avenue house. Shingled siding. Weathered from the consistently salty air. And like so many South Bay properties, it was constructed vertically to take full advantage of the slope overlooking the Pacific, with west-facing balconies on every floor but that of the two-car garage. When Lucky arrived he had no actual plan of action beyond the basic knock and talk. He'd identify himself as a police officer and ask a few questions. Authority plays would often turn into invitations inside with polite sit-downs and follow-up queries of a more incisive nature. It wasn't exactly illegal. He was still a sheriff's deputy investigating a crime. Who was to know he had been suspended and was breaking a cornucopia of regulations—rules and principled guidelines he generally regarded as sound and ethical.

But Lucky regarded Karrie that much more.

The front porch lamp was lit. Aside from that, there was no sign of activity. From the street he could see all the shades and curtains were drawn back—the windows like opaque, glassy eyes facing an overcast sea. Inert. As comatose as his daughter. Lucky knocked anyway, rung the bell three times without so much as hearing a shuffle from inside. A stalk to the rear revealed nothing more than a padlocked patio gate and more blank panes of glass. Whoever Frankie Coleman was, she wasn't home. Whether she was working late, out to dinner, or halfway across the planet, Lucky hadn't a wisp of evidence. He was left with choices. Stick around and wait or contact his Sheriff's resources and risk exposing himself to further departmental repercussions. The third option came with a constant tug. Karrie. Return to UCLA Med to be with her.

Lucky spotted a Mexican cantina called Don Julio's directly across the street. Resigning himself to an arbitrary deadline of midnight before moving on to some form of plan B, Lucky ordered a bottle of Dos Equis and sat at a tall bar table nestled against a street-facing window. He sipped the brew and kept his eyes on the darkened house, primarily skinned to the garage doors. He calculated that once the automated button was depressed and the gears to the motor engaged, he'd have thirty seconds to hustle from the restaurant to the threshold across the street. If the mechanism was up to code, there'd be a sensor to prevent the door from closing on a pet or a small child.

Or rule-busting rat bastards like me.

"You look like you're waiting for someone," said the woman, soft and from behind.

He expected the voice belonged to a cocktail waitress. As he turned he was struck to discover an intoxicated woman had already landed on the swiveling high stool opposite him. Her dark shoulder-length locks were a tumble, slightly wet as if she'd just come up for air after a long swim. She wore loose jeans and a tight white tank top revealing the straps of her black bra. The faux candle on the tabletop showed a stunner's face scrubbed of makeup with a light dusting of freckles arching between rich blue eyes and impossibly high cheekbones. He pegged her as an athlete or maybe a former model on the prowl.

Or Gonzo's sister from an Anglo mother?

"Waiting?" she continued. "Or drowning some kinda shit-ass sorrow?"

"Just hangin'," replied Lucky. She was distracting enough, yet he kept his face quartering to the window and beyond, not daring to miss a sweep of headlights nor the garage door opening.

"Mind if I hang with you?"

"Why not?" he relented. After all, she was probably a local. Knew people. She might even know the banker who lived across the way. Then he doubted himself. The odds seemed long.

"You native?" she asked.

"So Cal?" Lucky replied. "Or South Bay?"

"Neighborhood."

"Guess that makes me a tourist."

"Okayyyyyy," she slurred. "I'll continue the interrogation. What's out that window that's more interesting than me?"

It was the alcohol talking. At least that's what Lucky excused. By her looks, she was used to attention.

"Maybe I'm shy," he excused.

"You look like you surf."

"Guilty."

"Manhattan Beach. Come for the waves. Stay to get laid."

"Wow." Lucky followed with an involuntary chuckle. The stunner was past her limit, lonely, and trouble with a capital T.

"May I?" Without waiting for an answer, she lifted Lucky's half-supped long-neck beer. "Would you think me unladylike to drink from a bottle?"

"You're pretty drunk."

"You're pretty cute."

"And I'll bet you live around here."

"Walking distance."

"You're right," shifted Lucky. "I am waiting for someone. Maybe you know her."

"Another woman?" The stunner waved her index finger. "We are not gonna talk about anyone else. Not now. Not at this moment in time."

"Not a girlfriend," defended Lucky. "Don't even know her. Just lookin' for some information. Maybe she's a friend."

"Thing about lady friends," she turned, a dark mood lurking. "Women don't help other women. That means they can't be friends. Not for-real friends. Lovers? Okay. But real friends help friends. You with me?"

"Doesn't matter if you don't have any female friends. I just wanna know if you know this one lady."

"Why do you think they call us bitches?" she laughed.

"She lives right around here."

"Bitch got a name?" she laughed again.

"She does," smiled Lucky, feeling the thinnest traction. "Her name—"

"Screw her name," she swerved. "What's your name?"

"My name's Lucky."

"Really? Your name's Lucky?" she withered into a giggle fit. "Your momma named you Lucky? Damn."

"Just a nickname."

"And I love it like…Maybe you're my lucky star. Anybody ever call you that. Their lucky star?"

"Not ever," he fibbed.

"I'm the first?"

"You really are." He wanted to settle her, sink a hook and reel her in. Even flirt with her if she'd be willing to talk about the other woman, the neighbor who lived in the multimillion-dollar four-story only fifty yards away.

"Maybe you're *my* lucky star," she insisted.

"Okay," he teased. "And what do I call you?"

"My momma named me Francine," drawled the drunk

woman, offering a manicured hand. "But I like it when a man calls me Frankie. Frankie Coleman."

Lucky couldn't summon a memory when he'd felt so...well... *lucky.*

They nearly closed the joint, tipping long-necked Dos Equis until 1:30 a.m. All the while, despite her dizzy demeanor, Frankie kept up with the come-ons. And Lucky, no longer peeling an eye on that automated garage door, played along with her seduction game. He'd eventually had to help her cross the street. With her flip-flops stuffed into his jeans' back pocket, he tested the screws in his back by practically carrying her across the empty four lanes and up a set of switchback brick steps to the same landing where only hours earlier he'd stood at the door hoping for someone to hear the bell, throw the bolt, and answer.

"Can't get to my keys," she chortled.

More bad seduction play, thought Lucky. Yet he obliged, slipping a hand into her front right pocket for something that resembled a key. Frankie gently gyrated as if finding pleasure in his pursuit until Lucky's finger hooked a key ring. In the porch light, he noticed the orange and gold fifty cent piece–sized medallion that dangled from the metal loop, a keepsake of the University of Tennessee Volunteers.

"Go Vols!" she whooped before hushing herself. "Shhhhhh. I got neighbors and a rep. Need to main-taaain."

As Lucky worked the lock, Frankie took advantage, slipping her fingers down the front of his jeans in an awkward grope of his manhood.

"Hey, now," warned Lucky. "We're not even inside yet." He turned the key and gave the door an easy shove. It swung inward without a squeak. Before he could catch Frankie, she stumbled inward, finding her balance with assistance from the stairwell pilaster.

"Upstairs?" she asked. "Or we could do it *on* the stairs?"

"You're really drunk," said Lucky, overstating the obvious.

"You're hot." Frankie leaned into Lucky, fumbling for his belt.

"Slow your roll," he teased, turning her around as if wanting to take her from behind. Only he used the maneuver to hook an arm around her waist before starting the climb up the staircase. Through a skylight, the overcast sky provided enough lumens for Lucky to read the steps.

"Bedroom? Never a bad idea," she giggled. "It's a California King for my California king."

"Where?"

"Top floor. On left…wait. On right…or left. Shit, I got me the whirlies."

"One step at a time."

"Hope I don't puke on you. That wouldn't be sexy t'all."

"Don't talk. Just follow my lead."

By the top of the two-flight climb, Frankie was practically limp and Lucky's lumbar region felt as if it might architecturally pancake. Those unguarded windows Lucky had peered at from the outside offered just enough light for him to make out the doors to the master suite. In the scant light, he managed to read the impeccable décor, feminine yet strong, with furniture built from heavy beams of wood, softened with warm, ivory frills. The four-poster bed lay underneath a hand-painted canopy trimmed with Egyptian fringe.

"Bathroom or bed?" Lucky asked.

"Bed, please." Frankie's instincts took hold. Once at the edge of the bed she crawled into the middle of the mattress and patted the duvet with an open palm. "Right here. Next to me. Just a moment's rest. Then we can make out…"

Retreating to a pair of wingback reading chairs, Lucky eased himself into a sitting position, wincing away the pain in his lower back until he felt relief. He checked to make certain his phone was on vibrate, then checked for messages about Karrie. His screen was clean. Zero missives, as if the entire world was in a sightless slumber. He waited five minutes, eyes fixed on Frankie's silhouette, measuring the beauty queen's breathing and checking it against his watch. Thirty-two breaths a minute. A sign sleep was winning the fight against the ethanol in her bloodstream. He waited. Observed. Counted breaths. He needed her asleep, sound enough that she wouldn't hear him creep her house for clues regarding her relationship with Denny Teng. He hadn't a glimmer whether or not Frankie Coleman was the key to anything, let alone some kind of outcome that might clarify why his treasured Karrie was fighting for her life while in her own dream sleep—a medically induced hibernation.

What about you, Frankie? he wondered in the silver-gray cast of her bedroom. *Are you afraid of the dark? Does being a rich single banker allow you to make certain your nights are never ever black?*

After some thirty minutes counting off Frankie's inhales and exhales, Lucky was satisfied as to the depth of her sleep and left his seat. He engaged the flashlight function on his phone and began a closer inspection of his surroundings. The second bedroom had been turned into an extra closet, complete with rolling hanger racks and miles of clothes—gowns, business and cocktail dresses, women's suits and accessories, plus an entire wall of shelves stacked with shoes.

Frankie's home office was practically devoid of paper. The utilitarian space, absent the rest of the home's decorator flair, was all computers, monitors, separate hard drives, neatly bound wiring, and vertical cabinets better suited for the back room of a pawn shop than a home workstation. *Suspicious?* Lucky wondered. The most he knew about banking was the bottom line of his generally threadbare checking account.

With every tick of his internal clock, he was reminded of how dangerous the entire search was, bordering on downright stupid. Lucky didn't know if Frankie had a roommate or even a houseguest with a key. At any given moment, he had to fully expect discovery. Sure, she'd invited him in, meaning a breaking and entering or trespassing charge would never stick. The lady, though, had money and was connected to the mayor of Los Angeles. A victim with money and power always had enough political leverage to make life miserable for someone considered an enemy, even if that adversary had rescued her from a sordid crawl across the street to her own front door.

Because that's me, thought Lucky to himself. *I'm the good goddamn Samaritan.*

Thursday

23

Frankie awoke to a car crusher of a headache, the beginnings of what was sure to evolve into an epic hangover. She lay on her side just trying to breathe slowly and keep her eyes shut, certain if she allowed the faintest sunlight to invade her optical receptors it would feel like ice picks driven into her ear canals. By the color temperature inside her eyelids, she guessed it was between 6:00 and 7:00 a.m. That was her usual morning game. Before she actually opened her eyes, she made a bet against herself regarding the exact time. If her answer landed within fifteen minutes of the digits displayed on her bedside clock she'd treat herself to a toasted sesame-seed bagel with cream cheese. If wrong, she'd force herself to choke back a bowl of egg whites topped with parmesan, but only after she'd pedaled fifteen miles on her stationary road bike.

The pain in her skull, though. It felt far too ominous to risk opening her eyes. Not just yet. She rolled onto her back, leaden, setting off a wave in her head that felt like a five-pound ball bearing settling at the base of her neck. She groaned aloud, flipping an instinctive switch. Was she alone? She had vague recollections of a man, tallish with a buzz cut of sandy hair. *A surfer?* She pictured his faint smile beneath a permanently broken nose. She loved that in a man—a lack of vanity. In the plastic Los Angeles age, more men were giving themselves permission to go under the knife, fixing their flaws through cosmetic surgery, even going as far as implanting pectoral enhancements.

Is that man lying beside me? she wondered.

With eyes still shut, her fingertips slid across the duvet cover. Gently. Left hand then right, reaching for the touch of a bedmate. All she discovered was an empty plateau. Neat. Flat. The bedding under her felt like it was still made from the day before, snapped into uniform tidiness just as she'd left it nearly twenty-four hours earlier. Frankie's hand reached for herself, expecting some form of nakedness yet finding her loose-fit denims intact, as were her tank top and bra. Only her flip-flops appeared to be missing.

How the hell did I get home? she worried.

Had she dreamt the man? Was her slutty seduction act just random memory?

"Jesus, Frances," she flogged herself aloud. *Why can't you try sleeping alone for once in your grown-ass life?*

Her eyes fluttered open. The gray light across the canopy was deceiving. It could be dawn. It could be noon on a day when the South Bay sun hadn't yet burned off the morning cloud cover. Her phone wasn't where she last remembering leaving it—in her back pocket. Facing more physical anguish, Frankie found the edge of the bed and pushed up into a seated pose, her eyes squeezing shut as if to ward off the coming hurt. The agony came in a familiar wave, peaking at the top of her scalp as the blood drained. Her smartphone was on the nightstand, plugged into a power cable despite her having no memory of doing so. *Whatever.* When she finally glanced at the clock, the time read 7:11 a.m. Early. There would be no messages worth her effort at that hour. She would check after a long, stinging shower.

Before her feet touched the floor, habit took over. Work began to plague her. And with work came worry about her bank—her precious brainchild. The numbers flooded in. The negatives were at the forefront, the deficits, the demand for more high liquidity investors, and the constant shell game that was the Denny Teng business. Without the consistent drip of his offshore deposits, the façade cloaking her bank's dire circumstance would fail. The reveal would expose the beauty-queen-turned-banker as the trailer trash she was.

Trailer trash in Prada, Frankie corrected.

She stood, battled the next wave of pain, then wobbled her way toward the bathroom. She shucked her clothes. The jeans were expertly kicked away, followed by the tank top and underwear. Choosing to leave the bathroom light off, she started the water for her shower and waited for the steam to rise. Turning to face her expansive vanity mirror, replete with rows of extinguished glamour bulbs, she leveled her eyes for an inspection of her body, the dimness casting her in black and gray contours. At forty, her body remained supermodel lean, taut, while naturally fulsome in its femininity. But for the crow's feet at the corners of her eyes and the deepening worry lines on her forehead, Frankie's face remained a flawless beacon of classic American beauty.

This was a moment that would usually bootstrap her ego. But it wasn't her body that Frankie saw in the mirror. Initially, she thought it was just dripping condensation from the shower. But that would only have made sense if she'd just stepped out from twenty minutes under a savaging stream of hot water. She blamed the fog in her head and braved a half step forward. No. The anomaly in the mirror had a human touch. The moment she recognized it was writing, she spun, fingers scraping for the light switch. Those make-up bulbs ignited, leaving the lipstick-scrawled message in colorful relief.

NEVER FORGET. DENNY TENG HAS EYES ON YOU!

Frankie's knees nearly gave out. As she felt her body buckling under her own weight, she reached for the granite-topped vanity and held fast to the edge of the sink.

I'm dreaming. That's it. I'm still in bed and this is a just a nightmare.

Her body felt cold. Steam from the shower was licking at her skin, beading against it and turning cool from the rogue breeze filtering in through a bedroom window. Yes. She was, in fact, awake. Fully. Her arms straightened and she pushed up with her legs. The mirror was fogging up. It made the lipstick lettering appear to bleed a clear liquid, dripping from the bottom of each letter. The message, though, remained unchanged, chilling Frankie to her guilty soul.

24

Playa del Rey. 5:54 a.m.

Lucky was conflicted. Part of him wanted to let Emery sleep before knocking on her apartment door. He'd been parked there since around 4:00 a.m., excusing his lingering to a lagging mind that might've benefitted from a nod or two of sleep. Of course, he could've phoned Emery the moment he'd left Frankie's Manhattan Beach house after scouring the stair-happy home for anything he could relate to Denny Teng. If Emery weren't so prickly toward him, he might've discarded his concern for the early hour and just dialed her up. Only the last time he'd tried to connect with the self-described *geekette*, she'd practically hung up on him. In Lucky's admittedly narrow rationale, Emery deserved some face time, if not a few extra hours of her own precious sleep.

But Lucky's every attempt to close his eyes was met with

subconscious resistance. Images blew by as if speed-projected on the insides of his eyelids.

Karrie surfing.

Karrie struck by the car and flipped into the air.

Karrie immobilized, fully ventilated, shaved of all hair and wearing that orbital crown of skull screws.

And when his eyes would inadvertently snap open, Lucky would see the street lamps of Playa del Rey glowing in the rolling fog. Fifties-era apartment buildings striped both sides of the thin roadway, the fronting palm trees locked in a time warp. The partly lowered window of his '99 invited a nostalgic scent from the nearby ocean mixed with recently mown grass and dew.

As a frustrating distraction, he kept replaying the creep he'd made through Frankie's beach house. From the top floor down, bedroom to the garage, he'd uncovered nothing obvious he could use as a sharp angle on Denny Teng. If Frankie had been sober and answered the front door when he'd knocked, he might've found a verbal crack he could pry apart. Or he might've offered some line of bull that could have rattled her. Worse, though, he might have been scouring the privacy of someone with nothing but nothing to hide. An awful violation, entirely based on a suggestion from Cat Rincon—not exactly the most certified of resources. Lucky regretted that rooftop tune he'd played on gimpy Wang, Denny Teng's yellow-toothed associate. Denny Teng may have been cloaked in power, but before Lucky messed with Wang he might have been approachable.

By now he's deployed full armor, Lucky reasoned, leaving him with only an indirect track to investigate.

And what lousy track is that, dammit?

Wang's reaction to Lucky's interrogation had revealed that he was some flavor of bad guy—but not necessarily *the* bad guy. The same assumption could be applied to Denny Teng.

Lucky felt he was merely grasping at straws and had boxed himself into a sideways approach. Girlfriends, lovers, wives, mothers, and silent partners were the soft points he could poke with a bayonet.

Only Frankie's house had given up nothing whatsoever that linked to Denny Teng. Nothing Lucky could exploit. He had been a hip-turn from leaving when he'd decided to return to the master bedroom, where an unconscious Frankie appeared not to have moved a millimeter. From those loose jeans revealing her lacy thong's whale tail, he'd eased the phone from her back pocket and gently maneuvered her thumb to the touchpad, unlocking the device.

There you are, you...

Denny Teng—listed as Denny T. on Frankie's phone—appeared to be her most-dialed person. His ten digits were interspersed with dozens of other calls, both incoming and outgoing, but most of those were between 9:00 a.m. and 5:00 p.m. Frankie and Denny spoke at all hours—fitting, if they were having an affair. Next, Lucky had opened Frankie's text and email feeds and, as busy as they were, there was nary a single missive listed as sent or received from the man in question.

Erased? wondered Lucky. *What two people talk that much via mobile phone without sending or receiving a singular text?*

That's when Lucky had decided to scrawl the lipstick note on the bathroom mirror. At worst it was guaranteed to unnerve Frankie into a hasty response. If there were nothing illicit between the ex-beauty queen and Denny Teng, the message would come off as no more than creepy—unsettlingly so. Any self-respecting woman living alone would be quick to dial up the local police department and report the deranged stranger who'd assisted her home. But if there were something dark between Frankie and Denny—something that might be liable to fissure under the stress of distrust—Lucky wanted to be there to wedge his steel-toed boot into the crack.

Screw this, thought Lucky, his eyes popping open to the digital clock read-out on his dash.

4:16 a.m.

* * *

Emery. She wasn't a morning person. And Lucky knew as much. Nonetheless, he hit the door buzzer at the uncaring hour of 4:18 a.m. He waited twenty seconds and pressed again. After four rings, a tinny voice finally sounded from the speaker.

"Whoever the hell this is," said Emery, barely audible but aggravated, "stop it before I call a cop."

"It is a cop," he leaned in. "It's Lucky."

"It's four in the fucking morning!" groused Emery. "Jesus. You got my number. Why not just phone me?"

"Said the girl who complains I never come round."

"Well, this sure as shit cured that jones."

Before Lucky could answer, he heard another voice in the background. *Aha*, he reasoned, Emery was having a sleepover. A half second before he could suggest returning to his car so he could phone her, the lock release buzzed, noisily reverberating the old wrought-iron gate. Lucky swung it aside, journeyed forward, and let the gate slam shut behind him.

Emery was waiting in the coffin-like vestibule outside her upstairs unit, the door to her apartment fully open. Lucky could see all the way to the kitchen. Emery's oversized T-shirt was so slight and thin that, even in the dimness, he could practically read the cartoon tattoos that adorned her skin. With fuschia and bottle-blonde streaked hair, an adorably round face, and a landscape of body ink fashioned entirely out of comic strip characters, to say Emery stood out from the crowd would have been a gross under-statement.

"Need I remind you of the hour?" Emery repositioned her heavy-rimmed glasses. "What the fuck, Lucky?"

"The nose ring," noticed Lucky. "That's new."

"How long since you seen me? Two years? Three?"

"New to me," Lucky corrected.

"Who you know this time of day?" called a voice from inside

the apartment. Female. A figure crossed in front of the kitchen window. Leggy. Naked. There and gone. "You need help out there?"

"I'm taking care of it," called Emery. "Go back to sleep."

"Whatever," was the woman's simple reply.

"Not how it looks," suggested Emery.

"None of my business," shrugged Lucky.

"It's an experiment," she shifted. "I keep attracting gay girls so maybe there's something there, you know?"

"Seriously, Em. Not here for a 4:00 a.m. booty call."

"Right. You *need* something and couldn't wait for a decent hour." She crossed her arms. "Bet you got a number or somethin' you need a track on."

It was painfully obvious. Emery's job working for an NSA subcontractor gave her access to a variety of digital tracking technologies. Time after time, Lucky had abused the privilege, not to mention her good nature, mostly during exigent circumstances.

Mostly, he excused.

"I know I'm out of favors," he admitted. "But this one's important. It's about my daughter."

"Like I knew you got one? Anyway, here's bad news. I lost the job *and* my clearance cuzza the *last* thing I did for you."

Emery was slowly twisting in place, bare feet quietly shuffling against the cold concrete. Meanwhile, Lucky's guilt was riding up his solar plexus.

"Sorry—"

"My own stupid fault," she interrupted. "You didn't make me do it. No gun to my head."

"Charges?"

"Company buried it. Nobody wants a Snowden thing. Gave me a year's severance if I signed the NDA and promised to keep my mouth shut. Whoops. There I go. Messed up again."

"Looks like you got company. I just poked a bear," admitted Lucky. "If I can't spy on the phone number to see how the bear reacts…"

"Lucky is shit outta luck?" she gibed.

"Somethin' like that."

"I'm no help. Maybe you can buy some Bitcoin, troll the dark web for a Russian hacker. My last free advice. Time for Lucky to get off my porch." Emery retreated, turning an about-face and slamming her door shut. The deadbolt sounded for punctuation.

Lucky stood there, looking as if he'd just taken a wet slap to the face, deserving every pained lick of punishment. He'd gone to the Emery well too many times and it had not only lost her a government subcontractor gig but it had blown up in his face.

Without being able to hack Denny's phone number, the creep of Frankie's beach house, along with the cryptic message he'd lipsticked on her bathroom mirror, appeared to have been utterly for naught.

As for Emery's tech advice, she'd lost Lucky at *Bitcoin*. Nor would he have an inkling how to access the dark web. To make matters worse, he felt as if he were running on empty and bereft of actionable options.

"Sorry, Karrie," Lucky said softly as if conversing with her. "I got nothin'."

25

Babylon had been up all night. But that wasn't at all strange for the detective. He was famous for going two to three days without a minute of slumber. A four- to six-hour nap and he'd be up and ready to go another fifty or sixty hours. As sleep disorders went, his condition had no name. The tens of thousands of dollars he'd spent out of pocket on sleep clinics could've made a healthy down payment on his dream retirement cabin in Coeur d'Alene, Idaho. Instead, he lived at the cottage home he'd grown up in with his poker-playing mother's name still on the deed. Once he kicked drinking and self-medicating, he'd come to appreciate his special insomnia as a gift. Sure, he reckoned, he might not live as long. But he'd get in twice the living—or in Babylon's case, double the work.

By day, Babylon was a background investigator at the Public Safety Division of the City of Los Angeles's Personnel Department.

It made for a hell of a business card. The shorter, condensed description of his job was that he investigated everybody and anybody within the city government, from would-be politicians to private contractors hoping to catch a piece of the metro's nine-billion-dollar annual budget. He was part of a team of ex-sheriff's deputies and LAPD officers assigned to look under the rocks of anybody the government demanded intel on. After his day job, instead of putting his feet up in a glove-leather Barcalounger and surfing TV sports channels, Babylon turned his attention to his off-the-books gigs—private detective work…with all the city's resources at his disposal.

He'd been reading, ingesting police reports, news accounts, and any and all public records regarding Sheriff's Deputy Lucky Dey for hours. Babylon had met Lucky, but most of what he knew was by reputation, the lion's share stemming from the man's years as a Lennox Reaper. Lucky was a legend of certified *badassery*. In the urban jungle of South Los Angeles, Lucky Dey was known for dealing street justice when none other was available. And it mattered not the color of a man's skin or uniform. If you were on the wrong side of things, the Lucky Dey Babylon knew had never hesitated to drive the first justified nail into a deserving coffin.

Yet, as Babylon continued to tiptoe through Lucky's history, a different impression began to form. A reluctant admiration. Empathy, even. Babylon pored over Lucky's two-year stint in Kern County. By the looks of it, Lucky had accompanied his younger brother up north, where they had both signed up as sheriffs. When the younger brother was murdered, Lucky had chased the killer all the way back to Los Angeles.

There were more files. Gunfights. Deathly scrapes. Reports often began with suspected impropriety, but somehow seemed to go nowhere. Babylon discovered Lucky was presently on leave—or suspension, most likely—following a bloody mess involving the Armenian mob and four dead police officers. Having investigated cops of all flavors, it was a dance with which Babylon was more than familiar. He rightly guessed Lucky was in that delicate place where the department brass wanted to retire a cop without having to go through the legal hellfire of issuing a decorated deputy a pink slip.

A public records search revealed that Lucky had recently adopted a seventeen-year-old girl named Karrie, an emancipated teenager with the last name of Kaarlsen. Babylon was going to leave things there when he came across a *Malibu Times* story regarding a recent hit and run. A seventeen-year-old named Karrie Dey had suffered a near-fatal car collision. There were vehicle descriptions and BOLOs, otherwise known as Be On the Look-Outs. A few keystrokes later, Babylon learned the teenager was currently in critical condition at UCLA Medical Center.

Is this the string? he wondered.

Could the hit and run have something to do with his only-hours-old client, Denny Teng? It was a stretch, yet a place to begin, as well as an efficient way to get eyes on Lucky.

First gotta tank up the Yom Kippur Clipper, Babylon told himself.

That's what he called his roomy sedan, a creamy 2002 Cadillac El Dorado. The old invective of calling the car a *Jew canoe* sounded racist coming off his tongue, this despite "Tribe" credentials on his mother's side. Instead, he called his fat Caddy the Yom Kippur Clipper. It often raised belly laughs when he timed the phrase well. Babylon had noticed the gas hog's fuel needle was practically pointing to empty when he'd dropped his mom off at her assisted living home. Traffic to Westwood was sure to be bruising so he decided to pit stop at his favorite filling station, a depot that doubled as a 7-Eleven. While gasoline poured into his Caddy he'd fuel himself on a glazed donut, a teriyaki SlimJim, and an extra-large black coffee.

That oughta ready me, he agreed. *Ready me for a Lynwood versus Lennox reunion with Deputy Lucky Dey.*

Of the many open-ended questions, one lingered at the back of Babylon's skull. Would the reunion be a simple stalk? Or would it somehow turn into two old-school freight trains hell-bent on colliding? Just the thought of a throw-down with Lucky gave Babylon a tingle to his armpits. Palpable. Excited, even.

26

San Gabriel. 8:13 a.m.

"LIKE I GIVE A TENNESSEE *SHIT* WHAT YOUR NEIGHBORS THINK?" shouted Frankie.

She stood on the asphalt of a stately Southern California street, inches from the curb. Denny was half dressed for work in a button-down shirt and slacks, but shoeless. His front lawn's Bermuda grass sprouted between his toes. Behind him, cowering, yapping like a dog five times its size, was a black and brown Chihuahua.

The former Miss Runner-Up was in full regalia—plaid skirt, silk blouse, impeccable makeup, and hair trussed to perfection. Though she was towering in a pair of extra-high heels, the rise of Denny Teng's own stature and the slightly sloping sod gave him an advantage. Hands in pockets, he tried to look cool, lowering his voice.

"If you could *pleeease* watch your voice," he directed.

"Your stupid animal's louder than me!"

"Topsy!" he ordered the dog. "Back in the house."

The little dog retreated to the front porch, but not the house. It paced back and forth along the brick, wary of the brassy intruder.

Frankie's plan had been to drive directly to Ninth Street, where her private bank occupied the top floor's corner of a historic ten-story downtown location. Once in her office, she was going to summon Denny via text message. To the casual observer, it would appear as nothing more than business as usual. Banker meets her big depositor. But the more eastbound road she covered, the angrier she had become. Beyond steamed. Practically unhinged, she would later admit.

"This is my home," calmed Denny, his words unfolding slowly, hoping the depth of his tone would throw a blanket over her hysteria.

"*YOUR* HOME IS OFF LIMITS?" she screeched. "BUT *MINE* IS A-OKAY FOR YOU TO INVADE?"

"Frankie. I seriously don't have a clue—"

"What we do is about trust!" she pointed, at last putting the brakes on her volume.

"Exactly," Denny said, hands exiting his pockets in an arms-wide gesture, another attempt to remind her that she'd stepped far out of bounds. Multi-storied, multimillion-dollar prewar homes stood left and right, the Spanish arched windows and clay-tiled roof of his own prized dwelling rising behind him. The palm trees dated back nearly one hundred years.

"But you sent that man to my house!" Frankie pressed.

"What man?" wondered Denny, chin jutted forward in abject confusion.

"The man who delivered your message, asshole. You're 'watching me'?"

"Frankie. What the…?" Denny eased closer to the sidewalk. "Be clean with me. Are you high?"

"You're a really good liar."

"Whatever this is, we will get to the bottom of it. But later. It's my morning to take my daughter to school."

"We are in this shit *together!*" she spat, trying to be hushed but failing. "I go under, you go under!"

Denny remained stoic, his head aimed at her while his eyes swept side to side. Beyond Frankie was the ten-foot ivy-covered fence that separated the residential street from the eighteenth fairway of the storied San Gabriel Country Club. When Denny had bought the house some two years earlier, he imagined himself applying for membership and upping the social side of his game— a reminder that came with every out-of-bounds little white golf ball he discovered on his front lawn. In the still of that moment, between verbal volley and counterpunch, Denny prayed that a stray golf ball would strike the beauty queen in the soft part of her skull.

It might knock some sense into her, he fantasized. *Or even kill her dead.*

"My office," she spun on a stilted heel, climbing back into her Porsche SUV. "Twelve o'clock. And I don't care what's on your calendar. You cancel it and be there."

Denny remained in place until the Cayenne made it to the corner, turning sharply onto Las Tunas Boulevard. Frankie's tires chirped against the asphalt as she accelerated. Denny's chest rose and released in a significant exhalation. Her accusation had been dizzying. Out of the blue. And prompted by what? Had the pressure of their illicit banking game become too much for her to handle? Had she simply snapped shortly after his unromantic departure the day prior, when he'd left her alone between the sheets in the Downtown Crown?

Topsy, the Chihuahua, spun and skittered ahead of Denny as he walked the twenty paces along the driveway to the home's rear door. The little beast, hopeful for some playtime while oblivious to the worry Denny harbored, growled and nipped at his master's ankles. Denny was half tempted to kick the animal all the way into the next county.

"Daddy!" cried Min. "I go school now!"

"I see you are," faked Denny while wiping the grass clippings from his bare feet on the doormat. "Daddy just needs some shoes and a coffee and we're good to go."

Jiao, Denny's Chinese-born wife, didn't so much as look up when her husband entered, choosing to keep her attention on loading the dishwasher. The porcelain beauty was in a chenille robe, her silken black hair hanging over her face, disguising any noticeable reaction to Denny's combustible encounter outside.

"*Tā zǒu le?*—she is gone?" asked Jiao.

"*Shì*—yes," answered Denny in perfect Mandarin, just as his parents had drilled. "*Tā xiǎnrán shì gēngniánqí tíqián le*—she is obviously going through early menopause."

"So young," added Jiao, her accented English hardly covering up her disbelief. She had no illusions that her husband, a rich American businessman, hadn't come with all the entrapments common of successful men. Her father, an enormously prosperous medical equipment distributor in Shanghai, had more than once cautioned his daughter with sage advice: "*Wèile àiqíng jiéhūn, jiù zhǔnbèi hǎo shòuqióng. Wèile jīnqián jiéhūn, jiù dé yǒu róngrénzhīliàng*—marry for love and prepare to be poor. Marry for money and prepare to forgive."

Jiao's patience had been tested throughout their marriage. Most recently by the lady banker whose scent she'd more than once smelled on her husband. That statuesque *Ex-Miss-American-Fried-Chicken,* as Jiao had once slipped after too many margaritas, reeked of sex. Without the memory of her father's wise words to chill her temper, Jiao might've very well wrapped her delicate fingers around one of her Henckels chef's knives and plunged it into the bitch's chest.

"You late," reminded Jiao. It was Denny's day to hand-deliver Min to school.

"C'mon, lamb chop," Denny swerved to Min after slipping on a set of loafers.

"Piggy, please?" Min asked, climbing onto the countertop, arms spread and waiting to climb aboard.

"No shoe on table!" angered Jiao.

"Too late," said Denny, securing the kindergartner, whose arms were in a monkey grip around his head. He brushed his wife goodbye. *"Wǒ ài nǐ."*

"I love you too!" answered the child for her mother, showing off a rare understanding of the foreign language.

A proud smile appeared on Jiao's clear face. Radiant. Naturally rosy cheeks. The kind of beaming reserved for her one and only baby girl.

"Have a good school day," waved the mother, showing all the warmth she could muster until Denny and Min disappeared out the kitchen door. With that, she leaned against the granite countertop, allowing it to hold her upright. She wanted to cry. The violation she felt. Peering from the dining room window at her husband with his mistress, Jiao had felt a rush of heat come over her along with the pain of a thousand pinpricks. Unable to watch, she had hurried back to the kitchen and thrown the freezer door open to cool her face.

But with Min and her cheating husband gone, Jiao returned to the freezer, only this time it was to reach inside for a bottle of Maotai, the distilled rice and sorghum *baijiu*—or vodka—popularized and bottled in China. She poured a couple ounces of the liquor into one of her daughter's plastic sippy cups, added a squeeze of lemon juice, and screwed on the lid. Liquid courage in hand, Jiao chose to ignore her father's words and take advantage of a rare opportunity.

When Frankie arrived that morning, hell-bent on whatever leather she hoped to lash upon Denny, he had been in his backyard office, a retreat he never—ever—left unlocked—at least not until that morning, when he'd been so conspicuously interrupted.

There were two entries to Denny's secret domain: through the garage—where the interior door was always dead-bolted—and via a side entrance, a glass slider that led out to the pool area. Jiao had often been tempted to sneak inside through the outside door. She'd even researched YouTube videos on the most efficient ways to jimmy the lock. Wisdom, she reasoned, was why she'd never chosen to betray her husband's privacy—though she'd later admit it was more out of fear than logic.

As Denny backed out of the driveway, Jiao waved at her daughter, trying to refrain from turning back to the wide-mouthed garage door and what she'd spied when Denny had bolted from his back office to confront his banker on their front lawn. While the inner door had been left unlocked and open, Jiao had seen minute strobes of green and red light emanating from inside her husband's private sanctuary. In Denny's effort to appear composed in front his wife and young daughter, he'd been shaken just enough to have forgotten to shut the door and key the deadbolt.

Whoops.

The yard had a classic old Hollywood–style swimming and sunning area, with a barbecue and dining patio shaded by queen palms and jacaranda trees. The sun reflected off a gated kidney-shaped, turquoise pool nearly as old as the house. Denny's hidden home office was directly behind the detached garage, tucked in the rear corner of the lot.

Jiao had put eyeballs on the secret room but twice: once when they'd first toured the house when it was on the market, and again, late one night when little Min was inconsolable and she herself had run out of patience. Jiao had marched in through the open garage, stood at the closed inner door next to the permanently humming second refrigerator, screaming three-year-old in her arms, and demanded Min's father deal with his child. When Denny had finally appeared, her eyes had slipped past him. But for the collection of computer screens detailing graphs and numbers she couldn't decipher, the home office was practically pitch black. Since that night, when it was Denny's turn to mind his little daughter, the two would sometimes vanish into the digital cave for hours leaving Jiao relieved, yet horribly lost and isolated.

After a few more sips of liquid courage, Jiao padded out the back door, down the bricked steps, and crossed the half basketball court–sized slab that separated the house from the garage. With the garage door retracted and the blinking red and green lights beckoning, she braved the entrance, stepping into a near-blackened room. Two monitors were tuned to Bloomberg stock market indicators—one in English, the other in Chinese. A third stand-alone screen, framed into nine separate cells, appeared to be dedicated to the security cameras outside their house. But for the displays, her husband's inner sanctum appeared devoid of comforts. No photos of Min or Jiao. Nor were there the ubiquitous neon or antique beer signs often relegated to man caves.

Then Jiao heard voices. Thin, as if projected from a pair of ear buds. Turning slowly, careful not to bump anything, she noted a fourth computer monitor opposite the others, propped on a folding buffet table. The room's one seat—a single, comfortable swivel chair—appeared as if spun away in a hurry.

Easing nearer to the screen, Jiao searched within the fourth monitor's borders. On the screen was a dull, colored image playing back in what appeared to be a digital loop. Distant. Wide-angled. It looked like an extra security camera feed of some sort, with sketchy wifi resolution. Revealed was an interior room Jiao did not recognize. Foot over tiny foot, she eased closer, neck crooked, eyes gazing up at the story unfolding on the monitor. Children were dragged into frame, bound, then gagged by black men in blue baseball hats and wraparound sunglasses. Though she couldn't make out the muted audio, Jiao understood the images. Slowly, her almond-shaped eyes grew into worried orbs. On-screen, a terrified man was seated in a chair, visibly upset as he seemed to be interrogated by a black man in sunglasses attired in a Hawaiian-print shirt. Then suddenly, in a blur followed by muffled cries, a woman was struck, a smear of saturated red pooling on her face.

With that, Jiao gasped. Had her husband been viewing this moments prior to the rude front-lawn interruption by Frankie Coleman? But why? And to what end? Eyes wet in fear, Jiao backed away from the monitor. She fled Denny's secret office for the sanctum of her house, praying all the way that her husband would never figure out she'd breached the darkness of his privacy.

27

Westwood.

Recognition came in an instant. Lucky had marked the grizzled Lynwood Viking from fifty feet down UCLA Medical Center's magnificent, museum-like first-floor corridor, as wide as a boulevard. Despite all the foot traffic during morning shift changes—doctors and medical techs arriving for their workdays—plus the ever-present visitors and office staff, Lucky was able to pluck Babylon from the throng. It might have been the way the man's bowlegged gait advanced his hulking pair of shoulders. Babylon was moving slowly in the flow in and out of the cafeteria, breaking free of the crowd with a coffee in a tall to-go cup. Lucky couldn't produce the man's name. All he managed to summon was *Lynwood* and *Viking*. Meanwhile, Babylon had stopped in place, zeroing a semi-surprised smile in Lucky's direction along with an index finger aimed like a gun.

"Hey," called out Babylon, "I know that deputy."

Lucky acknowledged with an up-tilt of his chin and slowed his feet to a stall as Babylon strode toward him.

"Lennox, right?" faked Babylon.

"You're Lynwood," confirmed Lucky.

"Million goddamn years ago," grumbled Babylon, that pointed finger turned into an outstretched hand. "Mark Baba."

"Lucky Dey," returned Lucky. "You have someone here?"

"Naw. On the job. Hadda get some go-juice first."

"Deputy biz?"

"Retired," replied Babylon. "City work now."

"Whereabouts?" asked Lucky, not so much curious, but more reflexive without his usual armor. Inside that particular hospital, Lucky's skin felt thin.

"Personnel office. Safety investigator."

Lucky nodded. He knew enough about the desk gig and it dawned on him that his run-in with Babylon might not be entirely coincidental. Could the old deputy have been assigned to the pending litigation between Lucky and the Sheriff's Department?

Babylon, assembled Lucky. *They called him that because the man could chew a rag until it was in shreds.*

"What about you?" asked Babylon.

"What about me?" Lucky dodged.

"You just get here?" broke in Gonzo, appearing from the cafeteria. She clutched a paper coffee cup identical to Babylon's. Her face was drawn.

"Lydia?" swiveled Lucky. "Mark Baba. Mark? Lydia."

Gonzo was garbed for work in her LAPD Air Support jumpsuit, unzipped to her waist with a slender white T-shirt underneath.

"Officer Gonzalez," cued Babylon, reading the name below her embroidered shield. He offered his free hand. "Friends call me Babylon."

Normally, Gonzo would've come back with "and just call me Gonzo." But by the look of her, Lucky surmised that she was feeling as equally antisocial as he and equally eager to see their comatose daughter, three floors overhead and hanging to life by a fraying thread.

"So?" asked Gonzo.

"Just got here," answered Lucky. "Was just heading up."

Gonzo's shift in posture was as obvious as a billboard, as if to say, *If you just got here then where the hell were you?*

"You have people here?" asked Babylon, feigning ignorance.

"Injured kid," deflected Lucky.

"Oh, hey. You're together?" played Babylon, regarding them as a couple. "Just got the man and missus picture. Hey. Hope your girl's okay."

"Hit and run," said Gonzo. "Sorry. Tight window. Nice meeting you, Mark. If you'll please excuse us?"

"Of course," agreed Babylon. "Hey, pal. Nice runnin' into you."

"Sure," said Lucky, allowing Gonzo to nudge him toward the elevators.

"Who's he?" she finally asked when far enough away from Babylon that she wouldn't be overheard through the echo of voices.

"Viking," answered Lucky. "Lynwood. Way back whenever."

"Just bumped into him?"

"What I thought." Lucky punched the up elevator button with his fist. "But then he said, 'Hope your girl's okay.'"

"So?"

"So, I didn't say Karrie was a girl, teenager, nothin'. Neither had you. Just said 'injured kid.'"

"Coulda been a guess. What's it matter?"

"I don't trust it."

In that one instant, Lucky had painted a target on Babylon's back. Was the retired Lynwood Viking part of the city's investigation against him? Or was he working for someone else?

"Yeah. What do the hairs on the back of your neck say about me?" asked Gonzo. "You trust me anymore?"

"What's that got to do with anything?"

"I know I told you to go out and run this thing down," she

explained. "But if this goes south? With Karrie? And you weren't here when it happened? Could you live with yourself?"

"First you suggest I stick close. Then that I go and run down the bad guy. Now you're back to this?"

"Forgive me for giving a shit about your mortal soul," she defended. "That and like there's some kinda playbook for all this?"

Playbook? No. That had been flushed when Emery had turned him away. But Babylon was a brand-new thread that Lucky was considering pulling to see if anything unraveled.

At last, the elevator arrived. The doors slid wide. Gonzo and Lucky filed in along with four doctors wearing surgical booties. Lucky stuffed his desire to answer her "playbook" question with, *"You have no clue how much dust I've tried to kick up since Karrie was run down!"*

He was there for Karrie now. On his way up to the ICU alongside his ex-common-law-wife. That's when he felt Gonzo's hand touch his, her fingers seeking a connection. They intertwined. With that, Gonzo gave a white-knuckle squeeze. It was a grip loaded with more fear than hope, a hanging-on kind of grab. As always, Lucky felt the fit of her hand in his as an inescapable reality. They were destined to be together. Bound by history. Together or apart. Until death.

28

Calabasas.

Austin Andrews woke that dawn with an unusual hope. It was odd because it had been so damned long since the excitement of a sale had buoyed him. Back in the go-go days before the Great Recession when he was at the top of his game and the West Valley's number-one real estate agent, selling—and the fat commissions that had accompanied it—had been as easy as breathing. He had started each day with a phone sheet of incoming calls, potential high-dollar clients, and more multimillion-dollar sales than he could honestly manage. No. Those days when his heart raced with rapid anticipation were pretty much gone. That had been when he was still closeted, pretending to be heterosexual and hoping financial success would flush off the stink from flunking out of Cal State Northridge just eight units shy of graduation.

For the previous pair of nights, his bed had been a couch in the Keller-Williams real estate office. After parking in front of the Calabasas Commons' Barnes and Noble he would cross through the Commons parking lot on foot until he was back in the office. Tonight, the lights were already extinguished and the darkness masked his presence. He'd been readying himself for sleep, fitting a Vicodin between his wired teeth and chasing it with a bend-able straw stuck in a carton of Ensure, when his phone trilled. It was one of the detectives from the Lost Hills Sheriff's Station. The deputy was hoping Austin could stop by to eyeball a series of photographs. Conscious that he'd just ingested enough medication to impair a buffalo, Austin asked if the deputy could email him the images. Perhaps he could examine the pics on his computer screen. Less than a minute later, Austin was staring back at what the detective referred to as a six pack—a lineup of similar-looking mug shots. Recognition came in an instant. The fifth picture, at bottom center, showed an African-American thug with hair knot-ted in neon-colored rubber bands. He was leveling the same callous glare at the camera that he'd given Austin.

Austin electronically circled and initialed the photo before returning it via email. The deputy replied with a curt thanks. Only the rejoinder came with an attachment, as if he had accidentally cc'd Austin along with the other detectives. The photo Austin had circled was enlarged. Next to it was the suspect's details:

Ernest Joel Selfridge, a.k.a. Neon, a known member
of Lakewood's Mac Mafia Crips.

In an instant Austin was texting Zipper Ling with a tease.

> just id'd one of your baddies to detectives.
> you ready to buy some property?

While a sack full of payoff cash stashed under his bed would've served him nicely, it felt like a dirty line not to be crossed. That was how criminals behaved, not white-collar professionals who didn't want to get caught.

Thus the transaction Austin planned was far more complicated than necessary, but it was legitimate. And somehow, he convinced himself it would work. If he could rope Zipper's mom into buying a house—one of his own listings, no less—he'd make commissions on both sides of the deal, she'd own some great investment property, and Zipper would get the information he wanted, all while Austin held on to what little integrity he had left. Plus, the deal would add a notch on his lagging sales chart. Everybody wins.

Austin planned to show Zipper the home on Paul Revere Drive—not so coincidentally the very three-bedroom fixer he had been on his way to seconds before the pickup truck rollover and double murder that had begun this whole nasty affair. Once inside, Austin would give Zipper a look at the information he had to sell. If Zipper deemed the info worthy, he would make a deposit subject to inspections, escrow, loan approval, etcetera. With each step, more money would be transferred to Austin who reasoned that this protected both himself and Zipper's mother from illicit exposure. Zipper had already agreed to an initial down payment of twenty thousand dollars—a healthy start toward Austin's short-term financial survival. He would clear over a hundred grand in commission when all was said and done.

And selling the same property only doors down from where the nightmare had all begun? *Kismet*, Austin marveled.

Austin realized he was already breaking his promise to himself and Zipper that he would only meet in public, where there were security cameras. He thought of fixing his phone somewhere out of sight, lens aimed and uploading to the internet. But a hidden camera was hardly a deterrent against violence. The worry had woken him over and over again until the solution had come to him in the dark. He remembered an office colleague, a squat and annoying agent by the name of Joanie, who was constantly bragging about a grandson whose tuition she'd been partially financing at one of L.A.'s private film schools. She'd been obnoxiously hawking his services as a videographer for entrepreneurial realtors seeking ways to put visual helium into their social media profiles. Austin texted her, promising a quarter point of the sale plus a hundred dollars cash for her grandson to tag along and videotape him in the act of doing what he did best—closing real estate deals. Joanie had responded in the affirmative, forgiving Austin's pre-dawn plea with a string of annoying emojis—thumbs up, googly-eyed happy faces, hearts, confetti horns, and gilded dollar signs.

It was 9:30 a.m. when Austin arrived at the Paul Revere address, only to discover Joanie was running late. He'd insisted on timeliness from both Joanie and Zipper, the latter scheduled for arrival at 10:00 straight up. Austin broke out in perspiration, already beginning to sweat through his pink Geoffrey Beene dress shirt. What if Joanie was late and the buyer was early? After all, it was Los Angeles, where traffic jams could whip up out of nowhere like an Oklahoma funnel cloud.

Jesus, he cried on the inside. *I might've just screwed myself.* Then he soothed, *Trust, Austin. Trust in the transaction. You have the leverage. The info. Zipper is just bringing the down payment.*

Eleven minutes of mental panic was remedied when the rounded headlamps of Joanie's vintage Mercedes pulled into the driveway. The jet black, late nineties–model sedan was in mint condition. Yet, from Austin's perspective, it reeked of stale real estate lady. Joanie's outfits were like her personality, loud and with big patterns. Her hair was home colored, the gray leaking through to give a shade Austin chided as *bleached squirrel*.

Annoyance aside, Austin greeted her with a surgically wired grin as she rolled into the driveway. He bent down and kissed her on the cheek, then moved on to her grandson, a willowy lad with a face covered in artsy, cocoa-shaded peach fuzz. The youngster, whom Austin took to calling "Spielberg" in a display of his most kiss-ass salesman side, lugged a pair of Pelican cases loaded with camera and sound equipment from his trunk up the short walk and into the vacant house.

"My God!" blasted Joanie after getting a look at Austin's bruised face. "What happened to you?"

"Trip and fall," replied Austin.

"I didn't get that," said Joanie, unable to decipher his words. "You sure you want to be filmed looking like that?"

"Spielberg can figure it out," grumbled Austin.

"Still can't understand you. Who are your buyers?"

"Investment people," gritted Austin. "Asian fella. Represents his mother."

"Agent fella?" asked Joanie.

"Need ventriloquist lessons," annoyed Austin.

"*When Phillips asked?*" guessed Joanie of the word "ventriloquist."

Frustrated, Austin indicated they'd continue the conversation—such as it was—once inside the house. He was stepping across the home's welcome mat, perhaps the only remaining furnishing, when he heard the whine of a badly tuned engine shifting into park. He swerved and saw Zipper easing from the passenger side of a road-weary Honda Civic. Sun-weathered silver. Fungo squeezed out from behind the wheel—almost cartoonish in the manner in which he exhumed his sizable self—stiff, as if his back were in spasm. A chill shot through Austin's broken jaw, flaring into a deep ache when he saw Fungo, whose colossal fists were concealed in his hoodie's front pocket.

Fungo and Zipper both wore dark sweats and hoodies as if they were embarrassed to be seen so far west of the SGV.

Swell, thought Austin. *One look at them and their car and Joanie's gonna think these yokels aren't for real.*

"My man!" hailed Zipper. "Is this my new house?"

"It's got a pool, dude," added Fungo, noting the red-worded shingle fitted atop the realtor's sign.

"Let's do this," cued Zipper with a friendly pat to Austin's collarbone.

The front door led directly into a broad living room with a fireplace, canted and open beam ceilings, and hardwood floors speckled at the edges from a sloppy paint job on the Sheetrocked walls. The college filmmaker, crouched over his Pelican cases, assembled a hand-held grip on his SLR video camera in the center of the room.

"Never told me it was a party," said Zipper with an air of annoyance.

"They're making a documentary," excused Austin.

"I'm Joanie Dunford!" The squat real estate gal stuck out an equally stubby hand in greeting. "This is my grandson—"

"There a bedroom where you and me can have a one-on-one?" Zipper's question was directed at Austin, fully ignoring Joanie, not to mention her equipment-preoccupied grandchild.

Even though he couldn't imagine he was in any immediate danger, Austin attempted to signal the kid in hopes of accelerating his readiness to film. He was of value to Zipper. Joanie and her boy were mere props. Witnesses. Unofficial human shields in his defensive chess match. Austin led Zipper around two tight corners into the master bedroom, where French doors led to a scruffy backyard overgrown with trees in dire need of a trim. Zipper instantly began to twist the rods and close the venetian blinds.

"So, why'd you gotta bring Urkel and Driving Miss Daisy?" he angered.

"Told you why," answered Austin. "Security blanket."

"Like they could protect you from a flea bite," groused Zipper before a come-hither gesture. "So, give it up. Whadda you got?"

"Whadda you got for me?" suggested Austin, the clamps on his jaw keeping his teeth from chattering in fear.

From his hoodie's front pocket, Zipper removed a gallon-sized plastic baggie filled with rolls of rubber-banded twenty-, fifty-, and hundred-dollar bills. He tossed it at Austin, who snagged it out of the air.

"Twenty large," said Zipper, repeating the come-closer gesture. "Now, your turn, fag-man."

Austin stiffened at the insult, instantly sucked back to the schoolyard days of junior high. He found himself sing-songing inside his head:

Sticks and stones can break my bones but names can never hurt me.

Given the circumstances, Austin might've called bullshit on that old panacea.

In lieu of trying to communicate clearly and succinctly through his busted mandible, Austin produced a black-and-white printout of the email the sheriff's detective had sent him. The fifth photo in the six-pack was circled in green Sharpie.

> *Ernest Joel Selfridge, a.k.a. Neon, a known member*
> *of Lakewood's Mac Mafia Crips.*

"Sure about this?" confirmed Zipper, his eyes perusing the printed sheet.

"That's the guy," Austin nodded before switching into his patented sales mode. "Now I got mine and you got yours. How 'bout we get a look at this hot property?"

"GOOD TO GO," called out Zipper, loud enough for Fungo to hear.

"YUUUP!" returned Fungo, who'd been standing over Joanie's grandson, appearing to be interested in all the filmmaking gadgetry.

"So soon?" asked Joanie. "You all just got here. How about we get a looksee at the kitchen—"

The aging agent was shifting her weight towards the kitchen door when Fungo pulled out the machete. The machine-sharpened blade had been concealed inside his hoodie, sheathed in a scabbard duct-taped to his spine—explaining why the big Samoan appeared so rigid in posture. In a move he'd practiced a thousand times on his backyard tree trunk, Fungo unsheathed and delivered the machete at a downward angle. Forty-five degrees. The blade entered Joanie's neck at the nape, penetrating almost to her windpipe and separating her spinal cord from her brain stem. The pull from her sinking body discharged the machete. Arterial spray fountained all the way to the ceiling.

Per Linh Ling's instructions, Austin had to be killed. He was both a witness and an extortionist. Not to be trusted. The muscle side of things had always been up to Fungo. Zipper was management, after all.

Fingernail Rancher/Flunky Number One.

Zipper had successfully concealed his anger since catching an eyeful of the real estate marm and her grandson. But the math had instantly added up to his getting his hands bloody, both figuratively and literally. Austin was supposed to have come alone and Zipper had never killed anyone before.

Killing is my mother's thing. Not mine.

When the opportunity came, Zipper's body shook. He drew Austin in for what appeared to be a deal-sealing embrace. But instead, plunged a six-inch Ka-Bar blade into Austin's chest. He withdrew the knife and sunk it again in speedy successions until Austin's legs gave away, blood spilling from his mouth.

The gurgling and choking sickened Zipper to near vomiting. His stomach practically flipped and locked in a spasmodic cramp, sending him down to one knee. He caught his breath—his mental equilibrium—and wiped the knife against his black shirt before standing and retracing his path back to the living room. He found Fungo standing between the two nearly decapitated bodies of Joanie and her grandson, the ceiling and walls dripping in oxygenated crimson.

"Holy shit," cried Zipper.

"What this shit looks like, bro-heem," shrugged Fungo. "Besides...*your* fuckup. We were only supposed to do the fag."

Zipper gathered himself, checked the front windows, eyes scouring the surrounding neighborhood. He repeated the act at the front door's threshold. He could see no traffic whatsoever and the sidewalks were clear of pedestrians. The two killers proceeded to follow Zipper's mom's instructions. They were to keep their eyes forward. No darting eyeballs or sketchy body language. The plan was to drive carefully along the old Mulholland Highway due west into the Santa Monica Mountains. After checking for hikers, they'd abandon the stolen Honda on the rocky bed of Las Virgenes Creek, strip off their bloody clothes, dress into trekking gear— hiking shorts, daypacks, etcetera—and dump three milk jugs filled with toluene, the aromatic hydrocarbon used in nail salons to remove polish, into the car—one in the trunk, two in the interior. After tossing in a match, they'd walk the creek bed for a quarter mile back to Fungo's waiting truck.

Simple as pie, Zipper's mother had dismissively shrugged before sending them off with a wave of her decorated fingernails.

My mom, the dragon lady.

Easy as pie, Zipper had corrected.

Fungo's feelings were his own as was his comfort with violence. And though all Zipper had to do now was follow Linh Ling's instructions, he remained rattled and nearly breathless. Zipper liked to think of himself as *gangsta*, but was more accustomed to pimping girls and collecting debts. He wasn't muscle. He wasn't a killer. *She* was the gangster.

"Waitin' on you, bro," said Fungo in a whisper from behind. "Need a push?"

"Just checkin' to see if we're clear," faked Zipper.

"Longer we wait…"

"Right. Okay," nodded Zipper. "Here we go."

With that, Zipper stepped out of the Calabasas house. His eyes were swimming, trying like hell to focus on the Honda and the thirty-five feet he needed to travel. There was a trombone effect to his vision. His focal plane continued to drift. He felt light-headed. Weak.

Eyes on the prize. Don't trip, he told himself. *Follow the plan.*

Those words of self-comfort were the last thing Zipper remembered before he lost consciousness.

29

It was the ugliest Hawaiian shirt ever—at least according to his mother. Twenty-four-year-old Howard Bokeem Morris, otherwise called Aloha or Mr. Aloha by his high school and college pals, had worn the electric blue and green shirt throughout his academic career. Every time he'd fished it out of the rag bin or trash heap he'd argue to his mom that it was his superhero shirt—his trademark.

"Shirt's so damn ugly," Howie's mom would say. "You walk into a bank they'd turn off the cameras."

Oddly enough, his mother's words had prompted his light-bulb moment. Besides a baseball hat and wraparound sunglasses, a breeze-flapping Hawaiian shirt might be the best disguise ever. Witnesses would be so distracted by the garish garb, they'd never key in the few recognizable features of his face. *Especially the FOBs.* Beyond the ugly garment, all they'd recall was a black man. That's just how the Chinese were—or so his boss and mentor, Denny Teng, had detailed.

"Chinese don't see beyond the black," Denny had waxed. "Think they never heard of Bloods or Crips? They see black and they see danger."

"Unless they're skyscrapers like you," Howie had joked back.

"Maybe," Denny had replied. "But the race shit goes both ways. I robbed a liquor store in someplace like Compton or Inglewood? Police description of me would be a yardstick with a socket face."

Howie recalled laughing at the joke despite his guilty measure of racism. The good-natured business wannabe had grown up upper-middle-class in Northridge, the heart of the San Fernando Valley. Both his parents were science and technology nerds who'd met at Cal Tech. His father had recently retired after a long and fruitful engineering career at Lockheed Martin. His mother had risen through the ranks to become Assistant Headmaster at the Buckley School, a tony private institution in tony Sherman Oaks young Howie had attended on a teacher's scholarship. His dad would often remark that "Howie B. hadn't inherited the geek gene" and that his son was academically challenged, money-obsessed, and admittedly influenced by all the millionaires and showbiz kids alongside whom he'd learned to read, write, and smoke designer weed. In another city and school, Howie might have been considered the rich kid. At Buckley, though, he couldn't help but feel like a second-rate mercy case.

Two years of junior college allowed him to up his academic game enough to get into USC. Howie met Denny Teng on a summer business internship in Hong Kong. A relationship bloomed between the self-styled mergers and acquisition consultant and the ambitious intern. Mentor and mentee became drinking buddies, with Denny plying his young charge with top-shelf tequilas.

In Denny, Howie thought he'd found his express elevator ride to the luxe life.

In Howie, Denny had discovered a willing tool.

The internship had carried over into a part-time job stateside. When Howie wasn't in class, he was at Denny Teng's downtown consulting firm. That was where Howie kept the offending Hawaiian shirt. It was folded inside a paper sack hidden in the air conditioning duct connected to his office. After his first extortion sortie—that's how Howie had always characterized Denny's scheme, as *extortion sorties*—he found he couldn't sleep with the garment hanging in his dorm room closet. So, he'd stashed it at work without ever informing the boss.

"Howie?" a voice chirped over the phone speaker. "Mr. Teng needs you to drive him to an appointment."

Howie's "office," a converted, bricked-in space he'd bifurcated by reorganizing the supply room so he could shoehorn in a desk and chair, had a row of thin windows at eye level and a bamboo screen for a door. This act of squatting, usurping his own private space in lieu of the cubicles manned by the other interns, part-timers, and full-fledged employees, was cause for significant inter-office sniping. It hardly bothered Howie. Business wasn't for pussies, or so Denny had coined. Howie wasn't there to make friends. And unless Mr. Wang or Denny himself complained, he was going to keep up his game and remain boss's favorite golden boy.

But then came Monday and the Calabasas disaster. Instead of riding with Tung Chee to the West Valley bank, he'd handed the assignment to Lil Rod and Neon hoping that in the two-hour stretch babysitting Tung Chee's frightened family, he might be able to catch up on some studying. It had been a horrible error in judgment. In the days since he hadn't spoken a word to either Denny or Wang Zhang.

"My car or Denny's?" returned Howie over the comm.

"I'll ask," she said. "But get up here now because he wants to go *now*."

Howie nervously scrambled through the cubicle maze to the front desk, where a pair of Budget Rent a Car keys waited for him.

"What about the Range Rover?" asked Howie, who often relished driving the opulent beast.

"Fender bender," said the receptionist with the burgundy hair. "In for repairs."

"Which intern?" Howie's competitive tone revealed his loathing. "Keith, right? Had to be Keith."

"Not anybody's business." Ever politic, she had no interest whatsoever in adding fuel to the inter-office fire. "Mr. Teng asked to have the air conditioner set on sixty-two degrees. So, best you get to it."

Howie waited in the rental car parked at the building's back exit—a new Buick Enclave, generic white, engine running, cool air blowing on high. At the moment he was worrying that he should've brought a sweater, Denny pulled open the rear right door, hopped into the seat, and pulled the seat belt across himself. *Click.*

"Know where we're going?" asked Denny.

"No, sir."

"Good," said Denny. "Gonna go left at the corner then left at the light."

"You got it." Howie depressed the brake and dropped the car into gear.

"Not yet," said Denny. "Wait for the Wang."

Hobbling up to the front passenger door was Wang Zhang. Howie bent, reached across, popped the lock, and received the injured man's aluminum crutch. Zhang fell into the seat with a decided groan and struggled to buckle himself. When Howie leaned in to assist, Wang grunted and waved him off.

"How's my drinking buddy?" asked Denny, unspooling a pair of ear buds. "Things good with you?"

This is where I get fired, thought Howie. *Or worse.*

"Okay," returned Howie. A big lie.

"Sure about that?" questioned Denny.

Howie threw Denny an unconscious glance, a peek through the rearview mirror, checking to see if the boss was just busting his balls or seriously expecting Howie's confession for Monday's super fail. Casually open-collared, with his sunglasses hiding any intent,

Denny was facing dead ahead, wholly without a discernible expression as he plugged his headphones into his ears.

"Look. About Monday?" worried Howie, his voice automatically elevating. "I had no idea—"

"Not him. You tell *me*," inserted Wang before adding another navigation point. "Five blocks, make right on Sixth."

"Man. I called you right after it all went to shit," reminded Howie. "You never called me back."

"What happen Monday cannot be repaired," said Wang.

"What about…" Howie thumb-gestured to the rear, always keen to remember that Denny *never* wanted to hear about his extracurricular's details. "Thought we weren't supposed to talk deets in front of the boss."

"Earphones," gestured Wang. "He hear nothing."

Howie shot another look into the mirror. Denny appeared in a trance. Face slack. Checked out.

"What happened is in the past," said Wang. "It's what you do next that determine your future."

"Anything!"

Howie's tone sounded so desperate. He threw a beseeching look at Denny. He didn't like following Zhang's orders. In fact, he abhorred Zhang's ever-present scowl. Howie was there because of Denny and under his keen tutelage. But Denny had wisely set up a series of buffers to protect himself. Zhang was a buffer. And Howie's leaving information out of certain equations was a buffer. As in, "the less said, the less known, the better for all." Sure, he'd eventually realized he'd been set up as a potential patsy. But the trade-off was a resume of experience.

"We weren't the only ones sitting on the mark," relented Howie. "Either somebody else was planning to rip the dude or somebody was sitting on our thing."

"Our thing?"

"Our mark. Our scheme. Whatever you want to call it."

Extortion sorties. Or as Denny had once phrased as a joke, *We're gonna put the Asian in home invasion.*

"It's in the past," forced Wang. "We talk about future now."

Howie made the right turn on Sixth, waited for Wang's next direction, and continued to flick looks in his rearview mirror at the boss. In the back seat, Denny continued that stare into nowhere, his affect remaining as blank as it had begun while unknown tunes tickled his eardrums. The shadows from the skyward buildings that lined both sides of the boulevard crossed his face.

"Right lane. Put it behind FedEx truck," ordered Wang.

After executing the maneuver, Howie slid the rental over to the curb and geared it into park.

"Last few days?" said Wang after a few quiet heartbeats. "We discuss. Things too tangled. And Mr. Denny don't like tangled. Know what I mean?"

"Sir?"

"Your Crip friends—"

"*Not* my friends," shot Howie, quick to differentiate himself from the ghetto gangbangers he'd been paying as muscle. He regretted his tone instantly. "Just day hires. Not my people. I'm from Northridge, remember?"

"Like I knows Northridge from Nanchang," argued Wang. "What I'm say is that you need to fix."

"Like, let 'em go? My day hires?"

Wang's head swiveled, glowering. It disturbed Howie to his intestines. His stomach flipped. He kept waiting for Denny to pull back Wang's leash and bail him out.

"I'm not telling you how to manage *your* people," said Wang. "But Mr. Denny say in business we do what we need to do when we need to do it. All for future of business. Cut through unpleasantness. Get things done. Understood? Can't do nothing about Calabasas bullshit. But can do something about people who might get big mouths."

Howie could only nod. Denny opened the rear door and was gone in a flash, rewinding his earbuds as he walked. Wang exited as well, but slower. He shut the door and stood on the sidewalk. Through the window, Howie could only see from Wang's pocket to his armpits, his suit jacket flapping as he expertly balanced on his cane while blazing up a cigarette. Howie was left to stew. He had no instructions other than to "get it done." His face felt flush. His heart thrummed with the realization of what he'd been ordered. The words were squishy enough. That's how the Wang liked to phrase things. Just like Denny, he didn't like to be specific. His mandates were often wordy, full of implied directives, and always a buffer for deniability's sake. *The Chinese way?* Howie wondered. Yet, he didn't question. Because Wang's message was unambiguous when put in context of the larger business plan.

I need you to kill the killers.

And not just the *killers. But* my *killers*, Howie had concluded. He could practically hear Denny at the helm, whispering into his ear, *It's not like you haven't done it before. You know? Taken a life?* How often had Howie regretted that drunken confession in Hong Kong? For so long he'd believed his winning, go-to personality had snagged his ride on the Denny Teng train. But over time, Howie had come to realize it had been the disclosure of his irreparable indiscretion that had most likely sealed the deal.

And why not?

If Denny had hammered one thing into Howie's young skull it was his take on the ancient Chinese methodology of leverage. Learning it. Probing for soft spots in the enemy. Finding a fulcrum point. And applying pressure until the adversary acquiesced into unmitigated compliance.

Jesus, thought Howie. *What the hell have I gotten myself into? Denny Teng hadn't needed to seek out my weakness. Immature and ambitious, I served it up like a ripe slice of melon.*

30

Westwood.

Lucky smuggled a second chair into Karrie's ICU unit. There, he and Gonzo sat next to each other, silently in their own thoughts, fingers still intertwined.

"You can't both be in here," interrupted the Mighty Mouse of a nursing assistant. Her tone had been nothing near polite. "Only *one* family member at a time."

Lucky was about to push himself out of his seat, plead their case, and if need be, upshift into authority mode when Gonzo beat him to the verbal punch. She was up like a shot, towering over the barking autocrat, her embroidered LAPD badge the height of the nurse's nose.

"We're her parents," growled Gonzo. "Both of us. We belong to her—and her us."

"Yes," returned the nurse, her kelly green smock not budging, her smug face unimpressed. "ICU is for family only. But one at a time."

"Is that a rule?" pressed Gonzo. "Or a just a guideline?"

"Medical center policy, ma'am."

"I'm not a *ma'am*. I'm Officer Gonzalez. This is Sheriff's Deputy Dey. And we will be breaking hospital policy and staying with our daughter when and how we choose. Now, do you need to write that down so you can inform your supervisor? I wouldn't want you to get my words wrong—"

An alarm sounded—electronic, accompanied by a loud buzzing. Gonzo whipped her head in the direction of the noise as the nursing assistant brushed past.

"What's going on?" burst Gonzo, her eyes glazing into tears.

The unit's glass door slid open and a stream of intensive care practitioners hurried inside. Lucky gripped Gonzo by the bicep and gently eased her backward.

"What's *happening*?" she cried, her mettle cracking with her voice.

"Let 'em work," whispered Lucky, guiding her toward the automated exit doors.

Like that, they were sucked back into the family waiting room. Lucky stood, leaning into the thin window frame, his focus resigned to infinity and recording nothing whatsoever to memory. His mind was in overdrive, preoccupied with one undoable solution after another. After twenty minutes, the attending physician, a pugnacious woman of Pakistani extraction, thick from shoulders to waist, swept into the space with an air of command.

"She's okay," eased the doctor, comforting in her accented English. "She's on an anti-clotting drip. Her blood pressure dropped again and set off an alarm. We're balancing her out with Levophed. See if we can raise her numbers. We have Adrenaline at the ready if it happens again."

"What does that do to her brain?" asked Gonzo. "All the extra meds?"

"No effect, considering."

"Considering what?"

"Your neurosurgeon informed you, yes?" prodded the doctor, arms crossed and girding herself. She didn't like delivering the bad news. "Prognosis for a TBI?"

"While in the induced coma," recalled Gonzo, "prognosis was impossible to judge."

"That's correct. But she's no longer induced. The swelling decreased enough for us to turn off the Propofol. The coma is *her* coma now."

"What's that supposed to mean?" concerned Lucky.

"It means she wakes up when she wakes up," the doc indicated with an eyebrow shrug. "She's in ICU until she stabilizes. By then if she hasn't come out of it we'll move her to a stasis facility. Now, I can see by the look on your faces that this is a surprise and I'm sorry to be the one to bring you up to speed. She's young and strong and she *should* wake up. And when she does, she will most likely require some significant rehab. Physio. Speech. And time. That's most important. Time and support."

"Of course," said Gonzo, reality appearing to have slugged all the hope from her face.

"And you can't take care of her if you don't take care of yourselves," explained the doctor. "Go home. Rest. That's what your daughter needs you to do."

"Gotcha," signaled Lucky, stalled hand as if to say, *Thanks. That's enough.*

The doctor vanished the way she had come in, leaving Lucky and Gonzo alone again. Feeling caged in every which way, Lucky suggested they follow her advice—or at least get out and find some decent coffee. Gonzo shook her head, hands still stuck to her face. Seconds later, she forced a change of mind—as if realizing that sitting still in her own stew was no solution. They strolled to Westwood Village to find a cafe. There was no handholding as Gonzo kept her arms bound tightly around herself as if chilled or stuck her hands securely into her jumpsuit pockets.

Both sat solemnly at a sidewalk table, warm air tickling their skin—Lucky with black coffee and Gonzo barely sipping at a straw stuck in a blended iced mocha topped with caramel and whipped cream.

"This is what she wanted," said Gonzo with a weak chuckle, breaking minutes of silence.

"She wanted an ice-blended caramel mocha?" Lucky's glibness didn't quite land.

"You and me. Together. Like this. But *not* like this, you know? I don't know if she hit you up about it, but with me it's been a broken record. 'You and Lucky. When you gonna swallow your stupid pride and put our lives back together?'"

Lucky shook his head as if to say no, she hadn't pressed it.

"Guess that pretty much says where she thinks the blame lies," added Gonzo.

"Not your fault."

"Whatever," snapped Gonzo in an attitude shift. "I need to know what's going on with you."

"Whadda you mean? Same as you, I think."

"Not that," she backspaced, her fingers splayed to their tensile length. "With the hit and run. Tell me you're getting someplace."

Lucky reached for a suitable answer—some kind of floatation to keep him from sinking any further. Instead, he slumped two inches and offered little more than open hands.

"What's that mean?" she pressed.

"So far it means zero. I'm shaking trees and nothing's fallin' out. Sources aren't getting back to me. Nothing but threads leading nowhere."

Grinding out the miles to and from downtown, back and forth from the South Bay, Lucky had dialed up every cop connection he could. Half or more couldn't even muster the stones to return his call. Lucky suspected it was because of something he called *drowning syndrome*, a political malady that strikes when

LAPD and sheriff's officers suspect another deputy is circling the drain. Fearing the cop might pull them under too, weak careerists kept a safe distance.

The few willing to assist Lucky hadn't returned a scintilla of insight to the hit and run. The names Denny Teng, Wang Zhang, and Frankie Coleman had rung no bells whatsoever, returning nothing more than speeding tickets and parking violations. And without help from Emery, Lucky hadn't been able to reap a single slice of fruit from the creepy message he'd planted on the banker's bathroom mirror. As far as he knew, any fissure he'd pried open between Denny Teng and Frankie Coleman had already been filled or stitched back together.

He was neck deep in doubting his own instincts.

"I'm almost a dry hole," he confessed. "Getting nowhere. Not even close to a driver or a link back to whoever ordered this thing." He paused, then added, "That's even if it's a thing other than what it looks like. Stolen fucking car. Hit and run. Random. Shit."

"But you said you thought there might be something with that retired Viking—"

"Babylon. Yeah, I said. Not like I've ever been wrong," he dripped sarcastically.

"Look. And listen." Gonzo was gripping the sides of the sidewalk table. Were it not bolted into the concrete, Lucky wouldn't have been surprised to see her lift it over her head and chuck it in disgust. "She's gonna wake up. We have to believe that. And whether she needs rehab or snaps to the second her eyes open, we both know her. She's gonna wanna know what happened. She's gonna demand an answer to make up for what she's already lost, not to mention all the other shit she's had to survive. Karrie is gonna want to *know*."

"I'm with you—"

"No. You're not." Gonzo leaned in, deep brown eyes fully searching, pupils seeking a complete connection. "You gotta do what you do. Whoever the son of a bitch is, we gotta know. *She's* gotta know."

"Says you to the 'human shit magnet.'"

"This isn't about me and you. It's about *her*."

"You saying I'm not trying hard enough?"

"I'm telling you to stop being careful. Stop trying to protect us by playing it safe. You are what you are. Don't stop being you on my account."

"I haven't laid back. Believe me. I've been leaning plenty. Just without results—"

"Then lean harder!" she pressed. "All the way."

She didn't know what she was asking. Or so Lucky had to assume. Gonzo hadn't witnessed his foolish showdown in the desert with that O.G., Mr. Teardrops—two grown men with shovels, opening up a six-foot-long space of jagged earth to fashion a grave. In Lucky's opinion, she hadn't a flicker of a clue just how far over the edge he could take something.

Then a deeper doubt was triggered in Lucky. *Had* he been wasting time playing it safe, tiptoeing with the likes of Cat Rincon and Frankie Coleman? He wondered if he should've finished hard with Wang and pushed on to a direct confrontation with Denny Teng.

"This isn't you," Lucky pushed back. "You don't like messy."

"You think?"

"Then why this all of a sudden?"

"Because we took her in. She's our girl now. And she deserves all we have."

"All *I* have."

"No. *We*. I'm in this too," she pleaded. "Whatever it takes."

31

Downtown.

Frankie Coleman's corner office was stately, designed to impress with views both to the north and west. When she'd chosen the space and ordered up the build-out, she'd insisted on leasing half the historic building's top floor. She wanted her customers to subconsciously experience some old-money, institutional-styled grandeur. The double-height ceilings trimmed in hand-carved crown molding subtly spoke "money." The remaining offices were generous, well appointed, and individualized to fit each employee's tastes though still approved by the boss. She wanted feminine flourishes, opting for sprays of fresh fragrant flowers at every corridor's turn. This went double for her own suite with bouquets near her desk, at each end of the opposing leather sofas on the opposite side of the space, and centered on the heavy oak conference oval beyond.

Denny Teng was buttressed against that conference table,

hands resting gently on the edges, consciously postured to appear open, confident, as if hiding absolutely nothing whatsoever—all this despite his damp palms.

"Now that *we're* calm," began Denny, euphemistically including himself, "you wanna tell me what this is all about?"

He couldn't tell if Frankie was as icy as she appeared—a demonstrable contrast from her ambush-like visit to his house earlier that morning. From behind her desk, an airy library table, her shapely legs shot out from underneath her almost girlish skirt. The mesh headrest of her Herman Miller desk chair royally framed her head.

"You tell me," she replied, twirling a pen like a baton in her fingers. Her air of quiet control was no accident.

"You recording this conversation?"

"No. Are you?"

The air of distrust hung heavier than their usual desperation. Theirs was a relationship built on both trust and suspicion, a marriage in mutual profit that had begun at a fundraiser for the Los Angeles chapter of the Democratic National Committee. They'd found themselves strolling under the twinkling lights of the Music Center's plaza—the Dorothy Chandler Pavilion at one end, the Ahmanson Theatre at the other. It had been an instant mix of romantic flirtation and lust as the pair discussed each other's businesses. Frankie had only recently founded her bank and was seeking deep-pocket depositors in search of greater returns along with the maximum privacy allowed under US regulations. Denny's consulting business put him in the precarious position of advising his clients the best way to move cash assets from China to the United States.

Lawfully, he'd said.

Of course, she'd replied.

The affair had come first and fast. Intimacy had led to confessions. Not of love. Or even affection. But need. Denny had been charmed as much by Frankie's banking acumen as by her looks and ambition. He'd teased her with the swarms of Chinese nationals he knew looking to offshore their money into legitimate American banks. He had the cash. Frankie had the bank and a shortfall of assets. Thus, a second illicit partnership formed as they stretched from friends with benefits to flout the Fed's sticky bank regulations. Frankie rationalized the first five million dollars as a one-time deal, a gap loan so her fledgling depository would appear cash flush.

Pushing money through the tight legal loopholes placed by the US government was a complicated endeavor. Frankie modeled her system on that of the drug cartels, utilizing "smurfs"—otherwise known as proxy depositors—who would open legit bank accounts in Mexico and make small under-the-federal-radar cash drops. The amassing funds would be legally wired to Frankie's private institution into dummy accounts. The money would then be loaned to fictitious shell companies to make the bank appear profitable. Without a balance sheet that screamed her financial entity was on a rising sea of success, there would have been no public offering.

Frankie's scheme was so cleverly layered, proving so slick, so undetectable—*so easy*—that it was hard not to do it again and again and again. To date, Denny had run over forty-five million dollars through her doors. Frankie reckoned fifty cents on every dollar was a violation of federal law, adding up to felonies upon felonies. She didn't know if Denny was ripping off his clients or 7-Elevens, but the distrust between the two trembled like a Cold War detente with both parties forced to reside under an understanding that one couldn't destroy the other without risking mutual annihilation.

"As you can see," continued Frankie, "I'm no longer a scream-ing bitch in front of your house."

"Thank God," said Denny, remaining cool.

"Don't let my chill fool you," she dripped. "I'm still raging. But I think I know why you did it."

Denny was a reflex away from asking *What did I do?* for the umpteenth time. But didn't want to trigger any unwarranted rage.

So, "Okay" was all he replied.

"Considering the depth of our involvement…" she said. "Thinking about it, I can understand that one of us might have to go through a kind of gut check."

"Gut check," repeated Denny, leaving a question mark off the end of his sentence.

"If this thing between us breaks down?" Frankie stood, slowly circumventing her desk. "We're both screwed. So, denial…and I'm talkin' the psychotherapy kind of denial…is a lot about what the two of us do every day. At some point, reality has gotta turn one of us into a boot-sniffin' pussy."

"Pussy," repeated Denny, thinking, *There's that trailer-trash mouth out of a Miss America package.*

"It's okay. You turned pussy," she repeated, her voice full of a strange empathy. "If it didn't happen to you, it was gonna be me. Just happened to you first. That's all. Don't blame you."

"And because it happened to me first," he said, trying to follow her tortured logic. "That's why you knocked down my door this morning screaming like a banshee?"

"Well?" squared Frankie. "That's the only way I can wrap my head around this shit without wishing you'd choke on your own puke."

"Right," nodded Denny. He attempted to swallow a saliva-load of condescension before he let his next words loose. "At the risk of pissing you off even further, I have to ask this one salient question."

"Ask!" she rose to the bait.

"As a result of me turning 'pussy,' what shit am I supposed to have done?"

"Really? This again?"

"You showed up at my house. We don't want to relive that. Then you summoned me here. At your appointed time. Here I am. Calm. Not yelling. Absolutely without a fucking clue what you think…or *know*…that I did."

"Asshole. You sent that man," she hissed.

"One of my men?"

"Who else would you send? Some wetback you picked up at Home Depot? Of course he's your goddamn man. And believe you me, he delivered your message!"

"Frank—"

"Jesus Christ! We're back where we started!" Frankie angrily stomped a spiked heel.

"No," cautioned Denny. "This is progress. We're just not on the same page yet."

"*Your guy*, you condescending prick!"

"Okay," conceded Denny. "The message. What exactly was it?"

"'Denny…Teng…is watching.'"

"That was the message?"

Frankie's head cocked to the side in disbelief. Yet somehow, Denny appeared convincing in his act of ignorance.

"The 'message,'" he air quoted, "was that I am supposed to be watching you?"

"In lipstick," she pointed a sharpened fingernail at him. "On my bathroom mirror."

"You wouldn't have taken a picture of it?"

"Wouldn't that just get you off? Seeing the sick-ass way he delivered your message?"

Denny released a deep sigh, shaking his head from side to side in frustration. Meanwhile, Frankie marched back around to the opposite side of her desk and spun her laptop screen to face him. Denny eased a few steps forward as Frankie's nightmare came into actual relief. In unsaturated color, the photo depicted a block letter scrawl in burgundy red on a steamed and dripping mirror above a vanity full of makeup and beauty products. Instinct led Denny to mark his own name before confirming the context of the words.

"What the hell?" he mouthed.

"Yeah." Frankie slammed the laptop shut. "Memorandum served."

"Serious, Frankie," surrendered Denny. "That wasn't me."

"Bullshit."

"So…what? I send some evil minion to deliver a memo in

lipstick on your bathroom mirror? All the while knowing you'd be sure to lose your shit, show up at my house in front of my wife and baby girl, only to get summoned here and dressed down like a schoolboy? With my only excuse being it wasn't me? Jesus, Frankie, think about it."

Indeed, Frankie was mulling over the lousy logic. Making sense of it was deflating, as if the air in her legs had sprung a silent leak, returning her slowly into the ergonomic arms of that desk chair. It gave Denny a moment to reflect on Babylon. Had something in his instructions gotten so mixed up that the chatterbox had perceived Frankie as a threat? But then again, he'd never even *told* Babylon about Frankie. It made no sense whatsoever. Babylon had come as a man highly recommended by none other than Mayor Ramon Avila. Denny's head spun with permutations. Somebody…somehow…was dogging him and his business with Frankie or *through* Frankie. Who? And just who would know? There had to be a Judas within his orbit. A betrayer.

Denny ran the exponential math. Since Monday he learned someone had been poaching on his FOBs. There'd been the meltdown in Calabasas. Wang had been mysteriously kneecapped, then roughed up and interrogated by a mysterious sheriff's deputy named Lucky Dey. And then Frankie shows up at his curb screeching about some man who'd scrawled his name on her mirror. Deeper in his brain was a tangential niggling over the treatment Min had received for drawing something the private school had deemed objectionable. *A private school I pay a lot of money for!* In a matter of days, life had turned from methodical and systematic to downright sloppy. Denny didn't like sloppy. And sloppy didn't happen because of accidents.

"If this isn't you, who did this…" trailed Frankie. "Someone knows."

"But knows what? You and me? Our thing? It might be…" Denny snapped his fingers. "Extortion? Somebody who knows something but might not know everything? Maybe just enough to rattle our pockets. See what falls out."

"Somebody of the *Chinese* persuasion?"

Denny instantly resented the insinuation.

"But for me?" Frankie's fingers spread across her blouse. "My bank is clean. That's the only way it works on my side. Me. I'm the *only* villain in my bank."

"I need to think," snapped Denny, already starting for the door. "Talk tonight. No phones for now. Only face to face."

"Where?"

"Let ya know."

"How?"

Thunk. The office door closed behind him. The quick exit left Frankie in a cold sweat egged on by her lingering hangover.

"LINDSAYYYYY?" she shouted loud enough to be heard through the hardwood panels. "NEED TYLENOL NOW!"

32

The eighty-two former LAPD and sheriff's deputies in the Los Angeles City Personnel Department were warehoused in the basement of 700 East Temple Street, a nondescript three-story monolith just a stone's throw from downtown's Little Tokyo.

"If all those files down there could talk," Babylon would sometimes joke to his colleagues, "it would be the end of all faith in the goddamn city governance."

Security in the basement facility was standard. Visitors were required to leave a valid driver's license or ID with the armed security guard manning an incongruously placed desk in front of the elevator bank. Only cops weren't known to bother with such protocols. A badge fixed to either a uniform or belt was often ID enough for a wave-through. No signing in. No declaration of whom they were visiting.

Same shit, different building, mused Lucky as he strolled past the security guard, an elephantine fellow with three chins and two folding chairs parked side by side to support the broad cheeks of his backside. The guard nodded and smiled at Lucky as if they were brethren in blue, quickly returning to the Sudoku puzzle on his computer screen.

Lucky skipped the elevator in favor of the stairs, then criss-crossed the dull fluorescent-lit government-issue corridors until he found Babylon's office. The detective's name—Mark Baba—was spelled out on a standard three-by-five card framed next to the jamb. The door itself was propped open and the desk inside empty. There was a couch—not standard—vacant, wellworn, and shoe-horned into the space. Babylon's neighbor across the hall remarked to Lucky that the investigator was likely imbibing his ritual sushi lunch. After a few minutes of cop-to-cop small talk with Lucky, the neighbor left to grab a burrito from the Mexican food truck outside the building's west entrance.

Babylon's desk was neat. The files currently under investigation were ordered alphabetically, feathered across the tabletop like a gin rummy hand. The names were tabbed, last name first. Not a single folder bore Lucky's name. Lucky took up residence in Babylon's chair, opening drawers until he found a box of unused file folders, removing one for his own use. He uncapped a red Sharpie from the LAPD Memorial Fund mug Babylon utilized as a pen and pencil holder and, in block lettering, began writing his own name. That's when he heard Babylon's voice, as distant as it was distinct and longwinded, growing closer with every phrase.

"…don't go to movies no more," sounded Babylon, ever nearer but still well beyond the frame of his office door. "What they're charging for a ticket? Senior discount only a buck? Forget that shit. I got movies on my big screen at home. Better sound. Better food. And nobody but nobody talkin' during the show. Seriously. Home theater? Best thing since toaster ovens."

Lucky jabbed the Sharpie back in the cup, casually swiveled and leaned back in the chair, putting his feet up and crossing his ankles with the heels of his boots hanging over the corner of Babylon's desk.

"Ever cook your popcorn in coconut oil?" carried on Babylon to some other compatriot beyond the door. "Swear to baby Jesus there's no goin' back to the Orville Redenbacher in the microwave. From the stovetop to a bowl, sprinkle curry and sea salt? Boom goes the dynamite, *know what I mean*?"

If Babylon was in a conversation or just talking to himself, Lucky would never know, not having heard any other voice. When Babylon eventually turned his brick-like torso into his office it was as if the monologue had barely paused, the Lynwood Viking in him registering little, if any, surprise.

"Lucky damn Dey in da house," remarked Babylon. "Wait. I can do better. Lucky twice-in-a-Dey. How's that?" He belly-laughed at his own joke.

"Keep goin'," said Lucky. "You might drop a line I haven't heard."

"Comfy?" Babylon regarded his desk and chair.

"Decent digs. Might have to look into this gig once my cop career goes terminal."

"That why you here? Lookin' to make a change?"

"Stopped by to see an ol' deputy dog pal."

"Yeah. Who?"

"Rangel."

"Good guy. Call him Sir Robert the Rangel."

"You share with him any of that home brew you guys used to distill?"

"You're talkin' 'bout that South L.A. moonshine?"

"We heard stories. Over at Lennox."

"I am a reformed, sober-till-I'm-over Viking," mugged Babylon, proud of his cleaned-up act. "But those were some days."

"That they were," agreed Lucky.

"And you came all the way 'cross town to see Sir Robert, huh?"

"Naw. I'm bullshitting," switched up Lucky. "Just like you were bullshitting me at the hospital."

"Busted," shrugged Babylon. "Suppose you figured out already that we city-side *detectivas* were asked to open an investigation on you. Over that thing you got going with the Sheriff's. Pretty standard."

"Wondered about that," said Lucky. "But my deputy dog pal, you know? Sir Robert of Rangel? Says there's no such open file. Then there's that catching up with me at the hospital. How'd you know I'd be there?"

"I'm a great goddamn detective, ass hat."

"You were there about my daughter."

Babylon's mouth stopped moving. His face looked like putty troweled onto rough granite. He turned and ever-so-quietly began to shut his office door until the latch softly clicked. After that Babylon threw the bolt.

"That little girl of yours caught a bad one—"

Lucky's fist landed before Babylon could turn back to him, leaving the old fireplug to later contemplate just how the hell Lucky had covered the distance between them with such velocity. From that leaned-back posture, feet up on Babylon's desk to cocked and firing a fully weighted fist, Lucky appeared to have reflexes and a will way beyond his dossier of injuries. It was like walking into a punch, the blow catching Babylon fully in the crease between his nose and cheek. His neck snapped back. His brain went black. He came to, rocking on the floor, disoriented, with Lucky's face close enough to lick. Before Babylon's faculties returned, Lucky had fistfuls of his collar and was yanking him up and over to the couch. The ball of Lucky's knee pressed against Babylon's sternum.

"I hear you do private work," hissed Lucky. "And I got a good guess who's paying you. So, go tell him. Enough with the mini moves and let's get on with the big dance."

Lucky released his grip on Babylon, stepped off, and straightened himself.

"You like to talk, right?" finished Lucky. "Talk your client into making things right."

"And what if being right has nothin' to do with nothin'?" coughed Babylon.

"Then buckle the fuck up. 'Cause shit's gonna get bumpy."

Babylon didn't protest. He lay half on/half off the couch, rumpled, face beginning to redden and throb, and observed Lucky unlock the door and let himself out. He knew he could've had Lucky arrested fast enough. From what he knew, a formal complaint against the deputy would be enough to put some serious topspin on the county's case. But Babylon was still in a brain stew. He tried to shake off the sucker punch as just another back-alley scrape. It sure as hell wasn't the first time he'd been clocked, let alone by a fellow cop. *Hell, I probably had it comin'*, forgave Babylon, grateful Lucky had no clue about his ICU visit with his daughter. Babylon had even stood over Karrie, listening to the sounds of the machinery as if they were ghostly whispers, beckoning the girl to let go and succumb to her mortality.

But the Viking's anger began to swell in time with his face. Whatever recompense he would choose to visit upon Lucky would need to wait for another day and more clarity of thought. First he needed a cold pack. Walking behind his desk, he searched for a plastic bag for ice. He stopped cold when he saw what had been left on his desk. There, centered, was a new vanilla-colored file folder with Lucky Dey's name inked in red on the tab. Gently, with the tip of his finger, Babylon touched the top right corner and pulled the flap. Inside lay a single sheet of paper crayoned by a child. Depicted was a box-shaped house under a lemon-yellow sun. Within the walls of the house appeared to be a family of huddled bees under the watchful eyes of black, red-eyed dinosaurs.

"Sweet mother of Ghandi," remarked Babylon to nobody but himself. "What the hell are you supposed to be?"

33

Lowbrow apartment buildings inhabited by low-budget USC students living outside campus boundaries, and Hispanic and African-Americans barely keeping their heads above the poverty line, flanked the quiet, potholed street. A violent gust of wind whipped a pair of palm trees like a cheerleader's pompoms. Parked on Hoover Avenue, a nondescript stripe of urban black-top that abutted Martin Luther King Jr. Boulevard, Howie's view kept shifting from the shaking fronds above to the outline of the Los Angeles Memorial Coliseum. He worried one of those heavy fronds might cut loose and come crashing down onto the hood of his borrowed VW Jetta.

Borrowed my ass, spanked Howie's subconscious. The truth was that he'd technically stolen it from a girl at USC.

Acknowledgment of his crime delivered Howie back to his

first—the one that had started the whole damned snowball that had defined his young life. His senior year in high school, Howie had volunteered to drive some classmates home from a party. The '92 Jeep Wrangler, his father's weekend toy, had a roll cage but no electronic warning that a passenger might not have secured his or her seat belt. Skating along the twists of Mulholland Drive, Howie had gotten distracted and caught a sandy shoulder. The Jeep swerved then flipped, rolling over three times. The two rear passengers, the Buckley School's prom king and queen, were ejected into the blackness. While the girl was found in a crevasse full of chaparral and suffered a broken pelvis, the popular senior boy had bounced off the pavement, crushed his skull, and been declared dead before EMS could scoop him into an ambulance.

When tested by the LAPD, Howie had registered .09 on the breathalyzer, one hundredth of a point from being on the legal side of sober. The prom king's father, a politically connected television producer, had insisted on a vigorous prosecution. Howie pled out to felony involuntary manslaughter and received a sentence of eighteen months in county jail. After serving ten months, he'd been released to a year of semi-supervised probation. The past was behind him.

Or so he had thought.

It was dusk. The street where Howie had parked was appropriately dim. Gray. An internet search had informed him that twilight was statistically the hardest time of day for an eyewitness to identify a suspect. It weakened the eyes. The lack of contrast turned even a light-skinned black man opaque. In Howie's lap was his father's .22-caliber semi-automatic, a lightweight Ruger—and the only gun he'd ever fired. Though not the mightiest weapon, it was a far cry more deadly than the replica he carried on his *extortion sorties*. He'd bought the fake gun online. It required no registration. It looked so authentic he imagined he'd fooled true-blue gangbangers Neon and Lil Rod, his Asian Invasion comrades who he'd eventually blamed for the meltdown in Calabasas. Neon's and Lil Rod's guns had always been the real McCoys, loaded with hot shit and ready to drop a man. Howie's rationale was that as the operations manager of Denny Teng's extortion scheme, he was only a poseur—or pretend gangster—the proof was that he'd never come to a job actually armed. If arrested, Howie hoped that single fact would serve as a legal modifier.

Your honor? I'm just a dummy from the Valley with dummy bullets in my dummy gun.

But the Ruger .22 was no dummy gun. And as the moment of truth neared, Howie noticed his palm sweat smearing the weapon's oily bluing. 8:00 p.m. approached, the hour Howie had requested Neon and Lil Rod to meet at the corner of Hoover and MLK. Howie's nerves accelerated from light jangling to endless vibrations—this despite popping two Xanax tabs twenty minutes prior. Upon scoping the spot, Howie's plot had been hatched in a matter of minutes. Scarily quick, he stressed. Yet everything about it seemed to pencil out to near perfection. He had called Lil Rod from a disposable phone and summoned him and Neon for an urgent meetup, promising more money than the $10K per job the pair had been splitting. The duo viewed Howie not as a threat, but as exactly what he was—a college boy, a pretender, a middle-class coconut from the white suburbs of the San Fernando Valley. They had no reason not to trust him.

What Neon and Lil Rod took seriously about Howie was the cash flow. The green. Sure, Howie had been locked up on a technical homicide beef. But it was a car accident, plain and end of any argument. Lil Rod had known Howie was nothing close to hardcore the second they met when sharing a two-man pod at the Men's Central Jail and working roadside cleanups on a county service crew by day.

Lil Rod, a self-described bona fide *killin' jellybean*, had notched four kills onto his metaphoric gun handle since first murdering a defenseless homeless man. After gunning down his second unarmed man, *a lily white ghetto tourist*, for stealing his bicycle, he'd been officially jumped in as a Nutty Bloc Compton Crip. But two months later, he got jammed up in nearby South Gate for stealing and joyriding a street-racing Camry that belonged to an affiliated gang member.

After his stint in jail, Lil Rod had been shunned by his home set and was more than happy to reconnect with his homogenous homey from Northridge. Howie had reached out through a prepaid mobile phone. A burner. Nearly impossible to trace. All that mattered to Lil Rod was that his chocolate-covered marshmallow of a bunk buddy was offering strong dollars in exchange for genuine South Los Angeles black man muscle in an extortion scheme against a bunch of slant-eyed seaweed suckers out in the SGV. And the paydays that had eventually come had been epic. Lil Rod had conscripted a muscle-head steroid addict known as Neon, another gang outcast lacking in human remorse.

Before the rendezvous, Neon picked up Lil Rod in his vintage Pontiac Trans Am, the original 1977 *Smokey and the Bandit* edition. He'd dropped forty grand in cash for it. Legit. But for the GPS device guiding Neon to the meetup at Hoover Street and MLK Boulevard, the interior appeared original and loved up by the previous owner.

Lil Rod wasn't impressed.

"Smokey and the what?" he bugged.

"Jus' 'cause you a nigga who don' know his movies," rebuffed Neon, "don't give you no right to complain on my classic."

Lil Rod lit up a spliff, offering a hit of the hand-rolled marijuana and tobacco blend to Neon.

"Shit may be legal now," refused Neon. "But cops catch me up on the wrong side they can impound my Bandit."

"Call it Bandit already? You ain't stole nothin' with it."

"Bandit, as in *Smokey and the Bandit*. The Burt Reynolds movie. You know nothin' 'bout nothin', Jar Jar."

"Jar Jar? I'm a flippin' Jar Jar now? Why I gotta be all that?"

"'Cause you both little *and* stupid sometime."

"You a *fugly* ass mud duck, then," shot back Lil Rod.

"In my very own bandit car, I am," grinned Neon.

Neon rolled the Trans Am up Hoover toward the Coliseum for the staff meeting with Junior Mint—Neon's derogatory name for Howie. A white wrought-iron fence circled an empty lot with scrub and weeds sprouting from the cracked asphalt. There was an empty space near the corner. Neon eased Bandit close, careful not to scrape his vintage tire rims against the curb. He checked the dash clock. It was 7:56 p.m.

"Early," muttered Neon.

Slipping down low in the Jetta, Southern Cal baseball cap pulled down to his eyebrows, Howie had watched the Trans Am slip past him, then park. He'd hoped they would stop behind him, climb out, and stroll toward the corner. That way he could have easily stepped from his own ride, left the car door open, walked up behind the gangbangers, and opened fire at the backs of their heads. Once the deed had been done, he could have rushed back to the Jetta and driven the two blocks to USC's southwest parking structure. To witnesses it would appear like a gang murder, a thug-life ending to a pair of "male usual" victims. Sure. The cops might trace the car to USC, but the last person they'd be looking for was some business major named Howie Morris.

Only the Trans Am had parked twenty paces in front of him. In a moment of unusual calm Howie came up with a new idea. *Let Neon and Lil Rod step out of the vehicle and begin their stroll to the corner. Then I call their names. They stop, turn, and I let 'em have it in their faces. Once they're down, I'll pop each of 'em one more time in the head. They'll be dead and Denny and Wang will be pleased at my efficiency.*

But Howie didn't notice the rental car. Deep blue. Metallic. A compact model. In the gray cast it would've been hard for a witness to make out its make or year or true color. Howie wasn't the only one to take advantage of that hard-to-read space between light and dark. The car stopped broadside the black Trans Am, the barrel of a rifle protruding from its rear passenger window. Assault-style. Muzzle flash suppressor. Howie couldn't miss the vomit of flame that spit from the weapon. As fast as the shooter could pull the trigger, the rifle spoke and the vintage Bandit car was punctured. Safety glass fell like curtains, a dull red mist coloring the air.

Howie's fight or flight impulse made the choice for him. He wouldn't even recall when he'd started the car. Was it before the gunfire erupted while preparing for his own getaway? Or had it been unconscious, in those first milliseconds of violence? He retracted the transmission lever with such force he lost his grip of the handle. He then gassed the Jetta so hard it leapt from forward and, before he could manage to steer around the blue compact, his right front end struck the compact's bumper with a decided thermoplastic and metallic crunch. Panicked, Howie gunned the Jetta and, instead of switching to reverse, plowed ahead, swiveling the lighter compact car clockwise until traction won out over friction. Sparks sprayed along Howie's right side, filling the windows and obscuring the face of the blue car's scowling driver. When the Jetta broke loose, Howie kept the accelerator down, ignoring the red light at MLK Boulevard.

Jesus, Howie thought later. *If there'd been cross traffic or a cop or...*

Two speedy right turns and a left and Howie was in the USC student lot with the automated gate safely dropped behind him. He parked on the second floor of the structure and wiped the car of his fingerprints. He hauled himself to the school gym, hid the pistol in a locker, and returned to his high-rise campus apartment. During the long shower that followed, he replayed the incident, the lead up to it, and the aftermath. He realized he hadn't yet figured a way to return the car keys. The damage to the car could easily be explained away with the usual college shenanigans involving drink and drugs. The entire sixth floor knew where she kept her car keys. A goody-goody like Mr. Aloha would be the last suspect.

And Neon and Lil Rod are dead!

Upon realizing he'd receive the credit without ever having touched the trigger, Howie experienced a heady contact high. Denny would be nothing but pleased. That prick Wang would be impressed. Howie let out an echoing, self-satisfying hoot from inside the shower stall. He fist-pounded the plastic enclosure as if it were the only friend he could share with.

Tracking down Ernest Joel Selfridge—a.k.a. Neon—had been so effortless for Zipper, he'd found himself repeating another English language malaprop his mother was so oft to overuse that her sensitive son had begged her to stop.

Easy trapezee.

He'd hated every time she uttered it. He'd even suggested she use different expressions. *Easy as pie. Piece of cake. Simple as ABC. Child's play.* Despite his pleas, that singsong rhyme of *easy trapezee* crept into nearly every conversation. She dropped it like periods at the end of her sentences. After a while, it appeared to have found a home under Zipper's tongue, lying in wait for the moment he and Fungo had identified Neon at a house in West Rancho Dominguez. The address had come up in a simple Google search. Neon's residence had been listed on a variety of public websites that identified sex offenders.

They hadn't had to sit on the tiny stucco bungalow for long before Neon had appeared in the driveway and untied the dust cover blanketing a black 1977 Pontiac Trans Am. They'd watched Neon neatly fold the cover, stow it in the trunk, and gingerly pilot the vehicle to a probation office in Inglewood. Twenty minutes later Neon was eastbound on Imperial, unwise to the blue rental compact that was quietly dogging him sixty yards to his rear. Neon stopped at a marijuana dispensary in Watts, where he picked up Lil Rod. Zipper had tailed them all the way to the meetup with Howie.

Only Zipper hadn't a notion that there was a Howie in the mix or that he was any kind of factor. The plan had been all about opportunity and that had come at the dusky stop on Hoover. Zipper had lowered the rear windows, maneuvered the rent-a-car up alongside the Trans Am, and given Fungo the green light. He'd fully intended to keep his eyes in scan mode, checking the surrounding landscape for witnesses, bogeys, and, most importantly, cops—specially since they were so close to USC. But the noise from the Chinese-manufactured AK-47 was almost ear busting—a high-pitched *SNAP-SNAP-SNAP*. Spent cartridges ricocheted and pinged throughout the rental's interior. A hot piece of ejected brass rebounded off a rear cushion, tumbling through the static air until it came to rest, wedging between the base of Zipper's neck and his collar. It burned his skin. He was sucking in air, about to release a pained yelp, when the sedan was rocked, slammed from behind and pushed like a clock hand demanding to spring ahead. In the panic, all Zipper could make out of the assaulting car was the VW medallion on the trunk as it sped away.

Jamming into reverse, Zipper had jerked the rental car backward before shoving it into drive and wheeling it in the direction from which they'd come. South, accelerating. Before the assault, Zipper had made certain to extinguish the headlamps. Come the first stop sign, he fumbled, found the switch, and turned them on, hoping to hell it wouldn't alert a police cruiser.

Had the headlights had been on and sweeping the street seconds earlier, Zipper might have noticed Lil Rod, the passenger Neon had picked up at the weed shop. He was belly down on the sidewalk and snaking his way from the bullet-riddled Trans Am, a track of smeared blood in his wake.

34

Downtown.

The sun dipped behind the downtown skyline, leaving a trail of jailed shadows across the vast array of less impressive architecture, industrial and otherwise, all the way to the railroad yards. Staked out on the street fronting the east side of the Personnel building, Lucky sat in his '99, eyes stuck on the building's exit and the crosswalk leading to an employee parking lot fenced in semi-rusted cyclone. It had been some six hours since he'd cracked a fist into Babylon's doughy face, threatened the Viking SOB, and left him with a question mark inside the folder he'd labeled "Lucky Dey." In the scheme of all things regarding Karrie and her coma, the child's drawing might have meant absolutely nothing. Lucky's gamble was that the scribbling deposited as a mysterious *leave behind* would motivate the gnarled detective into a face-to-face with his presumed client.

Lucky's lids kept dropping, demanding rest. Twice already he'd reentered the building to dump quarters into a vending machine that dispensed everything from canned sodas to sugar-free Red Bull. A few times, sleep overcame him. He'd wake with a start, uncertain how long he'd been unconscious. With every gap, he'd dial up his pal Robert Rangel, who'd put him on hold while checking around the corner to see if Babylon was still in the building. Each time, the answer was affirmative. When Rangel clocked out just shy of 6:30, Lucky was on his own. He chewed gum to stay awake and burned up cellular minutes chasing down other leads, leaving even more messages that would most surely go unreturned. Those on the inside who would talk to him knew nothing or found nothing beyond the Malibu police report: *Hit and run. Victim female. Seventeen. One witness: Lucky Dey.*

Night overtook day; the streetlights ignited. With that, sleep crashed into Lucky and with it came a shattering dream. In his subliminal fiction, he was seated in his '99 just as if he were on the same stake-out. But instead of Babylon escaping the Personnel building, it was Karrie. In a wet suit, dripping and barefoot, she carried her surfboard down the two steps that emptied to the crosswalk. The powerful Crown Vic suddenly roared and charged ahead like a surging shark. Jaws wide. Lucky pounded the failing brakes and spun a steering wheel that felt loose and without any connection to the tires. Karrie stopped mid-crosswalk, hair the color of straw, smile as wide as Kansas, beaming as if happily unbridled to see Lucky. The grille connected with his daughter. At the bone-crunching impact Lucky jolted awake, heart racing, his scalp tingling in sweat. He was back in the real world, escaped from the nightmare, in the exact spot where he'd nodded off.

And there was Babylon.

Leather shoulder bag in tow, the detective quick-stepped toward the employee parking lot. Lucky marked him all the way to his Cadillac El Dorado, turned over the '99's engine, and eased into a loose follow hoping that Babylon wouldn't be too curious about who or what might be stalking him in his rearview mirror. The tandem drive covered thirty-five minutes and two freeways, the last being the iconic 101.

Babylon's Caddy peeled off at a Studio City exit, ultimately arriving at a south-of-Ventura-Boulevard residence in Fryman Canyon Estates, a low-lying enclave at the base of the hills, populated by undulating lawns and ancient live oaks. Parked cars lined both sides of the narrow residential street. Nearly each and every vehicle was a luxury model. A regiment of red-vested parking valets waited outside a house—a certain sign of a high-roller gathering.

Babylon waved off the valet, instead setting the brake and switching on his flashers. Lucky hung back at a gentle curve about a hundred yards from the valet stand. He popped the glovebox and, without taking his eyes off his mark, felt around for his spotting scope. The light-gathering telephoto lens squeezed the image. A turn of the focus wheel crisped Babylon's shoulder bag into flattened relief. The former cop was climbing a long handcrafted flagstone staircase leading to the front entry of a warmly lit mansion. A towering Asian man in white linen slacks and a fashionably untucked dress shirt met Babylon halfway up the steps.

Denny Teng.

Lucky lingered with the long lens as Babylon produced the child's drawing from his shoulder bag, handing it off to Denny Teng. The child's father barely gave the artwork a once-over before folding it into a package small enough to fit in his shirt pocket. It was a reaction of insignificance. Dismissive? Or telling? Lucky couldn't hazard a guess. But by delivering the drawing, Babylon had proved he was in the employ of Denny Teng. At last, a clear connection.

As stoic as Denny Teng appeared, Babylon gestured in an aggravated manner. Denny placed an arm on the detective's shoulder and guided him back down the steps to his Cadillac. Babylon returned to the driver's seat while Denny slowly legged it around to sit shotgun. Lucky expected to see brake lights flaring before

Babylon set off again. But no. The car never budged. The best Lucky could make out was that both men were simply continuing the conversation that had begun on the steps.

Lucky lowered the scope, rubbed his eye, and, just as he was reorienting himself to the eyepiece, caught a glimpse of a statuesque woman standing on the lip of the hardscape that fronted the home's entry.

"Well, hello," breathed Lucky.

The woman was Frankie Coleman. She tipped a glass of white wine to her lips before perfectly securing her runner-up Miss America half smile, clearly pretending to listen to a duo of men busy chatting her into bored oblivion. Her eyes, though, looked keen, flicking every two or three seconds in the direction of Babylon's car. Lucky heard a car door slam and quickly panned his lens down the path. Denny Teng was already skipping back up the steps while Babylon's Caddy surged forward, wheels cranked into the nearest driveway in the beginning of a three-point turn before the sojourn back down the road's gentle slope.

Headlights blasted toward Lucky. He purposefully slumped in his seat as Babylon eased his *Yom* Kippur Clipper past, the space between the two ex-cops a matter of inches. Babylon was surely smart enough to spot the retired cop car amongst all the shiny, European imports—the indubitable turd in the proverbial punchbowl. The question was if he would tie the car to Lucky. If the ex-Viking detective was on his game, he'd be calling the Crown Vic's tags into a police connection with access to DMV records, producing Lucky's name, and confirming his skullduggery. Once the Cadillac was finally out of sight, Lucky regained his bearing, realigning the spotting scope to the front of the manse. But neither Denny nor Frankie were anywhere to be seen.

Now what? he asked himself.

A car horn from behind startled Lucky and he realized he was blocking traffic. He raised an apologizing hand to the offended driver. But when he checked his mirror he noticed a very particular shade of red. Candy apple. The elfin figure behind the wheel was easily identified. Catalina Rincon. She was both annoyed and behaving as if she had the right not to be delayed. Lucky watched her pull an angry face while she once again fist-punched her car horn.

Though Catalina Rincon could see him open his door, step out, and begin a languid approach, Lucky's face was in shadow. She was too incensed to recognize the car as the same one that had pinned hers in at the yoga studio. The man at her door bent at the waist and back-knuckled a non-threatening *rap-rap-rap* on her window. She defensively rolled the pane down just four short inches.

"Late to the party, huh?" smirked Lucky. "Guess that makes two of us."

35

"Wait in the kitchen. 'Round the corner to the right."

"Think I can't find my way to the fridge?" Fungo was already through the foyer.

Zipper paused at the threshold of the low-ceilinged, stone-faced entry to the house he'd grown up in. The Fernfield Drive domicile was in a 1950s-era time warp. As he stared inside to what should have been familiar, his eyes adjusted to the dark. He could barely see past the family room into the addition. Both spaces, once furnished with the warmth of a family—corduroy sofas, big floor pillows, milk crates full with Thomas the Tank Engine pieces, and an old tube color TV for a hearth—were now cramped with the silhouettes of Asian antiquities. Vases mostly. From inches tall to thigh high, the collection reeked of a hoarding condition rather than the investments his mother claimed them to be. She had rooms above and behind her numerous nail salons chock-full of eighteenth- and nineteenth-century pottery, bubble-wrapped and catalogued for her son—should he survive her—to auction off at a monstrous profit.

By memory, Zipper swivel-hipped his way through the mine-field of jade canisters and ginger jars to a pair of French doors leading to a manicured Vietnamese garden, magically lit with stringed white lights, and centered by the home's original figure 8–shaped swimming pool.

The pool glowed blue-green, the minuscule changes in sur-face tension delighting the surroundings in dancing reflections, the most pronounced of which moved across Linh Ling's stoic face. In tartan fleece pajamas she sat at her usual roost, a wide wicker chair arranged with outdoor blankets, a flute of half-supped Italian limoncello in her slender fingers. Zipper had often compared her nightly meditations to those of a black owl peacefully revisiting the place of her first kill: the very swimming pool where she'd drowned Zipper's dad.

"It is done?" asked the mother, the liqueur rising to her lips.

"Both," answered Zipper, preferring to remain to her rear and beneath the wisteria-choked pergola. His answers were flat. "They fit the descriptions."

"Not a virgin no more," she said. "But an all-grown gangster. Veteran swordsman."

Zipper didn't miss the import of her reference. Days ago he'd been little more than a part-time pimp and errand boy. His moth-er's son. A criminal. But in his own mind, almost innocent.

"The number five comes to mind," said Linh.

"To be accurate, only one," clarified Zipper, as if he still pos-sessed a measure of chastity. "The other four were just assists."

"Kills are kills. A mother is proud of her grown-up boy."

Rocking nervously from the balls of his feet to his heels, Zip-per tried to picture his mother's face. As a child he'd thought of her blank-faced demeanor as tough love. That was until his step-father had confided that his wife believed all expressions created unflattering lines on a woman's face. Her theory had been that the quieter the skin, the younger a lady's visage. Despite her vain attempt, Zipper thought his forty-four-year-old mother, her inky hair reinforced with black dye, looked north of sixty.

Your true frickin' hair is gray with guilt.

"Tell me about them," said Linh, her voice a gentle demand.

"Which ones?"

"Start with the real estate queer." Linh broke into a soft laugh. "The one who imagined he was going to sell me a house."

"And if I don't feel like it? Tellin' you?"

"Are you denying your mother the pleasure of your experience? These are men who stole from me."

"Like we weren't the one's stealing in the first place?"

"I steal nothing," she snapped. "I make investments for people. That Calabasas money was from that fobby franchisee—Tung Chee Liu—to me for a salon in Fullerton."

"You seriously won't admit to stealing but you want me to detail for you the murders I did?" The indignation of it elevated in Zipper. *"For you?"*

"Not murders. Revenge. Those were *your* cousins got ambushed in Calabasas."

Zipper's mom was a repository of rationalizations. *The stupid lies she tells herself,* he groused in his head. Here Linh Ling was, asking her only boy for details about the murders he'd done for her.

Linh's game was to lure some unfortunate FOB into investing in one of her seedy, strip mall nail salons. If they balked, she'd threaten to inform her Beijing connections about the unreported cash they'd taken into the US. They didn't know that Zipper's mother wasn't connected to anything beyond the pay-for-information pipeline that identified off-the-boat marks who had arrived in the SGV with suitcases of bundled hundred-dollar bills. Zipper guessed that such a conduit had to service a litany of predators. Poor Tung Chee had been just another Chinaman who'd spirited millions in cash from the mainland. It had only been a matter of time before Linh Ling's extortion scam collided with another's.

And that day had come on Monday.

Linh had sent Zipper's cousins, Billy B. and Tu'an, to meet her newest nail salon franchisee at the Calabasas bank, where he kept his stash of undeclared bills. It was either fate or just really bad luck that a few hours before the scheduled appointment, Tung Chee Liu had found himself and his family held at gunpoint by three black thugs. Then, upon stepping out of the bank with the duffle bag, an addled Tung Chee had recognized Billy B. and Tu'an rolling up to him in a Dodge Ram pickup. Whether it was due to fear or instinct or maybe even the idea that he needed to honor his agreement with Linh Ling, Tung Chee simply passed the duffel stuffed with cash through the pickup's open window. He did this only thirty short paces from the two black gangbangers waiting in the white sedan. Stupefied by the audacity of it all, the gangsters had gassed the sedan, leaving black trail marks behind their smoking tires. Within minutes, Linh's unarmed nephews were upside-down and bleeding out from their gunshot wounds.

"Don't wanna be your push-button killer," declared Zipper. "Not so you can add another fingernail ranch."

"Don't like when you call it that," she snapped. "It's a business. Family business. *Our* business."

"Mom. You only pay me fifteen dollars an hour."

"Would you rather pay taxes on what I invest for you?" Linh's question trailed as she silently slurped more limoncello. "When I die, all this is yours. The salons. The cash. My art."

"You never asked me."

"Didn't know a mother had to ask. And what is mine is yours."

"What does all your shit buy me if I get jammed up?"

"Are you?" Her voice had a ring to it. "Going to get arrested? Did you make a mistake?"

"No," he dodged. And left it at that.

As he worked his way back through the maze of ancient vases,

Zipper felt an itching at his own confidence. He'd seen the head of the man Austin had ID'd practically explode under the onslaught of Fungo's gunfire. But after their rented compact had been spun by the asshole in the Volkswagen, could he confirm the second man's demise? No. If he were a betting man, he'd have laid strong odds on the second killer's end. Still, there was that tapping at the back of his skull. Had he been wrong?

Something told him…*yes*.

Zipper was halfway to the front door when he realized that he'd forgotten Fungo was midway through a refrigerator raid. In shifting direction, his elbow grazed a clay vase near the center of the room. It was taller than the rest and heavy at the top, the narrow base requiring hardly any force to send it tipping. Instead of sliding left to save it, Zipper twisted at the waist and rotated his shoulders. The heavy vessel, brittle from eons of dry air, crashed into a table of smaller jars. The sound was monstrous as well as a delight to Zipper's ears. The rest was knee-jerk, a remnant of the teenage boy who snapped back at his mom. Zipper bent at the waist, recalling his martial arts years as a preteen. The sweeping leg kick he envisioned was a sloppy copy of Jet Li, yet more satisfying than any color belt he'd ever earned. His right foot and calf connected with more pottery, blindly flailing, but sweeping more precious jars to their demise. The clamor of breakage had a short but thrilling domino effect as the space surrounding him was cleared of all obstacles.

He twisted toward those open French doors leading to the pool area. If he'd expected to see his mother, angry and rising from her wicker niche, he was disappointed. She'd surely heard the racket. And all without any visible reaction.

"Whoops!" Zipper sarcastically shouted toward her.

Even after he'd vacated the house with lumbering Fungo at his heels, Zipper couldn't escape the feeling of failure. He'd left something undone. Near the Coliseum. Not just the witness in the VW, but one of his two targets. He had no evidence. Just a sensation that somewhere out there was an untied shoelace waiting to trip him into some inescapable pit.

* * *

Fungo's second target, the short gangster called Lil Rod, had indeed survived. Most of what he'd witnessed had been glimpsed through muzzle flashes. Lil Rod had still been high from an afternoon inhaling premium bud. He'd smoked so much weed his throat was like sandpaper and he had been begging Neon to make a liquor store stop for a forty-ounce salve of malt liquor all the way to the meetup.

"Nuh uh," Neon had said. "No food in the Bandit sled."

"Not even a Big Gulp?" Lil Rod had argued.

"Get a ride back with college boy and have a picnic for all I give."

Brain buzzing, gullet dry, Lil Rod had been just hanging on until their meetup with Aloha-shirted Howie. After Neon had carefully wheeled his Bandit car to the Hoover Street curb, something innate in Lil Rod, be it curiosity, habit, or self-preservation, had directed his eyes to the side-view mirror. He thought he'd recognized Howie behind the wheel of the car parked behind them. Before he could strain his dilated pupils to focus, one of those matching rubber bands in Neon's hair had come dislodged and stuck to the window—affixed by its owner's blood and brain matter. Lil Rod had recoiled, racking his head ninety degrees to the left. Between the flashes from the AK-47 he had somehow distinguished a cartoon face. Animalistic.

Russel Hobbs. The synapses in Lil Rod's brain had reduced everything down to slow motion. Hobbs wasn't real. And Lil Rod knew as much. Hobbs was an animated character in music videos for a British virtual band called Gorillaz. He'd loved them as a boy. In those blank spaces between the gunpowder afterburn and another spinning bullet, how Lil Rod had pictured a fictitious musical cartoon character was either a riddle or a testament to how stoned he truly was.

Lil Rod's mental slowness had ended when he'd thrown himself against the door. It swung open under all 130 pounds of him and he sprawled to the sidewalk. With only the use of his arms, he dragged his body along the concrete. His lower limbs had stopped operating and acted more like anchors. He couldn't feel so much as a nerve ending below his belt loop. He saw wheels churning against the asphalt as the blue compact and a guy who looked like Howie peeled away. The stink of burnt rubber hung in the air. Instinct told Lil Rod to get up and run, beat his feet until he was far away from the scene. Only his legs refused. His muscles failed to reply to his brain's command. Then a pain bubbled up from the small of his back. It began to spread upward, thorax to neck.

Jesus Christ, he cried to himself. *I'm shot. But not dead. At least not yet.*

He reached behind himself, feeling his pants for the warm stickiness of fresh blood. The gangster Crip in him raged. It was that ugly rush for revenge. The voice in him screamed that should he survive, Howie and his Aloha shirt would need to be capped. Killed ten times over. Made seriously dead in a way the world would know that nobody but nobody messed with Lil Rod.

36

Studio City.

The Studio City function was a private fundraiser for Lilly Zoller. The cost per attendee and a plus-one was a donation of ten thousand dollars to her political fund. For their contribution they were plied with free liquor, tapas prepared by one of L.A.'s most famous chefs, and a chance to cross-pollinate with a cornucopia of the city's political and cultural elite.

Lilly, the former US Attorney and Department of Justice's shooting star, had been conscripted to run for the office of California Attorney General. Host for the evening was a big-time talent manager whose clientele ranged from movie and television stars to famed athletes, a few who could be seen engaged in cocktails and conversation throughout the modern mid-century home. The interior was shallow, long, and sleekly remodeled with polished concrete to accentuate every angle. Contrasting the home's breathtaking horizontalism was the verticality of the mostly standing guests. The geometrically pleasing picture was not lost on Frankie Coleman. She couldn't ever roam far enough from her Tennessee trailer park to fully forget the grotesque confines of worn shag carpet and fake wood paneling.

With some three hundred or so Lilly Zoller supporters packing the property from the front door to the deck surrounding an infinity-styled pool, Frankie was having issues putting eyes on Denny. Someone as tall as he should've stood out like Snow White amongst her seven dwarves. Tired of waiting for him to exhume himself from whatever he was discussing with the man in the Cadillac El Dorado, Frankie had returned to one of the three hosted bars for a third cosmopolitan. At her request, each drink was more vodka-infused than the last. She wandered from room to room, overtly aware of her counterclockwise pattern. She needed to speak with Denny face to face and apologize for their last two encounters. She hadn't expected to run into him at the event. But once she'd caught sight of him across the immense sunken living room, Frankie had been angling for some clarifying words.

My dear Mister Cock-Asian must be avoiding me.

Shit, she then mouthed. For all Frankie knew, Denny had either left with the Cadillac man or already tipped the valet for his own car and shuffled off to his next destination.

Where? Home? Another cocktail meet and greet? An appointment with a different mistress?

"Frankie!" sounded Ram behind her, climbing the stairwell from the downstairs game room. Taking up the mayor's rear was Denny, lips clamped tightly as if he were being led to the executioner.

"*Raaaaam*," she dripped, red lips gliding across her perfect Miss-almost-America teeth.

The mayor's arm wrapped around Frankie's waist, drawing her close for a cheek kiss.

"Denny and I were checking out the man cave," he remarked.

"Do gay men have man caves?" joked Frankie, nervous and

knowingly off-color. "I mean, I know they're men 'n' all. But man caves I picture have big-screen TVs, beer taps, 'n' posters of swimsuit models spread across Lamborghinis."

"Yeah," answered Denny. "Just like that, only higher class. No chicks. No sports cars."

"Y'all saved me the trip down a set of stairs in heels too high for this time of day," she over-twanged.

"And perhaps one too many cosmos." Denny's joke was sharpened with a wink.

"Last one 'n' done, hon." Frankie raised her clear martini glass in gleaming reply.

"Lookee lookee. It's my Tuesday lunch bunch!" announced Catalina Rincon, squeezing her bantam frame past a huddled trio of former college football heroes.

"Cat!" exclaimed Ram, pleased and grinning his approval.

"And I brought a date," added Cat. "C'mon, big fellas. Let my man pass."

The former star players parted just enough for Lucky to join the circle. Attire for the party was L.A. casual, meaning Lucky was demonstrably underdressed.

"Lucky Dey?" introduced Cat. "Mayor Ramon Avila. Denny Teng. And this is Frankie Coleman."

"Good to meetcha," greeted Lucky, sporting an imposter's smile that looked surprisingly genuine. He gripped the mayor's hand then bypassed Denny's conspicuously open mitt in exchange for Frankie's trembling fingers. Lucky looked her dead in the eye and said in a way meant entirely to unnerve her, "How's that hangover?"

Frankie, who considered herself a skilled cocktail party socialista, suffered a sudden attack of confusion. It was out of body. She didn't recognize Lucky. Nor did his voice register any significant memory. She did, though, feel gooseflesh traveling south, from the base of her neck along the bones of her spine, spreading out to her thighs and forearms.

Then there was Denny Teng. He'd patiently offered his

friendly grip by rote, unthinkingly jutting his open palm forward
well before the name had fully registered. *Did she say his name
was Lucky Dey?* A bolt of electricity surged through him. His heart
skipped awkwardly before gearing into a speed twice its normal
rhythm. Denny's mind tripped backward, as if he were stumbling
in reverse back down those stone steps and into Babylon's Cadillac
El Dorado. How long ago had that been? Fifteen minutes? A full
half hour? It had been an unplanned confab, with the insistent city
detective forcing the Lucky Dey issue with discomforting urgency.

After an awkward meal at home with his wife and Min, Denny
had changed clothes into something that connoted Hollywood
aloof and hurried off to make an appearance at the fundraiser.
Supporting candidate Lilly Zoller wasn't even secondary on his
agenda. There was certain to be showbiz people there. Agents. Producers. Studio honchos. And Denny wanted them to know that
if the numbers were right, his cash was available for certain slices
of the movie game. No sooner had he handed off his keys to the
valet than his phone had begun to blow up with messages from
Babylon:

Where are you?

Gotta talk now!

Coming to you. Be avail!

Nearly forty minutes later, Denny had been seated in the
roomy passenger seat of Babylon's Cadillac, the burgundy leather
slick and cracking from years of wear, the emergency flashers
sounding with every electronic connection.

Tick-tick, tick-tick, tick-tick.

Even in the dull blink of amber light, the reddened lump
underneath Babylon's left eye shined as if polished with hard
wax. The detective had replayed both his morning and afternoon
encounters with Lucky, beginning with the one at UCLA and the

revelations concerning his comatose daughter, and finishing with the assault in his downtown office. That's when he showed Denny the drawing Lucky had left in the folder.

Min's drawing.

"What the hell is this supposed to be?" Babylon had forced. "And what does this have to do with our Lucky Dey problem?"

"Not *our* Lucky Dey problem. *My* problem."

"And you made *your* problem *my* problem by hiring me. You're holding out puts me in your shit. That's why this, right here and now, is your goddamn come-to-Jesus moment."

"The Jesus in this moment being you?" Denny had asked.

"I don't particularly dig gettin' my ass kicked in my own office by Lucky fuckin' Dey. Yeah, I'll be your Lord and fucking savior. All you gotta do is come clean and pay in cash."

With his hand still extended, frozen, and bypassed by Lucky for Frankie's, Denny sucked in a lungful of air and held his breath as the nightmare came to life, his personal devil in the flesh only feet away.

"Denny Teng," remarked Lucky. "Think we might've met."

"I don't recall being introduced..." claimed Denny.

"Wasn't me," defended Cat, jazz hands comically raised. Mayor Ram laughed at her gesture, hardly in on the joke, but instinctively trying to keep the conversation buoyant.

"You two are friends?" Frankie found herself asking, her index finger waving between Lucky and Cat.

"We go back a couple years," Lucky answered.

"Never thought he was the fundraiser type," Cat added with a wink.

"Politics? Rather have my eyes gouged out with a spork," smirked Lucky. "But then I heard Denny would be here so I got over my unease."

"So, you and Denny *do* know each other?" confirmed Mayor Ram, entirely lost on the social connectivity.

"I—" Denny began.

"Our daughters," Lucky cut in, "they know each other pretty good. And you know what I hear? Somebody…please ask me *what?*"

"What?" bit Frankie.

"That Denny's little girl is one hell of an artist," Lucky said.

To the others it appeared that Lucky's pointed finger, articulated in the guise of a pretend gun, was aimed at Denny's sternum. But both Denny and Lucky knew the location was off by a few inches. Lucky's eyes were fixed on Denny's shirt pocket, where Min's drawing remained folded.

Lucky may as well have been pushing a big red button. The picture in Denny's pocket was the only possible link between the hit and run and Denny Teng. Why? He still didn't know. But Lucky could practically smell the fight or flight pheromones leaking from Denny's pores.

"It's true," Denny swallowed. "My Min loves doing school art. She has such a huge imagination."

"Do you also have a kindergartner?" the mayor innocently asked.

"Almost eighteen," corrected Lucky. "She works part-time at the grade school. She's what they call a shadow."

"Shadow?" asked Cat. "What's that?"

"Teacher's assistant," said Denny, his hackles beginning to show in both tone and posture. "My Min says your girl hasn't been at school much this week."

"Car accident," chilled Lucky. "Hit 'n' run."

"Oh my," worried Mayor Ram. "I hope she's okay."

"Well, he's here, right?" injected Denny with a defending smile. "If it were serious he'd be by her side. She must be fine, I assume."

"So, that's how Mr. Teng goes through life?" shifted Lucky, a half step forward, chest out. "Assuming shit?"

"Mr. Mayor?" swerved Denny. "Did you know Lucky is one of your boys in blue?"

"Sheriff's," corrected Lucky. "We're the guys in the uniforms that look like park rangers instead of real police."

"So, technically, you're *not* one of mine," said Mayor Ram. "Sheriffs are County authority. All the same, deputy, your service is appreciated."

"But not for long. Right, Lucky? Retiring? Have I heard right?" recalled Denny from his debrief with Babylon. "Oh, wait. Isn't it more like they're buying you off to avoid any more million-dollar payouts for all the civil suits you've incurred?"

The tone had clearly flip-flopped from cordial to downright cutting. There was an awkward pause where nobody had a syllable to contribute.

"Funny thing about all that," shrugged Lucky, his words full of bite. "Nobody ever sent me a bill."

"So, what does a deputy do after retirement?" The mayor's question lifted in tenor, trying to segue out of the obvious rancor between the men.

"Maybe I'll turn debt collector," answered Lucky, his eyes never once leaving Denny's. "And I'll give you one guess where I'm making my first stop."

Lucky was pushing it. Not physically. At least not yet. Or in the way Gonzo had suggested—Lucky being Lucky. He was, though, shaking the tree to see if any fruit would fall—action in search of reaction.

"Know what? Been a pleasure bumping into you," snapped off Denny, open hand in a faux show of detente. "Time I rubbed shoulders with the candidate."

Touching Frankie by the elbow, Denny signaled for her to follow. Holding his hand, she was led deep into a crowd that had swollen into the hundreds. In a serpentine line, they appeared to be aimed for one of the hosted bars. But halfway across the room she stalled, heels dug in.

"That was him, wasn't it?" she forced.

"That was who?" Denny shot back.

"The man who wrote on my mirror!"

"Which brings up the question of how drunk were you last night that you didn't even recognize him?"

"Fuck you," she spat. "You wanna tell me what that was about back there?"

"No business of yours."

"You mean no business of ours?"

"It's personal," guessed Denny. "Nothing to do with us."

"Then why come at me?"

Denny ignored, pulling her again. Only Frankie yanked back, breaking the link while leaning into him with the harshest of scowls. Next, she pivoted as if on a high-fashion runway, and used the crowded space to create distance between herself and her sometime lover.

Mayor Ram found a reason to excuse himself, once again thanking Lucky for his service before kissing Cat on the cheek and shouldering his way back into the throng.

"That went well," joked Cat, lost as to the true gist of what had just transpired but feeling altogether used. "My guess is that you'll be leaving now?"

Her question sounded more like a strong suggestion.

"Arrived together," said Lucky. "Better we bug-out the same way."

"Maybe you didn't get my not-so-subtle drift," she hissed in only a half whisper. "Whatever milk you just spilled, I don't want any part of it."

"Walk out with me, get me to my car, and you and me are square. At least for now."

"For now? That's all the points I've earned?"

"Did you or did you not once nearly have me murdered?"

"My official answer is no. But can't say the present temptation isn't goddamn palpable."

Lucky gestured toward the front door. Cat began to snake her way there. Lucky followed until Frankie stepped out from a crush of flesh pressers and stepped in front of him.

"That was you, wasn't it?" she accused Lucky.

"Me what?" replied Lucky, despite being certain of her meaning.

"Last night. You were in my house," she clarified in no uncertain terms.

"Couldn't stand on your own," said Lucky. "So, yeah. I might've played Good Samaritan and helped you across the boulevard."

"Forgive me if I didn't say thanks. But what the hell was that about? The message in the mirror?"

"Ask your boyfriend."

"I did," she angered before pushing up so close to Lucky he could smell the vodka on her tongue.

In heels, Frankie was well over six feet and slightly taller than Lucky. *Gonzo territory*, he thought, *but with way more makeup.*

"Am I under some kind of investigation?" Frankie asked.

"I dunno," said Lucky. "Should you be?"

"Know what? I'm just a banker," she said, clearly fearful. "I'm not part of anything else that might be considered—"

"Criminal?" finished Lucky, as if setting a fishhook in her.

Her lips pressed together, tight, practically deflating their normal bloom. She was out of words.

"You heard your friend," gambled Lucky. "I'm on the way out. I'm no real threat to you unless—"

"Unless what?"

"Another time," promised Lucky.

Lucky left it there, tipping an imaginary hat before easing past Frankie to catch up with Cat Rincon. Frankie, standing well above the crowd, kept an eye on him until he'd completely disappeared out the front door. She spun again, twice turning a full three-sixty, this time on the lookout for Denny. Her head hurt from the dehydration induced by twenty-four hours of too much liquor followed by caffeine delivered via untold cups of coffee. That and her mental equilibrium had received one off-balance shove after the other.

Goddamn you, Denny, she pissed to herself, unconsciously

assigning tonnages of blame. *And goddamn you, Frankie, for placing your future in the hands of a con man.*

Frankie never found Denny. Seeking privacy, he'd made his way to the backyard and through a gate in the hedge that led to an unlit tennis court. There, in the dark, he dialed a number.

"Already?" Babylon answered his mobile phone.

"Thought about it. I think we should do it," said Denny, crossing the Rubicon that Lucky needed to be murdered.

"The thing we talked about just now?" confirmed Babylon. "When you were in my car?"

"Yeah," conceded Denny.

"You got a timetable for me?"

"Soonest," impressed Denny. "Yesterday, if I could."

"Consider it done."

Lucky tipped the valet five dollars, climbed into the passenger seat of Cat Rincon's convertible, and snapped the seat belt tongue into the receiver. There'd been no conversation whatsoever between the duo since they'd left through the front door. Lucky noted that every visible square inch of Cat's body appeared tension-struck, like that of a hostage but without obvious binds. Once behind the wheel of her own car and out of earshot of anybody from the party, the scrappy little operator was none too shy to express herself.

"That was fucking humiliating!" she seethed while pulling the switch that lowered the Audi's soft top, as if she were afraid Lucky's cop stink would overwhelm her. "For the life of me I don't know why you just didn't whip out your junk and pee on the man's shoes."

"Hmm," replied Lucky as if to imply that the option hadn't occurred to him and maybe wasn't such a bad idea.

"We are square, get me?" Cat carried on, full of grit. "I have more than made up for whatever you think I owe you."

"You wanna take this to mediation? I can find us a judge or a therapist—"

"Go screw yourself."

"And I thought we were getting along so good."

"Jesus!" she popped, almost unglued. "Why couldn't you have died that night with him?"

Lucky turned to face her. It was as close to a confession as he would ever receive from her. Nonetheless, he'd practically dragged her by the ponytail into that party and used her as both a shill and a shield. He was considering keeping his word that from then on—or until she transgressed again—her debt to him had been wiped clean.

Foot on the gas, Cat urged the Audi down the slope, barely braking into the right turn to Brookdale Lane. Lucky's '99 was where he had left it, grille aimed in the opposite direction. A canopy of drooping pepper trees blanketed an elbow-shaped section of the road, making good cover from helicopters, driveways, and the ubiquitous security cameras attached to most upscale neighborhood homes—which was exactly why Lucky had chosen it.

"Out!" ordered Cat before her foot had fully stomped on the brake.

Lucky unhitched his belt. His head swung left. He wanted to end the fake date with a pithy line like, "'Til we meet again." Instead, he settled on something more flattering.

"You did good," settled Lucky.

"More than I can say for—"

Cat's eyes swerved from the flood of her car's high beams, blasting what little asphalt could be seen through the dripping strands of pepper tree leaves. It was an intuitive move. Or maybe an impulse. She had inadvertently locked on to some movement in her rearview mirror.

Lucky's pupils flicked right to zero in on the sideview mirror. But the housing had been folded into the door. He hadn't time to wonder if it was something the valet had done to defend the car from damage. In his periphery, he caught a shadow crossing the faint cast of red from the Audi's taillights.

Whatever—or whoever—it was, they were closing in quickly.

Then came the scent of gun oil. Lucky's nostrils flared. In one move he twisted his neck left and away while throwing up his right arm past his own ear. His fingers felt the shooter's cuff the moment the trigger was pulled. *CRACK!* The muzzle sounded, rupturing Lucky's eardrum. Not knowing if he'd been struck by a bullet or not, Lucky hooked the man's arm under his own and pinned it to the top of the doorframe.

CRACK! CRACK! CRACK!

Three more shots busted the night air. Wild. Uncontrolled.

"DRIVE!" Lucky begged.

The car lurched ahead as if Cat were miles ahead of him. Lucky felt heat on his face, plus a fan of liquid, glass, and metal. He recalled sparks as the Audi bucked hard to the right, ditched and pitched, engine screaming, rear wheels spinning without road for purchase. Somehow he'd let go of the man's arm. The side of his head roared in pain as a double frequency sound—like that of a ten-story-high gong—kept ringing alongside a high-pitched hiss. The car was tilted to the right and angled down. Instead of throwing the lock and falling from the door, Lucky somehow rolled out over the frame, his right hand reaching for his ankle holster. In a blink, his junior-sized Sig .45 was in hand, leveled and sighted down the right rear of the car. Yet, in the wash of red brake lights, he saw nothing. No movement. No shadows. Only dust that hung in the air like a dirty sea mist.

"Stay down and in the car!" he ordered, feet under him and slinking along the ditch. He cleared the Audi's rear and backed onto the roadbed, his gun muzzle tracing the edges of dark.

Shit, thought Lucky. The assassin could still be there. Unconscious. Or lying in wait. Somewhere beyond the limits of the light. He needed Cat out of the car, huddled behind the door, and dialing 911. So, walking backward, Lucky rotated around to the driver's side.

"Can you get out?" he asked, short of breath. "Pop the door, stay low!"

Eyes and gun still trained in the direction of the attacker, Lucky used his left hand to feel along the door panel until he landed on the latch. He pulled and swung the door wide.

"Let's go! Let's go!" he urged, his left hand reaching to grab some part of her. He found her hair and his fingers were instantly slicked with goo. It was warm.

Then, at last, he looked.

The headlight beams, switched on high and directed into the ditch and pepper trees, reflected back a luminescent greenish-brown haze. Cat hung halfway out of the door, her body slung sideways, suspended by her seat belt. Her head lolled at the full reach of her neck's flexibility, a bloody cavity where her left eye used to be. Her other eyeball was exposed, lids wide, but blackened from an eight-ball hemorrhage. She was gone. Dead. Lucky knew it with zero ambiguity. Her nervous motors had been cut the moment the bullet had landed. Staying wary of the shadows, Lucky shoved a hand into his pocket for his cell phone. He didn't recall dialing the emergency digits. Nor even talking to the 911 operator. However, there would be a digital record in perpetuity of yet another Lucky Dey missive.

"Nine-nine-nine!" Lucky relayed, the code for *deputy needs help urgently*. "Shots fired! Civilian down! Suspect unknown! Brookdale and Fryman."

37

I'm your Lord and fucking savior. All you gotta do is pay in cash, is
what Babylon had said.

The moment the words floated across Babylon's tongue he'd
both savored and regretted them. His mother, the Jewish side of
his religious cocktail, would've slapped his cheek hard for blas-
pheming, leaving her fingerprints as a marked reminder. Even at
her advanced age she wasn't shy about poking him with a fork
or picking up the nearest object and hurling it at his head for
engaging his filthy mouth. The other side of him, the practical,
agnostic side he'd excused because of all his years as a rough trade
street cop, would never forget the look on Denny Teng's face. It
was priceless, witnessing the moment a man considered crossing
over into the ethos of a killer. The realization of it all. Denny's lips
and cheekbones had lost all artifice in a slackening of skin as the

man's face turned blank with remorseless resolve. But Denny had wavered, replying that he needed time to think. And despite not being asked, Babylon had included the price tag and given his client a number to chew on. $100,000. It was a high-dollar ask. Then again, Babylon reminded him that the target was a cop. A fellow sheriff's deputy. Any remorse Babylon imagined he might suffer came with an automatic upcharge.

Or so he excused.

Since leaving his downtown office, Babylon knew the Reaper was a few cars behind his Yom Kippur Clipper—loosely tailing him, as if magnetically pulled along in his wake. Though Babylon hadn't actually seen Lucky's face behind the wheel of the darkened Crown Vic, Babylon had a keen eye for cars. His connection at the DMV had found the make and model of the vehicle registered to Lucky Dey. After receiving Lucky's hard fist to his face and the child's drawing, Babylon figured Lucky was doing more than playing defense. If Lucky were smart—at least as smart as Babylon—he'd do what Babylon would do: squeeze hard and watch to see what the subject does next. So, it was no shock that Lucky had followed him all the way to the Fryman Canyon party.

In a matter of hours, his two-thousand-dollar private eye gig had ballooned into a fifty-fold bounty on Lucky's head. A bargain, reasoned Babylon, considering the obvious complications that came with killing for hire. Over his post–police officer career, he'd arranged only three such hits. With a sage understanding of nearly every in and out of a successful snuff ploy, Babylon had planned each to the micro-moment, enlisting help from a number of trusted lawmen, all retirees, each a sworn member of the Lynwood Viking brotherhood. Babylon always split his fees down to the penny with his accomplices.

After giving Denny Teng the curious drawing, Babylon had driven right by Lucky's double-parked Crown Vic. He had cruised a few hundred yards down the slope, before backing the Caddy into a driveway, cutting his headlights, and wheeling back up the hill. From a darkened distance he'd watched Lucky step

out of his Crown Vic to converse with a petite woman in a red
Audi convertible. She had followed Lucky's Crown Vic to nearby
Brookdale Lane, a winding hillside street that dead-ended after
less than a mile. After Lucky had parked, Babylon watched Lucky
squeeze into the woman's car for the quarter-mile return to the
party's valet stand.

There was nowhere he had to be, so Babylon decided to wait
for Lucky to return to his car, and tuned his radio to the Dodgers'
season opener. *God*, he thought. *I so miss Vin Scully*. The Hall of
Fame broadcaster had been in Babylon's ear for his entire life. Five
months out of every year, Vin's soothing play-calling of America's
game had been a constant. A serviceable former ESPN stalwart
and a once-great Dodger had replaced baseball's Dutch uncle and
provided enough audio wallpaper to allow Babylon space to ponder. Scheme. Contemplate the options for the Lucky problem he
had yet to fully understand.

Then, during the seventh-inning stretch, the call had come.
Denny Teng wanted the deed done. There came a rush of blood to
Babylon's brain and with it a heady notion. Opportunity. By park-
ing in a secluded spot, Lucky had chosen a residential blind spot
perfect for an ambush. It was a titillating prospect. Efficient. And
Babylon wouldn't have to split the $100,000.

Perhaps his rush to pull off the murder by himself had been
informed by the throbbing ache Babylon felt under his left eye. It
pissed him off. Sucker punched by a fellow deputy. A Reaper, no
less. Babylon shook the feeling off. He was, after all, an old hand at
skullduggery. He wouldn't make an emotional mistake.

No. Not me.

In the dark, Babylon had circled back to the Caddy's spacious
trunk. Inside was a brand-new golf bag loaded with good inten-
tions to learn the game. It had been gifted to him by a famous
PGA tour pro for whom he'd relieved a few "female problems."
Babylon had never gotten beyond the lesson stage. He did recall,
though, that he'd stuffed a Gore-Tex rain suit in a side pocket of

the bag. The pants and zippered jacket were designed to be slipped on over a golfer's clothes. With latex gloves and a baseball hat pulled low, Babylon would be unrecognizable and impossible to ID by witnesses, CSIs, or hidden video cameras. For his getaway, he disconnected the tiny bulbs that illuminated the Cadillac's rear license plate.

Babylon armed himself with a vintage AMT .380-caliber pistol. Palm-sized. The gun was from his collection of weapons confiscated from Lynwood gangbangers during his years on the job. Untraceable. *Back pocket throw-downs* just in case a fellow Viking needed to put a gun in the hand of a bad boy who came up shot by a cop but with no *pistola* in hand.

Cloaked by a redundancy of darkness, the rain suit, and a four-foot stand of blooming desert paintbrush, Babylon crouched near Lucky's Crown Vic and reminded himself to stay present. If the situation didn't unfold cleanly, he wouldn't make a move. Plan A would be back on track. He kept his mind busy, imagining plots, situations, circumstances ripe for Lucky's end. The most opportune places and times. He was sketching out a possible motorcycle-assisted assassination like those often utilized in South America when the headlights flared. A car was rising up the first of two steep turns. The shadows of those dripping pepper tree branches skittered to the right in a sweeping pattern. Babylon glimpsed a red reflection. It had to be the Audi returning Lucky to his Crown Vic.

And that's when the flaw revealed itself.

The plot had seemed so perfectly simple. Lucky would return to his parked car and when he keyed the door, his back would be turned, his primary hand engaged. That was when Babylon would step from the darkness, calmly cross the twenty feet of blacktop, and unload all six shots of the .380 into his target. But the Audi put a serious wrinkle in Babylon's plan. After dropping Lucky off, that pixie of a woman would probably continue up the hill to turn her car around. By the time she U-turned and headed back down,

Lucky would be lying in a bloody heap, dead on the blacktop. Predictably, she'd stop and dial 911. Upon questioning, she might recall seeing a highly identifiable Cadillac at the top of the hill.

The flaw in Babylon's fast-hatched plot hadn't yet crossed the synapse from subconscious thought to reason. Before he could reach the sensible mental reply to *abort, quit, walk away*, a secondary contingency had presented itself. Despite the spring chill and dew point, the woman's soft-top was down. As she slowed to stop parallel to Lucky's car, Babylon found himself only yards from his target—and far closer than he'd anticipated to the back of Lucky's exposed head.

Only later would Babylon be reminded of an axiom he'd once coined for Viking recruits:

Trusting your instincts doesn't mean every instinct deserves your trust.

Before he could second-guess his already clouded judgment, Babylon emerged from cover, stepped onto the road's shoulder, and calmly walked toward the Audi. He recalled the car's exhaust steaming the air, obscuring the cherry ember from the applied brake lights. He quickened his pace, raised the pistol, and pushed the muzzle at Lucky's right ear while squeezing the trigger. The dirty Viking could've sworn he'd hit his bull's-eye with the first shot.

The rest was a blurry mess. Babylon knew instantly that his arm had been dislocated. His shoulder socket had popped when Lucky had somehow managed to pull his gun to the side and pinned his limb. Babylon didn't remember any more trigger pulls, though evidence would later prove he'd emptied the magazine. The Audi jolted forward and ditched. Babylon felt as if his arm had been torn clean from his torso—like he'd received a heavy jolt of electricity. He was in the drainage ditch, his face smothered in dirt and wet leaves. From there he crawled forward, around the front carriage of the Audi, up alongside the road until it curved to the right. He didn't know how far. Behind, he heard Lucky's shouts and a phone call to the emergency operator. The woman had been shot. *Was she injured or dead?* When he reached his Cadillac, Babylon made certain the headlights remained extinguished. He turned the ignition, geared it into reverse, and slowly backed up the hill, guided only by the twin white backup lights. At the first turnout, he flipped the car around and drove normally, climbing up Brookdale Lane for nearly two miles until it dead-ended at a fire road just below Mulholland. There he parked and switched off his lights. After stripping out of the rain suit and rubber gloves, he balled them up and pitched everything into a roll-away debris container on the street in front of a house under construction.

The mistakes were already piling up. But instead of berating himself and sinking further into an all-consuming swill of regret, Babylon set his imagination on how the LAPD would respond. The 911 call would summon the nearest black-and-white units. By the sound of the sirens, they were already closing in on the crime scene—LAPD plus fire department first responders. The arriving cops would set up a cordon, ribboning the crime scene with yellow tape and road barricades. Robbery-homicide detectives would be dispatched from nearby Van Nuys. That would take fifteen minutes tops, unless the investigators were busy elsewhere. Once the detectives took possession of the striped half acre, some of the uniforms would search for signs of a single or multiple assailants, witnesses, and the all-important home-security footage.

Babylon was certain that his ill-conceived attack hadn't been anywhere close to an incriminating camera lens. His easy-to-spot white Caddy, dark as it was, might've been recorded driving up the street. Suspicious? For certain. But not incriminating—especially if Babylon was nowhere to be found during the initial search. He emptied his bladder in some nearby brush, opened the trunk, locked the doors to the Cadillac, pushed his golf clubs aside, and crawled into the trunk, pulling the lid shut. It was a clever move. Babylon knew that the most any cop would do was flashlight the interior, record and process the license plate tag number for wants and warrants, and drive off.

Four hours, figured Babylon. Maybe five. With complications?

Six hours at the most. He could wait that out. Lying in the dark of the trunk, he opened a police scanner app on his cell phone, tuned it to the LAPD's Valley Division, and plugged in the single earpiece he often used to listen to Dodgers games. The chatter would tell him when the coast was clear. His mistakes would most likely fall by the wayside. Then he could carry on.

38

For Lucky it wasn't so much a sinking feeling. It was more a sense of having already being sunk. Bottomed out. Swallowed by a wave and stuck in a churn of sand with the taste of salt burning the back of his throat. To make matters incredibly worse, nearly five months to the day after his last violent conflagration, he was in the very same LAPD station, in the exact same interrogation room, being questioned by the very same robbery-homicide detective in regards to yet another Lucky Dey–involved murder.

"Jesus," said the detective Lucky had nicknamed Mr. TV Detective for his actor good looks and streaks of gray in his comb of jet-black hair. "You really are some kinda human shit magnet, aren't you?"

Tell me about it, sighed Lucky to himself.

He was aware there was a video recording being made of the

interview. Considering what his civil attorney had advised, he chose to be circumspect about his answer to the detective's question.

"Seriously, dude," continued the detective. "In my career? Never seen a cop get dipped in it as much as you."

"That a question that pertains to your investigation?" annoyed Lucky. "Or just a sum-up of my lousy character?"

"Just feel for ya," shrugged the detective. "Wouldn't wanna be ya. Like that." He rapped the metal table with his knuckles then rose to his feet in a demonstration that the interview had concluded.

Like that, repeated Lucky to himself.

"Ear okay?" asked the detective, pointing to his own ear.

"Still buzzing." Lucky knew he'd suffered some sort of tear in his right eardrum. He felt fluid leaking, draining like it would after being held under by a bad wave. To muffle the fizzle that accompanied every tiny noise, he'd wet a tissue and wadded it into his ear canal.

His equilibrium had been screwed with.

He'd spent hours at the Van Nuys station. From stem to stern he'd pored over the events of the evening, doing his level best to minimize his sins of omission. The story he told was accurate enough. He'd attended the political event as a guest of the victim, Catalina Rincon. They'd met near the address. To save on valet costs, they'd come and gone from the fundraiser in Cat's convertible. At the party he'd been introduced to a number of people including Mayor Ramon Avila, Denny Teng, and Frankie Coleman. In his signed and recorded statements, Lucky suggested that though he never saw the attacker, he was the most likely target considering the first bullet appeared meant for him. Cat Rincon, in his estimation, was an accident—the would-be assassin's collateral damage. To verify his story, the CSIs at the scene had performed gunshot residue tests on both Lucky's hands and face.

As for who and why someone might want to kill Lucky, he'd let the obvious be his answer: his less-than-noble history. After all, Mr. TV Detective had said it himself. Lucky Dey was a human shit magnet. Why else would the Sheriff's Department have been looking to flush him down the nearest toilet?

Excluded from his recollections were his motives, his suspicions regarding Denny Teng, and his involvement with Karrie's hit and run and former Sheriff's Deputy Mark Baba, as well as any elements of his one-man-mission to rip the skin off the truth. Lucky's gut was screaming that Denny Teng was the culprit who wanted to cap him for getting too close. But too close to what? Lucky was in the dark. But he'd venture an educated guess that the gunman had been either Babylon himself or one of his old Viking associates.

"You're free to go," ushered the detective, holding the interview room's door open.

Invitation aside, Lucky remained seated, his eyes stuck on the same point of reference he'd noticed during his last stint in that confined room. Just left of the doorjamb was a defect in the drywall—the shape of a balled fist. Despite having been painted over, the impression was clear. Interrogation spaces were usually built with soundproof insulation, the sheetrock nailed and sealed to a solid surface. Lucky imagined that whoever had been angry enough to punch the wall had probably walked away from the frustrated incident with a shattered hand. He couldn't help but think that, given the right kind of push, the wall fossil could easily have belonged to him.

Before carving a hard left down the fluorescent-striped corridor, Lucky glimpsed Frankie Coleman waiting outside the women's restroom, anxiously ping-ponging from wall to wall. *Smoker*, he pegged. Nicotine deprived. Anxious. Craving a cigarette. As he took the stairs he wondered who else the PD had dragged from the party to the division. Everybody Cat Rincon and Lucky had come in contact with? Or only those they could get their hands on? It was a long list, a paper-load for detectives to sort through. Add to that Cat Rincon's history and enemies list and there just might've been enough dust in the air for the spotlight to shift away from Lucky.

Please, Jesus, to anywhere but my thing.

It was a minute past midnight when Lucky's boots carried him out of the Van Nuys cop shop and into the night air. The division HQ opened to a grass and concrete plaza fronted by two courthouse buildings on the southern side—a ten- and a seven-story structure. Opposite were a public library and one of the city attorney's offices. Sandwiched between were tended trees and a park-like atmosphere so dimly lit that anybody, unless armed, might express the need for an escort.

At least he was outside. The open air softened the pressure on his ruptured ear. To his immediate right was the east courthouse's back patio. Lucky stuffed the hard memories that lay there and headed for the curb, where he hoped his Uber would be waiting. His Crown Vic, caught inside the yellow-ribboned crime scene cordon, was considered part of the investigation. No telling how long before the car would be returned. Before being escorted to the Van Nuys Division Station, Lucky had requested to remove one item from his vehicle: Karrie's backpack. This allowed him to disable the booby-trapped pepper spray canisters underneath the '99's trunk lid without the CSIs getting a surprise face full of chemical capsicum. After the backpack had been photographed he was free to leave with it. The item had either sat innocently at his feet or been slung across his shoulder ever since.

As he approached a streetlamp, his good ear heard the quick clicking of footsteps from behind. High heels. *Frankie Coleman*, he rightly guessed. He half turned to the left, catching her rushing into the light like a missile closing on its target.

"You 'n' me!" she spat. "We need to talk right now!"

Lucky knew that look well, a lanky, long-legged woman on the warpath. Her sharpened eyebrows narrowed over a pair of angry eyelashes. He knew he didn't have to reply before another salvo was launched.

"'Bout time someone explains to me just what the Jesus is going on!" she seethed.

"Someone's dead," Lucky said, all affect dried from his tongue. "There's an investigation. That's what cops do."

"Before that!" she cleared. "Last night. This morning. Tonight. I don't know you. But you show up and all my shit hits the fan."

"All your shit?" Lucky repeated.

The misty air made it appear as if they were standing in an illuminated cone cast from a high overhead lamp. Spotlit.

"Who the fuck are you?" she circled, jabbing a finger at Lucky's sternum. The pointed gesture thickened his feeling of being totally exposed.

"Got a car?" Lucky asked.

"What's that have to do with what I asked you?"

"I need a ride. You need answers." The sideways query left Frankie searching for context. So, Lucky explained while holding up his cell phone, the app's map aglow with his driver's approach. "Waiting for an Uber 'cause my car's part of the crime scene."

"You creep. You want a ride after what you did to my bathroom mirror?"

"Fine," shrugged Lucky. "I'll just wait here."

Frankie spun on a sharpened heel.

"I give you a ride and you answer everything? Ev—ree—thing!"

"Over the hill. Westwood," Lucky nodded. "I got somebody in the hospital."

"No funky business," she warned.

"As long as we got between here and UCLA?" Lucky said. "Give you all the answers you want."

"I'm in the parking structure," Frankie pointed.

Lucky indicated for her to lead the way. He trailed her across Delano Street to the three-story concrete structure, where she'd parked on the first floor. The space was dangerously dark, a veritable trap for vulnerable women either coming or going from their vehicles. Lucky had already strongly instructed Karrie on how unsafe it was to park in certain locations. And even though both

Karrie and Gonzo could clearly take care of themselves, neither would have been foolish enough to have selected Frankie's parking spot. It left Lucky wondering if Miss Tennessee was myopic or just plain dumb.

The Porsche SUV's lights double-flashed as Frankie unlocked the car remotely. She climbed into the driver's seat while Lucky circled around the vehicle, scraping his gaze over the dim concrete for potential dangers. He'd already escaped one attempt on his life. He wasn't going to bet against a second attack.

The car smelled of new leather, the upholstery as creamy as Frankie's skin. She pressed the ignition button. Before she could put it in gear, Lucky touched her hand. She instinctively recoiled.

"Don't back out," he eased. "Not yet."

"You said between here and Westwood—"

"Change of plan," said Lucky. "Talk first. Drive after."

"Okay—"

"You wired?" Lucky asked.

"Wired?" she shook her head. "What?"

"How do I know you're not wearing a wire?"

"I'm not. Why would I be—"

"You just spent two hours with LAPD detectives."

"Answering some uncomfortable goddamn questions."

"So, answer my uncomfortable question. Are you wired?"

"No."

Lucky found the lever that opened the Cayenne's sunroof. There was a sleek hum as the panel retreated ten inches.

"Phone," said Lucky. "On the roof."

In a show of good faith, Lucky stuck his own device through the space, setting it on the SUV's roof.

"Gotta pay to play," prodded Lucky.

"Whatever," moaned Frankie, extracting her phone from her purse.

"Let's make it the whole damn purse. For safety's sake," said Lucky, hands waiting.

She relinquished her bag, a Prada number, and Lucky placed it on the roof and toggled the switch for the panel to close.

"Okay. First question" said Frankie. "Why me? What do I have to do with all this shit?"

"Not yet."

"Not yet what?"

"Listen to me carefully," he said, deadly in his seriousness. "Whatever you do. Don't flinch."

"Don't wha—"

Faster than she could imagine, Lucky shot his left arm out and snagged her wrist. Vise-like, as if in the unyielding jaws of a pit bull. The grip was so firm that she stiffened, but didn't retreat. He slid his right hand up the sleeve of her blouse, felt around her collar and down her other arm. Next he undid her top two buttons and began working his fingers around the architecture of her bra.

"This is called assault," she burned.

"This is called looking for a listening device," explained Lucky. "What you did to me last night after I helped you to your front door? You grabbing my junk? *That* was assault, but I'm not going to file a complaint."

Nearly finished, he twisted her away from him and ran his hands along her shoulders, working down to the small of her back.

"Satisfied?" she said, buttoning up her blouse.

"For now."

"And how do I know *you're* not wearing a wire?"

"You don't," he said, digging into the backpack.

"Fine. Foreplay's over. You wanna tell me what this is all about now?"

"It's all about why my daughter is in the ICU. Screws drilled into her skull," said Lucky before aiming his index finger like a gun barrel at the side of his head. "It's about your man, Denny Teng, trying to put a bullet in my ear."

"No, no," she shook her head. "It wasn't him. He was at the party—"

"Quid pro quo time," switched Lucky, fingers snapping. "Denny Teng. Him, you, everything right here and now."

Frankie swallowed. A heavy lump traced her elegant neck.

"You're a cop," she said, as if it were her excuse for caution.

"Not after this week. And I don't give a rat's ass anymore. You're gonna to tell me all of it. Now."

"I don't know anything—"

"That's probably what you just said to the LAPD. But I know that's a lie. Same as you didn't tell them about you and me last night. Otherwise they'd have tag-teamed us both until we were locked into different stories."

"You don't know shit about what I said."

"I know the only reason Denny Teng would wanna have me dead is because he thinks I'm a threat. You just spent two hours getting questioned by cops. When he finds out...and that's only if he already doesn't know...who's gonna be the bigger threat? You? Or me?"

"Maybe I'm not a threat because he's as afraid of me as I am of him."

"Keep telling yourself that."

"Why did you do that to me?" she elevated. "What you did at my house?"

"I've got nothin' but my girl in a coma and my gut telling me Denny Teng had something to do with it. I pushed your buttons. My guess is what followed is that you pushed his."

"Of course I did!" she spat. "What does my business have to do with any of this?"

"You tell me."

"I'm just a private banker. Denny Teng is one of my depositors. That's all."

"He's scared 'cause he's dirty," surmised Lucky. "You're scared because you're dirty. I can smell it on the both of you."

"That's bullshit."

"Know what? Whether you're washing his cash or his goddamn underwear? I seriously don't fucking care. Really. I don't. I just wanna know why one minute I'm sittin' on a wave. And the next, my girl's nearly dead."

Frankie leaned hard against the door, pressed against it as if to make the most of what little distance she could find. She wanted to pull the lever, get out, and start running. Anywhere. In any direction as long as it was away from him. But he was in *her* car. She'd *invited* him inside. She thought of tripping the car alarm. Or pounding on the horn to alert somebody. Anybody. A woman crying rape was a surefire route to attention.

Then it was as if he'd read her mind.

"You could do that," he agreed, hushed.

"Do what?" she defended.

"Sound an alarm. Make it look like I'm assaulting you. Just more fuel to the fire. That woman who was murdered tonight? She had powerful friends. It's gonna get real investigated. Your dirty laundry? Mine? It's all getting a good, long sniff."

Lucky pulled one of Min Lee's cryptic drawings from out of Karrie's backpack. He held it up for Frankie to see.

"Do you know what this is?"

"No."

"Look harder."

"What's to see? It's kiddie art."

"But what's it about?"

Frankie could only shake her head. Lost. Lucky could see it on her face, her posture. Zero recognition. The picture meant nothing at all to her.

39

San Gabriel.

Denny Teng couldn't sleep.

Since the LAPD had claimed it was required to interview nearly the entire cocktail party, those swept up in the investigation were shuttled off to different divisions and divvied up amongst the available robbery-homicide detectives. Denny waited nearly two hours for his interview. Making matters even more insulting, a junior detective had mistaken him as one of the parking valets who'd been working the event.

At last he'd returned home, entered through the kitchen door in the dark, slipped off his loafers, and padded up the antique stairs. Usually, that late at night he paid mind to the squeaky boards, sometimes gaming himself into a near creak-less climb. It was all about Min. If the little girl heard her daddy, she'd wake and cry out for him. Ignoring his own rules about a quiet entry, he'd already let the back door slam. Topsy the Chihuahua was atop the stairs, barking.

"Shut up, Topsy," Denny had hissed.

Despite the racket, Min miraculously did not wake. But Jiao did.

"Go back to sleep," Denny demanded, letting his tone indicate that a marital battle at two in the morning was not going to happen. He shucked his clothes on the bathroom floor, showered, and eventually climbed naked into bed. Tired as he was, his mind hurtled ahead without slowing.

After ordering up the murder, Denny had segued back into social mode. When the rumor floated that a homicide had taken place just down the road, Denny somehow knew. It was as if within seconds after giving Babylon the go-ahead, his command had been obeyed. Could Babylon really have worked that quickly? Jesus! Worried gossip travelled through the party like a savannah fire. When uniformed LAPD officers entered the house, Denny's armpits dripped with perspiration. The room had begun to swim. Feeling light-headed, he worked to control his breath.

When word returned that the victim was none other than Catalina Rincon, it came as hard as a slap across the face. The LAPD was being tight-lipped and Denny didn't know what to think. Was it a coincidence? Or had Denny's crime gone sideways? The LAPD peeled off patrons one by one for initial questioning— a form of investigative triage. Surely the police would eventually land on guests who'd been seen with Cat Rincon. His thoughts whipsawed to both Frankie and Mayor Ram, whom Denny later discovered had slipped out of the event with his bodyguards. So had most of the other luminaries, Lilly Zoller included. From a distance he'd watched Frankie escorted out the front door by a uniformed female officer. When it came his turn to respond to the queries, he had chosen to stick to the simplest truth. He didn't know the victim well, but during the party they'd shared some small talk. That was all there was to tell.

At LAPD's downtown Parker Center, Denny had been

required to be more descriptive regarding his brief encounter with Cat Rincon and Lucky Dey. Again, he kept his facts plain and on the surface, except for the places where he continued to drop Mayor Ramon Avila's name, hoping to paint himself with the same untouchable brush strokes. Yet as often as he mentioned the mayor, the downtown police detectives showed equal measure of disinterest.

As he lay in bed, Denny pushed away his fear of getting caught up in the murder by pure will. It was a mental exercise. He'd picture his fear—himself in handcuffs, incarcerated. Then he'd freeze it, box it up, label it to some distant address, and ship it off via a white and orange FedEx package. It was one of the many self-actualization techniques he'd read about on those crushing flights to Hong Kong and Shanghai. With practice, he'd employed his developed skills in his daily routine. His notable calmness and ease hadn't come naturally. They had been learned, mastered.

However, once his anxiety over the murder subsided, his brain was overtaken by a secondary, more subversive emotion. It had been crystal clear that the LAPD had excluded the party's political and celebrity elite from their dragnet. The *names*, so to speak, had been allowed their cars and their liberty. Denny hadn't. Worse, he'd been mistaken for a service employee. When he tried to visualize his worry, the picture kept dissolving into a crayon-like drawing his five-year-old daughter had dreamed up. There were no lemon-yellow suns, though. The artwork he saw when his eyelids shut was a sparkling image of downtown Los Angeles, the skyline in happy hues. Between the city and a tall, socket-faced stick figure that was him lay a black scribbled chasm. Hard as he tried with every mental purge, the drawing returned, the bottomless gorge deepening with every rendering.

Denny could've taken some prescribed sleeping meds—the ones that helped with the time zone changes that came with his business travel. Instead, he abandoned his bed and stepped through the gauzy bedroom curtains onto the balcony that overlooked his backyard. He descended the twisting, spiral staircase, the semi-darkness cloaking his nakedness. He crossed the basketball court to the garage and keyed the combination to open the retractable door. Ducking under before it had fully opened, he used the sound of that buzzing old refrigerator to guide him through the blackness to his home office.

The leather of his desk chair felt cool and sticky against his bare skin. He turned to the monitor with the security cameras, those nine external lenses revealing little more than hovering gnats. Using the keyboard as a toggle, he switched the screens to the interior cameras he'd secreted inside the house, ostensibly to keep an eye on Min's babysitters. But the voyeur in him had shifted his focus to following the movements of his wife. Jiao hadn't a clue her husband had been spying. Denny rolled his chair over to the lone computer on the folding banquet table and punched up a series of keyboard passwords to engage his most private hard drive. Once the system was fully booted and his monitors aglow, he performed an encrypted search for a special drawer. A list of numbered files unfolded on the left screen. All videos. With a mouse click, the right-hand screen lit up with a high-definition image in a 16:9 aspect ratio. The wide-angle laptop lens had recorded Denny's first home invasion heist.

My virgin voyage.

Because his safety depended on his fingerprints being miles away, Denny had armed Howie and his crew with a laptop as an intimidating, all-powerful eye. It was certain to terrify the FOBs. Fear of an all-knowing communist regime linked to the camera's lens would overwhelm the average paranoid Chinese newbie into instant compliance. After all, they were from a culture where neighbor spied on neighbor. From his backyard office, Denny could observe. Learn. He would give notes to Howie in the aftermath.

During that first invasion, Denny's fingers had trembled—not with fear, but sheer exhilaration. It reminded him of his teenage years and the anticipation of sexual intercourse. His breathing had shallowed. His heartbeat elevated. And when the robbery was over and the video feed extinguished, Denny had been embarrassed to discover he was left with an erection.

From that day on, he never missed an event, sometimes even pleasuring himself to the live images of families pleading for their lives in high-pitched Mandarin or Cantonese.

That dark shit turned me on like nothin' else, he sadly confessed to himself.

He'd originally planned to erase the video files, but instead had kept all of them—locked away behind firewalls, encryptions, and complicated, impossible-to-break passcodes.

My personal porn, he had excused. *Mine.*

Naked, with his heart pounding and perspiration dripping, Denny dared himself to execute the program he'd installed to destroy the evidence. Once he'd chosen to relegate the files to the digital shredder, each multi-hour robbery would be reduced to virtual dust, impossible to reassemble. The ultimate delete.

But could he? They were, after all, his trophies. Fifty-seven robberies in all, representing more than twenty-eight million dollars of pure, untaxed, untraceable cash, expertly laundered through the electronic tills of Frankie Coleman's bank.

40

Sherman Oaks.

True to her promise, Frankie drove Lucky to the UCLA Medical Center. Expressing his preference for surface streets, Lucky directed her through Beverly Glen, a canyon that cut through the natty neighborhoods of Sherman Oaks and the estates of Bel-Air. As they wound their way up the Santa Monica Mountains, Lucky's eyes ticked off a landmark only crime buffs or cops would know—the forested, hairpin turn where Tex Watson had tossed the gun he'd used to kill Rosemary and Leno Labianca, just one night after he and the other Manson-ettes had slaughtered pregnant Sharon Tate. As if Lucky needed another murderous connection in his life.

"Tell me about your daughter," broke in Frankie in an attempt to disturb the silence.

Lost in his thoughts, Lucky didn't answer.

"Your little girl?" continued Frankie. "The one who's hurt?"

"Not so little," said Lucky.

"How old again?" she asked, relieved to have perhaps jump-started a conversation.

"Seventeen."

"Senior? High school?"

"Coma. In the hospital," replied Lucky as a way of putting a cork in the subject.

"When you're at the hospital," she added, undaunted, "maybe you should get that bad ear looked at."

Lucky's phone buzzed and he checked the screen. Despite not recognizing the number, he answered, "This is Lucky."

"Deputy Dey?" returned the woman's voice. "I'm Sergeant Hidalgo from down in Southwest Comm."

Lucky's brain auto-mapped the call as if he had a GPS locator implanted in his hypothalamus. As a trainee he'd been required to build territorial street grids in his gray matter and be able to zero in on a street address in an eyeblink. Southwest Comm was a small community station housed on MLK between Western and Normandie Avenues. After hours getting grilled by detectives in the Van Nuys Division, why the hell was some Southwest Comm sergeant calling him in the wee morning hours?

"What can I do for you, sergeant?" he replied cautiously.

"Quiet night down here," said the sergeant. "I'm just reading through the dailies and I see you left a voice note with one of my day officers regarding any hits under known nicknames and aliases—and forgive me if I'm reading this wrong—a Mister Chihuahua?"

"Monster Chihuahua," corrected Lucky, partially relieved that the call was nothing related to the ambush or the still-dead Cat Rincon. "My thinking was it might've been a gang name or something in the database."

"Probably not your guy," she said.

"Who's probably not my guy?" queried Lucky, just to play it out.

"I'm only reading," she said. "But I got a gunshot vic near

the Coliseum. In the report it says while in the trauma center and under sedation, the vic was possibly identifying his shooter as a 'Mister Aloha.' "

"Mister Aloha," repeated Lucky, just to make certain he'd heard right.

"It reads that 'the vic was mumbling.' Like I said, he was sedated. Thought it might be something, but now that I look at it I'm thinking I shouldn't have risked waking you up. Sorry."

"Don't be," said Lucky, curious.

Was he grasping at straws yet again?

"The vic a walkout or has he been admitted?" he asked.

"Downtown," she said. "California Hospital. Victim's name is...wait...had it under here...Okay...Got it. Vic's name is a known gang associate. Maleek Radon Lewis."

Inside Lucky, a bell clanged.

"Crip affiliate?" confirmed Lucky. "Goes by Lil Rod?"

"With tattoos to match, at least according to my officer's shitty typing skills," relayed the sergeant.

"Really appreciate it," said Lucky.

"Monster Chihuahua," she laughed. "If that's a gang name, it's a friggin' winner."

No sooner had Lucky hung up than he gestured with a finger point in front of Frankie's nose.

"Change of destination," he said. "Make a left up here on Mulholland."

"I said I'd take you to UCLA." Frankie's voice had turned from inquisitive and conversational to immediate and terse. "C'mon."

"Think of me as a friend," issued Lucky. "As in *you're making a friend* by helping me out. Friends help friends, right?"

"Were you *friends* with Cat Rincon?" The cutting in Frankie's voice was obvious.

"Nope."

"Coulda fooled me. Didn't she introduce you as her date?"

"It was a bullshit play. She owed me. Getting me into the party was just her paying down a debt."

"And look where it got her." If her words were meant as daggers aimed at Lucky's conscience, each hit the mark.

Nevertheless, Frankie reluctantly made the sweeping left onto the twisting tightrope that was Mulholland Drive. The two lanes scored a serpentine route across the top of the Santa Monica Mountains. For the shortest glimpse, the lights from the Valley on the left and the Basin on the right were visible. The view beckoned.

"Eyes on the road," reminded Lucky.

"Quid pro quo," she shot back.

Lucky mulled over a response. That's if he was going to answer at all. Eyes forward, he watched the white from the halogen headlamps sweep the mix of desert scrub, mailboxes, and iron-gated drives.

"She tried to have me killed," said Lucky, final and flat. He caught Frankie glancing his way. Her face was hardened.

"So, this is a thing of yours?" she asked, incredulity straining her voice. "People trying to have you killed?"

"Yeah…" he eventually conceded. "It's a thing."

The California Hospital Medical Center was one of Los Angeles's oldest infirmaries. The original house of healing had long since been replaced by a nine-story brick façade just a few short blocks from downtown's convention center. In those early hours it was shrouded in a sticky fog that appeared to radiate from the atmospheric light spilling from the surrounding skyscrapers. Just beyond the red-and-white glow of the emergency entrance, Lucky slid from the Cayenne's passenger seat, boot soles touching the asphalt.

"Thanks for going out of your way," said Lucky. And he meant it.

"Did I really have a choice?" Frankie asked, her voice more syrupy sweet than aggrieved.

"Always a better way to imagine things," he said. "Thinking there's a choice and all that."

"What happens next?"

"You go home. Hope your phone doesn't ring."

"What about my bank?"

"What about it?"

"Do I have a problem with you?" she asked.

"Did your bank have anything to do with what happened to my daughter?" postured Lucky.

"Not a damn thing."

"Then you and me don't have a problem."

"Well, all right…" Frankie revealed a hopeful smile, this despite the beauty in her looking as if drained from every vessel. Lucky could see her age was creeping in, as well as loneliness.

It was nearly 3:15 a.m. He'd thanked her, but the parting was as awkward as everything else in their three encounters. Neither knew if they'd see each other again or really cared. Frankie had her bank to save. Lucky had guilty parties to run down—though he hadn't yet planned what he'd do once he discovered the actual truth.

But it will sure as shit be a reckoning.

The usual badge play allowed Lucky pretty much the run of the hospital without having to sign in. After checking with the emergency room staff, he was directed to a third-floor recovery room, where Lil Rod had been placed after the surgery to remove the bullet fragments lodged near his spinal cord. Though the hospital was fully functioning, there was a quiet pall down every half-lit corridor, as if death were ready to rub up against any willing soul.

The recovery suite was spacious, with a ceiling tracked for curtaining off beds. Lucky discovered only one nurse was present—a stout grandmotherly sort with a Czech accent. He identified himself in a polite whisper. She beamed back at the tall deputy as if he were her long forgotten son, something Lucky knew he'd miss once the sheriff's job was over. In some parts of Luckyland, cops were still more revered than they were reviled.

"Your little man is getting an MRI," said the nurse, helpful to a fault. "You want I can get you a coffee and a sweet while you wait?"

"Thanks," said Lucky. "I'll hit the cafeteria and come back."

The lie was closer to a fib. He didn't want to wait, nor did he want to lose the element of surprise. It had been a few years since he'd crossed paths with Lil Rod and he was hoping his appearance would land with the fully intended effect. That was, of course, if the result would get him any positive traction. *Mister Aloha* was a long stretch from *Monster Chihuahua*.

Objectively speaking, it was as if Lucky were trying to lasso air molecules with a garden hose.

Friday

Index

41

Downtown.

Lil Rod had been drifting in and out of consciousness. In part, it had felt like a wild high—somewhere in that lucid in-between of being self-aware and floating away on a cloud of marijuana. He recalled struggling in the trauma suite. And the horrible pain. "If you're screaming, you're breathing," he'd heard a doctor reply right before he passed out, begging for more drugs. When he woke, it had been either the Nigerian-looking ER nurse or the Hindu-toned surgeon who'd informed him that he needed emergency surgery. When he asked when he'd be able to walk again, they'd somehow found ways to change the subject to "Think positive thoughts" and "Is there a relative we can call for you?"

Since surgery, he'd been fuzzy but generally happy while lying parked in a basement corridor, his rolling bed braked against a fresh-painted cinderblock wall. Immobilized by a nerve block that was beginning to wear thin, Lil Rod blinked at the light refracting dully through a hanging bag of IV fluid. Of the four fluorescent lights overhead, only one was lit, saving electricity and casting everything in a gray hue. In that morphined and post-anesthesia netherworld, Lil Rod felt unable—or unwilling—to ponder what had happened. The drive-by. The blood. That cartoon Gorillaz face. It was behind him now. And the land ahead felt sad. It was painfully clear the home invasion gig was over. *Cash and release*, he'd named it. Though he'd earned five thousand dollars per hit, he'd blown most of it on top-shelf weed and designer gangsta wear. He wondered if he'd be able to get decent eBay dollars for a closet full of size 6½ Jordans and Yeezys.

The slight gangster couldn't remember if he'd already received the MRI or not. Nor how long he'd been left alone in a corridor so broad Neon could've driven his prized Bandit car though it. Then things went almost dark. Had the lights been halved again? Lil Rod blinked until his lenses cleared. He forced the muscles in his orbital cavity to squeeze his eyeballs until they focused through his tears.

"Remember me?" a voice whispered.

Hovering over Lil Rod, face upside-down, was a white man with days of unshaven stubble, blue eyes, and a painfully crooked nose.

"No," said the gangster, oblivious from the drugs.

"Won't take long for you to remember," smiled Lucky.

Lil Rod felt the brake release before the cot swiveled from its mooring. He spun.

"Wait, what…" grogged Lil Rod. "Who you again? You gonna gimme my MRI?" The acronym came out sounding more like *emmmm-rye*.

"Shhh," warned Lucky.

"Where we goin'?"

Lil Rod received nothing in reply. It seemed that things were getting darker, as if he were being pushed by the devil himself into further blackness. The bed slowed at an intersection. The patient twisted his head. Down another corridor was an abundance of light pooled in front of a pair of freight-sized elevator doors. As the doors slid open, Lil Rod gasped.

"I said shut up," whispered Lucky, seeking an empty underground space where he could conduct his interrogation.

"It's the guy," wheezed Lil Rod, slurring his words. "The Gorillaz guy who shot my damn legs off."

Lucky snapped his eyes toward the elevators. An imposing figure lumbered forward, slowly, as if lost and searching for something. It was Fungo, hands in his hoodie's pockets. Though the man ticked off none of Lucky's bad guy boxes, Lil Rod had turned from placid to vibrating. Lucky pushed the bed deeper into the basement recesses, backing Lil Rod into a blackened X-ray pod. Hydraulic hinges hissed as the door swung until it latched shut. *Click—clack.*

Lucky kept an eye out through the wire-meshed industrial glass window in the lead door. He changed his attack.

"You sure?" he asked. "He's the one who shot you?"

"Gorillaz motherfucker," groaned Lil Rod.

"Hey! Lower your volume or he's gonna find the both of us."

"No, no, no, no," pleaded Lil Rod, his words turning to mere breaths. "He gonna finish me and you."

"Who is he?"

"Dunno."

"But he shot you…"

"Yeah, yeah. He did it for Howie."

"Howie?"

"College boy. Mister fuckin' Aloha. He ambushed me 'n' Neon."

"Neon the dead guy in the Trans Am?" asked Lucky.

"My man. Neon? He die in his Bandit car? Shit, shit, shit."

"And this Mister Aloha is Howie?"

"College boy. Yeah," Lil Rod broke. "Pussy fake gun pretender. He thought we din't know. But sheeeit. He was strappin' only a kiddie toy."

"Right," said Lucky, playing along. "And what'd you 'n' Neon do with *your* guns?"

Before Lil Rod could muster an answer, his demi-sized body stiffened, his legs planking to his toes. Then came a shudder followed by a wave of intense spinal pain.

Lucky muffled Lil Rod's scream with a hand over the gangbanger's mouth and nose. He put his lips to Lil Rod's ear.

"Ssshhh. You want that big man out there to know who's in here?" he hushed.

"It hurts." Still, Lil Rod shook his head no.

"I wanna know what you did with the guns."

Lucky expected a vanilla answer—some flavor of gangbang retaliation having nothing whatsoever to do with his mission. He'd gone from grasping at nothing to practically strangling an injured nemesis from two years ago. The odds that Lil Rod possessed any information with strings to Karrie scored near a million to one.

"I remember you," grimaced Lil Rod, as if the pain had shocked him into consciousness. His face slackened. "You that Reaper motherfucker."

"Much as I dig a stroll down memory lane, I got shit to do." Lucky swiveled the bed ninety degrees to give Lil Rod a look out the sliver of glass. "See that guy out there? He here to finish you?"

"I dunno…"

"Here's what's gonna happen. You start talkin' or I'm gonna do some surgery of my own."

"And I'll scream my ass! Then he come 'n' cap us both."

Lucky dropped one hand again over Lil Rod's mouth and slipped the other between the mattress and the gangbanger's back. Lil Rod issued a muffled howl.

"Here's the thing." Lucky kept his grip on Lil Rod's mouth while breathing the rest of his words into his ear. "I got my own reasons to finish you. So, give it up."

Lucky released his hand from over Lil Rod's mouth. Lil Rod nodded.

"Why does this Howie guy want you dead?"

"Not cuzza my fuckup. That for sure. Wasn't me."

"Not my problem. Details. Now."

"We been rippin' the FOBs."

"FOBs?"

"Fuckin' Chinese. All of 'em. Soy suckers, you know? New moneys from China and shit. Bags of it."

"Where? When?"

"Everywhere. In the SGV. Home invasions," Lil Rod rushed. "Dunno how Howie know it. Who's got the cash. But it was regular. 'Most every week. Early morning. Different family, same money. Big, big money. *Cash and release.* That's what I call it. Howie call it *puttin' da Asian in Invasion.*"

With an eye out the window, Lucky was able to follow Fungo as he wandered further away, checking doors one at a time.

"Don't stop now," continued Lucky. "You seriously have my attention."

Little Rod spilled it in quick relief. From where and how he met college boy Howie—a.k.a. Mr. Aloha—to the home invasions, to Tung Chee and Calabasas, to getting shot up near the Coliseum. After the download, Lucky left him in the X-ray pod. He'd eventually call the hospital to inform them where—but not how—their tattooed patient had been misplaced.

As Lucky humped it down the corridor, he called out.

"Hold the elevator, will ya?" he shouted.

The over-stuffed man in the lift thrust his hand out to stop the closing doors. Whether it was because he was commanded or polite or a little bit of both, Lucky didn't know or care. He acted grateful and slightly winded upon arrival.

"Thanks," wheezed Lucky.

"Not a problem," returned Fungo.

Lucky punched the ground-floor button. The door closed. He felt gravity defied as the cables began to smoothly lift the car. The big man to Lucky's rear and left was even more imposing up close, about four inches taller and outweighing Lucky by at least a hundred pounds. The last thing Lucky wanted was to tangle with the beast. *Samoan or Polynesian*, he guessed from the forearm tats and the necklace strung with teeth. He suspected the screws in his back were unlikely to remain fastened in any kind of wrestling test.

"So, what did the fat Samoan say to the fat Polynesian?" Lucky suddenly asked.

"What you say?" quizzed the big man, wondering if his ears were working.

Lucky already had his .45 Sig in hand, hidden from Fungo's view. He bent at the waist, leaned forward, and pulled the emergency stop button. Before Fungo could react, Lucky spun and smashed the gun's heavy frame directly into the giant's flat nose. Blood squished. The rest was about inertia. The elevator slammed to a stop and with Fungo already off balance, Lucky kept moving forward. Fungo tripped backward as Lucky landed with his full weight on his chest. Fungo's head slapped the deck with a resonant *thunk* and his eyes squeezed shut.

"What the fu—"

"Feel the pressure against your eye socket?" grit Lucky. "That's a fuckin' gun muzzle."

"Didn't do nothin'—"

"Shut the fuck up or you won't hear the joke's punchline."

42

San Gabriel.

Jiao woke to a splash. Loud. In her dream she'd heard the distinct sound and lurched from her bed to the French doors that led to the backyard balcony and overlooked the gated pool. Floating face down was five-year-old Min, her black hair and frilly leopard pajamas all that were visible to the eye. Floating. Helpless.

Dying.

It was when Jiao forced a scream of Min's name that she woke, breathing rapidly, relieved to see sunlight streaking across the bedroom. After noting that Denny wasn't next to her, she shook off the nightmare and listened to the rhythmic splashes coming through the open French doors. Mystery solved: her husband swimming his morning laps.

By rote, Jiao started her morning routine by going to wake her daughter. But Min was already up, seated on the floor of her bedroom, playing one of her favorite pretend games. She called it "Dollhouse and Barbies."

"Teeth brush, dress for school, downstairs," ushered Jiao before turning around and shuffling back toward the master bathroom.

Denny's clothes lay precisely where he'd shucked them on the porcelain-tiled floor. Jiao crouched, gathered the discards, and dared herself to sniff the linen shirt for traces of a woman's smell. Perfume. She pushed her nose into the fabric, breathed in, and thought she caught a faint but familiar whiff. But she was more curious about the crinkling sound she heard. She looked into the shirt pocket and found little Min's folded drawing.

Resting her knees on the small pile of clothes, Jiao unfurled the picture, gently flattening it against the cool tiles. Her eyes scanned the paper, top to bottom, edge to edge, examining every stroke. Though she surely recognized the art as Min's she hadn't yet seen that particular drawing. It was thematically familiar, not at all unlike the rendering that had concerned the school. A box house with bumblebees with blacked-out eyes inside. Centered and large was a toothy, blue and green dinosaur holding a black crayon-scratched gun.

Jiao's eyes were blown wide as she remembered the day before, when Denny had left his office unguarded. In the darkness she breeched, she had discovered nothing of interest until she'd spotted the computer on the banquet table. She'd stared, at first in curiosity, but moments later in horror. She's seen men with guns. A family bound, gagged, and beaten, their faces racked with severe distress, holding back their muffled whimpers.

In the hours since, Jiao hadn't been able to process the significance of the video feed. But it had so frightened her that she'd stuffed it, excusing whatever she'd seen as merely something she didn't comprehend. And there would be no way to confront her husband or ask him for context without revealing that she'd broken his golden rule of never, ever entering his backyard office without his express permission.

Now there was Min's drawing. The subject matter, so unmistakably familiar.

"It's mine, mommy!" announced Min. The child was half-dressed and behind her, broad grin sliced across her face.

"Mini," spun Jiao. "Where? Where you see this?"

"You like?" asked the child.

"Very much," faked the mom, verging on tears. "But did you see this?"

"Uh…" Min answered.

"Where you see?"

"On TV. In Daddy's office."

Jiao swallowed the confirmation. She could feel a surge of electricity pulsating to her fingertips.

"It's okay, Mommy," claimed Min. "It's jus' a TV show. Daddy tol' me."

"Who's not getting ready for school?" veered Jiao.

"Mini is!" The child laughed at her own reply before rushing back to her room.

For Denny, those last hours of darkness had brought no sleep or rest. Instead of erasing *all* the incriminating files, he'd saved his favorite ten invasions and buried them deeper into his hard drives. Those he'd eliminated had been scrubbed with a deletion program that overwrote the data with digital gobbledygook. Task completed, he'd retrieved the pair of swim trunks he'd left to dry on the shower head of his office bathroom. He hoped to cleanse his mind of all fear and worthlessness with what he liked to call a maximum dip—a mix of unheated pool water and triple his usual number of reps starting with breaststroke, followed by backstroke, crawl, and some body-slapping butterflies. If that kind of punishment didn't purge him of what ailed his soul, nothing would.

As he ticked off laps, Denny began to feel the weight of things release. It was probably only the opioid-like endorphins. *But damn*, he thought. *If everything goes to shit, I could always start shooting up heroin.* The thought made him lose count. As self-punishment, he added another set of laps.

The old-style pool was woefully short for proper lap work and the kidney shape made it hard to keep his lines straight. Yet it was water. It was cold. And after every kick-turn there were moments of blissful, perfect quiet. Two feet to the right of the deep end's intake was where he liked to throw himself over, plant his feet, and tumble turn back in the direction of the house. But his moment of silence was interrupted by the sound of screeching. It penetrated the surface tension of the water and elevated to an ear-piercing pitch the moment his head broke water.

Jiao!

Denny buried his head and ears and plowed forward with his arms. He wasn't going to let his unhinged wife ruin his morning effort. *What was she angry at now? Did she find Frankie's lipstick on my collar? Smell her perfume again?* In that moment he hated her. Loathed the air she breathed. That and his maximum dip hadn't yet produced the guaranteed calm he'd hoped for.

Nearing the shallow end, he saw Jiao's bare feet first. Her toes curled around the edges of the brick coping. With the swim goggles' magnification, Jiao's tiny feet looked huge. Untidy. Not at all like the ones he'd stroked so lovingly on their wedding night. Denny lifted his neck, allowing his eyes to fully breach the water in nothing more than acknowledgment. He was about to speak Chinese to her. Mandarin. Sternly, in hopes of flipping her *off* switch. His focus shifted. But it wasn't his wife's face he was seeing through the oval lenses. It was her fingers, nails fancily decorated in sparkly polish. Pinched between her thumbs and index fingers was Min's folded drawing. Its yellow sun ignited by the very real morning sunlight reflecting off the choppy surface.

For the life of him Denny couldn't distinguish her words. They were angry. Chinese. But with such a machine-gun force that his brain couldn't keep up. Topping that was her volume and tone. It was both disrespectful and embarrassing. How long had she been hollering at him with that horrific, bilious screed? What neighbors were listening?

Jiao! You need to shut the fuck up!

Denny's feet found the pool's bottom. Smooth. He pushed upward, standing, using the force of movement to reach out and snatch the squealing banshee by the same pigtails she'd let her daughter braid the night before. She felt as light as the offending paper she held forth. Denny pulled. He recalled her scream peaking at the point she hit the water.

He held her under, fighting off her struggle and appreciating the silence he was creating.

Aaahhh, he told himself. *Peaceful again.*

The moment was broken by the pet Chihuahua's yapping. Sudden and nonstop, as if the damned animal had no concept of punctuation. The pet stood outside the doggy door on the top step leading into the kitchen. Then the door swung outward, revealing Min, dressed and ready for school.

"Daddy?" called the child. "Where's Mommy?"

"What do you need?" His retort was remarkably free of tonality considering he was still holding the child's mother under water.

"Need to go to school." Min remained framed in the kitchen door, strange worry forcing her tiny mouth to practically disappear into her face.

"Daddy's taking you!" shouted Denny, releasing Jiao's lifeless body and rushing up the pool steps.

Denny made sure to shut the pool gate behind him, not daring to look over his shoulder to see if Jiao's body had already floated to the surface. Still wet, he grabbed a T-shirt from the basket of clean laundry atop the dryer just inside the kitchen, pulled it over his head, and snatched his wife's car keys in one hand while whirling Min into his arms with the other.

His child let out a happy "Wheee" as the pair hopped off the back step towards Jiao's Jaguar.

"But what about breakfast?" Min added.

"Starbucks!" said Denny. "Special treat. Don't tell Mommy."

"Where she go?"

"Taking a bath, I think," lied Denny, buckling Min into her booster seat. "She had a real big headache this morning."

"That why she was crying so loud?"

"Crying, yes." He slammed his door shut and turned over the engine, his wet swim trunks dripping onto the leather seat and carpet.

"I thought all that was yelling," giggled Min.

"That's right. It's funny, isn't it?" pretended Denny. "But Mommy is okay now. Feeling lots better in her bath."

43

None of them were cops anymore. Yet they still met up at Tom's Burgers in the big corner booth with windows facing busy Imperial Highway. If asked, each of the former sheriff's deputies would say it was a Vikings thing. Tom's Burgers was where they had eaten, schemed, and told tall tales back when they were all on the job. And it had remained that way well into each of their retirements. Not one of them ever called it Tom's or Tom's Burgers.

They called it *the Spot*.

The four retirees were slumped into the slick brown vinyl seating. Babylon sat nearest the edge as it was too painful for him to take his usual center post. His right arm hung in a sling purchased that morning at CVS. He wasn't at all keen on giving up to the jaded crew exactly how he'd come to receive the badly dislocated shoulder or the shiner under his eye.

The fellow Lynwood Vikings with whom Babylon shared the booth were appropriately nicknamed. That's because at the Lynwood station—and if you were a Viking—you had a nickname.

Babylon's pals were, clockwise, Stricks, Mooch, and Guava.

"C'mon, Babs," goaded Mooch, the self-professed fat man of the crew, his broad face pocked by horrible teenage cystic acne, a brush of a mustache shrouding his upper lip. "We're all old. Shit, think I once tore my rotator cuff beating off."

Guava and Stricks rolled with laughter while Babylon barely cracked a smile. He was in awful pain and craving a handful of Vicodin. Before pulling the trunk lid on himself in Fryman Canyon, he'd forgotten to resocket his shoulder. He had lain there for five hours, his prostate pushing on his bladder and his right arm feeling like it was aflame. And now his stomach was in tumult from a thousand too many milligrams of self-prescribed ibuprofen. In his left hand he held his eleven-year sobriety coin like a totem to ward off the evil sirens of potential drug abuse. He anxiously rolled it back and forth across the top of his knuckles like a practiced magician.

"Babylon lost his babble," laughed Stricks, lean, gracefully mustached in charcoal gray bristles that matched his buzzed afro. "And I think I like it."

"Fuck you," grumbled Babylon.

"He's back!" pointed Guava. "Hey, Stricks. You got two syllables out of him."

"Think we can get back to it?" asked Babylon.

"Dunno," Stricks said, leaning in, his voice lowered. "Lucky Dey, man. He's one of us."

"Yeah," agreed Guava.

"What's it matter?" growled Babylon. "We do it or somebody else will. He's dead. Buried. Over and out. And the list of folks who want him dead? Endless."

"He's a cop." Guava's arms were crossed. He wasn't at all at ease with Babylon's proposal.

"I don't got no problem," shrugged Mooch. "I'll do it. Take the whole hundred large. Shit man. That's a cabin on ten acres in Montana."

"Can't be no fuckups," stressed Babylon. "Not a one-man thing."

"You're way too fat anyway," said Stricks.

"What's fat got to do with pulling a trigger?" returned Mooch.

"Nothin'," joked Stricks. "It's the getaway where you got problems."

The line was met with more belly laughs, Babylon included. He winced at the pain it triggered.

"Thinkin' I could just propylene glycol the SOB," Mooch offered, referring to the poisonous chemical in commercial antifreeze, sweet to the taste, and easily accessed.

"The fuck did you do to your shoulder?" Stricks shifted back to Babylon.

"You guys don't want in, more Vikes where you assholes came from," parried Babylon.

"What's your end?" asked Guava.

"Nothin'," said Babylon. "All yours. I need to be far away on this. I get up from this table and I don't see you all for six months. I'll make sure the cash lands, though. Guaranteed."

"I'm not worried about getting paid," said Guava. "Still stuck on the cop thing."

"Nobody's gonna make you," annoyed Mooch. "You can stay on your taco truck for all I give."

"Third of a hundred K buy you a second taco truck?" argued Stricks.

"Maybe, maybe not," replied Guava before an autonomic smile. "But after trade-in it maybe gets me an upgraded truck."

"Well, there you go," goaded Mooch as if it were already decided.

"It's called a mitzvah," Babylon nodded. "Yiddish. Means 'a good deed done.'"

"And where's the good deed in *assassinating* a cop?" Guava leaned, his voice dropping to a whisper when wording the criminal act.

"So, you're out?" asked Babylon.

Guava sat back, slumped slightly, and glanced left and right at Stricks and Mooch. Neither offered a degree of consolation.

"Taco truck, taco truck, taco truck," Mooch chanted, fists drumming the tabletop.

"Fine," shrugged Guava. "You're my guys. I roll how you roll."

"Small caliber. Back of the head," Babylon urged. "And he won't be hard to find."

A sinking silence set in, leaving the ancient exhaust fan coming from the kitchen as practically the only sound. Each man was nodding in his own unconscious way.

"Hey," snapped Stricks. "He's still a deputy brother. So, let's drink to him, okay?"

"Drink to Lucky Dey?" asked Mooch.

"Why the hell not?" Babylon finished before raising his good arm and hailing the waitress. "Brayonna! Darlin'! Three beers and a coffee, will ya? We got us a toast to make."

"Celebratin' what?" she cheerfully called back.

"A fallen brother!" Babylon revealed.

Brayonna, the kind of waitress who didn't mind slipping her thick curves into a two-sizes-too-small uniform, arrived with three cold ones in one hand and a coffee pot in the other.

"I know this fallen fella?" she asked.

"Comrade from a long time ago," said Babylon in a semi-lie.

"Be that as it may," she said, "beer's gonna be on me."

"Too, too kind, sweetheart," said Stricks. "Big tip comin'."

"No shit, Sherlock," she grinned before sashaying back towards the kitchen.

"To Lucky." Mooch raised his beer.

"To Lucky," said Guava and Stricks.

Babylon raised his cup of black stuff, holding it level.

"To Lucky."

44

South L.A.

Howie couldn't erase his case of the shakes. He lay awake all night on a single mattress opposite his sleeping roommate in their campus apartment. There were moments he was shuddering so hard that the bedframe rattled against the wall. Still, his roommate snored on. Howie viewed it as another lucky break. He had been moments from emptying a full clip from his father's .22 Ruger into Neon and Lil Rod when a pair of armed angels had swooped in from out of nowhere to take care of his business.

It made sense, he reasoned. After all, he had hired a pair of bona fide South L.A. bad boys to act as muscle on his *Asian invasions*. Gangbangers. Crips. They'd led violent lives and died fittingly.

And I'm still clean. Well, relatively, I guess.

He pulled the covers over his head, turning his body toward

the darkness of the wall, and imagined himself in his Northridge bedroom. Safe. He hadn't yet returned his father's pistol. It remained locked up in the gym. And as far as he knew, his upstairs gal pal hadn't yet discovered the damage done to her Jetta.

"It's all good," he kept mumbling to himself.

But his nervous system was in full riot. After a night without sleep, he showered in scalding water thinking it might finally warm him up. It didn't. The bowl of cereal he tried to ingest came back up in a stream of Froot Loops–colored vomit. Waves of diarrhea topped off his dismal state. Plus, he had an afternoon midterm in Marketing 406 following an 11:00 a.m. lecture. He decided to do some last-minute cramming at the campus Jamba Juice. Under the patio's propane heater, he reviewed his class notes but was unable to decipher his own handwriting. It was a nightmare. His own words became jumbled. It was so bad Howie wondered if he had post-traumatic dyslexia. *Is that even a thing?* He tried to look up the condition on his iPhone, but couldn't even read the results.

He texted a study partner he knew who doubled as a walking pharmacy, serving up chemical remedies for overstressed students willing to pay in cash. After listing his symptoms—all of which he claimed were triggered by test anxiety—the student suggested Klonopin, a benzodiazepine known to quell nerves. Inside the hour, Howie was set up with the drug, trading a hundred-dollar bill for an unmarked bottle of twenty 5-milligram tablets. He chased two pills with a Strawberry Surf Rider, then trudged off to the Stauffer Lecture Hall.

The Klonopin might have taken the edge off, but it hadn't helped his attentiveness. Less than ten minutes into the white-headed professor's soliloquy on building global brands, Howie began to nod off. As the beginning of a deep sleep escaped his nostrils in a snort, the curly-haired coed to his left poked him with her stylus.

"Snoring," she whispered.

"Jesus," popped Howie, straightening in his seat. "Thanks."

"Anybody want to share their conversations?" interrupted the professor, eyes firmly on Howie and the coed. "You're welcome to come up here, stand in my shoes, and take over my lecture."

Howie held up a single open palm, shaking his head apologetically, shrinking back into the nearly 175 other students packed into the canted theater.

Then, when a voice loudly announced Howie by his full name, it so startled the business student that he first feared he'd fallen asleep and was being called out again. He looked around. Nobody was looking at him. All eyes and necks were craned to the rear landing.

"Howard Bokeem Morris!" repeated the man, loud, but not yelling. Firm. Authoritative.

The voice cut right through Howie, who turned and strained to see just who was asking for him.

Lucky's visit to USC was prompted by the information he'd extracted from Lil Rod. After waiting around for the Administration Office to open, Lucky queried a marmish bureaucrat at reception for info on a business student named Howie Morris. His questions were rebuffed with a civil libertarian's officiousness. Without a warrant, the school would not disclose any information regarding an enrolled student. And that was no matter who was doing the asking. As was his habit in such circumstances, Lucky positioned himself in a fashion where he could see the bureaucrat's computer screen. Upon hearing Howie's name, she'd unconsciously keyed a search. And while she was condescendingly lambasting Lucky for seeking private data on a student, he was scanning what he could on her screen. He'd caught glimpses of the student's five-day class grid. On the Friday block was an 11:00 a.m. class in SLH-200.

Despite her rebuff, Lucky thanked the woman, vacated the administration building, and found a building legend for the 226-acre main campus. A quick perusal through Howie's Facebook page and Lucky knew precisely who he was looking for. But rousting the man Lil Rod called *College Boy* and *Mr. Aloha* from a lecture hall chock-full of entitled, easily bruised, potential cop-loathing *snowflakes* required a quick decision: Wait until the conclusion of the class—precious minutes Lucky didn't care to waste—or clip his badge to his belt and make an audacious entrance?

"Howard Bokeem Morris?" Lucky intoned, his register low, feet on the top step, back ramrod straight.

"S'cuse me?" shot the professor, indifferent to Lucky's authority play. "Whoever you are, whatever you want, you surely don't belong in here."

"I'm very happy to talk to Mr. Morris outside if he wouldn't mind?" Lucky trolled the upturned faces searching for the smiling boy next door he'd pegged on Facebook.

"Well, I do mind!" rankled the professor, voice raised in a heroic pose for the classroom.

"Expect you do," replied Lucky, taking in the entire class. "Howard? Howie? Mr. Aloha? Wherever you are, maybe you'd like me to explain to your classmates why someone with a badge wants a chat with you."

"It's okay!" said Howie, his arm shooting up into the air. He was fumbling with his computer and backpack as he found his feet.

"Howie?" called out the professor. "You do not have to leave my class like this. The officer can wait—"

"No, sir!" defended Howie, overly anxious to appease. "I wanna help. I'll get the lecture notes. Sorry for the interruption, sir."

Howie slid down the row, past the other students, but didn't quite get his first eyeful of Lucky until he found the steps. The deputy in front of him was tall, unshaven, drawn around the eyes, and holding the door open.

"Sorry again!" Howie called back, his eyes level with the shield on Lucky's belt.

I'm fucking got, Howie said to himself, the gangster vernacular coming right out of Lil Rod's mouth.

Beyond the threshold, and just after the door closed behind them both, Howie felt himself rocked forward and thrown slightly off balance as Lucky manhandled him by grabbing hold of his backpack. In a matter of steps, Howie was manipulated through a bathroom door marked as gender neutral. The motion-operated light flicked on as Lucky twisted the locking deadbolt.

"Drop the backpack," Lucky demanded, "and grab the wall."

Lucky wrenched Howie's backpack from him and pointed.

"I said, grab the fucking wall."

Howie turned awkwardly, bungling the placement of his hands against the wall.

"Jeeezus," Lucky breathed as he began a standard frisk for weapons. "You really are an amateur."

"Amateur what?"

"That's what you're gonna tell me," returned Lucky. "But not now. You carrying?"

"Drugs?" Howie was confused, thinking maybe he'd been busted for purchasing the Klonopin.

"Weapons. Guns. Knives—"

"Uh, no," said Howie, almost relieved. "You're a campus cop?"

"Don't move," said Lucky, having finished the frisk and moving on to backpack.

"The pills!" Howie pled. "I got 'em from a friend."

"Like I give a fuck."

"Who are you again?"

After a quick backpack search, Lucky spun Howie around so the college boy could look him in the eye and imagine Lucky's rough world and what it had taken to have earned such a badly broken nose.

"Who I am depends how much you tell me," burned Lucky. "Right now, I could be either the best or the worst thing that ever happened to you."

45

San Gabriel.

In his frantic rush to evacuate himself and Min from their San Gabriel home, Denny had grabbed his phone but forgotten his wallet. He hadn't noticed until one of the teachers at the school had hit him up for tickets to the annual spring fundraiser. Denny had reached into his back pocket, realizing that he was still wearing swim trunks and his wallet was where he usually left it—in the decorative dish at the end of the kitchen counter.

The kitchen counter in my house with my wife's body floating in the swimming pool.

Denny used his missing wallet as an excuse to quickly withdraw and hurry home, where he'd need to collect himself and figure out just what to do with his murdered wife. Then a new worry broke through. What if he were randomly pulled over by a cop only to be dinged for driving without a license? A traffic stop would mark the time, place, and direction Denny was traveling in his wife's car in only a T-shirt and damp swim trunks. So, Denny drove five miles an hour under the speed limit, making the return leg feel like a slog through wet cement.

All the while, his mind raced.

Denny called Wang. Without giving up a morsel of incriminating information, he instructed his chief lieutenant to come to his house and back his car deep into the driveway until he reached the detached garage. Denny clocked his entire trip to the primary school and back at roughly an hour and five minutes.

He'd return to the scene of his crime. And what then? The pool? *No*, he reasoned. He'd wait for Wang. If anything, it was an excuse to avoid what he could never un-see—his wife, the murdered mother of his baby girl—lifeless and what? Floating? Or would she be resting on the bottom? Denny hadn't a notion how long dead bodies floated before sinking in pool water. Or, for that matter, how long before the gasses in them expanded, sending the deceased carcass back to the surface. He'd seen enough crime shows to understand some of the basic mechanics of death and decomposition. Nothing though, as it might relate to his own ugly deed.

He crossed back to the house without once glancing at the pool and launched himself up the stairs to the master bedroom. He showered quickly and dressed in fresh jeans and a polo shirt, all the time plotting what he and Wang should do with Jiao's body.

Why think? his mind would counterpunch. *Wang will know what to do. That's why he's your number two. Don't. Even. Try.*

He chose his most worn pair of sneakers, somehow worrying about footprints and how easy it would be to discard his shoes if things got messy. When he snapped a shoelace, he pulled one from his newer Reeboks, threaded it quickly, and inhaled and exhaled deeply as if that might somehow dry the perspiration that seemed in constant flush on his forehead. After checking the front window for signs of Wang, he dared traverse the generous master suite to the balcony that overlooked the basketball court and pool area beyond.

As he eased nearer the French doors, both still open from the night before, the diaphanous drapery slow-danced in the breeze. Denny imagined what he might see. He rationalized that it might be better for his first look at his dead wife to be from a distance. A far-away glimpse might not be as hurtful a shock. That can't-un-see-it moment might be seared into his corneas in a less-offending image.

Yes, he reasoned. *I can do the balcony.*

Denny pushed the curtains aside, squinted at the daylight, and tilted his view. Only the sun was at the perfect azimuth to turn the pool surface into a mirror. The balcony was practically ablaze. Denny might as well have been staring directly into the sun. He tried to shade off the light by cupping his hands around his eyes. It proved no use. The sun was where it was. The pool was calm, undisturbed, as reflective as a sheet of fresh aluminum foil.

And Denny couldn't see her.

Something pulled at him, reaching into his core and yanking him off the balcony and back through the double doors. Instead of taking the shortcut down those exterior spiral stairs, he charged out of the bedroom, down the main staircase, and out through the kitchen. He burst through the rear door and rushed to the pool gate.

But why the rush, Denny?

He wasn't in a hurry to save Jiao. She was dead. Sunken for at least an hour and a half. Yet he hurried all the same in a breathless surge to the pool. He threw the wrought-iron gate wide, crossing inside before the child-safety spring could snap it back, and stood with the toes of his shoes hanging over the edge of the shallow end's coping. He might've even been standing in the exact spot where Jiao had placed herself when she'd begun that screeching harangue that had gotten her killed.

The pool spread out before him. Placid. Barely a ripple. And

Denny's jaw dropped. That's because there was no body. No floating nightgown. Nary a remnant of his dead wife. He circled to the left, clockwise, checking the pool bottom from every conceivable angle. His heart pounded all the way into his throat. Every hair follicle tingled with fright. Denny revolved around the pool three times, certain his eyes—or the light—were playing tricks. The smooth plaster was sun-streaked in languid stripes of turquoise and light. The surrounding pavers were bone dry, any moisture having long since evaporated or trickled down the drains.

"Boss?" Wang called out in sharpened Mandarin.

Denny spun toward the driveway. Wang's Lexus was already parked, backed nearly up to the Jag. The gimpy, smoker's-toothed man leaned on his crutch. Denny stared at him, lost for words.

"I'm here," added Wang.

"Right," answered Denny, jump-starting his wits back into the present, purposefully speaking in Wang's native language in case neighbors were listening. "Right, right."

"You okay?"

"My wife," nodded Denny as he strode to the driveway. "She's…missing."

"Kidnapped?" snapped Wang.

"I took her car to drop Min off at school. Came home and she's gone."

"You need me to find her?"

"I need you…" Denny stalled, collecting his thoughts. "Look around my house. See if there's anything that says where she's gone."

"You've called her on her mobile phone?"

Denny hadn't. After all, he had thought he was returning home to find her dead and drowned exactly where he'd left her. The ramifications of Jiao having crawled out of the pool—alive—and God knows where—were unfolding at an exponential speed inside his brain. He imagined the doorbell ringing at any moment with a phalanx of San Gabriel PD uniforms, guns drawn. Was it time to run? But to where? And how? Denny had been so secure in his criminal operation that he'd never planned anything like a criminal's "go bag"—an insurance duffel—packed with thousands in cash and a valid passport.

"Just look for her!" he demanded. Denny hooked past Wang into the open garage. He needed to destroy those incriminating files. All of them. The rest of the digital footprint he should have expunged the night before. Then he'd have Wang drive him to the airport on an emergency business trip. Whatever Jiao had planned for him could be managed from a distance. All his troubles could be handled from afar. Until things cooled off, he could run his office from extradition-free Shanghai.

And Frankie would keep an eye on his money.

Upon his return to his backyard lair, the glow from the security monitor beckoned Denny's eyes. There was movement on the interior house screens. In wide-angled frames, Wang was working his way through the house, poking at papers, and going through Jiao's purse, left on the kitchen counter. Wang had found Jiao's cell phone, wallet, credit cards. Over the speakers, Denny heard the wingman muttering indecipherable curses to nobody but himself.

Then the doorbell rang. Denny toggled to view the exterior cameras. Howie was on the front porch. Beyond the camera's focus, he thought he saw a pair of interns in lousy fitting suits.

Wheeling to his keyboard, Denny immediately texted Wang:

why are howie & interns at front door?

The wingman's reply was equally speedy:

no idea

Denny keyed a reply meant to be efficient and final:

get rid of them

Pushing off with those beat-up sneakers, Denny slung his chair over to his second keyboard. He began entering the complicated series of passwords that gave him access to his home invasion files, his priceless cache of personal pornography. It required memory and concentration to get the codes right. In doing so, Denny ignored the cameras. Over his shoulder, the boxed image from the front door lens revealed Howie stepping aside for the two unknown interns. One of them, rail thin; the other much larger than he'd appeared through the warp of the wide security lens. Bootlegged to the big man's heavy thigh was a black aluminum baseball bat.

If Denny had entered his passwords faster, he would've seen more. Only he hadn't, and the external camera views of his property had turned visually benign. Then again, if curiosity had piqued him—just enough to use that keyboard toggle function to shift the view to the indoor cameras—his reaction might've been altogether different.

But he hadn't.

Denny finished keying the code to the hidden files then dropped them into a folder, where he applied the delete/overwriting program. The application reported in countdown digits that the process would take twenty minutes, thirty-seven seconds... thirty-six...thirty-five...Denny pushed his chair to the left, rolling it back to the security monitor. The outdoor cameras appeared clear of obvious dangers—no San Gabriel PD radio car parked at the curb. So, he found the toggle key and flipped screens to the interior views. He was about to scan from upper left to right, as he would often do when spying on Jiao or Min. The nine screens were laid out in the orderly form he'd designed, the top three boxes: Kitchen. Dining room. Foyer—

And Denny froze on the foyer camera.

It appeared as it usually did—still—the front door framed by a pair of spiraling artificial boxwood trees. The generous Persian rug was in the center, but there, in the five o'clock position, lay two motionless legs in shoes shined to perfection.

Wang.

46

The plan was Lucky's. After months executing Denny's crimes, the final act of Howie's *Asian invasion* story had been schemed by the sheriff's deputy who'd practically plucked him by the ear and walked him off campus. During their stroll, Lucky had filled up Howie with what he'd learned from Lil Rod, Fungo, and Zipper Ling. In turn, Howie had been compelled to fill in the empty spaces in Lucky's timeline. Calabasas. Tung Chee. The biggest confession was the breadth of Denny's extortion game.

But not a hint about a hit and run in Malibu. Nothing. Zilch.

"I stole millions for him," Howie had admitted under much less duress than he'd imagined. Perhaps his decision to spill all had been about relieving some guilt. Then again, Lucky's threat to unleash the wrath of those same assassins who'd blasted Neon and Lil Rod to kingdom come had been pretty convincing.

As Lucky described it, Howie's redemption would begin with a possible combination of forces. With the promise that Lucky wouldn't inform Zipper or Fungo of Howie's involvement in what had happened in Calabasas, hasty introductions had been made.

As per the quickly evolved game plan, Howie had rung Denny Teng's doorbell, waited for the door to open, and stepped to the side. If Denny's wife or daughter or even the twice-per-week housekeeper were to answer, they were to be rushed and subdued. Howie knew the drill, having worked versions of it for nearly a year on every one of his home invasions. This final suburban assault, however, was demonstrably different. For one, he was in that off-the-rack suit he wore to the office. Secondly, he'd left behind the replica firearm with which he'd intimidated so many of the FOBs. Thirdly, his criminal cohorts had been replaced by a duo he'd only just met via the compelling hand of Lucky Dey.

Lucky had strongly suggested Howie, Zipper, and Fungo dispense with trading names in lieu of expediting the revenge and redemption ahead. Howie guessed the hipster with the anime-inspired haircut was Vietnamese in origin. The other man, a mountain of a specimen with Samoan tattoos and human teeth for a necklace, was the obvious muscle. Howie wondered how a man like that found suits that fit for under a thousand dollars.

But their masquerade as a trio of interns had worked.

To Howie's surprise, it had been Wang who opened the door, his yellow teeth already exposed in a sneer meant to forbid. Howie simply nodded and the big man had shown remarkable speed and dexterity, taking possession of the porch and doorway with terrifying swiftness. The Samoan's bat had come up from a low position, shocking Denny's number two with a short-armed blow. Already unsteady on his feet, Wang fell and began to crawl backward on his elbows. The hulk of a man finished Wang in two successive strikes.

While the one with the anime hair worked his way down the driveway, Howie entered the house. He shut the front door and let his eyes slip sideways, taking in the nearly dead body of Wang Zhang. Despite the man's skull having been crushed like a melon,

Howie heard active gurgling and caught a singular rise and fall in Wang's chest—his last involuntary gulp at life.

"Office is behind the garage." Howie gestured. The big man showed his physical deftness again, swerving a pair of tight turns before busting through the spring-loaded saloon doors that led to the kitchen. Howie vaulted up the stairs to make sure Denny wasn't hiding in one of the four bedrooms. If he encountered his boss, he was going to have to subdue him. For that, Howie was prepared. And strangely, his nerves weren't an issue whatsoever—a stark contrast to the assassination he'd attempted the day before, a cluster of a calamity where he'd first encountered the deadly pair he was somehow now partnered with.

So much killing, he calmly mouthed almost as if in shock. Only Howie wasn't in shock at all.

Halfway up the stairs, he heard shouts from behind the house. Denny's voice. Howie reversed direction, rushing through the kitchen and the gaping back door. Opposite him was the detached garage. The Jaguar's car door was swung wide. Denny was on the asphalt, propelled only by his indifferent hands and knees, blood draining from a gash to his forehead. In the millisecond before the Samoan had squared up the barrel of the bat with the left side of Denny's cranium, Howie thought he saw Denny flick him one last look. The boss's eyes weren't so much filled with an accusation of betrayal—or even recognition—as much as with a plea for help. Then the bat landed with a soft, penetrating crunch. Denny's body rolled to the right, twitching next to the Jag's rear tire.

And Howie just stared, none of it quite landing. In a matter of seconds, his mentor and master, Denny Teng, had been reduced to a quivering corpse. The man for whom Howie had allowed himself be turned from intern to tool to criminal.

"It's done, dude," said the man with the anime hair. "Now, do your job!"

Howie's job, as they had discussed earlier, was to rush into Denny's office and disconnect the hard drive from the security cameras. Howie knew exactly where to look. Months before,

Denny had sent him to Best Buy to purchase a bigger external hard drive and connect it to the existing security system. At the time, the invite into the boss's private sanctum had felt like a perk. But now, removing the hardware felt like he was carving out his own heart. It was a feeling that fit. Deserved.

"Did you hear me?" pressed Zipper.

"Yeah," replied Howie, stepping into the garage and strolling forward.

"Get your bunny hop on!"

What followed had not been planned. At least not by Lucky Dey. The rest had all been Howie's doing.

From the space between his belt and the small of his back, Howie withdrew that .22 Ruger pistol he'd brought to murder Lil Rod and Neon. His father's small-caliber target gun. It was the first time Howie had come fully armed to a home invasion. No longer carrying the replica play gun, in his hand was the real deal. Loaded. And it felt as comfortable as holding a can of soda. Because the man with the anime hair was closer, Howie chose him as his first target, squeezing off shots using the point on that swoop of hair a target. Zipper dropped straight to the concrete like a lead curtain, clearing Howie's gun's sight for the Samoan. But the big man turned to run. Only there wasn't much room to maneuver in the garage. So, Howie kept moving forward and pulling the .22's trigger until he watched the Samoan collapse against that obnoxious humming refrigerator. Blood smeared against the fridge's white skin as Fungo tried to hold on before slumping into a muscled, motionless heap.

Considering the three bodies that lay before him, Howie spoke aloud to nobody but himself. "My job is done." With that, he stuck the gun muzzle under his chin, aimed the barrel vertically, and gave the trigger one last pull.

47

Westwood.

"I keep thinking it's her crown of thorns," whispered Gonzo, referring to the apparatus encircling Karrie's cranium. "I know it's there to help her. But it feels like it's some kind of punishment for her being so perfect."

"She's anything but perfect," Lucky reminded. "But she's still alive."

In adjacent chairs, Lucky and Gonzo held hands in the near dark, gazing upon their unconscious daughter. The beeps and quiet whooshes of the life-sustaining equipment provided an odd but hopeful rhythm. Gonzo checked her watch.

"Ugh," she said. "Travis needs to get home. Test tomorrow." Her teenaged boy was supposed to be studying in the family waiting room. But Gonzo knew better and couldn't blame him for distracting himself from fear and/or panic by playing endless loops of games on his phone.

"I'll stay." Lucky sounded sanguine. He hadn't yet shared with Gonzo what he'd discovered in regards to Denny Teng, his *Asian invasion* scheme, and the illicit banking connection with Frankie Coleman, let alone Zipper or Fungo or sad, college-boy Howie. It was all still a big question mark as it related to Karrie.

All Lucky had truly achieved was identifying a nest of villainy. In doing so, he'd entangled himself in something ugly with ripple effects that might even penetrate the armor of City Hall. Despite some relative certainty as to Denny Teng's bloody fate, Lucky hadn't been able to directly connect him to the hit and run on Karrie. The only thread remained Denny Teng's daughter's drawings.

Lucky didn't know if he'd be scooped up by the LAPD for additional questioning about Cat Rincon's murder—or even arrested. Because he knew more answers would come, either in an avalanche or a trickle, he felt he'd run out the string as far as he could. Now he was determined to spend as much time as he could with Karrie.

"You need a shower," volunteered Gonzo.

"That bad, huh?"

"You've smelled worse," she teased. "Worried Karrie's care will suffer, though."

"Because I stink?"

"Let us drive you home. You can clean up, maybe catch a few Zs, and resume your post."

"Already called Frosty for a lift."

"Still don't trust that guy."

"You don't have to. But trust me. He's all right."

"You're such a sucker for lowlifes on the rebound," she nudged.

"That why we found each other?"

"Come home with me and Trav. Let the docs do their thing. She's in good hands."

"Whose home?" Lucky wondered. "Mine or yours?"

"We can decide on the drive." Gonzo intertwined her fingers

with his and let out a deep sigh. "She's gonna be okay. She *has* to be okay, right?"

Footsteps. Squeaky sneakers. Travis appeared behind them, placing a hand on each of their shoulders.

"Jesus, Trav," said Gonzo. "You scared me."

"Hey," switched Travis. "Look at all of us."

"What do you mean?"

"We're all together. We're a family again."

Lucky let the moment sink in. Travis was nearly correct. The hit and run might have brought the four of them back into immediate proximity. Tragically, yet somehow buoyed by the revelation, the three conscious members of Lucky's improvised clan spent ten more silent minutes with Karrie before taking turns kissing her hand and offering a goodnight squeeze.

The trio ambled from the hospital to the parking structure. Lucky showed exhausted surprise when Gonzo chirped the alarm to a practically brand-new Toyota Tundra pickup. Double cab. White. Black rims.

"You?" offered Lucky. "In a pickup?"

"Snatched up the lease off another pilot in a shitty divorce," she replied. "Poor guy's back to driving a Honda."

"She's giving it to me when I turn eighteen," Travis said.

"Not," nudged Gonzo before putting on a coquettish pose in the driver's seat. "But I can tell Lucky likes it on me."

"Lucky does," agreed the deputy, succumbing to a rare feeling of normalcy. A strange peace.

The Friday-night traffic was thin. Gonzo's solicitations for Lucky to spend the night at their Altadena bungalow were met with awkward giggles from Travis in the back seat. Lucky compromised, requesting to be dropped off at his Eagle Rock apartment. He promised to be quick. He'd clean up and borrow Karrie's Prius.

The winding drive to Lucky's hilltop apartment complex emptied into a cul de sac. Gonzo needed to execute a seven-point turn to maneuver the big truck around until it was pointing back down the road.

"Don't laugh at me," she blushed at her tentative driving. "Had it barely a week."

"Your mom," directed Lucky to Travis, "can fly a helo through a hula hoop but couldn't drive her way out of a Trader Joe's parking lot."

There were no kisses so long. It was too soon for that kind of display. Lucky drummed his hand on the Tundra's hood, lingering on the warmth from Gonzo's face on the other side of the windshield, and mouthed, "Thirty, forty minutes tops."

"Promises, promises," she mouthed back. In her sideview mirror, she watched him disappear into the stairway that sliced between the covered carports.

"Think it's gonna happen?" asked Travis. "Lucky actually gonna stay over with us? At our home?"

Gonzo exhaled before finding her curly-haired boy out of the corner of her eye.

"It's the Lucky we all know and love," she shrugged, resolved. "Hope for the best, endure the heartache." With that, Gonzo dropped the big pickup into gear, eased off the brake, and crept the big tires back down the slope.

Travis was vacillating between the excitement of being a nearly whole family again and girding his emotions against disappointment and flat-out calamity. The rear passenger window felt cool as he rested his forehead against it, his eyes locked onto the slow-moving landscape of city lights filtered through the nearer trees and brush. At a dirt turnout, Travis noticed a parked car. The vehicle was his favorite color of maroon, but paint-challenged from bumper to bumper with Southern California sun damage. Travis clocked it as a Mercury Grand Marquis, the knock-off sister of Ford's Crown Vic, Lucky Dey's preferred ride.

So sad was the boy's initial thought. A cool car left to rot by its owner. Then Travis got an eyeful of the driver. Chill bumps erupted on his young skin. The two-seconds-long encounter felt as if in ultra-slow motion, especially the moment when the driver's eyes caught the teen's.

"Mom!" he sparked.

"Yeah?"

"The guy in the Marquis."

"Don't tell me he's got a for sale sign in the window."

"Big fat guy with a mustache. I saw him at the hospital!"

"Sorry?"

"He came into the waiting room."

"Believe me. A lotta fat guys look the same—"

"Mom! He was in the waiting room. He was asking all about Lucky."

Gonzo flicked her eyes into the rearview mirror and tapped her brakes for some light. The Marquis in the cutout was hard to make out. With the headlamps extinguished, the man behind the wheel was impossible to see.

"You sure?" asked Gonzo.

"I said I was sure. And he was asking about Lucky!"

Lucky's injured eardrum was pounding with a constant, high-pitched hum layered over the bass of his pulse. It sounded like distant electronic feedback and was annoying as hell if he allowed himself to focus on it. Instead he stayed on task—climbing up those tight three flights of stairs to his apartment for a shower and shave.

And there was so much more of Karrie yet to worry over.

He damned the planked staircase and, at every turn, the dark, unlit corners. It seemed a miracle he hadn't tripped before. The only saving grace of the crummy design was that it was barely more than a shoulder and a half wide. In a fall he might be able to catch himself. With his ear throbbing, Lucky was beginning to feel off-balance. On the final turn before his apartment, the usual flood from his yellow porch light was nowhere to be seen. The bulb was either extinguished or dead…

…*or unscrewed.*

Lucky slowed two steps shy of the top landing, his eyes level with the deadbolt lock. He swiped the flashlight function on his phone to get a look at the keyhole. He couldn't recall if he'd applied that safety film of lip balm when he'd last departed the apartment when he'd been rushing out to UCLA. He took another step, hyperaware of the creaks underfoot that could alert anybody who might be lying in wait inside the sublet or outside.

The keyhole. It was clean of any balm. Lucky could read tiny, fresh scratches around the lock, a probable sign it had been either bumped or picked. Flicking off the flashlight, he pictured the rental's interior. There was plenty of room to the left of the jamb for a concealed assassin to stand flattened against the wall, gun muzzle aimed at temple height. That flavor of ambush was nearly impossible to defend against.

I'm hesitating, thought Lucky.

His hand found his pistol's grip behind his right hip. Lucky pulled at the same moment he heard the footsteps, a fleet pair of feet charging up the stairs from below. Lucky spun around. His equilibrium was gone. He fell to the left, hoping the plywood wall of the stairwell would prop him up. He saw only a shadow. Small. Black-clad. His trigger finger showed experience and wisdom, held at a half-squeeze until he saw the first muzzle flash. Mid-caliber. *Probably a 9mm*, he guessed. Double taps—*Bam bam! Bam bam!*

Still leaning, Lucky pulled. One squeeze—a loud .45-caliber *BOOM*—dropped the figure. And though the gunshots masked the sound of the apartment door being thrown open, Lucky sensed another presence. He twisted back toward the landing as a silhouette as black as black emerged. Faceless almost. With all ballast gone, Lucky felt gravity pulling him backward. He saw another muzzle flash, feeling the sting of spent powder on his face and the spin of a bullet missing his hairline by fractions.

Whatever you do, thought Lucky, *don't let go of your weapon.*

What followed could only be described as a tangle. The intruder on the landing lost his bearings. Just when he was adjusting his aim he missed the first step. His 210 pounds of muscle carried him over in a cartwheel of momentum, none of it interrupting the rhythm of his trigger pulls.

To Lucky it sounded as if a string of firecrackers had been set off in his pocket. As the trio collided and tumbled down the stairwell, Lucky couldn't tell if the sting he felt was from hitting the stairs or bullets striking his flesh. He felt the splinters of plywood spitting like sparks and the uncoordinated flailing of arms and shoe heels. Then he found himself on his back, halfway past the ninety-degree turn and down the next flight toward the second floor. The yellow bug lamp outside that apartment blazed, bleeding mustard-colored light onto the melee. One of Lucky's legs was trapped underneath the first black-clad assailant, whose face was obscured by a gaping bullet hole and a geyser of pulsing blood. Beyond, at the bare reach of the amber illumination, was the second man—the one who had been lying in wait. He was dark, his features obscured by a nylon stocking, his eyes appeared stunned, but recovering.

Do I know you? wondered Lucky.

The man's focus returned in an instant. Alert. Lucky could see him searching for his weapon so Lucky didn't wait. He lifted his Sig and instinct guided his aim. He let the bullet fly. The pulp-wood sheering behind the assassin became instantly painted in a mix of the man's brains and some salt and pepper hair. The body tilted away, the dead man's arm involuntarily rising, revealing the Beretta pistol in his grip.

Lucky's head spilled back. He was about to release a sigh when he noted a figure standing eight feet behind him. It was the nosy neighbor in a periwinkle fleece housecoat. The old bat herself, with a shocked, slack-jawed face frozen into a silent scream befitting all those failed face-lifts.

"Get inside…Shut your damn door…Call 911!" wheezed Lucky, fresh wind not yet having filled his lungs.

She withdrew and the door banged shut with a hollow *whap*. Lucky twisted free, his left leg strangely feeling both numb and on fire. He turned himself and began examining his first kill, the man called Guava. Both forearms were clean of ink. Lucky pulled up both his pant legs, searching for a tattoo.

"C'mon, asshole. Show me," angered Lucky.

Lucky rolled the body onto its side, pulling up the fleece hoodie to reveal the telltale body art branded between the would-be assassin's shoulder blades—a Viking helmet.

48

Eagle Rock.

Despite her doubts, Gonzo had turned the truck around at the first driveway. She'd known Travis to be stubborn about certain facts he thought to be true—insistent and rigid—only to later be proven wrong by his mother or Karrie. The teen was generally good humored about discovering he had been mistaken. Yet that didn't change his initial stubbornness. As a matter of process, Gonzo had aimed her Tundra back up the hill, fully expecting her headlamps to sweep around the corner, spotlighting the fat man in the maroon Mercury. All she'd need was to identify herself as a police officer, flash her brass LAPD shield, and the first blush of the man's reaction would most likely reveal his business.

As in probably "none of mine," she mimed to herself.

Only the turnout was empty and the car was gone. If the man in the car hadn't passed her, then he'd U-turned from his parking spot and hustled back up the slope. Gonzo punched the accelerator. The big V-8 engine thrummed, bolting the pickup back toward the hilltop apartment building. The end of the cul-de-sac appeared over the rise, the maroon Marquis stopped in front of the lone apartment building. The round ex-deputy—also known as Mooch—was at the open trunk. At the sound of the onrushing Tundra, he swept his heavy chin over his shoulder, then automatically bent down to the trunk well. He returned with a shotgun, expertly jacking a round into the chamber as he swiveled.

"DOWN!" Gonzo screamed at her son.

She had no time to reach for her service gun, which was safely locked away in the glove box. Nor did she have anywhere to find cover. Hers was a choice to either brake and duck, or drop the gas pedal to the floor and close the distance on the shotgun.

Gonzo chose option two.

The moment was framed by her windshield. Gonzo folded herself over the pickup's center console and out of the picture. The muzzle of the retired cop's sawed-off pump shotgun vomited flame and thumbnail-sized lead pellets. The Tundra's windshield imploded in a spray of shards and dust. And all Gonzo could imagine was her darling boy receiving a face full of deadly buckshot.

The pickup's grille slammed into the Marquis, practically swallowing the open trunk. Air bags deployed, exploding open in loud pops from every which direction. Then there was the grinding of metal, followed by an uneasy stillness and the whining of the Tundra's impaired engine.

"Travis?" groaned Gonzo. When she heard nothing from the back seat, she cried, "Travis!"

It was dark. And the deflated airbags obstructed Gonzo's view of the rear seat. Unbuckling, she shouldered her way out, scrambled to her feet, and opened the rear door of the extended cab. Expecting the worst—to see Travis bloodied—maybe even dead. Instead, the back seat was empty and Travis nowhere to be seen.

"Mom?"

Gonzo hurried around the truck bed to the other side. There

she found him standing in a wash of headlights and broken tail-lamps. He appeared stiff but uninjured, eyes glued to where the truck's grille had impaled the sedan's now-crumpled rear end. Pinned between both vehicles were the remains of Mooch—his flannel shirt and perhaps bits of flesh and sinew all that were keeping his upper torso from being completely severed in two.

With a motherly hand Gonzo covered the teen's eyes and turned him into her, pulling her son into a close embrace.

"Are you okay?" she asked. "Hurt? Anywhere?"

"Fine," he said. "What happened? Did he shoot at us?"

"Think so. Yeah…" said Gonzo, not entirely believing her boy was uninjured.

"Lucky?"

"I dunno."

"No…Lucky!"

Travis swerved and pointed at Lucky, hobbling down the steps between the carports. He slowed to assess the wreckage, gun in one hand, Karrie's car keys in the other, her neon pink pepper spray dangling brightly. Travis covered the short distance with a stumbling sprint.

"Did you see what mom did?" shouted the teen.

"You both okay?" asked Lucky.

"We're good. But the guy who was shooting at us…" said Travis, wheezing with excitement.

"Deep breaths," cautioned Lucky before addressing Gonzo. "You got a phone? Not sure my neighbor lady isn't dead from a heart attack."

Travis hadn't noticed the blood staining Lucky's jeans, but Gonzo had.

"That somebody else's blood?" she asked. "Or yours?"

"Caught a stinger in the hammy. Through 'n' through I think," revealed Lucky, his voice low and as calm as death. He shook the keys. "Gonna get me to the hospital."

"Like hell," said Gonzo. "You'll wait for the ambulance."

"Got two dead guys on the stairs I don't wanna explain right now. Ex-sheriffs," he reasoned.

"I'll drive you, then," suggested Gonzo.

"One of us leaving the crime scene is bad enough. Be a good cop. Stay."

"You're not going to the hospital," she accused, knowingly.

"'Course I am. I'm shot." Lucky spun toward Karrie's Prius. Gonzo could see an ooze of red staining the back of his jeans, the blotch showing signs of a slow spread.

"I'm not good with this!" Gonzo called after him.

"What's good about any of this?" bellowed Lucky, unlocking the car via the remote. He threw the door open, carelessly sweeping away the safety glass from when he'd broken the window three days earlier to retrieve Karrie's backpack. He dropped into the seat without remembering to adjust it for his size. In doing so he smacked his sore ear on the doorframe.

Lucky cursed himself with a sharp "Fuck!"

49

City of Commerce.

If Babylon's mother loved playing poker, she loved playing on Friday nights best of all. Her theory was that the perpetual losers worked all week to wager their salaries on the weekend. In her view, those pigeons were easier to pluck than true gambling addicts, who would at least display a measure or two of skill. The Friday Losers—as she joyously called them—were fatigued after a week toiling at their jobs and one or two drinks away from making one bad decision after another. So, the cotton-topped ninety-one-year-old was none too pleased when her sling-armed son tapped her on the shoulder and said it was time to bag her chips and cash in for the night.

"Friday night!" she snipped, hoping it would make her appear even more lacking in faculties to the six strangers at the table.

"I'm tired, Ma," begged Babylon.

"I don't know this man," she laughed to her fellow players.

"I'm her son," he deadpanned, "and she's gotta make curfew at the old poker player's home."

"One more time around the wheel," demanded Babylon's mom, meaning another seven hands of poker. "Got my social security check today."

"One more loop," relented Babylon. "And then it's a night."

The casino floor was so congested Babylon had to make a circuitous route back to the bar. The pouty-lipped bartender saw him coming, filled a fresh tumbler with ice, and started another soda and lime. Babylon parked himself on the same stool he'd been settled on for the past two hours. He'd been talking up the bartenders and anyone else within earshot—in part because that's just who he was, but mostly because he needed to be distracted while he waited for the text from Stricks that the deed had been done. Until he had confirmation of the kill he wasn't going to bother Denny Teng with details on how and where to transfer the cash.

Babylon slipped his oversized phone from inside his arm sling to the bar, swirled the ice in his drink with his pinky finger, and lifted the fizzy brew to his lips.

The last spin around the poker table proved profitable for his mom. He carried her chips, cashing them in for four hundred dollars and change, always with the promise that he'd bank the winnings and use them to pay for her incidentals at her pricey retirement living facility.

Babylon parked the Yom Kippur Clipper behind the three handicapped-access mini-buses the home owned for shuttling around their ancient clientele. He handed his mother off to the uniformed doorman, more fitting of a swanky high-rise apartment building along the Wilshire Corridor, and trudged back to his Cadillac, having left the engine running with the keys still dangling from the ignition as if to say, *Just try stealing my car, asshole.*

Because of his injured arm, Babylon had to pull the heavy door open with his left hand, twist ninety degrees, and back himself into the seat, butt cheeks first. Then he swung his legs inside and pulled the door shut. That's when he smelled the cigarette smoke.

"Put your good arm on the steering wheel," said Lucky, his voice a veritable flatline of emotion. He slipped the muzzle of his .45 between Babylon's headrest and the top of the seat until it touched the man's neck. "Don't cramp up. Just gonna help you with your seat belt."

With a long arm, Lucky reached around and slowly unfurled the seat belt, the vintage retractor counting off the *tick-tick-tick* of every distributed inch of reinforced stranded ribbon until the tongue of the locking mechanism clicked into the receptacle.

"Here's the clever part of the trick," said Lucky, revealing a tube of super glue. "Picked this up from the Armos."

Lucky squeezed the super glue into the space around the seatbelt fastener until the tube was empty.

"Don't worry," Lucky eased. "Got a blade. In a pinch, I can cut you out."

"But you're not gonna cut me out," growled Babylon.

"Night's still young," yucked Lucky. "I might bleed out and die before we're finished."

Babylon studied his rearview mirror. In the dark, he couldn't see much of Lucky but for a scalp rimmed in droplets of perspiration. His face appeared briefly in the glow of a cigarette cherry as he pulled another drag.

"Didn't take you for a smoker."

"Reformed. Like you. Except my vises were pain pills and cancer sticks." Lucky regarded the burning Marlboro. "Guess I'm off the wagon today."

"What do you want?"

"Right now I need a ride to the hospital," said Lucky, pumping a soft fist into the headrest. "Get me to your nearest, will ya?"

"You're hurt?"

"Gunshot. Thanks to some of your Viking pals."

"I don't—"

"Stop," interrupted Lucky. "Your bullshit don't float here." If Lucky had any doubt that the attack on him was coordinated by Babylon, seeing the man's right arm in that cheap sling had sealed the deal. Babylon must've been the assailant who had tried to put a bullet through his ear outside the swanky Fryman Canyon fundraiser.

Cranking the Cadillac into gear, Babylon eased the boat of a sedan into the street. As facile as he considered himself when it came to extricating himself from sticky situations, with only one arm and his seat belt acting as a permanent restraint, he couldn't figure an escape beyond surging into traffic and hoping for some kind of cataclysmic collision that killed Lucky and left him alive.

Low percentage play, he decided, setting his indicator for a right turn onto Firestone Boulevard, the map in his brain automatically setting a course for the Kaiser Hospital on Downey's Bellflower Boulevard. The retired deputy knew the way by heart, having made hundreds of trips there both on and off the job. The bright lights from fast food stands, discount furniture stores, and billboards streaked across the Caddy's windshield like low-speed tracer fire.

"Musta been painful," said Lucky. He waited for Babylon to flick his eyes into the rearview mirror. "Laying in the trunk of your car. It's just a guess, but I can't picture you hiding out anywhere else with every cop in the Valley looking for the shooter."

"How'd you know?"

"GPS locator," answered Lucky. It turned out the device he'd long ago planted on Cat Rincon's Audi had some battery left. After visiting Babylon at the personnel building, Lucky had tucked it just under the right rear fender of the man's Cadillac. The magnets attached easily. When he logged into the device's app, Lucky could find a record of the behemoth sedan's every movement. "What is it? Dislocated shoulder? Torn rotator? Whatever happened to you musta hurt like—"

"Like a hot knife dipped in rat poison," finished Babylon, not satisfied to be relegated to the conversational beta. "My Vikes?"

"Body bags," informed Lucky. "The fat dude I didn't do? Think they might've had to call the hazmat team."

"Mooch," conceded Babylon. "Too fat. Too slow."

"Your job at personnel," switched Lucky. "You like it?"

"It's okay." Babylon thought the change in subject curious. "You lookin' to make a move?"

"I'm out at Sheriff's."

"Want me to hook you up?"

"Who do you know?"

"Now, now," teased Babylon. "Can't give away all my secrets if I'm gonna get done dead by you. I mean, where's my leverage? Gimme something I want and I'll give you something you want."

"You and Denny Teng."

"What about?"

"You're not the kinda guy he just stumbles across. Who introduced you?"

"Show me you're my deputy brother? I'll tell all," bargained Babylon. "Get you in a desk in personnel. Your own investigative kingdom. I will answer all. Over a plate of sushi, no less. You like sushi?"

"I'd like my daughter to live."

"Had nothin' to do with that." Babylon put his one able hand in the air. "On my Jewish mom's poker-playin' life. Not a goddamn thing."

"What'd Denny Teng tell you?"

"Besides to put a bullet in your melon? None of my business. But, hey. Denny Teng who you wanna get down with? I can be a big help. I'll even wear a wire for you."

"Denny Teng's not my problem anymore. But there's still you."

"I'm not your problem starting five minutes ago," promised Babylon. "I'm here to help. What can the Mighty Babylon do for you?"

"Can you stop the bleeding?" When Lucky looked down, his left pant leg was heavy and soaked in blood. "Your car's gonna need to get detailed after I get out."

"Hospital's close. Comin' up on the right. You wanna get dropped at the ER entrance?"

"That'll work," said Lucky. But before he finished the cigarette, he used the embers to start a second butt. Smoke billowed. He lowered his window four inches.

"Thanks," dripped Babylon, the sarcasm unmistakable, seeping through his bravado and fear. "Thought you were gonna gag me to death with secondhand smoke."

Lucky saw the blazing red emergency room symbol and pointing arrow. Babylon wheeled the car into the drive. Behind the ER's awning was a white, floodlit, seven-story hospital rising from the Downey flatlands—almost as if it were advertising itself as a destination for hope.

"My fourth hospital in a week," mumbled Lucky.

"Helluva week," added Babylon. He was trying his level best to seem more earnest than evil. The nearer he rolled to the ER entrance, the safer he felt. But Lucky hadn't given up his game. Surely there must've been fifty hospitals closer to wherever Babylon's failed Vikings had chosen their badly executed whack attack.

Useless shitheels, Babylon cursed to himself. He was blaming Mooch over all of them. The *fat fuck* had screwed the pooch. Somehow, Babylon was certain. He stopped the Caddy under the ER awning and awkwardly cranked the column shifter into park with his left arm.

"Signed, sealed, delivered," said Babylon.

"You miss Lynwood?" asked Lucky, fully aware they were hardly more than a mile from the Lynwood Station.

"Best days of my life," answered Babylon.

"True you fellas had a moonshine still behind the motoryard?"

"Hey. Not just any ol' corn whiskey," defended Babylon. "Distilled twice over. Smelled like bread baking. Tasted like home cookin'. And Cappy never caught on."

"Good times."

"The best."

Lucky pushed his door out and hobbled around the rear to

the emergency room's sliding doors. In a matter of seconds, he was gone. Out of Babylon's sight. Babylon heaved his relief with a deflating exhale, then found himself glancing fully around, craning his neck, checking all his mirrors. Half of him expected a blockade of black-and-whites to descend upon him for the arrest, perhaps having listened to the last ten minutes of the conversation via some wireless recording trap. The other half of him could imagine some killer compatriot taking Lucky's exit as a cue to slip up next to the driver's side window and put five rounds of nasty lead into his idiotic skull.

Deservingly so, he reasoned.

But nothing came. Not even an ambulance. So, he steered his Yom Kippur Clipper away from the hospital. At the first stoplight, he reached across himself to release the seat belt. Only the super glue had already set. The lock was impossibly frozen.

"Of course," he bitched.

Once certain he wasn't being tailed, Babylon quickly pulled off onto a residential side street, hoping to figure a way to extricate himself from the belted confines of his seat. The neighborhood might well have been his own—squat, humble abodes with semi-generous lots. Sidewalks. The outlines of a few scraggly palm trees against a sky that wasn't quite black. Best of all, the street bore no streetlamps.

Struggling against the belt wasn't going to be an option, especially considering the extreme g-forces the mechanism was designed to withstand. A blade, he thought. Something sharp. Or hot, even. Maybe the cigarette lighter would melt through the nylon strapping bite by smelly bite?

Cigarette? Smell?

Lucky might've been gone but the stench of the enriched tobacco smoke remained. Not stale, but fresh, as if he were still in the back seat. Babylon couldn't recall seeing Lucky toss his smoke before entering the hospital. Had the son of a bitch left the burning butt in his back seat? And what else did his nostrils taste? Was that burning leather?

The prick!

But a new odor was fast to the nose and even more familiar. Sulfurous. Like a match strike. A picture popped into his brain like a random pull. A memory from way back. A series of arsons that had plagued South Los Angeles. Both LAPD and Sheriff's had been all over it. Every cop had been put on the lookout for the sick bastard who'd been burning down businesses using little more than a cigarette for a fuse, a match for ignition, and gallon milk jugs filled with ethyl alcohol for fuel. Lynwood deputies knew all about the method.

So did the deputies from Lennox.

By the time Babylon had figured out Lucky's end game, it was too late. The two jugs of clear corn whiskey—moonshine—placed in the footwell behind Babylon's driver's seat ignited in a slow-moving fireball that instantly enveloped the car's interior, sucking out all the available air in a half second. And that rear window that Lucky had lowered four inches? It fed just enough oxygen into the cabin to fuel the pyre into a rage, setting flame to every surface, including the leather seats, as well as Babylon's clothing and skin.

The subsequent report stated that no neighbors had heard the driver of the Cadillac scream. The victim in the front seat, identified as both a Downey resident and former Sheriff's Deputy Mark Baba, was a recovering alcoholic who'd been long rumored to have a private penchant for homemade corn liquor, otherwise known as South L.A. moonshine.

Saturday

50

Downey.

Lucky had guessed correctly. His bullet wound was a through and through. It had passed through his flesh, exiting cleanly with minimum damage. An X-ray revealed the slug had entered his upper quad, dodged the femur by a hair's width, and left through the back of his thigh. Because no metal fragments were detected, the ER doctor and nurses irrigated, disinfected, and plugged the wound. Further treatment required an MRI and ultrasound to better diagnose the measure of muscle damage. Lucky denied the extra care, informing the staff that he'd have the wound looked at by doctors at his next destination—UCLA Medical Center. While waiting for paperwork and discharge papers, his mobile phone buzzed. He didn't recognize the number.

Bad news, he instantly thought.

Considering the carnage left in his wake—righteous or otherwise—how could the call be anything but lousy? The cast of dubious characters that sprinted through his head seemed like an endless parade of bad guys or fellow cops looking to put an end to him. For a split second he even contemplated if it was Babylon at the other end of the line, phoning Lucky only to laugh at him for his failed incendiary device.

"Yeah," whispered Lucky into the phone, his voice box dry from lack of saliva.

"Mr. Dey?" asked the voice at the other end. "This is Deputy Lewis from the Malibu/Lost Hills Station. Have some information for you on that hit and run involving your daughter. How is she, by the way?"

"Hangin' in," crackled Lucky.

"The department's thoughts and prayers are with you," replied the deputy, genuine and not at all sounding as rote as cops sometimes do. "As it turns out, the drivers were local."

"Drivers?"

"Joyriders, actually. Pair of fifteen-year-old knuckleheads. One of them was the son of the car's owner. Looks like they dumped the car to make it look like it was stolen before humping it back to the neighborhood."

"Joyriders? Local?" repeated Lucky as if trying to believe it himself. "The story I got was the car was jacked in Culver."

"Think that might've been a story spun up by the parents. To protect the kids."

"Jesus."

"Picked both boys up earlier this evening. Spending a few nights at Nidorf in Sylmar. That's the juvenile—"

"Yeah. I know."

"Thought you'd wanna know sooner than later," apologized the deputy. "Sorry if the call comes at a bad hour."

"Not a problem," finished Lucky. "Thanks."

The ramifications of the call didn't quite land, at least not in the moment. Lucky couldn't even place it as either good or bad news. In pursuing justice for Karrie, he'd turned over enough rocks to find a nest of scorpions and stirred them up enough to crack their defensive veneers and let havoc reign. Except not a single one of them was guilty of the crime against his daughter. He knew the guilt from his actions would surely come. Of that he was secure. On that date, he'd add it to his box of transgressions.

In a pair of borrowed surgical scrubs, he caught a ride to Westwood, leaving his crutches behind in the cab's back seat. When he stepped off the fourth-floor elevators, he spotted Dr. Uziel, the neurosurgeon who'd first treated Karrie after the hit and run. After the good doctor's double-take at the gimping deputy in scrubs, he pointed and rushed toward Lucky.

"I'm fine," Lucky warned, not interested in another lick of attention.

"It's your daughter," returned Uziel. "She's awake!"

Lucky stalled, feet glued to the floor. There were eerie tingles in his scalp. Did he hear the doctor correctly?

"She's talking," continued Uziel, guiding Lucky by the elbow. "Some of it's nonsensical and gibberish, but that's expected with the trauma. Some's almost cogent. We've tried to explain to her what happened, but I think she needs a familiar face."

At the turn in the corridor near the first ICU pod was the ever-faithful Frosty. When he caught sight of Lucky, a gigantic grin creased his face.

"He tell you?" asked Frosty.

Lucky returned only a nod, gimping himself faster toward Karrie's cube. He could hear music playing from a small speaker. It was from a band Karrie liked; Lucky couldn't recall the name. She was flanked by two nurses, faces beaming toward her.

"Karrie," announced Uziel. "Look who I found."

Then Lucky saw her. Karrie's eyes swiveled to him, exploding in recognition, followed by a face wrenched in pain.

"Watch your head movements," cautioned a nurse. "Pretend it's as delicate as an egg."

"Egg," repeated Karrie, nodding with her eyes.

"Hey, kiddo," smiled Lucky, pupils wet.

"…happened…you?" Karrie asked softly.

"You know me," said Lucky. "My own worst enemy."

"…not…so…lucky," she forced.

"No," he agreed.

Karrie tried a laugh, but that hurt as well. Uziel pushed up a chair behind Lucky, who sat as if discarding a ton of weight.

"You told her?" Lucky asked, not certain he'd remembered what Uziel had told him only moments earlier.

"That there was an accident," said the doctor. "And that since Tuesday she's been here with us. Some surgeries. And that sometimes coma recoveries come slow."

Excited to add her own point of view, Karrie began muttering nonsensical words and noises. To her it made sense, but for Lucky and the medical staff surrounding her, it might as well have been a language unto itself. The looks on their faces put a scare into her.

"I jus' speak blah blah blahs?" said Karrie to much amusement. Then she squeezed Lucky's hand, firmly as if to get his attention. He stood again, bent over her. "Tuesday?"

"Yeah," said Lucky. "It's Saturday now."

"'Kay," nodded Karrie. "So…So…So…?"

"So?" repeated Lucky.

"So…So what…I…miss?"

51

San Gabriel.

When Jiao returned to Country Club Drive, the street was blocked and her house was taped off with crime-scene tape. Instead of identifying herself as a resident, she asked her friend Biyu to turn the car around and to please not ask her any more questions about her strange appearance on her doorstep that morning. Jiao was still organizing the pieces in her own mind. She thought it best to figure out as much for herself as she could before talking to the authorities.

As for Jiao's murder—as she would later come to call the episode—the details were a mix of searing images and fuzzy recall. It had been a shock when her husband pulled her underneath the pool's surface, holding her down to drown her. In the moment, though, it had made complete sense. She'd been howling at him, angry enough to kill him herself. So, why shouldn't Denny respond in kind? She remembered struggling as he'd forced her under, yet she had been unable to find the will to live. But instinctively, she had held her breath. Blackness surrounded her and she lost consciousness. All the while in her subconscious she was thinking, *This is it. This is my death.*

Her next memory was the sky, blue, over her head. She was coughing up chlorinated water. Her throat burned. A bearded man came into her view. Blond. Strong in build, forty years old, wet, and wearing board shorts, he was explaining that he'd just given her a dose of live-saving, mouth-to-mouth resuscitation. He'd feared she was dead. He wanted to call an ambulance.

Finding her bearings, Jiao noticed the man's pool cleaning equipment. Through her muddy ears, she heard him reminding her that her regular pool man, Mark, was away on vacation. Her savior, a total stranger, had arrived to tend the pool when he'd found her motionless at the bottom of the shallow end.

Despite hacking up a nonstop stream of phlegm and water, Jiao had asked the substitute pool man to drive her to Min's school. Denny's car was still in the shop and he must have taken her Jag. After a quick change of clothes, she was able to walk onto campus like she owned it and coolly signed her daughter out for the day. The final favor Jiao asked the pool man was to drive her and Min to the nearby town of Arcadia, where her friend Biyu lived. Biyu tipped the pool man two one-hundred-dollar bills. In exchange he left Jiao with his contact info.

"In case," he'd said.

"In case of what?" she'd asked.

"Dunno," said the pool man. "In case maybe you need a new pool guy?" Though by his maturity and pose, it was clear he expected there might be more to Jiao's damsel-in-distress story. He wouldn't have been the least bit surprised to eventually hear from the police regarding a domestic violence complaint.

Meanwhile, the San Gabriel PD was dealing with multiple homicides, the kind of crime to which both large and small police departments all over the Southland had become accustomed. After cordoning off the scene on Country Club Drive, crime scene techs on loan from Pasadena had flooded the address. Four bodies were discovered at the scene: one in the home's foyer and three others in or in front of the detached garage. The first call to 911 had been made by an anonymous tipster from a phone later identified as belonging to one of the victims.

As for when Howie had pulled the trigger on his father's Ruger .22 for the last time...he had been met with a metallic *clink*. He hadn't expected the magazine to be empty. The internal hammer landed with no bullet to strike. The twitch of Howie's index finger sent a harsh waking signal to his nervous system. It was as if he'd just injected ten shots of espresso into his bloodstream. Seconds before, he'd wanted to die. Or thought he had. It would have been the end of Howie's story, a righteous curtain to his misspent year with Denny Teng.

Yet alive he was, the sole survivor of a quadruple homicide. A kind of clarity overcame him. A calm. After pocketing his father's pistol, he rushed past the bodies into Denny's behind-the-garage office and dismantled all the hard drives containing what he thought might be incriminating. He made sure to touch nothing but what he would bring with him, then calmly walked down the driveway to his car. There, on the dash, he found the cell phone that belonged to the dead gangster called Zipper. As he drove, Howie dialed in the tip to the police. Some forty minutes later, he tossed both the gun and Zipper's cell phone out the car window while traveling across the Vincent Thomas Bridge, the suspension span over the deep waters between San Pedro and Terminal Island.

With that final task completed, Howie returned to his dorm and somehow fell into a deep, dreamless sleep. And though he fully expected to wake to the police pounding on his door, none came. Eventually, he would be questioned regarding his relationship with Denny Teng, but in a group setting with all the other interns. Nobody, including Howie, claimed to have a lick of info regarding the quadruple homicide. There would be no follow-up questions from anybody in authority.

For Frankie Coleman, there were no more interrogations. But that didn't keep her from lawyering up with a five-star criminal defense firm. Her well-connected legal team was able to source the reason for the LAPD's lack of interest in any further questioning: the mayor's office had suggested the narrative surrounding Denny Teng and the quadruple homicide had something to do with his involvement with Asian gangs in the SGV. Frankie Coleman was profiled as nothing more than a friend of Mayor Ram's and someone with whom Denny Teng did some banking. With the spotlight switched off, she thought it an opportune moment to cash out. In lieu of taking Aegis & Angels Partners, Ltd. public, she accepted a low-ball buyout from one of her larger depositors and walked away with twenty-two million dollars. With that, the former Miss Runner-Up sold her Manhattan Beach home, pulled up stakes, and bought a mansion on forty acres outside of Nashville. Not bad for trailer trash, she reasoned.

Not bad at all.

June

52

Downtown.

"You're late," said Winter. Lucky had finally remembered Ms. Vanilla's name, and restrained himself from asking if she had siblings branded after seasons. Winter stood, smoothed out her skirt, and tucked a leather valise under her arm.

"Traffic," shrugged Lucky as he stepped off the elevator. He scanned the firm's lobby. It was furnished in a sleek, gray and black industrial motif, a mix of brushed stainless steel and black leather. Cold. *Fitting*, thought Lucky, considering most of the law practice's business was at the expense of the County.

"I see you've lost the crutches," noted Winter.

"That's the easy part," said Lucky. "Losing the limp is gonna take some work."

"We're all here," spoke Winter to the receptionist before returning to Lucky. "Speaking of work, how's your girl?"

"Rehab's a bitch. Good thing Karrie's a bigger bitch. Her description. Not mine."

"So, her ability to speak is back to normal?"

"Getting there. Hardest part for her? Speech therapy. Physically, though, she's in a race to beat me to the beach."

"That's right. The two of you surf—"

"They're ready for you," interrupted the receptionist.

"Be right there," answered Winter. She stepped closer to Lucky and lowered her voice. "Here's what's gonna happen. They are going to give us everything we want. You get to keep your badge but only as a reserve deputy. You also get the job in personnel at your current salary. In exchange, you need to clear some things up for them."

"Clear up what for who?"

"Don't know yet. That's why we're here."

"This oughta be a kick," dripped Lucky.

"That's why you're here with your personal attorney," she eased. "Things get uncomfortable, we walk. What we have working for us is they want this to end. Same as us."

Lucky and Winter followed a young paralegal, who guided them through the busy law office to a corner conference room with a north- and east-facing sixty-first-floor view. The day outside was as gray as the décor. June gloom, it was called.

Waiting were a team of county and city lawyers—all men in dark suits like they were in uniform. The two exceptions were the only men Lucky recognized: the handsome LAPD detective who reminded him of a TV actor—the same cop who'd questioned him after the assault that had left him nearly deaf in his right ear and Catalina Rincon dead—and Mayor Ramon Avila, who was standing, arms crossed, leaning in the opposite corner.

Shit, Lucky said to himself. The mayor himself—Denny Teng's friend. Until that moment, Lucky hadn't put much thought into the city's top pol's character beyond the obvious assumptions. He was a politician. Slick. Two-faced. A man who might not have been of the people, but claimed publicly to be for the people. Typical. Disposable.

Given Mayor Avila's posture, his presence in the room spoke of something personal.

Lucky knew Cat Rincon's killing remained unsolved. Now, in exchange for keeping his shield, salary, benefits, and a new job in personnel, the powers in the room were going to want him to tell all. Solve the mystery. String together the events that had left Cat Rincon plus four retired deputies bearing Viking tattoos dead. In math it was called the common denominator. And Lucky was it.

If only they knew the true number, thought Lucky. Add Denny, Zipper, Fungo, and Babylon? The real tally of bodies was nine. And though he had no remorse or guilt for Cat's death—after all, she was every bit a deserving bad girl—he did have regret. He'd made a promise that her slate with him was clean. They were square.

Lucky seated himself next to Winter.

"You asked for a sit-down," began Winter. "We've tentatively agreed to terms. So, here we are."

"Mr. Dey," led the senior partner in the room, fiftyish, fit, and tan, with slicked back brown hair.

"My client is technically still a deputy sheriff," warned Winter in a simple display of leverage. "Please address him accordingly."

"Deputy. My name is Seth Rosenfeld. And I represent the mayor. The names Denny Teng and Catalina Rincon, I believe, are familiar to you?"

"Here it comes," mouthed Lucky to Winter.

"You don't have to answer anything you don't want to," she whispered back.

"Yeah," answered Lucky. "I know who they were."

"And you understand both of them are deceased?" asked Rosenfeld.

"I do."

In front of Rosenfeld was a thin stack of papers. He pushed them across to Lucky.

"These are NDAs," said Rosenfeld.

"Nondisclosure agreements? What for?" asked Winter.

"By signing these, Mister...Sorry. Deputy Dey agrees to speak nothing of Mr. Dennis Teng or Ms. Catalina Rincon beyond that he was acquainted with both. Of course, it is non-binding if the deputy is speaking under the condition of subpoena and under oath in a criminal matter. But we don't think that'll be an issue."

"May I confer with my client?" asked Winter.

Not waiting for an answer, she grabbed the arm of Lucky's chair and swiveled it so they were both turned away from the other attorneys.

"I wasn't expecting this," she whispered. "Do you know what this is about?"

Yes, Lucky answered inside his own skull. *They're burying it. The whole ugly damn mess.*

"Yeah," he whispered back. Meanwhile, his mind spun. The mayor somehow viewed his connections to the deceased Denny Teng and Cat Rincon as a danger to him, either politically or otherwise. They didn't want answers. They wanted closure.

"Are you good with this?" Winter asked.

"Sure I am," said Lucky, locking his eyes squarely on the mayor's, sarcasm on full wattage. "After all. If it's what our mayor wants, who am I to refuse?"

Mayor Ram's mouth tightened. It was, in the moment, his only tell.

"It's a here and now offer," added Rosenfeld. "As in signed. Or the offer is off the table."

Winter turned back around and began reading through the agreements as drafted. Lucky rotated his seat until he was facing the mayor. The tall, square-shouldered politician, handsome even in half shadow, continued to lock eyes with Lucky in an unwavering stare. The glare was malice free yet, somehow, loaded with unadulterated power. It was as if he were allowing Lucky to know him, see inside to his soul, learn what a man in charge of the city government was capable of.

"Docs look okay," said Winter. "If my client is willing?"

Without so much as perusing a word of the nondisclosure agreements, Lucky signed his name in the appropriate spaces. At the precise moment he put down the pen, a rear door was opened, giving way for the mayor to escape. All the lawyers in the room stood and silently followed, including Rosenfeld. There was not a single thank-you or goodbye, just a line of retreating suits.

"So, that's it?" asked Winter. "We're done?"

"Not quite yet," said the good-looking LAPD detective.

"Who are you again?" asked Winter.

"My name's Ron Alcala. I'm a robbery/homicide investigator with the LAPD. The deputy knows who I am."

"What can I do for you?" asked Lucky.

"Do you know a man named Austin Andrews?"

"Don't believe so," answered Lucky. "Should I?"

"Real estate broker. West Valley," said Detective Alcala. "He was one of the victims in a triple murder. Calabasas. Unsolved. No suspects."

"Calabasas," repeated Lucky. "That's Sheriff's territory."

"It is," replied Detective Alcala. "But your car was part of a crime scene in my jurisdiction. And the deputy on the Calabasas case is a pal of mine. If I can't close my Cat Rincon murder, I can help him close his."

From inside his jacket the detective removed a clear plastic evidence bag. Inside the bag was a formerly crumpled advertisement on slick card stock, flattened and officially sealed.

Austin Anderson
The West Valley's Number 1 Broker
"I guarantee top dollar for your house!"

"Found that in your car," said the detective. "1999 Crown Victoria. Balled on your back seat."

"Never seen it before," shrugged Lucky.

Lucky wasn't lying. He just didn't recall crumpling the advertisement and tossing it into the back of his sedan at the Thousand Oaks hospital.

"Your car," continued the detective. "Parked at a crime scene where a woman was murdered. Inside your car, a calling card from a dead body in Cala-fucking-basas that's part of an unsolved triphomicide. Big coincidence?"

"Coincidences happen," answered Lucky.

"Not to me," grilled the detective, obviously pissed over the mayor's snuff job on the Cat Rincon case.

"Don't recall the guy," said Lucky. "Or the calling card. Sorry. I seriously can't help you."

"What is it with you?" growled the detective. "Bodies pile up around you like fuckin' cordwood. And you get to walk outta here with your shield?"

"Just unlucky, I guess."

"Not funny."

"See me laughing? I don't know the guy."

"I think you're lying." The detective stood. "I got witness statements about the Calabasas doers that match two more dead bodies in a quadruple homicide in the SGV."

"That would be the other homicide I'm legally obligated *not* to talk about?"

Lucky looked to Winter. She nodded back, then pinched her fingers and smugly mimed zipping her mouth shut.

"And we're not under oath or subpoena," she added. "I think we're done here."

She stood, Lucky with her. As they neared the exit, Detective Alcala barked at Lucky. "I seriously don't know how you live with yourself," accused the detective.

Lucky Dey stalled at the door and limped a 180-degree turn so he could face the LAPD detective.

"One day at a time," returned Lucky, repeating the oft-repeated Alcoholics Anonymous aphorism. "One day at a time."

Join Doug's mailing list
for sneak previews, exclusive content, and
news on the release of the next Lucky Dey Thriller,

Hip, Slick, and Dead

visit www.eepurl.com/b93Bfr

About the Author

Doug cut his teeth writing movies like *Die Hard 2, Bad Boys,* and *Hostage* until sharp enough to pen the Lucky Dey crime thriller series. He lives in Southern California with his wife, two children, and three mutts.

You can learn more about Doug at www.dougrichardson.com and drop him a line at bydougrich@dougrichardson.com. You can also follow him at www.facebook.com/bydougrichardson, on Twitter @byDougRich, and on Instagram @bydougrich.